THE
GATEKEEPER

JAMES BYRNE

HEADLINE

First published in the USA in 2022 by Minatour Books
An imprint of St Martin's Publishing Group

First published in Great Britain in 2022 by
HEADLINE PUBLISHING GROUP

First published in paperback in 2023 by
HEADLINE PUBLISHING GROUP

1

Cataloguing in Publication Data is available from the British Library

ISBN 978 1 4722 8820 2

Offset in 9.79/14.23pt Bembo Std by Jouve (UK), Milton Keynes

Printed and bound in Great Britain by Clays Ltd, Elcograf S.p.A.

Headline's policy is to use papers that are natural, renewable and recyclable
products and made from wood grown in well-managed forests and other
controlled sources. The logging and manufacturing processes are expected to
conform to the environmental regulations of the country of origin.

HEADLINE PUBLISHING GROUP
An Hachette UK Company
Carmelite House
50 Victoria Embankment
London EC4Y 0DZ

www.headline.co.uk
www.hachette.co.uk

To Keith Kahla, for seeing the potential in Dez, long before others had met him.

To Janet Reid, for hanging in there during the lean years.

To Katy: "I do love nothing in the world so well as you."

—MUCH ADO ABOUT NOTHING

PROLOGUE

Algeria

SIX MONTHS AGO

Dez sits in a compound on the coast of Algeria. His back is to the door of a great house and his eyes are on the gate to the manor's walled grounds.

He has recently ushered fourteen mates through that gate into the compound, and then through the door into the house.

What they do inside is not his concern. The door and the gate are.

The compound is outside Oran and consists of the massive old house, four stories tall, with white sandstone walls and the ubiquitous sooty, dusty red terra-cotta roof of that coastal region of Algeria. The compound is surrounded by a wall, six meters high, crenellated in the old Moorish and French styles. The walkways atop the wall are lined with twelve earthen pots, all hand-fired a deep cinnamon and filled with flowering bougainvillea. The pots—each the size of a Smart car—were placed up there a decade ago so that riflemen could hide and shoot down and inward at marauders who'd breached the gate.

The grounds are a lovely mosaic of green grass laced with winding pathways of crushed white seashells. In the rear of the compound is a garage large enough for the owner's fleet of eleven vintage automobiles.

Outside the garage, the grounds are spacious enough to park twenty sedans, which the owner, Djamel M'Bolhi, often does when hosting like-minded criminals, or Eurotrash narcotics enthusiasts, or those who wish to monetize terrorism.

Dez and his mates arrived in Oran individually or in groups of two, spaced out over three days and two nights. They came by boat and train and jitney. Fourteen men, one woman. Some of them had worked together before; others were strangers. They come from eleven different countries, speaking about a dozen languages. But all of them understand English, so that's their language for this job.

Dez has his eyes on the gate to the grounds and the door to the house. The gate into the grounds and the door to the house are both painted red. While they belong to Djamel M'Bolhi, right now Dez owns them both. He is the gatekeeper.

Dez is powerfully built but not all that tall. He has sandy hair and ruddy, pinkish skin. He wears a black-and-white-checkered keffiyeh, plus fatigues the color and pattern of oil-fire smoke.

When Dez hears the first *pop pop pop* of small-arms fire from inside the house, he thinks, *Well, there goes Plan A.*

Now he can hear cars roaring up the dusty old cliffside road. More than four. As many as seven. Lots of cars with men carrying assault weapons, he assumes.

A tall and gangly man known by some as Rafik has been guarding the interior side of the front door of the manor house, as Dez has been guarding the exterior. Rafik steps outside now, dressed much like Dez. He's rail-thin, with a thick, matted beard and skin burned to dinosaur hide by desert work. He says, "Cars."

Dez checks the connections to the remote control in his lap. He's got great night vision. He says, "Aye."

"There's shooting inside. They ran into oppo."

"Aye."

"Wasn't supposed to be no oppo inside the house, *chef*."

"Aye."

"We get caught in a crossfire, all hell's to pay."

Dez nods but does not get up off his butt.

Rafik points to the remote. "What's that?"

Dez squints up at him. "Borrowed a couple of batteries from M'sieu M'Bolhi's fleet of cars. Also borrowed one of his lawn sprinklers. Buying us some time, should we need it."

"We safe to stay here, *chef*?"

"Safe is a relative word."

"True," Rafik says, scratching his beard, and now they both hear more of it; more opposition than their intelligence told them to expect inside the house. "Then again: shooting inside. Cars arriving outside. Starting to hot up a little. *N'est-ce pas?*"

Dez nods. But he still doesn't rise.

They hear a scrambling and the squeak of rubber soles on tile, and four of their mates burst out of the house, sweating, all dressed much like Dez and Rafik. Two of them are carrying a filing cabinet horizontally, like a coffin. They thump it down none too gently, draw their Belgian FN Minimi assault weapons, which are strapped to their bodies by leather cords. Two men stand and scope out the compound; two take a knee, eyes to their gunsights, and do the same.

One, a surly Basque, hunkers over, fists on his knees, dragging air into his lungs. Sweat pours off his face. He has a puckered scar running from his hairline, down his left cheek, to the point of his chin. He rasps, "Got it."

"Most excellent, squire." Dez, in fact, has no idea what *it* is. None of his business.

Fourteen went in, and so far five have emerged. Nine have not.

Rafik eyes the four newcomers. "You were with her. Where is she?"

The four shrug. The *her* in this case is the shot-caller from elsewhere for this little caper. They do not know her name. They do not know where *elsewhere* is. They do not know why she gets to call the shots, but they accept that she does. Well, most of them do.

The unidentified woman provided the details and the intelligence. She set the objectives. She established the definitions of *win* for this job.

One of the guys wipes blood off his lower lip with the back of a gloved hand and spits a pinkish gob on the oyster-shell walkway. He says, "The intel was shit."

Dez laughs. "The intel's always shit, sweetheart."

"Fucker's soldiers are supposed to be in Algiers."

Dez nods. So they'd been told. Oh well.

Two more of their group step out of the house and one of them, a Swede, has been shot in the thigh. He's cursing a blue streak. He's holding a hard drive the size of a hardback novel, two wires still dangling from the back of it, showing copper, ripped rather than disconnected from one of Djamel M'Bolhi's computers. The Swede waggles it in the air, shows Dez he has what he went in for. Plus, apparently, a bullet. His left fatigue pant leg glistens black in the darkness.

Seven out, seven still inside.

Rafik eyes the big red double gates of the walled compound. "They be on us soon, *chef.*"

Dez sits and says, "Them lot? Nah."

Outside the compound, seven Jeeps have arrived and two dozen armed men are dismounting. Dust roils and swirls in the air. Their radios crackle, telling them of the assault on their master's compound. One of the leaders of the group marches up to the great iron handles of the red double gates of the compound wall, grips them both in calloused fists, then screams, his body in spasm, swirls of smoke escaping his palms. His body stands, rigid, long muscles locked, a rictus of death transforming his face into a carnival mask.

Dez points to the car batteries that he's attached to the gate. Nobody on the outside is going to be opening those gates by hand. And Djamel M'Bolhi, that most paranoid of criminals, has hardened the gates so much that it would take a tank to knock them down.

The Basque spots the jerry-rigged trap. "You do that?"

Dez bunches up the right sleeve of his shirt and proudly displays the tattoo of Janus, the two-faced Roman god, on the inside of his forearm. He thrusts a chin toward the thick stone wall. "Doors an' gates, friend. Doors an' gates."

Three more of their team come scrambling out of the great house. One is wounded, hopping on one foot, supported by the other two. They carry an attaché case with a digital lock and half of a built-in handcuff.

The Basque says, "We got to go."

Dez says simply, "Can't."

Fourteen entered. Ten out. Four to go.

"Got what we came for. The boat's waiting."

Dez nods. They'll be heading due north via a small fishing boat, set to rendezvous with a larger boat steaming their way from the Spanish city of Adra.

The Basque says, "We got to get to the boat."

"All in good time, my darlin'."

Rafik lowers himself down onto his haunches, his face on a level with Dez's. He says, "Hear them cars, *chef*? We're outnumbered."

Dez says, "What d'you know about California?"

Rafik blinks several times. "Pardon?"

"California."

Rafik repeats that. "California."

"Aye."

"Dunno. Scenic, I hear. They make wine. Silicon Valley. Hollywood. Pretty girls."

"What I'm thinking," Dez speaks softly. "Lot of pretty girls in California. A strapping young man such as meself could do quite well there."

An American, a Texan, stumbles out of the house and hisses, "Shit on a shingle! That intel was fucked!"

Dez thinks: Fourteen in. Eleven out. Three to go.

"Plus," he says to Rafik, "there's a vibrant music scene. Buy myself a better guitar, find a band or two. Could be a laugh, yeah?"

The men flinch and hunch low as, beyond the compound, Djamel M'Bolhi's men begin firing automatic weapons at the great gates. Dez knows the gates are lined with metal and they can't shoot their way in. Djamel M'Bolhi's men know this, too, but they're a little panicky.

The Basque wipes sweat off his haggard face. "Won't hold them forever."

Dez says, "Won't need to," and touches one of the buttons on his remote control.

It takes a lot of petrol to own a fleet of eleven antique cars. It takes a lot of water to maintain a splendid lawn of green grass. Dez did some reconnaissance before the Shot-Caller from Elsewhere led the team into the great house. He used the lawn-maintenance water hoses, a drum of gasoline from the garage, and one of those oscillating garden sprinklers and set it all up outside the great gate. Now, with the push of a button on his remote, Dez activates the sprinkler, which sends out a fine, arcing fan of petrol, covering the seven cars and the two dozen criminals outside the wall.

The thugs sense a threat but misunderstand its nature. Several fire at the oscillating sprinkler. Their muzzle flash interacts with the petrol now drenching their clothes and their hair, and hanging as a fine mist in the night air. The sparks from their guns ignite the gas and immolate them.

Some fall. Two stagger around, screaming, fully engulfed in flames. One of them fails to release the trigger of his Uzi, and pirouettes, spraying his own men and the seven Jeeps with bullets.

It's pandemonium outside the compound.

Inside the compound, Dez says, "Plus, there's surfing. Never tried surfing. Might be fun."

The team members hear the screaming and the sporadic gunfire outside the gate. They eye one another in wonderment. The Basque says, "Contact the boat."

Dez squints up at him. "Soonish, squire."

Two more men emerge from the house, panting, guns to their shoulders. Dez thinks, *Fourteen went in, thirteen came out, one to go.* Sitting, looking serene, he smiles up at the Basque and shrugs.

"You think we can hold this position forever?" the Basque demanded.

"Don't need to hold it forever. Thinkin' of retiring. California, maybe."

The Swede grits his teeth and nods sagely. "A lot of pretty girls in California."

"What I was just saying. Also, surfing."

They hear more small-arms fire from inside the house. They hear shouting from outside the wall. The Basque is in a fury now. "Will you fools shut the fuck up! We get out! Now!" He gestures to the walkway atop the wall. "If they get up there, we'll be ducks in a barrel!"

Dez tsks. "It's fish in a barrel. Or sitting ducks."

The Basque draws his sidearm. "What the fuck are you talking about?"

Dez drapes his forearms over his upturned knees and smiles gently up at the man. "I mean, a sitting fish would be a silly image. Not a half-bad name for a pub, though." He turns to Rafik. "Could open a pub. The Sitting Fish. American girls like pubs, yeah?"

Rafik rubs a hand through his beard. "I see a flaw in your plan, vis-à-vis these California girls."

"Flaw?"

"Well, you're quite homely, *chef*."

The Basque looks like he's a hair's breadth away from a coronary.

Dez is aghast. "That's a terrible thing to say! I'm actually quite a handsome man. Rakish, even. Comely, if we're bein' honest. An' you, you've a face like an elbow! I'd do quite well in California, thank you. Starlets an' what have you."

Rafik grins through his grimy beard. "If you say so, *chef*."

The Basque aims his 9mm firearm at Dez, then at the crouching Rafik, then at Dez. "Call the boat! We are leaving! Now!"

Dez turns his smile to the big, angry man. "A firearm's not a toy, love. It's all fun an' games till someone puts an eye out."

The Basque presses the barrel of his sidearm into the top of Dez's skull, pushing down the black-and-white headscarf. "I should kill you now!"

They hear shouting near the top of the compound wall. The remains of Djamel M'Bolhi's men have finally figured out how to get up there. Well, they work there. Likely, they've trained for just this contingency.

The noise distracts the Basque. When he glances away, Dez grabs the man's right wrist, sliding his little finger into the trigger guard, blocking the trigger itself. The man's leaning forward, already a little off-balance. Dez yanks hard on his right arm and the Basque stumbles into him. Dez, arm crooked, slams his elbow into the supraorbital ridge over the Basque's left eye. He hears the bone crackle. The big man slumps to the ground, unconscious.

The tall, quiet beauty, the Shot-Caller from Elsewhere, steps out of the house, SIG Sauer in her fist. She's bleeding from her shoulder. She nudges the unconscious Basque with her boot. "What happened?"

Dez rises and brushes dust off his smoke-dark fatigues. "Someone put his eye out."

She nods. "Count?"

"Fourteen in," he says. "Fourteen out."

"Call the boat."

"Aye." Dez draws a ruggedized mobile from his trouser pocket.

She studies the courtyard and the sturdy wall. "They get up on the walkway, they can use those flowerpots as merlons."

Rafik rises, too. "Merlons?"

"Battlements," Dez says, hitting Send on his phone. His friend frowns. "Solid bits, to hide behind and peek out and shoot us to death."

"Ah." Rafik studies the dozen red pots. "Yes. That would be bad."

They see scuttling movement atop the walkways.

"Unless someone had the forethought to put pouches of white phosphorous on them pots," Dez says.

They see movement behind four of the pots. Five. Djamel M'Bolhi's men, showing a little unit discipline, waiting to get all their snipers in place before attacking.

The Shot-Caller from Elsewhere smiles. She aims her SIG at the nearest of the great red pots, twenty feet off the ground, and fires.

She hits the packet of phosphorous adhered to the pot. Everyone on the ground turns, throwing arms or hands over their eyes, as the pot explodes with a bluish-white fireball, sending a gout of potting soil and bougainvillea into the air. A man screams, his body arching back over the crenellated wall, falling, landing on one of the Jeeps below.

Dez has rigged the phosphorous pouches in tandem, like Christmas tree lights, and when one ignites, they all do. The air is thick with the peaty tang of potting soil, and a snowfall of red flowers drifts into the courtyard. The explosions have deafened everyone sufficiently that they don't have to hear the screams of the burning men.

When the last of the pots has exploded and the last of the fireballs has dissipated, the team brushes clods of dirt and pedals of bougainvillea and bits of sandstone and terra-cotta and terrorist off their fatigues.

They hear no more shooting or shouting from outside the compound.

His ears still ringing, Dez leans toward the woman and shouts, "M'sieu M'Bolhi?"

The Shot-Caller from Elsewhere mimes blowing smoke from the barrel of her SIG, Wild West style, and holsters it.

Dez nods.

Rafik drags a med kit out of his rucksack and, without asking, begins cleaning blood from the woman's shoulder. She says, "My intel wasn't perfect."

Dez says, "Few things in life are."

Rafik applies an adhesive pad to her wound. "*Chef* is thinking of retiring. To California."

She ponders that a moment. "A lot of pretty girls in California." She points, in this order, at the filing cabinet, the hard drive, and the unconscious Basque. "Get this shit to M'Bolhi's cars."

Men stow their rifles, pick up the loot and the wounded, head toward the garage.

The Shot-Caller from Elsewhere observes the walkway, the now-smoldering ruins of the crenellated walls, the car batteries attached to the great gate. She makes eye contact with Dez, then looks down at the tattoo of Janus on his inner forearm. She gives him only the second smile he's ever seen from her.

"Gatekeeper?"

"Beginnings an' gates," he says. "Transitions an' times. Duality an' doors. Passages an' endings."

She starts walking toward the garage. "California," she says. "You could do worse."

CHAPTER 1

California

SIX MONTHS LATER

Dez stands and yawns in front of one of six gilded elevator doors of the Hotel Tremaine in downtown Los Angeles, checks the paper sleeve of his room key, and stabs the up arrow.

It's one of those grand old hotels that hint of a more glamorous era, with WPA heft, and vaguely socialist workers murals, and a lovely old baroque lobby with green velvet furniture. Dez has just spent the past three hours in a club that shares part of the ground floor, playing bass guitar, covering American rock and blues and soul, laying down the support for a petite waif of a lead singer whose voice can growl and wail, can soar and sink, and can surprise Dez every single damn time he hears her.

Dez is five-eight but built like a tank, with a barrel chest, thick arms, and short, bowed legs. His inevitable uniform these days is jeans and a black T-shirt and boots. His hands are oversized, knuckles crisscrossed with fighting scars, and it's hard to imagine those fingers playing the guitar.

It was a good set, he thinks. The vocalist and percussionist and keyboards lad had headed off to another club to hear someone else play.

They'd invited Dez but he'd demurred. The elevator arrives and he enters, hits his floor, leans back against the frost-filigreed mirror, sets down his bass guitar case, and thinks deep thoughts about a tall beer.

Before the door closes, a hand slips through the door, breaking the light beam. The hand is tan and strong and feminine, with long fingers and no rings. A woman steps on board. The woman is tall and dark, angular and lithe, wearing a black power suit, a white shirt open low, and four-inch heels. She's, well, remarkable. Her eyes are expressive and very dark.

She's with two men who can only be described as bodyguards: tall, well-built, nice suits, eyes everywhere. They both tower over Dez.

Dez recognizes the woman. She'd been in the audience in the club. She'd been meeting an Asian gentleman who, himself, had had bodyguards. International trade of some sort. The Asian fella and his bodyguards left during the last set.

As the car rises, she makes eye contact with Dez's reflection in the mirror to the left of the door. "You were playing in the club." The voice is low and smoky.

"Aye."

"You sounded good."

"Ta. Appreciate it."

"From England?"

"Thereabouts."

The woman is classy and rich and exudes a level of sophistication Dez could never match. Her hair is up in a complicated chignon, pinioned by lacquered Chinese sticks. Her wristwatch is mannish and likely cost more money than Dez has ever owned at any one given time. Her perfume is a subtle gardenia. *Twenty thousand leagues out of me reach,* Dez thinks. *Not even worth considering.*

The car reaches the tenth floor, and he surprises himself. "Fancy a drink?"

Nothing ventured . . .

One of the bodyguards actually snorts a little laugh, and the other shakes his head in wonderment.

The woman, though, smiles and turns to face the real Dez, not his reflection.

"No, thanks."

The turndown is polite and polished. She gives it not one more erg of energy than needed.

The car slows at seventeen. The guards exit first. The woman steps out, turns, and smiles at Dez. "But I appreciate you asking."

Dez says, "Cheers, then."

The tall woman with black hair and black eyes and power suit gives him a smile over her shoulder and whispers down the corridor, out of sight.

That smile alone could power a small city overnight.

Dez shakes his head and rides up one more floor.

It's half midnight. Dez's room is quite nice, with a double bed and decent minifridge and a bathroom that's bigger than some flats he's lived in. He'd agreed to play the gig tonight because the lovely young singer is a mate and because the hotel offered to comp him a room. Plush digs for a guy like Dez. He doesn't mind living large for a night or two. Good for the soul.

He showers and throws on a pair of boxers. He cracks open a beer from the minifridge and stands at the window looking out at the night and the city of Los Angeles. It's been a fun visit but he could never live here. Too big. Too sprawling. Too new.

Standing in just boxers, Dez cuts a formidable figure. His scars, burns, tattoos, and bullet wounds paint a road map of the world's hot spots. His skin is surprisingly pinkish despite years of working outdoors. He's bowlegged, and that plus his very wide shoulders make him look like a cube of muscle. Ridiculously, something about his squarish face, his light blue eyes and dopey, lopsided grin, makes him look a bit like a kid on a joyride. People's first reaction is to wonder what he's just gotten away with.

Over his left pectoral is a tattoo of a fleur-de-lis. On the inside of his right forearm is Janus.

As he sips his beer and studies the city, he spots the sniper.

The guy is on the roof of the next building over, with a long gun and a scope, his gun on a short tripod. He's lying on his belly. The glint of the scope gave him away. Dez didn't even realize he'd been looking for that glint, but he had. He does every time he steps near a window or a door.

The scope isn't aimed at him. It's aimed at the roundabout in front of the Hotel Tremaine, the ground floor entrance with its rotating doors and its gold-and-white striped awning.

Dez sidesteps, out of view of the sniper but still at the window. He peers down and sees a large van pull up. He's staring almost straight down at it. The side door opens and four men pour out—one, two, three, four. No awkward spacing, no crowding. They don't step out of the van. They deploy.

All wear black. All wear jackets on a warm evening. All look athletic.

The sniper is their eye in the sky.

Los Angeles is a city of international commerce and it's inevitable that some people would have bodyguards, but not that many people. The tall, dark woman on seventeen had two of them.

So what are the odds the men in the van are here for her?

They're not cops. Cops don't deploy like this.

Dez reaches for the room phone.

No dial tone.

He rummages in the pockets of the jeans he'd dumped on the bed, checks his mobile—bulkier than most modern phones, with some aftermarket upgrades.

No signal.

He steps into the jeans and pulls on his boots and another black T-shirt. He has no weapons on him. He pockets his key card and his mobile, and steps into the corridor. His situational awareness has reminded him that there's a fire alarm in the corridor and a glass-fronted red box with a massive, wound-up fire hose and a red-handled fire ax. This hotel dates back to the 1930s. A newer hotel would have neither the hose nor the ax, and indeed, they've likely been maintained for their ambiance, not their usefulness. His room and the corridor both have twenty-first-century regulation sprinklers. The cloth–covered hose probably deteriorated decades ago. It might not even be connected to water.

But that ax is a beauty.

Dez smashes the glass with an elbow and pauses.

Silence. Breaking the glass should have triggered alarms. Yeah?

They've a sniper on overwatch and someone's bolloxed the phones and the fire alarm. Pros, them. They've done this before. They'll be ghosts before the cops arrive, and the next government vehicle to park out front will be a morgue wagon.

There's no reason in the world for Dez to get involved. The shooters aren't coming for him. *Why borrow another man's troubles,* his old mate Rafik used to say.

But the tall, dark woman had the decency to smile when he'd asked her for a drink, even though she was way, way out of his league. A small kindness. No mediocre commodity, that.

Dez shoulders open the stairwell door.

CHAPTER 2

Dez holds the ax, blade nearer the heel of his hand, the handle sticking up like a bobby stick. He takes the stairs down from eighteen to seventeen. He presses his ear against the door. He can hear an elevator *ding*. He hears the *whut-whut* of a sound suppressor and small-arms fire.

He hears a *thump*.

No grass growing under these lads' feet.

He waits a ten-count, then opens the door slowly.

A man's down. One of the bodyguards who rode up in the elevator with him. Double tap. One shot to the middle of his back, another to the back of his head. Dez can see a belt holster but no gun.

The door at the end of the corridor is one-third open. It's a suite. The kind of room a woman with those expensive clothes would want, for sure.

Dez enters the corridor, lets the stairwell door close very softly behind him. He moves quietly, sliding toward the suite and the open door, the fire ax back like a tennis racket, arm cocked. Everything about the shooters screams professionals, so he's positive they'll be wearing Kevlar under the dark coats he glimpsed from his window.

He hasn't heard any more suppressed gunfire but he does hear flesh-on-flesh and hears a woman grunt, hears a body hit the floor and the tinkle of glass breaking.

A male voice says, "Confirmed. . . . Moving now."

Fine.

The first man steps through the door, wearing all black, chest puffed up under the ballistic vest, carrying a long, silenced handgun. Smith M&P22 Compact. American-made, which suggests lots of interesting things to Dez.

The gunman isn't expecting a man with a billy club, and he hesitates a quarter second.

Dez slams the handle into the man's gut, using it like a rapier, hitting him above his belt but below his ballistic vest.

Body armor is all well and good, but if you rupture a man's internal organs, he becomes a sausage in Kevlar casing.

The man grunts, paralyzed with pain. Dez bulls forward, knees bent, hunkered low, shoulder down, catching the man in the belly and lifting him off his feet. Dez takes three powerful steps into the room, carrying the man over his shoulder like a sack of potatoes, and throws him forward.

Two more men in there. Also, the woman he'd met in the elevator, lying on the carpet, propped up on her elbows, blood trickling from the corner of her mouth.

The first guy, airborne, slams into the second guy, who goes sprawling facedown.

Dez has the advantage of surprise, but surprise evaporates fast. He wades into the third guy's space, grabbing his gun hand with his massive left paw and plowing his forearm into the man's windpipe. The man's eyes bug and he falls straight back.

The second guy is buried under the first guy, who's passed out from pain. Dez notices a spot of blood on the knuckles of the second guy's right hand. He'd spotted blood on the woman's lip, and she's now glaring at that man in particular.

"This one hit you?"

The woman's big, shocked eyes turn to Dez. After a moment, she nods.

Dez takes one knee and places a calloused hand on the back of the man's shoulder. He grips the man's wrist with his other hand and yanks straight up, rising to almost his full height as he does so, letting his legs provide the energy as he yanks the ball of the man's shoulder out of its socket, tendons shredding.

Americans think they invented shock and awe. They didn't.

Dez and his old crew didn't, either, but Dez likes to think they perfected it.

CHAPTER 3

Dez turns to the tall woman and says, "They've more men. Come on."

Her eyes are like saucers and her chest heaves as if she's about to go into shock. Dez offers her his hand.

"Let's go!"

She hesitates, then takes it.

When he lifts her up, he realizes she's doffed the killer heels and is still taller than he. She's got two inches on him barefoot. She wears the severe black trousers but has untucked her starched white blouse. Her hair is down and flows to the middle of her back.

And now he sees that the instant of fear is quickly being replaced by a righteous anger.

"Who . . . ?"

"Dunno." He kneels and takes all three of the men's suppressed weapons. Smith & Wessons. The man with the torn arm socket spits obscenities. The third man has his hands around his throat, his lips turning blue.

All three guys are wearing high-tech earjacks.

Dez says, "Where's your other lad?"

"Allen," she says. "He . . . went out for food."

"More on their way. Let's go."

She doesn't argue.

He leads her out into the corridor and she gasps when she sees her dead bodyguard.

Dez races for the stairs door, holds it open.

"Up."

She says, "Up?"

"They'll expect ye to go down. To get out."

She stares into his eyes and uses the back of her hand to wipe blood off her lip. She nods.

Her bare feet slap the stairs as she races upward, Dez in her wake.

They get to eighteen and he puts a hand on her arm, stops her. He tucks two guns in his belt—cumbersome, with the silencers. He pops the clip off the other, checks the load, slaps it home again. He opens the door at eighteen and steps out, quick-looking, checking his corners.

Clear.

He crosses the corridor, swipes his magnetic card, and hustles her into his room, closes the door behind them.

Her chest still heaves, but she's mastered her fear. "Who are you?"

"Dez. Pleased." He strides across the room and draws his curtains closed. "They've a lad watching from that roof across the way. I saw four alight and we've met only three. Plus, someone got the phones and fire alarms before all that. Best to wait here, hope someone calls one-twelve."

He corrects himself: 911 in the States.

He returns to the door, listening.

"Who *are* you!" she barks.

"Dez. Who're you?"

"Are you part of this?"

"Seems. Lucky bloody me. Know who them fuckers are?"

Her breathing is beginning to level out. He can see the anger rising. Good. Anger's the most useful emotion when under fire. Fear is the least useful. She's trending well.

Her fists curl tight. "You're not just a bass player."

"Well . . ." He shrugs. "Keyboards, a bit."

Outside, he hears the stairwell door open.

"Bloody hell," Dez whispers, then turns to her. "Strip."

CHAPTER 4

The woman says, "What?"

He crosses to her, drags the guns out of his belt, and unscrews their suppressors. "Bastards shoulda gone down, not up. You've a tracker, love."

To her credit, she gets it immediately. She unbuckles her belt, whips it off, holding it up like a dead snake in one hand, fingers of her other hand skimming along it.

A tracker will weigh down cloth, will unbalance well-designed, well-fitted clothes. You'd feel it when you walk. So it's shoes or belts; wallets or purses. She finds it.

He hands her one of the unsilenced guns. "Know how to—"

She pops the clip, checks it, slams it home, dogs the slide.

Okay, then.

Dez circles her, aims his silenced gun at the hotel room window, and fires.

The glass shatters.

"Watch the door."

He steps to the window but stands at an oblique angle so the sniper across the way can't get a look at him. He aims straight down, picks parked and empty cars, starts firing.

Hits windshields.

Even eighteen stories up, he hears people scream. He hears car alarms bleat.

He stalks back past her. He tosses the empty gun on the bed, picks up the third gun. He steps to the door and shouts, "Excuse me! Gentlemen!"

Then steps back and fires one round through the door.

He hits shite but intended that.

He steps to the door again.

"Got your attention, have I?" he shouts. "I just hit four or five cars on the street! Police are on their way! It's a siege now. Clock's in play! How d'you want to do this?"

He hears nothing. He crouches low. If they fire through the door, they'll fire for center mass, over his head.

Hopefully.

"Could storm the room!" he shouts. "Could hope we don't do to ye what we done to your mates on seventeen! Yeah?"

The *we* is a nice touch. They don't know how big the opposition is. Neither does Dez.

He waits. He hears nothing.

Except sirens. Lots of sirens, heading their way.

All three bastards in the woman's room wore earjacks. These guys are pros. Their lad on overwatch has told them the score by now. They know cops are en route. From here on out, it's all retail math: Does the value of the woman outweigh the cost of getting caught by the police? Do they fancy a running firefight on the streets of LA?

Still, he hears nothing from the corridor.

The police have arrived.

The gunmen are pros. They've long fled.

Dez and the woman standing behind him are in the clear.

He feels the pressure of a gun barrel against the back of his neck. Hears the hammer pull back. Feels the vibration.

"Who . . ."—her voice is low, powerful, and absolutely in control—"the fuck . . . are you?"

The woman uses Dez's room phone—which seems to be working now—to call the front desk and to report what happened. When the police arrive, they find her standing over Dez, who's on his knees, fingers laced behind his head. She holds a gun professionally, in both hands, but she throws it on the bed and shows her palms as soon as the police appear.

She identifies herself as Petra Alexandris. The name seems to mean something to the plod.

Dez is shoved onto his stomach and handcuffed.

He spends the remainder of the night in the LA County jail.

He's been in worse nicks. He sleeps fine.

CHAPTER 5

Ryerson Ranch, Boca Serpiente County, California

Jonesy wakes at noon.

He'd had the night watch until 3 a.m. and his head hadn't hit the pillow on his camp cot until nearly five. He slept well.

He's a tall and muscular man—six-four—with hair brushed back to his shoulders and a thick, full beard that would have looked at home in 1880s California. Almost no one at the Ryerson Ranch has ever seen him without his beloved Detroit Red Wings ball cap. He looks skinny under a plaid shirt but the loose-fitting clothes hide an athletic body. Two percent body fat, 90 percent badass, camouflaged by a soft smile, oversized shirts, and a stoic nature.

Jonesy showers and puts on a fresh white undershirt, one of his two plaid shirts, jeans, work boots, and his Red Wings cap. He's a smoker but has given it up and chain-chews wintergreen gum.

The ranch house is rambling, having been added on to, with no master plan, four or five times in its history. It's two stories tall and well maintained, the color exactly matching the adjacent horse barn and the short silo.

In the kitchen of the Ryerson Ranch, he checks the duty roster. He's on dishwashing today. He's fine with that. There's something Zen-like about washing the communal dishes. Laundry is the same. It's easy work, and it's appreciated by all eight adults at the Ryerson Ranch.

Not so much by the seven children, of course. They range in age from five to sixteen. And kids will be kids.

Jonesy pours himself a coffee in the spacious farm kitchen, with its huge, rough-hewn wooden table.

Molly Ryerson, ranch matriarch, wife of Joe, sits at the head of the table, going over paperwork. Not bills, since the ranch is off the grid and self-sustaining. She glances up, pencil behind her ear, her salt-and-pepper hair escaping a loose bun.

"Jonesy."

"Ma'am."

"Everything all right last night?"

Jonesy stares out the window at the flat, arid land and what he can see of the L-shaped ranch house, with its red wooden fence, and the paddock for the five horses, and the winding, gravel road that leads to an even taller fence a mile away. Beyond that wooden, handmade fence, and its gate that has to be lifted a few inches and dragged inward to open, Jonesy can see two Boca Serpiente County Sheriff's Office patrol cars keeping watch over the ranch, the eight adults and seven children, on what is now the twenty-seventh day of the government's siege.

"Everything's fine," Jonesy says, and sips his coffee.

CHAPTER 6

Midmorning in the LA County jail, a uniformed officer comes for Dez, cuffs his wrists in front of him, and hauls him to a perfect, made-for-TV cliché interrogation room. Two metal chairs. Metal table bolted down. One-way mirror. A bar to shackle him to. Dez can practically hear the two-beat scene-change music from *Law & Order. Bah-dun.*

A Black woman with a detective's badge clipped to her blazer pocket comes in and sets down a manila folder and a legal pad. Dez stands when she enters, sits when she does. She opens the folder and peruses it through half-glasses. She's about his age, with a well-fitted suit and asymmetrical hair. She looks all business. He waits.

She peers up at him over the tops of her designer eyeglasses. "I'm Detective Beth Swanson, LAPD."

"Pleased."

She says, "Desmond Aloysius Limerick."

He sits forward. "Yes, ma'am."

"No, I mean, you told the arresting officer your name was Limerick, comma, Desmond Aloysius. You want me to believe that's your real name?"

Dez looks a little hurt. "It's a perfectly fine name."

"If you're a character from *Yeoman of the Guard*."

"*Pirates of Penzance* man myself."

She studies him for a while. "You told the arresting officer you're from the UK?"

"I did."

"Whereabouts?"

"Lots of places. Moved a lot."

"Sounds rough."

"Cliché, that. Always had a roof and meals. Got as good an education as the next lad, I suppose."

"Why did you move so much?"

"This an' that."

Beth Swanson watches him, her pen hovering over the legal pad, upon which she has written not a single word.

"Do you know why we held you overnight, Mr. Limerick?"

"Aye. Because I attacked three men, possibly ruptured the lower GI of one, possibly crippled one, possibly caused one to suffocate and die, though I doubt it. Because I shot up a hotel room and a bunch of cars parked out front. Because I drank one of them hotel room beers, which was swill, by the way, and I forgot to tell anyone and the hotel people will think I scarpered with it. Which, can't blame them, yeah?"

She stares at him. Not with malice or frustration. Just a sort of curiosity. Detective Swanson has sat across this table from many, many people. She can barely remember one from the next. Most bored her. Limerick, Desmond Aloysius, is not one of them.

She reaches into the pocket of her fitted blazer and produces a handcuff key. "You're free to go."

"That's barking!" He yanks back his wrists so she can't reach them without rising from her chair. "I actually did all that stuff. Who'd want the likes of me on the streets?"

"You saved her life."

"The woman?"

Beth Swanson reaches across and uncuffs him. "'The woman?'"

"Tall bird. Dark eyes. Lovely."

"Mr. Limerick, are you telling me you don't know who that was?"

"Friends call me Dez," he says, and offers a boyish smile.

She closes her manila folder and gathers her legal pad and stands. She hands him her business card, embossed with the seal of the LAPD.

Dez stands, too, because he was taught to stand in the presence of women and, if he had a hat, he'd doff it.

"They pulled some strings. Near as I can tell, they pulled every string ever made. A car's waiting out front for you. Your stuff is at the second door on the left, and you have to sign for it."

Dez says, "Right. Cheers. Second door on left. Pardon, who pulled some strings?"

She shakes her head. "You risked your life to save someone you'd never met before, Mr. Limerick. I figure that makes you one of the good guys. Having said that, the sooner you can leave the city of Los Angeles, and the county of Los Angeles, and the state of California, the better."

He smiles again. "Fair, that."

CHAPTER 7

Dez takes the time to lace his boots and to slip his belt into place. He wears a vintage Ancre 15 Rubis watch that doesn't keep time all that well but has sentimental value. He winds it and buckles on the aging leather band. He hadn't had a wallet when they arrested him, so if there hadn't been a car waiting for him, Dez would have been out of luck.

But there is.

It's a shiny black Escalade that had been washed that morning. And every morning, like as not. Standing next to it is a man who served as a military officer. He's not dressed in uniform, but you'd have to be blind not to see it. He's in his midfifties, with a crew cut and a well-formed bushy mustache, and he stands at parade rest, wide shoulders back. He's two inches taller than Dez and powerfully built. He is, clearly, waiting for Dez.

The man says, "Vincent Guerrero."

"Dez. Wotcher." Dez offers his hand and the man doesn't acknowledge it. Instead, he circles the Escalade and climbs in.

Dez follows suit. "Staying at the Tremaine. Ta for the lift."

Vincent Guerrero wears an unremarkable black suit and a regimental tie and generic sunglasses. He pulls out into traffic. He drives to the international headquarters for Triton Expediters, which isn't in Los Angeles proper but in the enclave of Hawthorne. The drive takes forty minutes and he says not a word. The main building on the corporate campus looks like it had been sculpted from a single, seven-story-tall piece of sandstone. It's in the center of a twenty-five-building campus, the capital city of a multinational corporation.

The underground parking lot has plenty of security, and Dez clocks the ways to get out of the garage and alternative ways to get in.

Guerrero parks in a space that has been stenciled with the word GUERRERO. He turns off the engine. He takes off his seat belt. But he doesn't climb out of the car.

Dez waits, smiling.

Guerrero gives him the cold stare, with the aviators and military mustache. He wears them like a police anti-riot shield. He says, "I find out you have anything to do with those rat-fuckers, I will have you killed and your body will be dumped in the Imperial Valley. Are we clear?"

Dez says, "Aye."

Guerrero stares at him through the aviators. Dez takes it.

He keeps staring. Dez keeps smiling.

The engine ticks and cools.

Dez says, "Can I say something?"

Guerrero nods.

"I was raised by Jesuits. If it's intimidation you're trying for, I've a couple of nuns I'd like to introduce you to."

Guerrero reaches for his door and climbs out.

Dez, too.

Guerrero has a badge folder with an ID that identifies him as head of Triton Security, and the ID is magnetized; it gets them into an executive elevator. There, he says, "Guerrero. Seventh floor."

His face pops up on the monitor to the right of the door and the door hisses closed.

It's a decent security rig-up, Dez thinks. He sees two immediate ways to mess with it if he needs to.

The seventh floor is gorgeous and Spartan, with a stunning view of Los Angeles and a smudge of blue ocean to the west. Guerrero marches to a double door, redwood with gold knobs and hinges. The door doesn't have a plaque reading CHIEF EXECUTIVE OFFICER because it doesn't need one. Coals to Newcastle.

Inside, he discovers that the office is fully one quarter of the seventh floor. You could play cricket in here. Two walls are nothing but windows. He spots an area designed to look like a living room, with a fireplace and a wet bar. And on the other end of the room is a desk made, seemingly, of a single, massive piece of obsidian. The man behind the desk is in his late sixties, leathery skin, a thick mane of silver hair and a silver mustache. He's small and birdlike; Dez doubts he stands any taller than five-five. His skin is as browned and gnarled as an old olive tree. His suit is expensive. His watch is steel, high-end but battered. He does not rise and does not acknowledge their presence. He's writing something in a leather-bound journal, using a fountain pen that also appears to be made of obsidian, though Dez doubts it.

Guerrero waits at parade rest. Dez draws his phone and covertly checks football scores. Man City is at home that day. Dez needs them to lose.

Finally, the man caps the fountain pen, and slowly closes the ledger, and looks up.

He radiates anger.

"Limerick," he says.

Dez puts his phone away. "Pleased. And you'd be . . . ?"

He thinks there's one chance in three this old fella is going to stand up and punch him. Dez can practically see the anger rippling like heat over asphalt on a summer day.

"You saved my daughter's life."

"The bird, from last night?" Dez says. He remembers that she identified herself to police as Petra Alexandris. "Ah. Good, good. Glad she's safe. She's lovely, your daughter. Kept her head, too. Should be proud, you."

"What do you want?"

— 32 —

"Would kill for a coffee." He turns to Guerrero. "Milk, two sugars. Ta."

Guerrero tamps down a ripple of anger like a palsy tremor.

The old man—Mr. Alexandris, Dez assumes—says, "What do you want, Mr. Limerick? For saving my daughter's life from kidnappers. What's your price?"

"Ah. That. Mind if I sit?"

A two-beat, and the man nods. Dez sits. He leans forward, elbows on his knees, hands the size of catcher's mitts knitted together.

"First, ye have to understand, they comped me that room last night because I agreed to play bass for the band in the bar. But then, I shot up a window, and a door, and I shot some cars on hotel property, and well, frankly, it's doubtful they'll comp me for that shitstorm. And I wondered, having this fancy office and all, if it's not too much to ask . . . ?"

The seated man finally glances at Guerrero, who shrugs almost imperceptibly.

The seated man says, "You want us to pay for the damage to your room?"

"There's more."

"I thought so."

"They have me guitar. A Gibson Ripper. Cherry red. Not the best ever, but it's been with me ages. Sentimental, like. If you could put in a good word . . . ?"

The man finally moves. He shoots his cuffs. He adjusts the ledger and the fountain pen, his eyes obscured. If Dez had to guess, he'd say the man had been raised in the Med. Greece, maybe, or Italy. Macedonia's a possibility. He has an accent but Dez hasn't heard enough of it to lock it down. The man is used to getting his way. He's rich and he's CEO in a fabulous office in a fabulous building.

"I honestly don't know what your play is. That's rare, Mr. Limerick. If that is your real name."

"It's a perfectly fine name." Dez can't understand why Americans seem hung up about his name.

The older man looks up at Guerrero. "Who is he?"

Guerrero answers crisply, "We checked military records, sir. Here, UK, NATO. If he ever served, it isn't under that name. We checked criminal records, here and Europe. Nothing."

The old man stares at Dez. Dez leans forward, smiling. Objects at rest tend to stay at rest.

"You wish for a job?"

"Not from the likes of you." Dez speaks without anger. "California isn't what I expected. Been here months; haven't seen a single starlet. Passing through."

"Do you know who attacked my daughter last night?"

"Aye. Military-trained Americans."

Guerrero says, "How do you know they—"

"Deployed right smart. Good discipline. Had money, too; comms, weps, good kit. Carried Smith & Wessons. Who but Americans uses them these days?"

Guerrero says, "I lost two good men last night. If you know anything—"

"You lost one good man last night."

"What the hell—"

"Fully stocked fridge in the suite and all-night room service. Yet your lad goes walkabout for snacks just before the attack? Please."

Guerrero says, "Go fuck yourself."

Dez responds to the old man. "They had a tracker on your daughter, y'know. In her belt. Tell me that's not an inside job."

Guerrero is livid. "Jennings was found in a maintenance room, two shots to the base of his skull! You are besmirching the record of a fine soldier and veteran. Of a patriot."

Dez smiles up at him. "Besmirching?"

"Jennings was one of my best men."

Dez turns to the old man. "That'd keep me up nights, were I you."

Guerrero makes a fist and takes a step forward. But the old man raps his knuckles on the table twice, the way a poker player will when he passes. Guerrero halts.

"We're done here," the man says. "I still don't know what your play is. Make it a good one. Good day."

He reopens his ledger and reaches for his fountain pen. Guerrero takes a step closer, in case Dez causes trouble.

Dez stands. "Cheers, then."

Guerrero leads him out.

In the elevator, Dez nudges Guerrero. "Just asking, but who was that?"

Guerrero ignores him.

They ride down and step out in a lobby with a seven-story-tall atrium and lots and lots of tinted glass. Guerrero stops to take care of some paperwork at the first security station. Dez studies a massive bas-relief world map, three stories tall, dominating the wall opposite the windows. Triton Expediters has headquarters here, obviously, but also in London, Rome, Buenos Aires, Tokyo, Macau, Moscow, Tel Aviv, Sydney, and Johannesburg. He sees dozens of lesser holdings, ranging from a private seaport in the Gulf of Oman, to a server farm near a nuclear power plant in Central California, to the Russian spaceport facility at the Baikonur Cosmodrome.

As Guerrero finishes up, two people approach: one in front of the other. The first, a smartly dressed girl, late teens or early twenties, says, "Major?" and Guerrero turns. The ID on her lanyard says INTERN. She hands Guerrero a tablet computer. He scans it.

The second person who approaches is a thin man, late twenties, with an athletic bounce in his step, wearing skinny jeans, driving moccasins, and a sweater. His walk suggests supple strength. He flashes a business card, makes sure Dez sees it, and slips it, en passant, into Dez's hand.

Dez tucks it in the rear pocket of his jeans.

Guerrero e-signs something on the tablet and hands it back to the girl.

Guerrero points to the front door, which is on the far side of a metal detector and a weight-sensor carpet pad and cameras that, Dez knows, shoot in infrared and ultraviolet, as well as the visible spectrum.

Dez says, "Give us a lift to the hotel?"

Guerrero studies him a moment, then turns on his heels and heads back to the elevator.

Dez ambles out. As soon as he steps past the tinted-glass doors and windows, he wishes he'd had sunglasses or a brimmed hat.

He pulls the card out of his pocket.

It reads: *Parking lot to your left. Please come. Petra.*

CHAPTER 8

The tall bird from the night before stands leaning against a fire-engine-red Ferrari. She wears painted-on jeans and short, suede boots with Spanish heels and a white button-down men's shirt. Her sleeves are rolled up and the shirt is open quite low and he sees that her skin has the same Mediterranean cast as her father's, although his has been baked by the sun. She wears round, blue, mirrored sunglasses, and he can't see her eyes. She's . . . Dez tries to find the right word.

Radiant.

Dez circles the Ferrari, fingers snugged into the back pockets of his jeans for fear he'll leave smudges. He whistles, high-low.

She says, "Two-fifty GT Berlinetta. The fifty-nine."

"Explains the shorter wheelbase. Lovely sled, this."

She uses a fob to unlock the car. "You know your classics."

He climbs in on the passenger side, longing to be in the other seat but knowing better than to dare ask. "I know beauty when I see it."

He shouldn't be flirting with her. Absolutely should not.

Can't help it.

She pulls out quickly onto the streets and heads toward the ocean. The classic Ferrari is proof of a higher being. Dez grins like a kid at Disneyland.

The woman says, "Desmond Aloysius Limerick."

"And you are?"

"Petra Alexandris. Chief legal counsel, Triton Expediters. You met my father, Constantine Alexandris. He founded the company."

"Heard of it," he says. "Big military contractor."

"That's a bit of an understatement. What do you do, Mr. Limerick?"

"Dez, to me friends. Retired."

She smiles at him from behind her stylish sunglasses. "Retired at what? Thirty-five?"

"Aye."

"From what?"

"This an' that. Odd jobs. Was a line cook at a beach shack in Trinidad for a while. Quite liked that."

"Uh-huh," she says. "Why did you get involved in my kidnapping, Mr. Limerick?"

He shrugs. Los Angeles whisks past the windshield.

"As opposed to what?"

CHAPTER 9

The house is in Malibu Colony Beach. It's alabaster white. It stands on stilts and, when the tide is in, it juts out over the water from a cliff face, hovering above the Pacific as if an island unto itself. With the tide in, a clear glass floor in the living room creates the illusion of walking on water. All of the west-, north-, and south-facing walls are glass. The house is three stories tall, with a greater dining room and a lesser dining room, about a dozen bedrooms, give or take, and an office that is hardwired, lashed-up to give Petra real-time financial information on four continents. The place has an industrial kitchen for a staff of three or four, although she assures him she has a staff of only one man. There's a six-car garage, a dock and boathouse, plus an outdoor kitchen with barbecues and smokers and a fridge and freezer and a wet bar.

Petra shows him around the ground floor.

"Bloody amazing."

"It's not a museum. You don't have to whisper. Do you like tequila?"

"Dunno. Never tried it."

She pours him two fingers, and the same for herself. She shows him the bottle, thinking the label will be familiar and will impress him. He says, "Looks posh."

"It is."

"Cheers." He sips. He winces.

She grins mischievously. "You don't like it?"

He croaks, "Don't think anyone living in a wildfire state should serve butane."

She laughs, and it's musical. She stands bolt upright and removes her ankle boots by raising one leg behind her, bending at the knee, whisking off the boot with her hand, switching her glass to her other hand, and repeating. Her upper body barely moves throughout. *Takes years of yoga or ballet to be that flexible,* Dez thinks.

"Alonzo Diaz runs the household. He keeps beer in the fridge. Kitchen's that way. I'll be out on the deck. Join me."

Dez stops to adjust his bootlaces so that he can watch as she inputs a code on a ten-key pad before stepping onto the deck. She'd used a code after parking, to get into the house, too. Different pad, same code.

He finds the industrial kitchen so spotless it could double as an emergency room. A young man is cutting red and yellow bell peppers. It's the same guy who walked past Dez in the lobby of Triton Expediters and handed him Petra's card. He's thin, handsome, and Latino. His hair is moussed and slicked back. He's added an apron to his ensemble. Dez thinks he couldn't look that sophisticated on his best day, and his best day wouldn't involve an apron.

Dez says, "Cheers."

The man eyes him with nothing but unexpurgated suspicion.

"Herself said you've beer . . . ?"

The guy pauses, then nods toward the refrigerator. He never stops cutting the peppers.

Dez finds a beer, uses the trick of snapping off the cap by placing it against the edge of the counter and popping it with the butt of his hand. Dez hunts around for a garbage can and throws away the cap, rather than leaving it for the staff to clean up.

"Ta, then."

— 40 —

Chop chop chop. The guy never stops staring, never stops cutting. Dez nods and backs out of the kitchen.

He ambles back the way he came, taking in the art and the blond-wood floors, for sure, but also the placement of the cameras and air-pressure monitors. Whoever installed this security lash-up did right by Petra Alexandris. He finds her out on the deck, watching surfers. She leans back on a chaise longue, barefoot, legs crossed at the ankles, two fingers of the tequila resting on the arm of the chair. Dez drags over a second lounger and joins her. It's a glorious day but, then again, it's LA. Most of them are, if you get out from under the umbrella of smog.

"You met Alonzo?"

"We hit it off." Dez takes a slug from the bottle. "Best mates."

"Our lawyers spoke to the Hotel Tremaine," she says. "Triton Expediters does a lot of business there. We've covered the damages. Your belongings and your guitar are being delivered here within the hour."

"Ta," he says, and sips the cold Mexican beer. A little sweet for his taste, but fine.

"I have international resources. I've asked everyone who owes me a favor, and everyone who'd like to owe me a favor, to find out who you are, Mr. Limerick."

Dez says, "Dez."

"Dez." She concedes. "What will my contacts find?"

"Did I mention a little beach diner in Trinidad?"

"Remind me not to play poker with you."

He laughs. "I'm no big mystery. Honest. Just a bloke likes to play music an' doesn't mind getting paid for it."

They sip their drinks and enjoy the day.

"I reached out to a man who is a captain in the U.S. Navy," she says, addressing the ocean, not Dez. "He drives a destroyer. We dated awhile. I gave him your name."

Dez sips beer. "He get back to you, your captain?"

"He did not." She digs a slim cell phone out of the back pocket of her matchsticks. Dez doesn't know if they give out awards for jeans that do their job well, but if they do, Petra's jeans would be in the running, worldwide. He drags his eyes off her frame. Not without some difficulty. She thumbs her phone awake. Hands it to him.

"*He* got back to me."

Dez reads a name. Gerald Lighthouse. Below which are two words.

Trust him.

"Do you know who Gerald Lighthouse is?"

"Think he was an actor. Was in that thing, with the actress. Them two tykes. Big car chase?"

She says, "Gerald Lighthouse is the U.S. secretary of the Navy."

Dez hands the phone back. "So, not the actor?"

She smiles. She sips her drink.

They sit and enjoy the view awhile.

At some point, Dez says, "You're calm."

"I find this place calming."

"No, I mean you were almost abducted at gunpoint last night. Handled it well. Still are."

"Do you know how old I was when I was first kidnapped?"

He shakes his head.

"Twelve. It happened again the week I turned twenty-one. We have K&R insurance. You know . . . ?"

He nods. Kidnap-and-ransom.

"Triton deals with military contracts all over the planet. First-, second-, and third-world contracts. I've lived under the threat of kidnapping all my life. It's partly why I love this house. It's secure and safe."

"This your place or the company's?"

"My father's, but his second wife died here. Heart attack. He never comes here anymore."

"She wasn't your mum?"

She sips tequila. "No, they split up when I was eight. They were . . . incendiary. Both alpha-Greeks. It was every bit as dramatic as you imagine."

Dez says, "Who were them fellas last night? And why didn't you want to have this conversation with your man Guerrero?"

"Not sure. The first part, I mean. It all happened so damn fast! As for the second part . . ." She pauses, eyes on the roiling Pacific. "I just wanted to thank you in private."

"Trust Guerrero, do you?"

Petra studies him awhile. Surfers ride frothy curls, and gulls ride thermals. He can see a paraglider, far in the distance.

"Why do you ask?"

"Because you staged that bit of legerdemain with your man Alonzo to slip me a note and to distract Guerrero. Because one of his men betrayed you last night, and I'm bettin' Guerrero handpicks the lads on your security detail."

Petra goes back to watching the ocean and sipping tequila. Dez lets the moment ride out. She'll answer the primary question or she won't, and if she doesn't, that's an answer in and of itself.

"The second time I was kidnapped, when I was twenty-one. . . . God, I just realized that will be fifteen years ago next month." She shakes her head in wonderment. "The second time I was kidnapped, they held me for a little over ninety seconds and they got a little less than one block away before my security detail overwhelmed them. Vincent Guerrero was leading the team that day. He's a former Marine. He killed the men who tried to take me. He saved my life."

And there it is: the nonanswer that serves as an answer in and of itself. Dez finishes his beer. He watches the paraglider. He or she seems to handle the rig well. Dez has done that, but carrying ten kilos of high explosives. He suspects the experience here would be different. He's in no hurry. He's sitting outside a stunning home, with a gorgeous view, sipping decent beer, and he's chatting up a woman of beauty and class. His plans for the day had involved a breakfast burrito and buying toilet paper for his bedsitter so, on the whole, this is better.

"Were you a soldier, Dez?"

"Me? That'd be a laugh. Frightened of me own shadow."

She says, "Were you a cop?"

"I find law and order to be overrated concepts."

"Vincent tried to do a background check on you already. He found nothing. Including no criminal record. But you're trained. You know how to fight men with guns."

"I do know how to fight men with guns," he says. "Quickly."

"Where did you learn to do all that?"

Dez thinks about another in a long line of coy replies but there's . . . something going on here. He can't quite put his finger on it. Petra Alexandris isn't being nosy. She isn't being a spoiled rich girl, used to getting her way. She's not being pushy.

He thinks she's trying to figure out a way to ask for help. He thinks she's vastly inexperienced at doing that. Dez finds himself wanting to help her.

"Was a gatekeeper."

"What's that?"

He's already regretting the honesty. He sips his beer, watching the ocean. She waits, eyes on him, her lean body unmoving. Dez has no idea how many people Petra Alexandris has deposed, but he gets the sense that she could outwait him unto death. He sighs. "Had a job opening doors that others couldn't. Me mates called it the gatekeeper. I know, sounds silly."

"I think of gatekeepers as people who guard gates. Not people who open them."

"Aye, but the trick isn't opening doors. Any half-wit can do that. It's about keeping 'em open. Closing 'em when needed. Controlling who goes through and who doesn't. Owning 'em. For as long as needed."

"Which doors?"

He shrugs. "Them what needs a bit of egressin'."

"Sounds dangerous."

He grins at her. "Nah."

Petra nods toward his forearm and says, "Janus." She pronounces it *ya-noosh*.

Dez turns over his right arm, examines the tattoo of the two-faced Roman god. It's his only visible tattoo when he's wearing a shirt. He tips his empty bottle toward the tat. "Patron god o' beginnings an' gates. Transitions an' time. Duality an' doors. Passages an' endings. Mate of mine."

"So you open doors that can't be opened?"

"No. I *used* to open doors that couldn't be opened. Now I play guitar. Also, for a while, small engine repair."

She says, "And a line cook in Trinidad."

"Jack-of-all-trades," he says. "Master o' none."

Petra sips her drink and watches the ocean, and Dez does, too. Something like five quiet minutes pass.

When she speaks again, she says, "Something's going on with my company. With Triton Expediters. Something my father doesn't want me to know about. I began investigating, behind his back. I think . . ."

She pauses. She drains the tequila. She squints out at the ocean again.

"I need help. And everyone I know today is associated with my company. I have no idea who to trust."

"What sort of help?"

Petra rises fluidly, all core muscle and gymnast's balance. She snags her empty glass and his empty bottle en passant, pads barefoot back toward the house.

"I need some doors opened."

CHAPTER 10

Six months ago, Dez had fallen for every lovely fable doled out by the California tourism industry. But now he's been here a bit more than two months and doubts he'll be here two more. He's passing through, trying to figure out what life is like for a retired bloke with a bit of coin saved up.

He has a friend, an Ethiopian, Ephrem Kebede, living in Torrance. Ephrem has a garage, focusing on German automobiles. Dez has been staying in a room behind the garage, helping a bit with the car repair work. There's a gym nearby he can hit on the cheap. It's worked out fine. But now he's agreed to look into this mess for Petra Alexandris. She's offered him a detached guest room in a stucco cottage to the south of the great house for the duration of his efforts to help her root out the mystery of her company, and to figure out who sent armed men to her suite at the Tremaine. He accepts, and she writes down the eight-digit code for the property's wall-mounted keypads that will get him in and out without alerting police or Triton Security personnel. The cottage beats the ever-loving hell out of a room behind a garage in Torrance.

She says, "I'll pay you."

He says, "Then we're in agreement on that." Only an idiot fights someone else's battles for free.

She has calls to make to Asia, something about providing funding for a copper mine but the details go over Dez's head, so he moves his duffel bag and his guitar to the cottage, which has a view of the ocean and also of the big house. He marvels at it all, then catches a Lyft to the shop in Torrance.

He lets Ephrem Kebede know he's got a gig. Then he grabs the rest of his gear. Including a locking metal tool kit. Also a tablet computer, which is housed in a ruggedized rubber case, surrounded by leather, and showing the nicks and scratches of several violent incidents. Dez kisses the leather exterior but doesn't realize it. He'll tell anyone who asks that he isn't superstitious. Most superstitious people think the same.

Two locked metal boxes hide under the single bed. One belongs to his friend Ephrem Kebede. One belongs to Dez. Ephrem has offered him the use of anything he wants in the first box, because Ephrem knows that Dez knows how to use them.

He uses his thumb pads to spin six locking dials. Inside, wrapped in oilcloth, is Ephrem's PAMAS G1, 9mm, and five nine-cartridge magazines. The gun is an inelegant, clunky L-shaped chunk of iron, but it's been well cared for, oiled and cleaned lovingly. Under it is a *militärische schutzhülle* quick-draw holster.

Dez sets them both aside and draws back more oilcloth, two layers of it, one flap gingerly folded outside the box, over Dez's knee, the other flap folded the opposite direction, to reveal a FAMAS G2 bullpup rifle. It features the modified 30-round mag. It's 750 millimeters long, weighs 4,170 kilograms when empty, and has a muzzle velocity of 925 millimeters per second, and Dez has memorized all this because—like his friend—Dez has handled this particular assault rifle, and others identical to it, for most of his adult life. It's an extension of his body. It fits him and Dez fits it, and they've seen each other through a lot.

He closes Ephrem's box and opens the one that belongs to him. That box includes a variety of technical equipment he used when he was a gatekeeper. Some of the equipment he earned. Some of it he invented. Some he still owns the patents for. He's still a little shocked that he told Petra about being a 'keeper. He hasn't spoken about that life since he retired.

Within the lockbox is a 290-millimeter fixed-blade knife, made by Coltellerie Maserin, black-coated steel in an olive drab nylon sheath, lying cuddled in black foam. Next to that is a folding Raptor blade, with its steel cutting surface that glides into the anodized aluminum handle. It comes with a belt clip, and the belt clip hides an array of lockpicks.

Dez doesn't figure he'll need any of Ephrem Kebede's firepower, not today, but it's a comfort to know it's available should that change. He takes his knives.

Ephrem has a thirty-year-old Jeep that a customer had brought in for repairs three months ago but never showed up to claim. Dez borrows it off his friend, and now he has wheels.

Next, he makes a phone call to Triton Expediters and asks for Major Vincent Guerrero. The young intern who'd distracted Guerrero in the lobby, when Alonzo slipped Dez a note, had called him *Major*. Petra had said he'd been a Marine. Dez bandies Petra's name about and gets an appointment for 6 p.m.

Perfect.

He heads to the offices of Triton Expediters.

CHAPTER 11

At five minutes until 6 p.m., Dez is leaning against the side of Vincent Guerrero's shiny black Escalade, on the executive parking level of the underground garage, thumbing through his bulky, upgraded mobile and looking for Premier League scores. He's been a Liverpool man since forever. The team is killing him this season but what are you going to do?

Vincent Guerrero steps out of the executive elevator and stops short, startled. "What the fuck . . . ?"

Dez looks up, beams a smile, and slips his mobile into his pocket. "Major."

Guerrero glances around to see who else is on the executive level. He spots no one. "Limerick. The fuck are you doing down here?"

"You accept an appointment with someone you don't like, have an underling take the meeting whilst you slip out of the building. Let your staff say, 'Sorry. Got called away. What can we do ye for?'" Dez smiles. "That trick was old when Jesus was a lance corporal."

Guerrero studies him. Dez leans against the car and takes it.

"You broke in here?"

"I did, aye."

Guerrero points toward the keypad adjacent to the elevator. "That's a state-of-the-art security system!"

Dez turns and glances at it, eyebrows raised. "Tell me you didn't pay full retail."

Guerrero takes a pugnacious step closer. "Triton Security designed this tech!"

Dez offers his kindest smile. "Then I'm wishing you all the best luck with it, Major."

The man fairly vibrates. Dez can see Guerrero battle with himself over how to react.

"I'm watching you, Limerick. You had something to do with Petra's abduction. Either you stopped those assholes, or you were with them and used them to squirm your way into the Alexandris household. I'm going to give you the benefit of the doubt. Once. I'm going to let you walk out that door. You ever break into any other Triton Expediters property, ever again, and our first call isn't to the police. It's to the Pentagon. And to the people who use Triton Expediters' finances to buy technology. Army Intelligence has black-site prisons, and they owe this company big-time. This is your only warning."

Dez crosses his arms, his biceps flexing. "Petra asked me to look into them kidnappers."

"She called and told me. Leave it the fuck alone."

"Be a good idea to figure out who them lads were."

"That's our job. That's *my* job. Get the fuck out of here. Last warning. And get your ass off my car."

Dez doesn't move a muscle. "Had good tech, them. Had experience. Done this before."

"Are you listening to me, mister?"

"Took care of the fire alarms first. Knocked out cell reception and landlines. Sniper on overwatch."

"Your point?"

"That's the way you Marines might do it, yeah?"

Guerrero draws his handgun but does not touch the safety. He holds it by his thigh, finger indexed. Dez ignores the gesture.

"It'd be dead brilliant if someone who was there last night had the forethought to grab one of the bastard's wallets."

Guerrero's poker face isn't nearly as good as he thinks it is. He blanches a little. Then his eyes narrow again. "We have the full police report. None of them had ID on them."

Dez relaxes a little but doesn't show it. He has what he came for. He says, "Yeah, but it had you worried there for a second. Didn't it, Major."

Guerrero raises the weapon, points it at Dez's chest. "Get the fuck out of this building. Get the fuck off American soil. Do it fast."

Dez finally pushes himself off the Escalade. Which puts the muzzle of the gun within an inch of his barrel chest. He maintains eye contact with Guerrero, maintains the easy smile.

"She's impressive, Petra. Never seen the likes of her before. If she thinks something's rotten in the state of Denmark, who'm I to argue?" He starts ambling toward the street door.

"You don't want to fuck with me, Limerick." Guerrero spits it out between clenched teeth.

Dez is all smiles. "I sorta do."

CHAPTER 12

There was probably a time when being a gatekeeper didn't require one to be a hacker, but every good 'keeper Dez has ever met is also an amateur hacker. You can bash your way through a door, shoot your way through, explode your way through, or burn your way through. But if the people behind the door have a good computer security system, it's all for naught. And these days, too many people have excellent security systems. Getting in the door often means defeating their computers first.

And besides, Petra gave him temporary access to the Triton Expediters main server, so getting into Guerrero's system isn't difficult.

Dez has no intention of breaking into the computer system of the Los Angeles Police Department. It's not that he couldn't, it's just that the arresting officers at the Hotel Tremaine, the night before, had been quite polite. Same for the detective that morning, Beth Swanson. Dez has no beef with the LAPD.

The same can't be said for Vincent Guerrero.

In the garage, Guerrero had said that Triton Security had the full police report. Which is all Dez really wanted when he paid his little visit. That, and to rattle the man's cage. Petra doesn't entirely trust the ex-Marine security director. Dez isn't sure what to do with that little gem of knowledge just yet.

He finds a quiet, dark bar not far from the Triton Expediters headquarters and orders a stout and a fish-and-chips. Then he sets up his ruggedized tablet computer on the bar and breaks into Guerrero's system in about seven minutes.

Dez studies the LAPD files. The three men who'd been arrested at the hotel had no ID and have said not one word to police. There were no identifying tags in their clothes. They had a couple of tattoos between them but their ink is anonymous and generic.

The fish-and-chips are light and perfectly fried with a thin panko crust, and served with a habanero slaw. The whole thing has a weird feel of being, well, healthy, and Dez has to admit he's slightly annoyed by that. He also would kill for a good side of mushy peas but this is America and that's just not happening.

The nurse practitioner on duty at the LA County jail had checked one of the men for blunt force trauma to his lower intestinal tract. Turns out he'll be okay but in a lot of pain. One man was treated for a badly shredded right shoulder. That's the fella who backhanded Petra. His arm's unlikely to ever heal fully and Dez is fine with that. The third man has a bruised trachea: He hasn't said a word to the cops because he's disciplined, but also because he can't.

The three men have an attorney who had made an appointment to meet with them that afternoon. He'd called ahead to clear the visit. Jail officials had looked him up. His name was Robert Smith. Dez opens a new window on his computer and goes to the law firm's website. He pops the hood and is inside the website within seconds. The site had been created only about a dozen hours ago. The site lists seven attorneys and two paralegals. Dez does a Google search and finds several references to attorney Robert Smith. He searches for the other six attorneys and two paralegals, and finds zip. They don't exist. Dez sips the dark brown beer and shakes his head forlornly. "Fuckers weren't even trying," he mutters.

The attorney is visiting the three men at the Los Angeles County jail in about two hours, and Dez decides to be there.

CHAPTER 13

The three men aren't being held at the Police Administration Building, where Dez found himself staying the night on Monday, but in a more secure jail annex near LAX. The place is in a sea of anonymous warehouses and is, itself, designed to look like a warehouse. Very little overt security is visible from the street except for a metal wire fence topped with concertina wire, and you see that all over the area anyway. Dez spots a second-story catwalk with deputies in khakis walking the perimeter of the building; that's the only clue that this isn't a warehouse.

He leaves the Jeep in the car park and heads for the reception building. It's about one minute before eight. He gets told, as he expected, that visiting hours are over. He asks about a man being held there, uses the name of a mate he'd known years earlier. *"Sorry, sir, we don't have anyone here by that name. Can we check other area jails for you?"*

It's like talking to the concierge at a high-end hotel. Even the sheriff's deputy on duty in the visitors lounge at the local jail is unusually polite. That's America for you. Weird.

A black sedan pulls in next to the Jeep at eight precisely. Dez makes his apologies and leaves. The man claiming to be attorney Robert Smith brushes past him, entering as Dez leaves. Smith is white, thirty, put together like a soldier, with short hair and intense eyes. In other words: He looks just like the three fellas Dez tangoed with last night.

Before the man enters, he pauses, frowns, and turns back to study Dez.

Dez grins.

The people behind the attack on Petra Alexandris might have put out Dez's description. Robert Smith might've been part of the assault. Could be he was the one who bolloxed the phones and alarms in the hotel. He could have been the overwatch sniper.

Dez checks the man's hand clutching his attaché case. He spots the telltale yellow calluses around the webbing of the man's thumb. One way of getting that is by putting in hours upon hours on the firing range.

The guy's still staring at him.

Dez says, "Lovely evening."

Unsure, the man just nods.

Dez climbs into the Jeep and backs out of the jail's public parking lot.

Before he leaves, Dez notes the make and model of the sedan, and the license plate, and then takes the Jeep about two blocks away and waits where he can observe the jail parking lot entry gate.

He checks his bespoke tablet computer. He's still inside Guerrero's system. The LA Police have just informed Triton Security that the three men are being transferred to a holding facility owned by the Department of Defense.

He digs out his wallet. Most men's wallets are stuffed to bursting with the crap they gather over the years. Dez's wallet is new, thin, cheap, and empty of anything more than two months old. He's been in America two months. This wallet offers not one clue about the before-time.

The only card in the wallet is that of Detective Beth Swanson, LAPD.

His phone is like his tablet; a bit bulkier than average, with some after-market add-ons. Some of them quite illegal in most countries. Dez calls her and, to his surprise, the call goes directly to her.

"Remember me? I'm the fella what—"

She says, *"Yeoman of the Guard."*

"Them three fellas I danced with? DOD is moving them out of the secure LA County jail site near the airport. Right now." He reads her the make and model of Smith's car, and the license plate details.

Any humor that had been in Swanson's voice evaporates. "How do you know this, sir?"

"Petra Alexandris asked me to look into them guys. Doing it now." All of which is true and avoids the dicey issue of computer hacking. "Just met the lawyer at the jail. Fella name of Smith, first name Robert. He's military, for sure. Looks exactly like them others."

"What are you saying?"

"That if I had three highly trained fellas in a public lockup, I'd want to get them out before the plod starts asking too many questions. That if I wanted them out, I wouldn't be so daft as to try a feckin' jailbreak. Excuse my language. I'd either use a false flag to lure them out. Or I'd hit the van in transit. Is what I'd do. If I were the nefarious kind."

"Are you?" Beth Swanson asks. "Nefarious?"

"Occasionally, yeah."

He watches the public parking lot gate from two blocks away and listens to the silence on his mobile.

"I have to make a phone call, Mr. Limerick. Will you stay on the line?"

"Friends call me Dez. Aye."

The line clicks. Dez sets the phone down on the cracked leather dash of the old Jeep, speaker mode on. He's thinking about the weirdly healthy fish–and–chips, wondering why such a thing is even possible and who'd bother. You want to eat healthy, you order a salad. You don't eat in pubs. Makes no sense.

Three minutes later, a long black van pulls into the jail property. The men who climb out wear U.S. Army fatigues and black berets with some sort of shield-shaped patch on the front, but they're too far away for Dez to read them. They look like military police. He actually thinks they might be because they seem to be joshing around, looking a bit bored, searching under a seat for the clipboard with the paperwork. Prisoner transfer is the meat-and-two-veg of military police. It's scut work and dull as dishwater.

If this is a jailbreak, the villains of the piece have opted to ambush the convoy en route, rather than take the time to fake the paperwork necessary to let their men waltz out.

He hears Beth Swanson speaking. "Limerick?"

"Aye. Van's here. Transfer's happening."

"We know. Listen very, very carefully. You are to take the key out of your car and sit there, as is, for thirty minutes. Do not pursue. I have vehicles doing that and they're professionals. You are not."

"Yes, ma'am."

"I'm going to tell you this, then deny we ever talked. My captain and I had the same exact bad feeling you had. We're monitoring this thing, too. Now stand down, accept my off-the-record thanks, and let us handle this."

"Yes, ma'am."

Swanson hangs up.

Dez turns over the key, the well-maintained old Jeep purring.

There are a couple of Jesuit nuns in Merry Olde who'd rap him smart for lying to Beth Swanson. At some point, Dez is going to have to consider an act of contrition.

CHAPTER 14

The paperwork says the three men who attempted to abduct Petra Alexandris are being taken to a stockade at Point Mugu Naval Air Station. As that's north of Los Angeles, one could have expected the long, armored van to take Highway 101. Everyone in Beth Swanson's three-unit surveillance crew is surprised to see the van turn off onto Highway 1.

The attorney, Robert Smith, rides drag. When the prison transport van pulls onto Highway 1 without a turn indicator, Smith turns off fluidly in its wake. He'd expected the turn.

Dez has spotted the police follow-cars—they're watching the prisoner transport, not their own six, so they haven't made him yet. He sees two of Detective Beth Swanson's vehicles hopscotch northward on the 101 to get ahead of the van and sedan, using sirens and light bars when they're well clear. One cop car (Dez will find out later that the beat-to-crap Nissan Sentra has a good engine and four new tires, and was confiscated in a drug bust) stays with the van and sedan on the slow, meandering, and switchback-laden Highway 1.

Dez follows, well back, his aged and unwashed Jeep blending into highway traffic rather nicely. Everyone loves a parade.

It's a tough road for rolling surveillance. The traffic thins out. They come to a lot of switchbacks, which means losing visual on the transport van over and over.

The van is adjacent to Leo Carrillo State Park when it comes around a sharp corner and runs into a spike chain.

All four tires blow in less than a second.

The Army driver's good, and he keeps the ungainly van on a tight leash as it skids sideways, off the highway, onto the rest stop. The van just misses the guardrail and a seventy-foot drop into the Pacific.

There are five MPs in the van, either up front or with the prisoners, and they deploy quickly, sidearms extended, looking for trouble. They don't expect trouble to be one of their own, and the first man goes down when the guy who'd been seated next to him puts a .45 in the base of his spine.

The not-a-lawyer, Robert Smith, avoids the spike strip because he knew where it'd be. His sedan skids to a halt on the lay-by, behind the van. He jumps out with an AR-15, and another MP collapses in a spray of blood.

The beat-up Nissan loses one tire, spins one-eighty, and screeches to a halt behind the sedan. Two LAPD cops sit, frozen, eyes wide, hyperventilating. That two-second delay costs them.

Robert Smith swings back to fire at the cops.

The surviving MPs and the fake MP shoot it out, sandwiched between the tireless transport van and the palisades guardrail, beyond which is nothing but vertical sagebrush and boulders and a rocky beach way below.

One of the cops from the Nissan takes a bullet in the calf, and she collapses to the pavement. Her buddy scrambles behind the car, well outgunned by Robert Smith and his AR-15.

Then Dez's Jeep rounds the corner.

He sees the van, and the sedan, and the Nissan, all parked like crap, noses pointed everywhere, in the lay-by. He hears gunfire. He spots the busted tire on the Nissan and two of the busted tires on the van, sees the swirling dust of rapid deceleration on gravel. So he swings the Jeep to his left, sharpish, missing the spike strip.

He sees the fake attorney firing an AR-15 at Beth Swanson's detectives, and he turns the wheel toward him.

He smashes the Jeep's grille into the right-hand side of the sedan, a perfect T-bone, shoving the sedan to the west, where it acts like a snowplow, scooping up Robert Smith and his assault weapon and sending him, and the sedan, and the gun, through the guardrail and over the edge of the cliff.

Dez is braced for the impact but not the noise of it, which rattles his skeleton. His teeth clack together painfully. His palms sting from the kinetic energy transmitted up the steering column. He shakes it off, hops out of the passenger-side door of the old Jeep, marches around the transport van on its right, the highway side. He can hear the running gunfight on that side. He circles the cab and takes in the scene. There's one Army MP firing at the others, so Dez does his sums, figures out who's the villain of the piece. He shouts, "Oy!"

Startled, the fake MP turns, and Dez punches him in the nose.

The man's boots leave the ground, and he skids a good four feet on the gravel.

The shooting has stopped. Everyone left alive is safe.

So Dez does what Dez knows to do. He laces his fingers behind his head and kneels in the gravel.

This part, he's got down.

CHAPTER 15

It was his old mate Rafik who used to say, "The fecal matter has just collided with the air-conditioning unit, *chef*."

And indeed it has.

The first circle of officialdom consists of Army MPs, who are out of their jurisdiction but who nonetheless get Dez on the ground, facedown, and cuff him.

LAPD is on the scene next, Beth Swanson's other pursuit vehicles having circled back and rejoined the caravan. They take command from the MPs, who are too shell-shocked to complain.

California Highway Patrol is next, and they quickly take command from the city cops, blocking all traffic in both directions.

TV news helos arrive in record time to capture live footage. The sun has finally set, but the place is lit up like Old Trafford.

The Department of Defense gets to the scene twenty minutes later and quickly takes back operational command, which pisses off CHP to no end.

Someone from the California Attorney General's Office arrives in twenty-seven minutes and reverts control of the scene to CHP but, by then, LAPD Detective Beth Swanson, a lieutenant, and a captain have arrived, and CHP's feeling like, who needs to be drum major of this parade? They quickly concede the crime scene to the city cops.

Dez misses all this, catching a quick snooze in the back of a California Highway Patrol SUV. When he wakes, he's thinking about that stout he had at the pub and how it's no longer fair to say Americans can't make beer. It was true for decades but they're getting better all the time. Most of it's still horse piss, and that's a fact, but the microbrew industry seems to be revving along just fine. Impressive, that.

The scene on Highway 1 is now about one panto and a maypole away from being a village fete. Dez is surprised no one's sold him a raffle ticket.

At some point, the Department of Defense guys lined up on the east side of the highway are joined by Vincent Guerrero of Triton Security and some of his lads. Guerrero makes eye contact with Dez, and Dez winks at him. Guerrero appears not to find any of this amusing.

A uniformed cop politely transfers Dez to a big, brightly painted LAPD recreational vehicle with INCIDENT COMMAND written on the side, where he's met by Beth Swanson and her lieutenant and her captain. The captain is an impressively tall woman with a long face and half-glasses on a cloth lanyard, who nods to Swanson. Swanson removes Dez's cuffs.

The captain might be six-two. She's rail-thin. He pegs her age at fifty-five, give or take. She says, "Aloysius? Really?"

"It's a perfectly fine name!"

Swanson seethes with anger. "What's it short for? Dumb Ass?"

Dez says, "Oh yeah, an' what's Beth short for?"

"Elizabeth."

Dez pauses. Turns back to the captain. "Had a better comeback in me head but I lost it there for a second."

The tall woman says, "I'm Captain Naomi Cardona. Los Angeles Police."

"Dez. Pleased."

She says, "You saved a couple of lives today, Mr. Limerick."

"But I also lied to Beth, ma'am, and for that I apologize."

The three cops study him for a few seconds. The lieutenant, a wiry blond guy, shakes his head in amazement.

"We interviewed the officers on the scene. They saw it all. We're trying to decide if we should arrest you or thank you," Cardona says. "But right now, I think we have a window of about fifteen minutes before the military takes those guys out of here, and I have a very, very stupid idea."

The lieutenant says, "I'm against this."

"Duly noted, Stan." Naomi Cardona points out the window of the Incident Command vehicle at the prisoner transport with its four shredded tires. "Mr. Limerick, I'd like to put Swanson and you in that transport for the few moments we have. Those men haven't said a word to anyone since they were arrested at the Hotel Tremaine. You slammed into those guys like Hurricane Katrina. They're pretty pissed off, and they're in a lot of pain. I'm wondering if we can't make that work in our favor."

Dez smiles. "Can I hit 'em again?"

Cardona says, "No."

"Can Beth hit 'em?"

"No. But I want to see how they react to the two of you. Are you game for this?"

Dez's smile turns into a grin.

The captain has a word with the senior-most military man on the scene. He has the chevrons of a first sergeant, which means he's used to making snap decisions and living with them. He says, "I can't authorize this. Sorry."

Captain Cardona makes her case without emotion. "It could be important. We need to know something. We won't touch the prisoners. Promise."

The first sergeant chews his gum, eyeing her. Dez can tell he wants to believe her, to help. He can't find a legal reason to do so.

Dez says, "Gimme a sec?" and leads the Army sergeant about ten meters away. They huddle, speaking sotto voce. At one point, the sergeant draws his cell phone, taps on it, looks something up. He eyes Dez, then his phone, then Dez.

Under her breath, Cardona says, "This is beginning to feel like an eight-point-two on the Sphincter Scale."

Swanson nods.

The sergeant turns on his heel and marches back to the cops. "Jesus, why didn't you lead with that? The transport is yours, Captain. Good luck."

He walks away.

Beth says, "What just happened there?"

Dez shrugs. "Dunno. Said you two was upstanding police officers. LA's finest. He came 'round."

From the way she side-eyes him, he can tell that Cardona isn't buying it. But time's short, and she just got what she wanted. She and her lieutenant climb in the front of the transport van, from where they'll be able to hear what happens.

Beth Swanson and Dez wait in the back as an MP gets ready to unlock the transport. Dez whispers, "Aloysius. Latinized. Part an' parcel with Louis, Lewis, Luis, Luigi, Ludwig—"

"Shut up."

"From the Latin meaning *famous warrior*."

"Begging you to shut up."

Two MPs open the back of the van. Dez and Swanson use the hand-holds to lift themselves up onto the thigh-high bumper, and from there into the mobile holding cell.

Dez recognizes his three dance partners from the Hotel Tremaine. All three are in their late twenties or early thirties, white, with short hair and athletic builds. He hit one in the gut with an ax handle. He hit one in the throat. He separated the ball and the socket of the third guy's right shoulder. All three wear prisoner jumpsuits with LA COUNTY JAIL emblazoned on the front and back. The first two have their wrists cuffed in front of them and attached by chains to wide, locking leather belts around their waists. The third guy's right arm is in a sling and only his left is cuffed to the belt.

Dez can tell from the bloody noses and split lips that they went flying when the long van skidded off the highway.

The three guys aren't simply in a locked van, they're also behind bars.

It takes them a second to recognize who's just entered the van.

The man with his arm in the sling stands from the bolted-down bench, eyes burning. He's on some pretty powerful painkillers; Dez can tell by the dilation of his eyes. "You are a fucking dead man."

Dez winks. "How's the bowling arm, then?"

The man with the bruised trachea rises and stands with his mate. "You're gonna die badly," he croaks.

Beth Swanson flashes her ID. "We'd like to ask——"

Broken Shoulder speaks directly to Dez. "No one's talking to your colored bitch."

Swanson lowers her eyes and takes a meek step back.

It takes Dez all of a quarter second to get it: three very white guys. Four white guys, if you count the not-a-lawyer, Robert Smith. Five, if you count the MP who opened fire on his men. Swanson and Cardona had an inkling the common denominator was that they're violent racists. They sent Swanson in here to test that theory.

Broken Shoulder says, "You're fucking dead. Race traitor."

Bingo.

"Could be. Not from the likes of you ladies."

The man with the sore gut hasn't spoken yet, but when he finally does, Dez can tell he's the leader. "No talking."

Detective Swanson stands there, head down, and just listens. If the racist bullshit gets to her, Dez certainly can't tell.

"Time comes, we're gonna remember your kind," Bruised Trachea hisses.

The leader finally rises.

Broken Shoulder steps close to the bar. "We're gonna find you, and that bitch, and we're——"

The leader reaches up and grips Broken Shoulder's broken shoulder. He squeezes. The man turns parchment pale, eyes wide, body rigid. Despite the massive dosage of painkillers, he falls to his knees and dry heaves.

The leader keeps his voice low, eye-fucking the other man. "No. Talking."

Broken Shoulder, penitent, nods toward the floor. Bruised Trachea backs up.

Dez grins at the obvious leader. "Which'd make you the big dick in this lot." He takes a rambling step closer to the bars. If the man reached through, Dez would be within striking distance.

"Your lawyer mate is dead. Your MP mate is down. Ye've five shots on goal. Five misses. You're the saddest bunch of fighters it's been my pleasure to meet."

The man stares at him with dead eyes.

Dez steps closer, puffs out his chest, testing the durability of the stitching of his T-shirt. "Desmond Aloysius Limerick. Pleased as hell."

The man behind the bars nods only once. His meaning is clear: *I've heard your name. I can find you. And I will.*

From behind Dez, Detective Beth Swanson says, "Thank you, gentlemen. We appreciate your time."

She touches Dez's shoulder. They turn and walk out, step down onto the bumper, then onto the gravel of the shoulder of the highway, with the cliff and the ocean off to their right. This close to the Pacific, the air is crisp. The harsh lights of emergency vehicles and helicopters make the lay-by look like a movie set.

"Aloysius." Swanson shakes her head. "It's starting to grow on me."

CHAPTER 16

Ryerson Ranch, Boca Serpiente County, California

Jonesy has taken out one of the quad ATVs to check the perimeter of the Ryerson property. It's his turn, written in pencil on the duty roster in the communal kitchen.

Joe Ryerson is in that kitchen making eggs for the seven kids, all seated around the big wooden table, all doing their homework. The older kids help teach the younger ones. Today it's practical math, the kids working out the problems of feeding fifteen people during the siege by the Zionist Occupation Government. The siege is only on day twenty-nine but the people here can hold out for seven months easily. Nine, if they ration. And they do.

Joe will fry up rashers of bacon for the children. None of them have any experience buying bacon at Safeway. Each of them has been taught how to slaughter a hog; how the belly and ribs are removed from the loin; how the belly is trimmed for bacon. All of the adults and all of the older children can do this. It's part of the life they live.

The radio on the sill of the window overlooking the vegetable garden squawks. "Jonesy here. You copy? Over."

Joe wipes his hands on his apron and lowers the heat under the eggs. He crosses the kitchen and grabs the mic. "Go ahead, man. Over."

"Ah, you got a dead calf out here. Over."

Joe swears softly to himself and glances at the uneven wooden table that he and Molly built when they moved here, twenty-two years ago. The kids all heard Jonesy's call. They know it affects their calculations but they don't yet know how.

Joe toggles the switch. "Where are you at? Over."

"Sector Seven-A. Over."

The ranch has been gridded off into sectors, ever since the siege began. For security reasons. Joe looks at the hand-drawn diagram near the radio. Seven-A is right at the edge of the Ryerson property, and close to the big old fence put up by the *federales* back in the 1960s.

Jonesy speaks again. "Anybody know what coyote kill looks like? Over."

"Coyote? You sure? Over."

Jonesy laughs. "I'm from Rochester, New York, dude. Hell, no, I'm not sure. I'm asking. Coyote, wolf. Looks like a predator, is all. Over."

It's not a wolf. They're all about 120 years to the right of any wolf packs roaming the Boca Serpiente Valley. Joe says, "Hang loose, good buddy. We'll come take a look. Over."

"Roger that. Out."

Joe talks to Molly. They do rock, paper, scissors. That's how they've decided things for more than twenty-two years now. Molly pulls scissors, Joe rock, so Molly hops on the second of their three quads and rolls out to Sector Seven-A.

She's skilled on the four-wheel ATV, knows to bring her thick leather gloves and her tool belt, because it's going to be fifteen minutes out, then fifteen minutes back and fifteen more for the return trip if she needs to go retrieve any tools. Better to bring damn near everything on the first run. Including her Colt 1911. It's a beloved bit of single-action, recoil-operated, .45-caliber American technology. She's owned it since she was a teenager. All of the adults at the ranch carry, as do the four children ages fifteen and older. Ranch rules. The only thing the Zionist Occupation Government understands.

Freedom isn't free.

Molly Ryerson curves around the dry brush of the flat, arid land that they've ranched for two decades, avoiding the ravines she knows, an eye open for snakes. She spots Jonesy and the other ATV. Well, first, she spots that red baseball cap of his. Between that and his full beard, she's not 100 percent sure what Jonesy looks like, although he's been part of this siege since it started nearly a month ago. If he got gussied up for, like, a wedding, she wouldn't recognize him.

He's parked near a deep crevice. Molly knows this land like she knows her own handwriting. Jonesy's standing maybe all of ten yards from the long, rusty, unbroken fence that stretches clear to the horizon. Directly behind him is an old, metal sign, hung on the fence, round, blue and green, with a lightning bolt cut crosswise. The U.S. Department of Energy.

Molly's not happy being this close to the federal land. She pushes up her aged, sweat-stained outback hat and peers up at the cloudless blue sky, as if she could see the ZOG's surveillance satellites peering tirelessly down at them all.

Jonesy's standing, hands shoved into the rear pockets of his Levi's. She likes the young man. She likes that he's quiet and a hard worker. She suspects he's had military training and, when she asks, he admits to a tour in the Coast Guard. She likes that he calls her *ma'am*.

She pulls up so the quads are nose-to-nose and dismounts. Her back aches. Riding the quads always does that to her these days. She sighs. "Hey."

Jonesy looks a little sad to see her, oddly enough. He says, "You and Joe play rock, paper, scissors for this?"

She shrugs. "Same as always."

Jonesy seems to think about that a moment.

"Calf?"

He nods toward a shallow ravine.

Molly approaches the ravine and peers down.

She's surprised to see two U.S. Army soldiers, both staring up at her, looking nervous as hell.

Jonesy pulls a Beretta M9 out from beneath the tail of his shirt and shoots Molly in the back.

Molly is dead before she hits the red clay soil.

Jonesy walks over and puts two more slugs into the flank of his ATV. The sound of the shots echo over the flat land. It'll reach the ranch in a hot second. Old Joe will be scrambling for the kitchen radio any moment now. Jonesy wishes it hadn't been Molly who came.

He turns to the ravine. The two soldiers are climbing out, their camo tinted red by the clay soil.

"Captain," one of them says, his voice breaking. "Did . . . did you just shoot a civilian?"

Jonesy throws the Beretta into the ravine. He removes his thick work gloves. He has a second gun in the saddlebag of his ATV. It's a Smith & Wesson. He draws it now and calmly shoots both soldiers in the chest. He closes in, fires more shots, makes sure they're dead.

The radio starts squawking. "Molly? It's Joe! Molly! You copy? Over!"

Jonesy takes a switchblade knife out of his saddlebag. He braces himself, then slashes his left forearm. It begins to bleed quickly.

"Molly? Joe! Molly, come back! Over!"

Jonesy waits. He doesn't bother answering. Not yet. From where he stands, he can see the vertical slit cut into the long, imposing Department of Energy fence, through which his unit had made egress onto the ranch land, under his orders. The clipped wires are directly below the round DOE logo and the DO NOT TRESPASS sign that's been vigorously decorated with buckshot over the years.

And beyond the fence and the sign, Jonesy can see the cooling tower of the Boca Serpiente Valley Nuclear Power Station, two and a half miles away.

He stands there, bleeding, thinking, *Now it gets interesting.*

CHAPTER 17

Dez calls his friend Ephrem Kebede to inform him that his Jeep is both ruined and impounded as evidence. The Ethiopian gives his signature basso profundo laugh. "Usually not hard to see where you been, eh, *chef*? Just follow the debris."

From what Dez finds out later, Constantine Alexandris throws all of his considerable corporate weight behind a demand that a representative of the Department of Defense brief him, personally, the following morning on the assault against his daughter, and the subsequent assault against LA County Sheriff's deputies.

He can do this, Petra Alexandris explains, because Triton Expediters doesn't manufacture weaponry or military materiel. Rather, the company shepherds the money to manufacture such weapons and materiel, and shepherds the money for international sales of weapons and materiel. Petra explains all this to him that night, again out on the deck of the sprawling Malibu property, him with a beer, her with a single malt Irish whiskey, as the clock ticks over to tomorrow.

"Your company doesn't make war, it just markets it." He sips his beer and watches a vaporous, horizontal white line of ocean froth appear, then disappear into the dark, like the breath of a dragon. They sit on the same chaise longues as before. Petra studies his profile, backlit by the light from the interior of the great house.

He calls Triton *your company* and not *your father's company,* and Petra silently likes that. "You're cynical," she replies without heat.

"The cynic is the company that knows the caliber of everything but the value of nothing."

She laughs. "Did you just paraphrase Wilde?"

"Growing up where I did, learning to fight an' steal cigarettes only takes up so many hours of the day. After that, it's learn to read or go mad."

It's late but neither of them is tired. Dez has told her about the incident with the prisoner transport, and the current theory of the LAPD that her attackers appear to be white supremacists. She absorbs all that information. It doesn't make much sense to her but it also doesn't make much sense to Dez. Difference is, she has an international law degree from Oxford, and a keen analytical mind, and a predator's sense of situational awareness, and she's not used to being in the dark about critical matters. Dez is really, really used to being in the dark about critical matters. That's almost always the way it works.

"My father will have the DOD called on the carpet. Later this morning, I'm sure of it. Triton money isn't something the Pentagon can ignore."

Dez sips his beer and watches the ocean froth. He plays back everything he's experienced the past couple of days. He says, "Can you have a say in all that?"

"I can and I will."

"Good. Have the briefing here."

She turns to him again. Wearing black yoga pants and a black hoodie, barefoot, she's barely visible in the dark. "At the house?'

"Aye."

"Why?"

"Want to see something."

They're quiet for a while. They hear teenagers laughing and horsing

— 73 —

around on the beach, somewhere out of sight. They smell marijuana. They hear the hiss of surf on the beach.

"I'll arrange it," she says. "Here."

"Ta."

She sips her whiskey.

"I'm thinking a lot about kissing you," she says. "See how it goes."

"Jay-sus!" Dez looks exasperated. "About bleeding time! I haven't been kissed by anyone in days now!"

It catches her a little off guard, and she laughs. "You get kissed a lot?"

"I get kissed constantly." Dez sighs. "It's the cross I bear."

Now she really laughs. Petra Alexandris is tall and gorgeous and rich, and she's used to men putting her on a pedestal, or treating her as unobtainable, or using her to count coup. She's not used to simple flirting.

She stands and says, "Come inside."

Dez rises. "Yes, ma'am."

Dez is an expert in a handful of areas. Opening locked doors. Keeping them open. Linguistics. Throwing a punch. Taking a punch. Drinking.

He is not an expert in the art of making love, but likes to think of himself as an enthusiastic amateur.

They're an odd pairing. He's solid muscle but makes love gently. Petra is long and lean, with few curves, and she uses Dez the way her Ferrari uses the road: all speed and ferocity, gutsy and on the edge.

What Dez lacks in expertise, Petra makes up for in energy. And between the two of them, they make, Dez humbly believes, a pretty spectacular showing of it. Fireworks. The Earth moves. Angels sing. All the clichés.

Nicely done, he decides an hour later, grinning like a kid on Christmas morn. Ten for ten. Full marks.

CHAPTER 18

The Department of Defense promises to send a U.S. Navy captain at 10 a.m. sharp to brief the CEO of Triton Expediters on the incidents involving his company and his daughter—in that order.

When he hasn't arrived by 10:02 a.m., Vincent Guerrero gets on the horn to find out what's happened. He's informed that the captain has arrived, not at the Hawthorne headquarters of the company, but at the Alexandris compound in Malibu Colony Beach. He's there right now, wondering where the CEO is.

"On whose authority did he go there?" Guerrero bellows into his phone. Constantine sits behind his obsidian desk, fuming.

Guerrero lowers the phone to his chest and turns to him. "Petra."

The old man growls a long, low litany of Greek obscenities.

One would expect the CEO of a multinational corporation to employ a limousine and drivers, and indeed, Constantine Alexandris has those things. It's simply that he hates them. His menial labor jobs, starting at age thirteen, included driving dump trucks, farm trucks, tractors, backhoes, and even, briefly, a cement mixer. He finds solace behind the wheel.

Besides, the man owns seven classic cars. There seems little point in owning a forty-year-old, limited edition Lamborghini that once belonged to Cary Grant while sitting in the back of a limo like a potted plant.

So Vincent Guerrero's problem—year in and year out—is assigning a three-car convoy of security personnel to create a fast-moving cocoon around the CEO as he races around the California freeways.

Constantine gets to the gates of the Malibu Colony Beach community only seconds before the lead chase car. He has a brilliant business mind but has a terrible memory for mundane things; he can never remember the code to get into the Malibu house, and he waits, impatiently, for Petra to unlock it from within or for Vincent Guerrero to catch up and input his code. The latter wins out. Guerrero arrives, taps his code quickly, and the double redwood front doors clack open. The hyperactive little man with hair and eyebrows like steel wool storms in, Guerrero in his wake. Constantine has rarely been to the house since his second wife died of a heart attack, and if he notices the collection of new art, mostly by up-and-coming Mexican painters, he doesn't let on.

He finds the Navy captain and two aides in the spacious, sunny living room with its floor-to-ceiling windows and languid ceiling fans. They stand in a cluster, talking quietly to one another. They seem overly amazed by the room's thick glass floor; the tide is in and the ocean is under their feet, giving the illusion of standing over the moon pool of a submarine.

Petra wears sharply pressed trousers that flare widely at the cuff, stilettos, and a man's white shirt, like some vision from the 1940s. Dez stands, holding a cup of coffee with a dopey grin and hair that was desperate for a barber at least three weeks ago. Guerrero glowers. Dez's presence in this house is an affront to Constantine, and he bristles. But he has bigger fish to fry. When he speaks, it is to neither Petra nor Dez. It's to the U.S. Navy captain. "What the fuck are you doing here?"

Petra sits on a piano bench, in front of the room's grand piano, leaning far forward, head down, elbows on her knees, hands clenched, staring at the carpet as if praying for Tropical Storm Constantine to pass.

"We, ah, were ordered to meet—"

"No, what are you doing *here.* Why are you not at my office?"

"Father." Petra sits up straight and smiles. "The captain is waiting for his superior officer. Who needed to make a call and I offered him the phone in my office. Ah. Here he is."

Another person enters. African American, tall and slim, in a blue suit and striped tie. He smiles at Petra, nods to Constantine.

The old man glances his way. "Who the fuck are you?"

Dez comes close to snorting coffee across the room. The captain and his aides look thunderstruck.

"Father, may I introduce Admiral Gerald Lighthouse. Secretary of the Navy. Member of the Joint Chiefs of Staff. Killer backhand in tennis."

Dez enjoys seeing the shock ripple through Vincent Guerrero's body. Even the perpetually grumpy Constantine Alexandris looks stunned.

"Sir." Admiral Lighthouse offers a hand and, after a beat, Constantine accepts. "I was flying back from Tokyo when I heard Petra had asked for a debrief on this . . . situation."

Constantine is trying to catch up. "Wait . . . I asked . . ."

Petra stands. "The admiral and I have been negotiating the financing for the new Vermeer fast-attack helicopters, Father. The talks are at a critical stage. Since he was flying through LAX, I asked if he'd look into the attack on me . . . on the company. Personally."

"And unfortunately"—the admiral offers a brisk smile all around—"there's very little I can tell you. I apologize. We—"

Petra cuts him off, addressing her father. "The Pentagon is balking at the price tag for the new gunships. They're prototypes. Damn expensive."

Lighthouse tries to turn the conversation back. "We can talk about that in the next round of negotiations, Petra. If we—"

She turns to him and smiles brightly. "They'd be cheaper if Israel chipped in and bought twenty."

She has the admiral's attention now. "Ye-es," he drawls. "But the Likud has closed the door on that deal."

"Moshe Abramovich would have said yes."

"Moshe Abramovich retired from politics."

"Moshe Abramovich is waiting to see how Likud does in the next municipal elections."

"Moshe . . ." The admiral pauses. And then, slowly, smiles. "Is he planning a comeback?"

"So I hear."

"He's a very strong proponent of the next generation of helos."

"So he told me . . . over caviar and vodka, two weekends ago, in Oslo."

They pause, staring at each other.

Everyone's quiet.

Dez nudges Guerrero with his elbow. "Is this going to be on the final?"

Admiral Lighthouse narrows his eyes, and studies Petra. "That's . . . an interesting development."

"Thought it might be."

"And Israel could be convinced to go in on the prototype?"

"Honestly?" She sighs theatrically. "We're so tied up trying to find out what we can about the attack on our company, I haven't had the time to pursue it."

And Lighthouse very, very slowly sighs as well. He knows when he's been outplayed.

He turns to Constantine Alexandris.

"I . . . might be able to tell you a bit about what happened, sir. But it. Absolutely. Must. Stay. In. This. Room. Am I clear?"

Constantine nods, trying to regain the upper hand. "Get on with it."

Dez realizes that Petra did some sort of hocus-pocus there on some sort of Pentagon procurement deal, while he was standing and slurping coffee. Now this, he thinks, is how you play poker. Constantine had puffed up his chest and bellowed and demanded a meeting with a military officer. His daughter had called his bet and raised him to a member of the Joint Chiefs. Fecking brilliant.

The change of venue had been Dez's idea. Asking the secretary of the Navy to stop by during his layover from Tokyo? That wouldn't have dawned on Dez in a thousand years.

Petra picks up her mobile from off the piano and hits a single key. Alonzo, her house staff, enters from the kitchen in skinny black jeans, pristine white sneakers, and a neatly pressed but untucked raspberry shirt. He's carrying a tray of cups, cream and sugar, spoons, and honey and packets of chemical sweeteners, along with a gleaming, high-tech coffeepot. Dez is unsure why anyone needs a high-tech coffeepot. The technology to boil coffee is pre–Bronze Age.

The Kabuki of distributing coffee keeps Constantine Alexandris from ripping off anyone's head. Admiral Lighthouse waits, chatting with Petra about their recent negotiations. Guerrero looks like someone dipped his nuts in a blender but hasn't yet hit Puree. Dez helps himself to more coffee.

When the formalities are over, Lighthouse takes the stage the way only a career officer and politician can. "Before we begin, I want to express the concerns of the Navy, and of this administration, about the attack on Petra. To the extent that we can help, we will."

Petra touches his forearm, smiles. "Thank you, Gerald."

The junior officers look at the demonstrative display with something like awe.

"The bad news is: Much of what I know is highly classified and I can't share it all with you. I can share some of it. Like I said, I must insist that nobody—I mean nobody—discusses this outside this room."

He glances at everyone's faces. "All right. On Monday evening last, at least five people, and possibly more, launched an armed assault on the Hotel Tremaine in Los Angeles. Three of these people were, ah, detained by Mr. Limerick."

He turns to Limerick. "If I haven't said it yet: well done."

Dez nods. "Sir."

Constantine and Guerrero exchange surprised looks.

Lighthouse continues, "The assailants have been identified, thanks to their fingerprints. But the Pentagon is not ready to release their names to you."

Constantine bristles.

"This whole thing is being treated as beyond top secret," the admiral says.

Petra nods. "What *can* you tell us?"

Lighthouse steels himself. Everyone can tell he's treading on exceedingly thin ice. "All I can to tell you is this: The three men detained by Mr. Limerick have been identified as current members of U.S. military services."

Everyone looks a little shocked. Constantine says, "Current members?"

But Dez and Guerrero have leapfrogged ahead of that bombshell, directly to the next. They speak almost in harmony. "Services?"

"Current, yes," says the secretary of the Navy. "And services. Plural. Yes."

Constantine shakes his head viciously, like a dog that wandered into a sprinkler. "That makes no sense! Who are they?"

"I'm not at liberty to tell you which branches of the military. Nor where they are stationed. Only that they are all active-duty personnel."

"Them other two at the ambush?" Dez asks.

The admiral nods to him. "Those guys, too, *chef.*"

"Holy fuck." Dez turns to Petra. "Sorry."

"Word for word," says Lighthouse, "exactly what I said when I was briefed in Tokyo."

Constantine looks utterly lost at sea. "Are . . . What are you saying? This was a *sanctioned* military action?"

Petra speaks and she's as cool as lime sherbet. "No. What Gerald is saying is, all five of the men whom we know to be involved are current military personnel, and that they serve in different branches of the U.S. Armed Forces, and that the U.S. military and intelligence services are experiencing a collective myocardial infarction as we speak. What he's telling us is, we appear to be hip-deep in an illegal, unsanctioned operation that would be prohibited by the code of military conduct, by the Pentagon, by the Joint Chiefs, by the executive, congressional, and judicial branches of government, and by anyone who's ever studied military law. Is that close, Gerald?"

He smiles at her. "Absolutely one hundred percent accurate."

Constantine Alexandris and Vincent Guerrero—and even the Navy captain and his aides, who stand in the corner, unmoving like lawn gnomes—all look stunned.

The old man says, "That's . . . that's . . ."

Dez slurps coffee. "Well an' truly fecked?" He turns to Petra. "Sorry."

CHAPTER 19

Everyone lets the revelations stand a moment. Dez swears he can actually see the gears whirling in Petra's skull. She's calculating the odds.

Guerrero couldn't be more of a fish out of water if he'd tried. With the rank of major, retired, he's used to being the biggest swinging dick in any room. In this house, he's at least second highest in rank. And Petra, the youngest civilian in the room, just played the Pentagon brass like a fiddle. Guerrero may have watched Petra grow up, but he clearly didn't know what she's grown into.

Constantine finally inhales deeply and runs his hands over his face. He turns to Guerrero and says, "Get rid of the fool."

Dez says, "Hey, now. Admiral's just doing his job. Don't blame the messenger."

A little laugh bubbles out of Petra. "He means you."

"Oh." Dez turns to Constantine. "Sorry. Carry on."

Admiral Lighthouse says, "Mr. Alexandris? This is none of my business, but I'd let Limerick stay."

"This man may be part of the group that attacked my daughter!"

Lighthouse shakes his head. "He's not."

"You can't know that!"

Lighthouse takes no umbrage. He just shrugs.

Guerrero finds his voice. "Respectfully, Admiral. Do you know this man?"

Lighthouse turns to his aides and gently touches the face of his wristwatch. The captain nods, and everyone gets ready to decamp. The admiral turns back. "Know him? Sorry. No. Just a gut feeling."

Constantine claws for the upper hand that he's so used to owning. "I want constant updates, Admiral."

Lighthouse says, "Yes, sir. I know you do."

I know you do isn't the same as *you'll get them*. And everyone in the room catches the nuance.

Lighthouse shakes Petra's hand, holding it in both of his. "Are you all right?"

"I'm fine."

"And what you said . . . about Israel?"

She laughs and touches his shoulder. "I've already made the calls. I'll see you in DC next week, Gerald. Thank you."

The house staff, Alonzo, appears as if conjured. The admiral and his entourage exit. Constantine goes with them, and where Constantine goes, Guerrero goes.

Leaving Dez and Petra.

Who says, "So, you and Gerald don't know each other?"

"Me an' the admiral there? Not hardly!"

"He's the man who vouched for you. Remember the text?"

Dez shrugged. "Dunno how someone like that'd know the likes of me."

She leans a forearm across his massive shoulder, lips near his ear.

"So why'd he call you *chef*?"

CHAPTER 20

The Alexandris family take their conversation to Petra's office. The meeting is near useless. Petra showed up her father in front of a member of the Joint Chiefs of Staff, no less, and the old alpha bull's feelings are hurt. So rather than address the threat against Petra and Triton Expediters, it becomes a shouting match.

Dez announces he wants to check something out and he'll catch up to everyone later. Petra says, "You know the code to get into the garage. Keys are on the pegboard. Take any car you want."

"Lovely!" He grins and ambles out.

He heads first to the unattached guesthouse, his duffel on the bed and his guitar leaning against the wall. He uses the eight-digit code Petra gave him to come and go.

Once inside the guest cottage, he takes a knee next to the ten-key pad he had disassembled earlier that morning. He's attached tiny copper alligator clips, linked to his tablet computer via red and blue wires.

He checks the readout. When Guerrero unlocked the door for the old man, Dez captured his every keystroke. That's the reason he had asked Petra to divert the debrief to this spot.

The code Dez had been given has eight digits. He's watched Petra unlock doors; she uses the same eight-digit code.

Guerrero's code is twelve digits long.

Dez is interested in knowing what Guerrero can unlock with his code that the mistress of the house can't with hers.

He pees and washes up, then saunters into the kitchen. Alonzo, the household staff, is taking a peach galette out of the oven. Alonzo looks and moves like a ballet dancer; he's got that easy but unused strength hiding under a slim figure. Just walking, you know the guy's got a leap like a gazelle. He glances up, doffs oven mitts by pinching them between his ribs and upper arms. Dez has seen hockey players remove gloves that way.

"Can I help you?" His accent sounds Cubano.

Dez switches to Spanish; he sounds like he's from Valencia. "I'm just here to help, mate."

Alonzo switches to Spanish, too. "She likes you."

"I'm the likable sort."

"Alonzo."

Dez says, "Dez," and offers his hand. Alonzo's hand disappears inside his grip when they shake. Dez now knows the house staff has been listening in on the important conversation. That's mostly what he had hoped to find out.

"You going to keep her safe, Dez?"

"Gonna try."

"Make sure you do."

"Have my word. Herself offered me the use of her cars. Thing is, five'll get you ten them cars are all LoJacked by our mate Vincent in there. Yeah?"

Alonzo studies him. Dez can see the moment the young man makes up his mind. "What if they are?"

"Don't necessarily need him knowing where I'm going."

They stand like that for a while. Alonzo makes a play of doffing and folding his apron. Eventually, he smiles. "Bet your cute ass you don't."

Alonzo walks to a small, narrow closet near the door to the garage. He takes out a stylish leather jacket, digs out keys, and lobs them underhand.

Dez catches them one-handed.

"Mini Cooper. Behind the garage." There's a mischievous twinkle in his eyes.

"Ta, mate." Dez nods and heads back to the main house.

Guerrero catches up to him in the foyer, which features sparklingly waxed black-and-white parquetry inlaid with strips of gold. For all Dez knows, the gold strips are actual gold. The rich are weird. Guerrero jabs a finger at him. "What you heard here stays here, Limerick."

"What? That bit from the admiral?"

"You know what I'm talking about, asshole. If I read any of this shit on Facebook, I'm going to make sure the Pentagon knows exactly where it came from. You follow?"

Dez looks shocked. "I would never—and I mean never—talk to anyone about what Lighthouse told us. I gotta say, I'm a bit hurt you'd think otherwise."

Dez steps outside. He avoids the six-car garage, circles around it, and finds a Mini Cooper. It's a light lavender color with a rainbow flag sticker, and it makes him smile. He's worked under the bonnet of these modern Coopers. Good, reliable vehicles. Since it's Alonzo's, and not part of the fleet of Triton Expediters vehicles that Petra has access to, he assumes it isn't LoJacked. But he checks under the chassis and pops the bonnet to be sure.

Before climbing behind the wheel, he searches his phone's memory and hits Redial.

"Detective Swanson."

"Beth? Dez. Them boys we pissed off are active military. More than one branch. Meet me for a coffee, yeah? Got an idea."

CHAPTER 21

Dez meets Beth Swanson and her captain, Naomi Cardona, at a Seattle's Best near the Police Administration Building. They all order coffee and find a booth with some privacy—Cardona is six-two and has to wind herself into the booth. She kicks it off. "Active military. More than one branch. Bullshit."

"I shit you not, guv'nor."

"Your source?"

"You'd need oxygen to have a source that high up. Can't tell you who, but the man works in a building near the Potomac with one too many walls, yeah?"

Cardona and Swanson exchange looks. Swanson gives her superior a complicated shrug that says, *I'm Team Limerick . . . for now.*

Cardona says, "Spill."

"So we know them boys're all racists. Seriously so. Skinhead, Klan types, maybe. We don't know for sure. But my source says they're active military. Now, where would a lad find a critical mass of fine, upstanding arseholes like that?"

Cardona leans back. She's old enough to be Dez's mother, her hair iron gray and cropped short and badly, skin taut and California-tanned, eyes the palest blue, torso thin as a cypress. Not easy for a woman to rise to the rank of captain in any major metro police force, and Dez can see she did it the hardscrabble way. Cardona, he suspects, takes shite off no one and never has.

"You know JFTB Alamitos?"

"Don't."

"Joint Forces Training Base, Los Alamitos, south of the city. Used to be an Army airfield. Military is using it for training these days. There are a couple of bars down in that area that the various agencies watch. Any given night, could be a couple undercover cops in place. Local police, Justice, FBI, U.S. Marshals. There would be righteous hell to pay if anyone connected to my unit screwed with any ongoing investigation in places like that."

Dez smiles. "Wasn't planning on asking Beth along."

Swanson says, "She's not joking. If you're looking to stir up a hornet's nest—"

"I am."

"If that's your plan, you could screw up any number of other investigations into organized crime and militia types. Right now, you and me, we're pretty goddamn mad at the guys who attempted to kidnap Ms. Alexandris, shot a cop in the leg, and killed those transport officers on the highway. But law enforcement has bigger pictures to keep in mind."

"Other pictures," Dez counters. "Not necessarily bigger."

Cardona spins her coffee cup slowly, painting overlapping circles of coffee stain on the table. She thinks for a bit, then says to Swanson, "Then again . . . silver platter?"

Dez sits back. He's not a cop. Never was. He thinks it likely he can learn from these two. "Meaning?"

"Meaning, if we don't *send* you into a place like that . . . If you're not an official representative, well . . ." Cardona shrugs. "Anything you uncover is admissible in court. You're just a wrench thrown into a machine."

"Bull in a china shop," Swanson says.

"One more mindless twat in a sea o' twats." Dez grins. "Violence ensues. We've a word for that where I come from. Tuesday."

Cardona is deadpan. "Men who might or might not be active-duty military, and who might or might not be serious-as-shit racists, attacked a woman who's the chief counsel to a company that finances the goddamn Pentagon. These guys also staged a jailbreak and were willing to kill cops and MPs to do it. I've got twenty-two years in and six till my wife and I retire to this little golf course outside of Palm Springs and I get my handicap under five. I want you to hear me now, chief."

Dez nods.

"This has the potential to be a clusterfuck of epic proportions. If you make it worse, you are on my list. This is not a good list. There is weeping and rending of garments on this list. But if you can help us get a handle on just what the hell we're dealing with, you will have my gratitude."

Now, this is familiar territory to Dez. Do well, and people above you remember that you delivered. Do poorly, and the people above you feed you to the wolves. Same as it ever was.

"Deal."

CHAPTER 22

Los Alamitos is south of Los Angeles. Easy drive: I-5 to the 605. It takes Dez almost no time to get there in Alonzo's Cooper. But he's in no hurry. He wants the sun to set before he finds the three bars that Cardona and Swanson told him to try.

Petra texts him about two hours before dark and asks where he is. Dez texts back, telling her he's following a lead and will let her know if he finds anything.

For the last couple of years, he's been using an email server just outside Viljandi, Estonia. It offers a service that comes in handy from time to time. Dez logs in and watches a dashboard to see if anyone tries to trace his whereabouts based on his text to Petra.

Somebody does.

That somebody finds out Dez's text originated in La Paz, Bolivia. If they check again in ten minutes, it'll appear as if Dez is in Terre Haute, Indiana. Ten minutes after that, Lahore.

Vincent Guerrero is trying to keep Dez on a short leash.

Joint Forces Training Base, Los Alamitos, of course, has what the

Americans call an MWR, or Morale, Welfare, and Recreation center. It's got a perfectly fine little pub that caters to military personnel and their civilian families. It's got billeting for families. But that's not where Dez is headed.

The three bars that law enforcement officials suspect serves militia-type clientele are all well off the base, and away from anything even vaguely of interest to community leaders and tourists.

Orange County has large Hispanic, Asian, and African American populations. You wouldn't know any of that from these bars. The clientele is the driven snow.

In the first bar, the music is country western.

In the second bar, the music is white-power rock.

In the third bar, it's German thrash metal.

Dez is a bit old-school. The Jam, The Clash. Sublime. Foo Fighters. The music in these bars is gibberish to him.

He doesn't find anything helpful at any of the three bars, so he heads back to the first one. If he can't dig up the guys he's looking for, he'll have to encourage them to come find him.

The place is a shrine to *The Dukes of Hazzard,* with a replica muscle car hanging from guy wires over the bar, massive Confederate flags, stuffed animal heads, and a wide array of paper targets from shooting ranges.

Most of the guys in both bars look like chowderheads. Idiots proudly proclaiming their ignorance. Literally—as in, *literally*—card-carrying racists. One guy shows Dez his card. It's like they'd just taken their family on holiday to HitlerLand and hit the Intolerance Gift Shop on the way out.

Fecking posers.

Dez spots three obvious soldiers, sitting by themselves, chatting, drinking beer and eating fried food. All are wholesome-looking white boys with beefy builds and short haircuts. None of them sport racist graffiti on their clothes. They are not here to prove themselves to anyone. And it's also clear that the other dickheads give them a wide berth.

Dez moves to the counter to order a beer.

Finding out who attacked Petra is terribly important. Just not important enough to drink a typical American beer. Nothing's worth that.

Dez spots a half-decent German doppelbock and waits two minutes for the oxygen to seep out before he sips it. Pretty good.

He sits at the bar for close to an hour and nurses his beer. A couple of pretty girls swing by to chat him up. He politely blows off the first because she took a stool to his right, which would put the trio of soldiers at their table in his blind spot. The next takes a stool to his left so he flirts back a little. She wants to dance. Dez can't and doesn't. She notes his accent—a blend of Midlands English, Irish, and Scottish. She assures him she has nothing against immigrants, especially white guys. She bemoans all the terrible evils being imported by dark-skinned immigrants, including crime and diseases. Dez wonders exactly how hard you have to be hit on the head for this particular screw to jar loose, but it's none of his business. She doesn't have to make sense. She's a duck blind.

The three soldiers laugh among themselves. One of them talks with his hands and it's obvious they're discussing American football. They scan their smartphones a lot; all Yanks do. Dez has been playing guitar in bars the last couple of months and he no longer thinks it's weird or rude. It's just American.

Around 11 p.m., the trio signal for their check and reach for their wallets. Dez makes an excuse about an early morning at work. The duck blind offers to go home with him.

"Live with me mum," he says. "She'd be scandalized."

The duck blind is clearly disappointed. She writes her email and phone number on a beer coaster. He thanks her. He leaves his pint on that coaster as the three soldiers walk out.

Dez ambles in their wake.

The trio head to a gravel parking lot behind the tavern. Dez walks that way, too. He stays pretty close to them, close enough that the crunch of rocks under his boots catches their attention. He makes no effort at subterfuge. All three guys turn and spot him.

Dez grins. "Wotcher."

The guy on Dez's left says, "Help you?"

"Me? Nah. Well, yeah, maybe."

They wait. All three sense that something's up. Five-ten, five-eleven, and six-one, they're all taller than Dez. Dez out-masses each of them, the illusion being that he's damn near as broad at the shoulder as he is tall.

"What do you need?" the guy in the middle asks. There is no warmth in the question. He's not trying to be helpful.

"You see that story on the news? Fuckwits attacked a hotel in Los Angeles. Tried to scoop up some bird. Monday, it was."

It's in their eyes, in the tenseness of their shoulders and spines. It's in the way they square off their hips and plant their feet. It's in the way they separate a little from one another, creating three targets, not one big one.

They have heard about the attack on the hotel. They know something about it, even if they had nothing to do with it.

The guy in the middle repeats himself, but more slowly. "What do you need?"

"Peace in our time," Dez says. "Shirts that fit my neck. Coke with real goddamn sugar in it. Liverpool to trade for a half-decent striker. Same's everyone."

The three guys separate a few inches farther. They're in a semicircle around Dez. It's dark back here, and nobody else has emerged from the bar.

The guy on Dez's right says, "You're talking shit about shit you know nothing 'bout."

Dez says, "Tuplet."

"What?"

"Tuplet." He grins broadly. "Irrational rhythm. A rhythm that involves dividing the beat into a different number of unequal subdivisions. 'You're talking shit . . . about shit . . . you know nothing . . .'bout.' Three beats, two, three, and one. Tuplet, that."

The guy in the middle says, "I . . . wait . . . what?"

Dez hits him. He doubles over, folds in on himself like origami.

The guy on Dez's left goes for a knife clipped to his belt. No fault to be had there, provided your target isn't a better hand-to-hand fighter than you are. Dez wraps his left arm around the man's arm, locking him up, before he draws the weapon.

He uses that guy as a brace and kicks the third guy in the knee. The man's knee bends inward at an angle that the lord God never intended.

The guy on his left struggles to get his arm free and that gives Dez time to drive the heel of his hand up into the underside of the man's jaw. His head snaps straight back, his knife twirling away into the dark, clattering on gravel.

The guy on Dez's right has both hands wrapped around the torn ligaments of his knee, which puts his head down around belt height, which is about perfect for a short, fast rabbit punch to the ear. He's unconscious before he hits the ground.

Dez kneels over the first guy, the guy he hit in the gut. The guy still hasn't inhaled. He lies on his back, arms crossed over his stomach, face pinched in like a half lemon squeezed for its juice. Dez picks him up by his shirtfront, lifts his torso off the gravel, and cocks back a fist.

"The men attacked Petra Alexandris. Tell me about 'em."

"Don't . . . know . . . anyth—"

Dez hits him. He releases his shirt and he thumps back into the gravel, unconscious.

Dez rises, moves to the guy he chocked under the chin, kneels again. He lifts the guy by his shirtfront, cocks his fist in front of the guy's eyes.

"The men attacked Petra Alexandris. Tell me about 'em."

"Jesus . . . Heard they . . . heard they were soldiers."

"Heard where?"

"Around, man. Heard they were serving, is all. Heard . . ."

Dez cocks back his fist a couple of inches, the way you ratchet back the string of a crossbow. His fist is only ten inches from the guy's eyes and, from that angle, looks to be the size of a small moon.

"Heard what?"

"Bitch . . . some kinda raghead. Heard she had it coming."

"Raghead." Dez hits him in the nose, but softly. Just enough to break cartilage, not enough to concuss. "She's Greek, ye thick twat. Don't mind you bein' racist, but crack a feckin' book."

The guy spits up blood. "Don't . . . Jesus . . . stop . . ."

"Where do I find these soldiers you hear tell of?"

"Don't kn—"

Pop. More cartilage crackles. More blood arcs away from the guy's nose.

"Don't . . . know! Man! Don't know!"

Dez believes him. He hits the guy one more time. Animated bluebirds circle. He releases the guy's shirt and he falls back like a sack of laundry.

Dez rises. He checks the third man.

Out like a light.

Dez tsks. Oh well.

He didn't find anyone at any of the three bars who was helpful.

That's fine.

Come tomorrow, the blokes who'll be helpful will come looking for Dez.

CHAPTER 23

Dez stops by a Burger King and gets a cup of ice for his knuckles. He parks the Cooper and calls Petra.

It's half midnight and she answers on the first ring. "Where are you?"

"Looking at bars that cater to militia types. How're you?"

Petra's in her room, wearing a T-shirt and panties and reading glasses. She'd been sitting cross-legged in bed, laptop perched on her knees, communicating with Singapore. Her hair is back in a ponytail and it makes her look ten years younger. "I'm glad you're doing this, Dez. Thank you. Did you find anything?"

He removes the lid and distends the cup so he can fit his curled fingers in. The ice will reduce any swelling. "Guys talking, is all. Word is out that someone attacked you, an' that you did something to deserve it."

"Did what?"

"Dunno. Still haven't told me what's wrong with Triton."

"It's . . ." She pauses. She studies the thick cube of a glass between her fingers. "I found some missing funds. Very, very carefully camouflaged in the company's profit and loss statements. A little here, a little there. I've had a full forensic analysis done. I found money missing back as far as two-plus years ago."

"How much?"

She sips her drink. "To date? One point three billion."

Dez barks out a laugh. "You're joking!" When she doesn't answer, he sobers up. "You are joking. Aye? Nobody misplaces one an' a third billion dollars. The Vatican couldn't misplace one an' a third billion dollars!"

"Triton does several billion dollars' worth of deals across the globe every year. We are providing the funding for infrastructure projects like bridges and dams to third-world countries. We're arming first-world countries. My father had an attack of angina in a restaurant a year ago and the NASDAQ lost seven points. Triton is just a company. But if we were a sovereign nation, we'd be among the top-ten largest economies on the planet. We can lose one point three billion. We have. I just don't know how."

"Who would know how to hide something like that?" Dez asks.

"Very few people. I could. My father could. Maybe two other executives, acting alone. Or a dozen other executives acting in tandem."

"D'you have a board of directors?"

"Yes, but they're toothless. My father and I own fifty-five percent of the stock."

"Where's all this money going, then?"

"The concept of *misplaces* eludes you." She says it sharply, and quickly apologizes. "Sorry. I'm . . . scared, is all."

"You were attacked."

"I'm scared for Triton. I can handle myself."

"I seem to remember you putting a gun to the back of me head, so, yeah, I second that motion."

She smiles and swirls the liquor in her glass. "So what do you do now?"

"Keep watching. Keep asking questions. Find someone who knows someone, then find that someone, and find out what they know. It's pretty simple really."

"And people will just talk to you?"

Dez feels the swelling going down in his knuckles. "I'm likable."

"Okay. Are you coming here tonight?"

"No. Got a bit more hunting to do."

"Okay. Dez? Thank you. I mean it."

"I know. Sleep tight."

She hangs up, tosses the mobile to the foot of her bed. She thinks about it awhile, sips her drink.

Dez knows all this: about her being in bed, her wearing a baby blue T-shirt and blush pink panties, about the whiskey and the computer, because he's watching her. On his tablet computer.

He's sitting in Alonzo's Cooper, a block from the Malibu house, watching the feed off the house security cameras. Dez took the time, since barhopping in Los Alamitos, to download Vincent Guerrero's twelve-digit pass code to the house security system. Now he knows what his code nets him that Petra's eight-digit code doesn't net her.

Vincent Guerrero can spy on the inhabitants of the house. He can monitor all cell phone and computer activity. The Malibu Colony house may be the most gorgeous property Dez has ever been inside, but it's also a gilded cage. And Petra has been under surveillance in her own home for who knows how long.

Dez leaves the melting ice in the Mini Cooper and sneaks out, walking the perimeter of the house. It takes him the better part of two hours to do so without being seen, since making the full circle means slipping onto neighbors' property and walking the beach. But when he's done, he's spotted four outdoor cameras facing the house. He recognizes the make and model of the cameras; they're brand-new, state-of-the-art.

He hikes back to the borrowed Cooper around three in the morning and returns to Los Alamitos.

He's going to get some sleep, then hit the bars again.

Tried and true.

CHAPTER 24

Dez has a plan to hit the same three bars tonight in the same order he hit them last night.

Nothing happening at the first two.

The third bar is the one that wants to be a German thrash metal club. It's decorated as if by someone who once saw an episode of a television show set on a studio lot decorated to resemble a German thrash metal club. In fact, the owner likely hasn't taken the time to actually go to Germany and sit in an actual thrash metal club. Dez has. They look fuck-all like this sad lot.

This time, he spots several guys who could be active-duty military. They look fairly agitated.

Dez hears two longhaired guys talking about rugby at the bar. He joins the conversation, shows them a puckered scar on one arm he got from playing ruggers with some mates, and soon they're besties. He's not a loner with a foreign accent now. That's who the soldier types are talking about, but because he's in an animated conversation with two other blokes, their eyes pass right over him.

After a bit, he spots the reason the active-duty blokes looked agitated; they were meeting their marijuana dealer. Their agitation ain't his agitation, so after that, Dez kites out.

Back at the lavender Mini Cooper with its rainbow flag decal—it goes without saying, he's been parking the car several blocks from each tavern—he makes a phone call. Then he drives back to the first bar he'd been in the night before.

He gets to the *Dukes of Hazzard* bar and orders the same creamy German doppelbock as before. He lucks out and sits on the same stool. He ignores the same crappy music.

He gets spotted in under a minute.

Three soldier types sit at one table—opposite side as last night. They spot him but they play coy. One of them pulls out a phone and texts someone. Another stands and heads to the loo. After a sec, the other two rise, a little too casually, throw a twenty on the table and head out.

Dez follows.

The two guys head toward the gravel parking lot behind the bar, just like the lads from last night.

Once everyone's nicely isolated from street traffic, the two boys stop walking and turn around, facing Dez.

One of them slips on brass knuckles.

Three more guys—white, late twenties to early thirties, short hair, well built—emerge from a Ford F-250 Super Duty. The guy who'd slipped into the men's room emerges and stands guard at the edge of the bar to make sure no one comes near the parking lot. It's six to one now.

One of them is at least six-three and rangy, moving with the easy grace of a fighter. The way the others move out of his line of sight, Dez guesses he's the leader.

"You the fucking foreigner attacked some soldiers here last night?"

"Attacked? We was having a nice conversation. Chatty, that's what I am."

The leader says, "You were asking about that shit at the Hotel Tremaine on Monday. How come?"

"Naturally curious, is all."

— 100 —

The leader has sandy red hair and ears that stick straight out from his skull. He's got the muscles of a serious athlete—not like Dez's fireplug build, but put together pretty well. "We heard some English dude was involved in that shit on Highway 1, Tuesday. That you?"

"The one where someone rammed the fuck out of an arsehole and drove him over the guard railing and into the Pacific?" Dez asks. He ponders a moment. "Yeah. Now's you mention it. That was me."

The leader draws a fixed-blade knife. A good one, well designed, toughened.

All six of the men wear blue jeans and good civilian boots. It's tough to tell them apart. But one has a Hawaiian shirt. That's distinction enough. Dez speaks louder: *"Chemise Hawaïenne, s'il vous plait."*

The leader says, "The fuck are—"

And a fast-moving swarm of rock salt rips into the knee of the man in the Hawaiian shirt.

He screams and falls to the gravel. That seems to happen a lot back here, Dez thinks.

Ephrem Kebede emerges from the dark with a sawed-off shotgun in both hands. Two other lads, also Ethiopian immigrants, emerge from the other direction, also carrying shotguns.

The man on the ground keens in pain.

Dez takes three steps toward the leader. "Can I have that knife, kindly?"

Six-three, the man glares down at him. Dez smiles up at him, muscles loose, ready. The others are soldiers, and they've been trained to obey orders. Even facing shotguns, they'll fight if their leader tells them to. So Dez opts to take out the leader.

"The knife, my son."

The big man lunges at him, knife held professionally, blade toward the butt of his hand, quick slashing moves designed to draw first blood.

Dez grabs the wrist of the knife hand, digs his thick fingers into the man's flesh, and drives his other, comically large fist into the man's solar plexus.

The knife falls.

The guy's bent over so Dez steps in and head-butts him, cracking open his nose.

He falls straight back on his ass.

Dez picks up the knife, walks to the F-250, jams the blade between the bed frame and the rear gate, and puts his weight into it laterally. The knife snaps in two, the blade staying where it is, the bolster, tang, and butt in Dez's hand.

The other four men stand, dumbstruck.

Dez walks back and tosses the knife handle onto the ground between the leader's akimbo legs.

"*Chef,*" Ephrem Kebede drawls, and gives his usual low and rumbling laugh. "*C'est bon de te revoir.*"

"*Et toi, mon amie.*"

He turns to the other white supremacist goons. "On home with yourselves, now. Scoot, the lot of ye."

The Ethiopians take a few steps nearer. The man with rock salt buried in his thigh, knee, and calf lies in the fetal position, holding his leg, his denim oozing blood around his fingers.

The four men back away.

There's a rumble, and a van inches out of the dark. One of Ephrem's men opens the sliding side door.

Ephrem gestures toward the unconscious leader with the broken knife between his knees. Dez points to the crying man with rock salt in his leg. "*Non, prends celui-là, s'il te plaît.*"

The Ethiopians lift the keening guy up. He struggles a little. "Hey . . . wait . . . the fuck . . ." They toss him in the van. This has to be a racist's worst nightmare: wounded, abandoned by your mates, tossed into a van by Black men speaking a foreign language.

Dez circles the vehicle, checks the driver.

A cherubic face, a massive grin, and twinkling eyes.

He turns to Ephrem, aghast. "Ye brought Nyala!"

He shrugs. "Take your daughter to work day. It's an American thing."

CHAPTER 25

It's a complicated night. Dez and the Ethiopians—that'd be a killer name for a band, he thinks—need to get from Los Alamitos to Torrance, which normally would be a straight shot west on the 405, but Dez also wants to return Alonzo's Mini Cooper, which he's had for too long. And he wants to fill it up and wash it, because that's the polite thing to do, and Ephrem Kebede's guys know an all-night car wash, this being LA, so they get the Cooper back to Malibu Colony Beach around three in the morning. You don't want to be a Black guy driving a nice car in that neighborhood at night, so Dez makes the trek with Ephrem and his daughter, Nyala, riding drag in the stolen F-250 Super Duty.

They left the owner of the F-250 lying spread-eagled in the gravel parking lot. Taking out their leader had been good craft, and it'd been a bit of fun, but Dez is under no illusions: He's now a target.

Better him than Petra, he thinks.

On the way back to Torrance in the stolen pickup, Nyala sits in the middle and chatters away, telling Dez about her favorite bands and the latest role-playing video game and about running for treasurer in student government and about a paper she's writing on the #MeToo movement. "What's that?" Dez asks, although he knows perfect well, and she says that guys touch women in unwanted ways and that in the future they won't be able to get away with it. Dez asks, "What d'you do when that happens to you?" and she says, tell 'em to stop, tell someone in authority, tell Dad, tell Mom, tell Uncle Dez.

"So you stand up for yourself?" And she looks at him like he's dumb and shrugs and says, "'Course."

Dez and Ephrem exchange nods over her head.

Nyala falls asleep leaning on her dad's arm before Torrance, and they don't get back to the Quonset hut garage until nearly dawn.

The soldier they grabbed is named Tom Polhaus and, according to the information in his wallet, he's an E-5; petty officer second class, U.S. Navy. His left knee is an oozing mass of salt-rock-pitted meat, but the bone is fine and the deep muscles are fine, and he'll walk again. He'll limp, but *you pays your dime, you takes your chances,* as a Texan Dez knew used to say.

Dez is really not looking forward to questioning this guy. He's a gate-keeper, not an interrogation expert. But fortunately, Ephrem Kebede's wife, Beza, was an anesthesiologist in Cairo before immigrating to the States, and she gives Tom Polhaus a powerful painkiller that puts him instantly to sleep. She also treats his wound to avoid sepsis.

Everyone gets a couple hours' kip. As the sun rises, Dez calls Raziah Swann, the vocalist and lead guitarist of the band he'd played with Monday night. She's Black and Persian. Call her Iranian and she'll rip you a new one. She's lovely, a twenty-year-old, five-foot-tall bundle of TNT, and Dez is dead certain she's going to be a superstar in the not-too-distant future. She flirts crazy with him. She often asks Dez to sit in on gigs, not because he's the finest bass guitarist in town—he's not—but because he never, ever responds to her flirting. She's safe with him.

"Where are ye?" he asks.

"Vegas," she says. "Why, are you lonely?"

"No, love, I'm in a bit of a thing. Some people might start looking for me. If they do, they might start at the Hotel Tremaine."

"And . . . ?"

"And if they're looking for me, they might start with you an' the band."

Raziah's laughter always reminds him of wind chimes. "What did you do this time? Wait wait wait. Rescued a maiden from a drunk in the parking lot? Stood down an abusive boyfriend? I know there's a damsel in distress in there somewhere."

Dez makes a note to never, ever tell Petra Alexandris that she's been compared to a damsel in distress. "Me?" he bleats. "I lead a blameless life! You know that!"

She laughs. "Want do you need?"

"Keep an eye open. Stay out of LA for a couple weeks. Wouldn't be the worst idea in the world."

"I have a standing invite to play at a club in Portland. The owner of the joint wants to get in my pants."

"An' who doesn't?"

"Just say the word . . ."

He laughs her off. As he always does. "I've T-shirts older'n you, love! The gig in Portland? Can it last a week or two?"

"So this is serious?"

"A bit."

There's a pause. "Oh, holy fuck, Desmond! The dead guys, the shooting at the hotel that night . . . ?"

"It's connected to that, yeah."

"That was you? Are you in danger?"

"Don't be daft, ye brat. I'm fine. But, you know. Better safe than. Yeah?"

Raziah makes a snap decision. "Portland, it is. You can't beat the coffee or the cannabis."

Around 8 a.m., they start in. Ephrem and Beza fry up a massive *quraac,* or breakfast, of *quanta firfir,* a spicy dried beef, plus a goulash of sardines and chopped tomatoes, with berbere. Plus *shiro,* ground and reconstituted pea powder served over injera, or Ethiopian bread. Ephrem's men eat heartily, as does Dez, and Ephrem's wife teases him about being skin and bones, which makes everyone laugh.

"This is insane," Dez moans, gesturing toward the food. The word comes out *infane* because his mouth is full. "I'm about to cry."

Beza laughs and piles more on his plate.

"What'd you give our Navy lad, Doc?"

"Sodium thiopental," she says. "Eat up. More coffee?"

She had, indeed, given Petty Officer Polhaus sodium thiopental, and by the time Dez and Ephrem go to talk to the lad—lying handcuffed to Dez's old bed behind the garage—the man's positively effusive.

Dez hadn't wanted to torture the man, so the truth serum is a best-case scenario.

The information he shares is so crazy, Dez is forced to believe it's true.

CHAPTER 26

Midday Friday, Petra Alexandris's house staff, Alonzo, returns to the Malibu Colony house and spots Dez, leaning against the garage and checking scores on his mobile. Alonzo is just back from a rehearsal. He is a dancer, as Dez suspected when they met; Petra confirmed it. Singer, too. He's done some off-Broadway road shows and his career is on an uptick. His deal with Petra is: He runs her household until his agent calls. Then he's out the door in a nanosecond. She's agreed, and Dez can see why. Theirs may be an employee/employer relationship, but they've become family.

Alonzo looks a wreck. He's wearing an old, stretched-out T-shirt and gym shorts and sneakers, and it looks like rehearsal kicked his arse. He looked as willow slim when they met but Dez gets a look at the corded muscles of his legs and sees that's an illusion. Like with most dancers, the man's tightly kitted together.

"Well, well, well."

Dez says, "Look what I found in the guest cottage." He's carrying a soccer ball. He lets it drop and knees it in the direction of Alonzo.

Who deftly stops it with a side foot and boots it back. Alonzo's smiling now, but he looks a little confused.

Dez stops it with his thigh, dribbles the ball a bit with his boot. "Do us a favor, mate. See that power pole, behind ye and to the right, twenty meters?"

He sends the ball back. Alonzo stops it, dances around it a bit, his eyes sweeping behind him.

"Yeah?"

"Surveillance camera, fifteen meters up."

Alonzo's smile evaporates a little. He lets the ball escape his dribbling, retrieves it, glances at the power pole. Spots it.

"Dios."

"Got that right. Found more. Vincent Guerrero. The whole feckin' house's under twenty-four-seven surveillance. Inside and out. Can't use house phones or mobiles, either. Internet's the same. It's all monitored, mate."

They pass the ball back and forth. Two guys, just horsing around in the alley leading to the six-car garage of the estate. Alonzo is trying to keep up the easy smile. "Does she know?"

"Not yet." Dez stops the ball with a deft knee. "I don't trust Guerrero. She does. Puts me in a bind."

Alonzo's turn to stop the ball and kick it back.

"Do us a favor? Ask herself to meet me, sharpish, yeah?" Dez heels it back.

"Where?"

"Dunno Los Angeles all that well. Need it to be open. Public-like. A place she won't raise suspicions."

"The Getty." Alonzo doesn't hesitate. "It's perfect. She's a big donor. She goes there to clear her head a couple times a month."

"Done." Dez slices the ball back and Alonzo catches it in his hands. He's skilled. Dez outlines the steps he wants Petra to take to avoid detection. Alonzo writes none of it down but doesn't need to.

Dez steps closer and offers a hand. They turn it into a handshake–chest bump hug. "Owe you, mate."

"Do right by her."

Dez turns and walks back toward the stolen F-250 Super Duty with its new paint job and new plates.

CHAPTER 27

Petra Alexandris drives downtown and meets a girlfriend for coffee, leaves her car, and the girlfriend gives her a lift to the Getty. She's left her mobile in her glove box. Catching an Uber would've left a credit card trail. Dez had explained all this tradecraft nonsense to Alonzo, feeling foolish, melodramatic spy-craft, this, but he knows for a fact that Petra's under surveillance.

The J. Paul Getty Museum is perched on a hill with a sweeping view of Los Angeles and the ocean. It's easy enough to go there just to enjoy the view and the architecture, never mind the actual collection, which is world-class. Dez has visited it twice since hitting town.

Her hair is scraped back in a ponytail. She's wearing jeans and short suede boots with Spanish heels and, as usual, a man's white dress shirt. Dez wonders what kind of mutant power she's got. It's basics, yeah? Trousers, shirt, and boots. Dez wears the same, but he looks like a right thug. Petra looks like the raw energy and edgy sexiness of California rolled up into one person. If you could bottle that . . .

Petra air-kisses him, a long-fingered, pianist's hand on his beefy shoulder. They walk the grounds a bit. "Why are we meeting here?"

"Your lad Guerrero. The whole house in Malibu is under computer surveillance. He's been watching you. Live video streaming. Monitoring your phones an' internet. I've disabled it."

Petra pauses and squeezes the bridge of her nose, as if to fend off a migraine. Dez waits.

"That's . . ." But she gets no further. She has no words.

Another minute passes. She composes herself. "Okay. This other thing. How bad is it?"

"Pretty fecking bad. Sorry."

"You've slept with me, Desmond. You can swear in front of me."

"Sister Agnes would've approved of neither." He points to a stone bench, a bit separated from the tourists.

They sit. "Start at the beginning," she says. "Details matter. Impressions as well as facts."

Dez is reminded that she's a world-class lawyer.

"Ever hear of the State of Jefferson?"

She frowns. "The idea's been around for decades. Take the rural counties of Northern California and the rural counties of Eastern and Southern Oregon, and split them off into the fifty-first state. It'd be an ultraconservative enclave on the West Coast. Capital would be . . . Yreka, maybe? Or Roseville? I forget."

"Good marks t'you. The State of Lexington is similar. Only it's the arid parts of Central California. Oregon's not involved."

Petra nods. "Well, that'd be pretty dumb. The money in California is in the major cities, the high-tech corridor, and the agriculture sector. You're talking about the part of California that has none of the above. They'd be giving up more than they'd be gaining."

"Not how they see it. They'd be gaining independence."

"From what?"

"From Sacramento. From Democrats. From Congress. From atheists and Jews and people o' color and the LGBTQ lot."

"Fanciful." Petra has reached for her cell phone three times while they've talked, and three times remembered it's in the glove box of her car. She's like a smoker with no smokes. She'd planned to watch the dollar versus the Turkish lira today, because she's hoping to bankroll Ankara for a new antimissile system. "I'm guessing the State of Lexington is named for Lexington and Concord. The first battles of the Revolutionary War. What does any of this have to do with Triton Expediters?"

"Say you wanted to create a new state run by White Aryans. What would you need?"

She decides to play along. "I don't know. A constitution. A state assembly, or legislature. Infrastructure, I suppose. An economic plan. Interstate trade deals."

Dez says, "Probably, sure, but you'd also need law enforcement and a national guard, yeah? And you'd need some walking-around money. Say, one point three billion dollars. For starters."

Any lightness in her tone evaporates. Her eyes go flinty.

Dez waits.

"You're joking."

"Spoke to one of the arseholes in this Aryan bunch. He says a largish sector of the U.S. military is getting its waterfowl in a linear formation. Getting ready to help create the State of Lexington. Got the personnel. Got the funding. Waiting for the go-sign."

"That's . . . Dez, that's insane!"

"I know."

"That couldn't happen!"

"I know. It's bonkers. But there you go. If they weren't nuts, they wouldn't be white supremacists."

"Nuts or not, law enforcement would swat this stupid rebellion in about three minutes. I'm telling you, if that's what's really behind the attack on me, then we're fine. We tell Admiral Lighthouse. We'll alert the governor and the police. We'll alert the FBI. This thing goes away between news cycles."

Dez nods. "Yeah. That's almost, to the pound sterling, what I'd pay for it all, too."

She inhales, lets it out. "Whew. But these fools really believe they could split off from California?"

Dez shrugs.

"Well, they get points for thinking big. Even if they are living in fantasyland."

"S'pose you're right."

She studies him, cocks an eyebrow. "But . . . ?"

Again he shrugs. "Dunno. Feels like I'm not seeing the whole board. Feels like there are chess pieces moving about in the dark."

Petra takes his hand. "Hey. A revolt against Sacramento just might be the best-case scenario we could have hoped for. We call Gerald Lighthouse. You tell him what you know. Easy."

Dez squeezes her hand. She has long, strong hands, muscles delineated in her wrist and forearm; hands honed playing tennis and racquetball. But her hand looks comical inside his. She reaches over with her free hand and teases his unruly, wavy hair.

She sighs. "I've been trying to figure out what's behind all this for weeks now. Ever since I spotted the missing money. I haven't breathed normally in so long, I feel like I forgot how. Come on. I know a place we can call the admiral."

CHAPTER 28

Petra uses Dez's phone to text a girlfriend who is a pilot for United. She texts back from London: *Back on Tuesday—mi casa su casa.* The pilot keeps a bungalow in Venice, and Dez drives them there in the stolen F-250.

The place is small, a 1930s stucco cottage with a terra-cotta roof and a postage-stamp-sized garden, hidden down a backstreet and overlooking one of the many canals. Dez parks a block away; old habit. In front of the cottage, he peers at the store-bought security lash-up as Petra tries to remember the password to deactivate the friend's alarm. Dez reaches out to the ten-key pad, holds down the seven and the nine for three seconds, then taps five five five.

The door clacks open. Dez shakes his head sadly. "Shoddy, that."

Petra laughs. "Gatekeeper?"

He shrugs. "Force of habit."

Inside, the place has hardwood floors and arched, cutout stucco doorways with no doors between rooms. It's tiny, fit for a single person, but spotless and well aired-out. Still using Dez's phone, Petra texts Admiral Gerald Lighthouse in Washington. Not his secretary, not his aide, not his office. She has his personal phone. She reads his return text. "He's at the Capitol. Appropriations Committee. This'll take hours."

Dez steps into the tiny kitchen. "There's wine."

"Let's."

He opens and pours two glasses of a pinot grigio so colorless it looks like tap water, and so tasty that Petra groans a little, eyelids fluttering.

"How long a wait?" Dez asks.

She grins at him, slips out of her booties. "You're not good at downtime, are you, *chef*?"

"Never have been."

"What do you do when you're not playing guitar or rescuing women in hotels?"

"Laundry, mostly."

She takes his glass, sets both of them down, and begins unbuttoning her starched white shirt.

"Want to kill some time?"

Petra and the pilot, apparently, are very good friends, Dez thinks.

Petra makes love like it's a time trial, all energy and passion. Dez rolls out from under her at one point, leans up on one elbow, and says, "Slow down. It's the journey, not the destination."

She pushes him back down. "The destination's pretty damn important, *chef*."

They're lying there, drenched in sweat, naked. Dez is still breathing heavy from their lovemaking. Out of absolutely nowhere, Petra laughs. "You are by far the most bowlegged man I've ever slept with."

"You're not the first to observe that," he murmurs.

"If your knees touched, you'd be six-two."

It's his turn to laugh. She's not wrong.

"Your accent. Is that what they call Cockney?"

"It is not."

"What is it then?"

He thinks about it awhile. "Dunno, really. Grew up loads of places.

Liverpool, Ireland, Scotland, couple others. I sound like a Geordie to some; sound Irish to others. Total mutt, me."

She ponders that. Everything in Petra's life revolves around her Greek American heritage, her family, her father, the Alexandris company. To not know your own history . . . She can't imagine it.

Later, she gets up to quick-shower away her sweat, then lies back down next to him. Dez is now in his boxers, Petra in her once-pressed white shirt. Her razor-straight, pitch-black hair is a mess and looks spectacularly sexy. On the way back from the shower, she retrieves the pinot grigio.

She feels the tension in the corded muscles of his shoulder. "What?" she says, smiling over at him.

Dez has one forearm the size of cordwood behind his head. He's staring at the popcorn ceiling.

"What?" she pushes.

"I sort of understand wanting to start your own state. I realize there'd be pushback. But an armed cohort, pullin' off a kidnapping in a fancy hotel? A jailbreak that involved shooting cops an' soldiers? Seems overkill."

They lie like that, thinking about it.

Dez ruminates. "You'd need a constitution. You'd need a legislature or assembly. Infrastructure. An economic plan. Interstate trade deals. Law enforcement. National guard. Walking-around money . . ."

She says, "What else would you need?"

"A capital."

She thinks about it. He can practically see her drawing a geographic map of Central California against the backdrop of the off-white ceiling. She puts one arm behind her head, unconsciously mimicking him.

"Santa Margarita?" she says. "Paso Robles? Atascadero? What else is up there?"

"How about a server farm adjacent to a nuclear power plant?"

"Triton has a server farm up there."

"Aye. Saw it on that big map in the lobby of your headquarters."

She looks at him, a vertical crease of worry returning to the space between her brows.

"A Triton facility?"

"Said it yourself: Triton's a multinational corporation, love. But if it were a country, it'd have—"

"One of the ten largest economies on Earth." She gets up on one elbow, brushes hair away from her eyes, and studies his.

"Dez? What the hell?"

She's looming over him. He looks up, almost straight up, into her mahogany brown eyes. "You're missing a bit north of a billion dollars, yeah? What if it isn't missing? What if it's being repurposed? Within Triton?"

He can see the blood drain from Petra's face.

"What if your own company is behind this fecking mess?"

CHAPTER 29

Later, Petra hears Dez puttering around in the tiny kitchen, through the hobbit stucco cutout door. "Jennai told me her coffee machine is broken, so—"

She smells coffee. Dez has found two cups and is sniffing a half-pint of half-and-half from the fridge.

"Want some?"

"She said her machine was broken."

Dez says, "Was. Fixed."

"How?"

He pours two cups. "Are you interested in the forensic mechanics of coffee machines?"

"No."

"Then drink up and riddle me this: If Triton is involved in this shite—sorry—who could pull it off?"

Petra doctors her coffee. "My father could. I could. But this isn't possible. Triton is *not* part of this."

"Sure, are ye?"

Her eyes say no. "Absolutely."

"Humor me."

She uses both hands, alternating, to smooth her hair back and re-create her ponytail. "My father and I could. The CFO, Colin Frye, could. In theory? The chief technical officer, Brittany Kinney. She controls the computers that track the company's flow of money."

"What's a CFO?"

She looks at him over the rim of her cup. She says, "C. F. O.," but slower.

Dez blinks.

"Chief financial officer. How do you not know that?"

"Never worked anywhere that had a chief financial officer." He shrugs. "Never worked anywhere that had, y'know, finances t'speak of."

Petra releases her breath, realizing she's keyed up. Sex should do the opposite but it never has for her. "Sorry."

"So you four could've pulled off this caper?"

"Maybe. There could be others, if they were acting together. But again: It's not really possible. We're talking hypotheticals."

"Let's chat with your mate Lighthouse, yeah? Lay it out for him. If it's a lark, well, no harm no foul."

Petra agrees.

They sip their coffee and wait for Dez's phone to chirp back. As they wait, Petra uses it to check a dozen or more websites. Her thumb fairly flies across the screen.

Five minutes later, Admiral Lighthouse lets them know he's free, via text. Petra calls. The secretary of the Navy tells them he's just stepped out of Committee; he's in the House.

"This isn't a secure line. Desmond Limerick is with me. We're on speakerphone."

"Mr. Limerick. Did you find something?"

Dez steps closer to his phone in Petra's hand. "Aye. Sailor. Petty Officer Tom Polhaus. Assigned to Joint Base McKinzie-Clark, whatever the hell that is. Says a bunch of Nazi types swiped a huge amount of money and plan to break away from California."

He pauses.

Lighthouse says, "That's insane."

"Well, yeah. Nazis, them. Insanity is the baseline, innit."

"It would never work. Nothing like it is even remotely possible."

"Petra says the same, sir, an' she's smarter'n me. I buy stupid by the pint. But now you know what I know, so me part in it's done."

They waited through more quiet. Lighthouse finally speaks again. "Do I want to know how you came by this information, chief?"

"You do not, sir."

"But you're sure . . . ?"

"Sure that Polhaus is an idiot? Very. Sure that he was telling me the truth? Very."

"All right. Thank you. I'll pass this along to military intelligence, all branches. FBI, too. Just because it's impossible doesn't mean we can ignore it. Petra?"

"Yes?"

"Where's your gut in all this?"

She stares at Dez. "The threat's real. This stupid scheme is real. And Triton really is missing a lot of money. I don't for a second think anyone could pull this off, but they could pull off a *lot* with what we're missing. Whatever the scheme, I think it's worth stopping."

"Agreed," the admiral says. "Petra? Mr. Limerick? Thank you. I'll keep you posted."

"Thank you, Gerald."

She hangs up and hands the phone back to Dez, who promptly gets busy cleaning the coffeepot and the cups, and gingerly lifting the soppy filter into the garbage under the sink.

"Would love to talk to them two. Frye and Kinney, you said?"

"Ludicrous scheme or not, someone still stole from my company and sent armed men after me when I snooped into it. I want to talk to them as much as you do." She touches him on the arm. "You know, you've found out what I asked you to find. You could step away from this thing now with my gratitude."

He sets the cups upside down on the drainer. "Want to pop the sheets and pillowcases in the wash, if it's all the same to you. You take out the garbage, will ye? Then I'll tag along. If you don't mind."

She looks relieved. "Thank you."

CHAPTER 30

Petra says, and Dez agrees, that they need to reach out to her father and tell him what they know.

They return to Petra's car, parked in downtown LA, and find Triton Security guys hovering around it. A couple of the ex-soldiers working for Vincent Guerrero are going door-to-door around the block with photos of Petra.

Petra mutters, "That didn't take long."

"They have your car LoJacked, love. All your cars."

She studies him a minute. He can tell she's not surprised but royally pissed off.

She ignores the security men as she climbs into her fire-engine red Ferrari and peels away from the curb. Friday late-afternoon traffic is a horror. Despite that, it's a good thing Dez knows she's heading to the Triton campus in Hawthorne. She loses him inside of two blocks.

★ ★ ★

Constantine Alexandris had been planning to fly to Berlin that morning but canceled when Petra went "missing." Dez has only met the man twice and didn't get the impression of a jolly old elf. With the morning's news that his almost-kidnapped daughter's gone walkabout, Dez assumes that Constantine has cranked up the cranky to eleven.

Petra parks in the first level of the secure, underground, executive lot, in her reserved slot, and plans to take the elevator up to the lobby and meet Dez there. She's checking her makeup in the rearview as the image of the F-250 rolls behind her head.

Dez parks the beast in Guerrero's reserved slot.

They meet between the cars. "How the hell did you get down here?"

He turns his wrist, shows her the tattoo of Janus. "Beginnings an' gates. Transitions an' time. Duality an' doors. Passages an' endings. Not a place on Earth I can't get into."

She uses her swipe card to get them both up to the executive suite on seven. She'd called ahead to let her father know she was on her way in.

"Sunny disposition, is he?"

She smiles conspiratorially.

Petra marches straight to Constantine's corner office. He's on his feet before the grand onyx desk, radiating dark energy. He starts yelling before the door is closed. He yells in Greek, gesturing, jabbing a stubby, nicotine-yellowed finger in the direction of Dez.

"Speak English, Father. We have a story to tell you. Someone siphoned one point three billion dollars from Triton over a two-plus-year period. The money likely is being funneled to a group of extreme right-wing radicals in the U.S. military, who possibly want to split off a portion of California and create a new state."

Constantine blinks rapidly. "Bullshit!"

Dez says, "Took it better than I thought."

"You! You put this insane notion in my daughter's head!"

Dez laughs.

"He did no such thing, Father. I realized the funds were missing weeks ago. I didn't tell you because I thought it best to track it down first. I believe that's what triggered the kidnapping. Here: Get out of my way."

She circles the old man and the massive, pitch-black desk. She sits in his magnificent burnt-red leather chair and boots up his computer, her nails clicking like castanets.

It takes close to thirty minutes to convince her father. She shows him her research into the missing money, shows him how cleverly it was hidden in the multinational's domestic and foreign deals. At one point, Dez ambles over to the wet bar and spots damn near every type of liquor sold on Earth, including bottled beer. "D'you mind?" he asks.

Neither of them notice. He shrugs and pops the cap off one.

He stands at the floor-to-ceiling windows and admires the view. Heat shimmers off the city of Los Angeles. The ocean's a blue smudge to his left. He can spot five wide-body aircraft lined up to land at LAX, and two news helicopters in the air. That's LA for you. Even the airspace is gridlocked.

"Dez? Dez!"

"Hmm?" Petra has been calling him from the other side of the comically huge office.

Constantine looks his way with anger. "Pay attention."

Dez waves toward the majestic view. "'When Alexander saw the breadth of his domain, he wept, for there were no more worlds to conquer.'"

The old man eyes him. "Marcus Aurelius?"

"Hans Gruber, *Die Hard*."

He ambles their way.

Petra sits in Constantine's chair. The chair had seemed too big for the old man, the first time Dez was in this paddock-sized room. The CEO's chair fits Petra—physically and metaphorically, he thinks. Constantine studies his daughter. The skin around his eyes is rhino hide, deeply sun-tanned, thick with a world atlas of age lines. "Who took my money?"

"If it's a conspiracy, any of several people could have taken *our* money," she replies, punching that last bit. "If it's only one person, then the field of suspects narrows."

"You. Me. Colin Frye," her father says. "Who else?"

"Brittany Kinney."

He dismisses the notion with a short chop of his hand. "She knows next to nothing about international trade."

"She knows absolutely everything about the computer network we use to track international trade. Some of the theft definitely involved manipulating the data. I brought in my own forensic specialist to confirm."

"You let a stranger have access to our computers?" Constantine glares at his daughter, as if expecting her to look sorrowful and to admit her trespass. Dez wonders if these two have ever even met.

"No, Father, I let *three* strangers have access to our computers. Working independently. Each came to the same conclusions. My findings would stand up in court. *Will* stand up in court."

"Someone noticed," Dez cuts in. "Saw you snooping. Must've."

She nods in his direction.

Constantine marches over to his wet bar on short, fast-moving legs and splashes ouzo into a glass. He drains it at a go. Dez has tried ouzo in the past. He shudders.

"Why kidnap you?" Constantine asks, pouring himself a second glass and one for his daughter.

Petra says, "Good question. Dez?"

Dez rests his ass on the edge of the old man's pristine desk. The gesture annoys Constantine. Which is the point. "A: To kill you. B: To find out how much you know and who you'd told. C: To hold you hostage if they thought your da was behind the investigation. D: You staged it yourself because you stole the funds, and you were going to fake your death, freeing you up to work with the military conspirators at your leisure."

Constantine says, "Christ!"

Petra spins around in the big chair. "What?"

Dez shrugs. "Asked, didn't you."

Petra looks shaken, but only for a few seconds. Her eyes narrow. She studies him, then nods. "Good. Perfectly sound thinking. I'm glad you're considering every angle."

She accepts the glass her father hands her. "It wasn't me, by the way. Was it you?"

Constantine says, "That's not amusing."

And that, Dez thinks, *isn't an answer.*

He sets his beer bottle down on the beautiful desk and steps away from it. "Okay, then. Let's assume you're not Goneril, and he's not Lear."

Petra's eyes sparkle at the reference. "Good. Because I love my father more than words can wield the matter."

Constantine pats her on the shoulder and drains his glass. It's the first truly familial gesture Dez has observed. And clearly the leaden irony of quoting *King Lear* flies over the man's head. Petra and Dez exchange smiles.

"We've told Admiral Lighthouse," Petra says, and sips the clear liquor. "He's begun investigating this thing from the Pentagon's angle. I want to talk to Colin and Brittany."

The old man picks up the empty beer bottle from off his desk, holding it by the pad of a finger and thumb and eyeing it as if it were forensic evidence in a sex crime. He drops it in his trash, glowering at the condensation ring left behind. "I'll alert Vincent."

"Don't." Petra drains her glass. "I trust Vincent but he hires almost exclusively from ex-military personnel. This crazy idea includes the military, we think. Let's leave Vincent out of this for now."

"And him?" Constantine jabs a thumb in the general direction of Dez.

"Him, I trust."

Dez slaps the old man on the back. "Cheer up, mate. I grow on a person!"

Constantine glowers. "So does syphilis."

CHAPTER 31

The chief financial officer of Triton Expediters fancies himself Hugh Hefner for the twenty-first century, Dez thinks. Midsixties, he has tanning-bed skin and a carefully crafted crown of silver hair. His suit likely cost a small fortune, though Dez is no expert in such matters; he buys his black T-shirts three-to-a-pack online because he's only found one brand that can fit his neck and shoulders.

Dez and Petra can't meet with the CFO in person because he's in the Triton New York office. "He's back east negotiating a hostile takeover of Gamelan Avionics. It's a midsized company but it's poised for growth. Several government contracts are in the offing."

"An' you're buying it?"

"No, one of our high-tech partners is buying it. We're their bank."

As they talk, Petra marches Dez to her own office—a fraction the size of her father's, on the same floor, and uses her magnetic ID badge to get in.

Dez studies the door security system a moment, memorizing the design. Old habits die hard. Old habits can keep one from dying at all.

Petra's office is Spartan and spotless. Only two paintings: both small, both original works, both austere landscapes. She has a standing desk made of steel legs and a steel sheet platform. She boots up her eighty-inch-diagonal, flat, wall-mounted monitor using a keyboard on her desk and informs the CFO's executive assistant that she needs to talk to him right now.

It's nearing 11 p.m. in New York but still a workday for the Triton CFO. The aide says it will take forty-five minutes to get Colin Frye to the office.

"That's no problem. So long as he's in front of this camera within the next ninety fucking seconds."

Colin Frye appears in front of the aide's desktop computer pinhole camera approximately eighty-seven seconds later.

"Petra? My God, what's wrong?"

Petra folds her arms. Dez stands well clear of the camera mounted on her wall. Petra appears to be alone, but Dez can see the CFO at an angle. Frye has a clipped accent that reminds him of Yale for some reason.

"Someone has stolen one point three billion dollars, U.S., from Triton," Petra says with an absolute dearth of emotion. "It occurred over a two-year period. We think the money is being funneled into a right-wing military group here in the States."

Frye blinks at the screen. His suit is cream colored and his pocket square is baby blue. "Wait a minute. No. No, we're not missing more than a billion dollars. Pet, this is an accounting error. I can get on it right away. We—"

"We are missing the money," she says. "It's the reason I was attacked Monday. I've shown my father the evidence. Triton is at DEFCON 1."

Frye's eyes dart in every direction. Dez fears they might ricochet into each other and leave bruises.

"I'm . . . finding this hard to believe. I mean, it's just not credible."

Her voice drops half an octave. "You don't believe I was attacked by armed men at the Tremaine?"

"Yes, yes, oh my God, of course but—"

"I've shown my father the evidence. He believes it. Do you think he's credible?"

"Constantine? God, yes! But—"

"But what?"

Frye fidgets. "I can fly home immediately. I have one of the corporate jets."

"That's a good idea. And Colin?"

"Yes?"

"Two things."

He winks at her. "Shoot."

"One: Come prepared to convince me that you didn't steal the money."

"What? Pet, I—"

"And two: Never, ever call me *Pet*."

She'd been holding a tiny remote in her fist and Dez hadn't realized it. She disconnects the call in the same heartbeat as the final word.

Dez grins. "TSA will never let him board. Won't make it through the metal detectors with your boot so far up his arse."

CHAPTER 32

There's no need to hunt down Brittany Kinney, the Triton chief technical officer. She's on the campus.

Not in the architecturally important main building, but in a non-descript, two-story box of a building on the periphery of the twenty-five-building campus.

The Triton Expediters worldwide headquarters is so large that Petra and Dez take an electric golf cart to get there. Dez thinks it's silly not to walk, then remembers Petra's heels, so he acquiesces.

The company's tech center occupies the entire bland building on the edge of the campus, surrounded on two sides by high metal fence and on two sides by a Sargasso Sea of parking lots. Even from across the lot, Dez can hear the industrial air-conditioning on the roof and can see ripples of heat radiating into the sky.

"Heard of climate change, have you?"

Petra parks the cart. "You believe in climate change?"

He climbs out. "Also gravity."

Petra's magnetic ID card gets them into the building, naturally. She draws some surprising looks and Dez imagines the rank and file have never seen the head legal counsel and heir presumptive of Triton in jeans and a ponytail. Several people are on their phones and are chatting animatedly. Dez hears the words "shooting" and "standoff" and makes a note to check his mobile when he gets a chance.

Brittany Kinney's office is half-circular, on the second floor, and extends out over a bullpen of technical workers like the pit boss over a casino floor.

She's an intense woman, small-boned, athletically built, maybe five-two and compact. Her hair is a vivid red, clipped short and asymmetrical, stylish but low-maintenance. She wears a white tank, black yoga pants, and black sneakers. There is not one note of color—not a belt, not a collar piping—in her wardrobe. Dez suspects she dresses in black and white to accentuate the crimson dye of her hair. Like everyone else, she wears her ID on a lanyard. It's a building full of mainframes, in Southern California, and even the massive air-conditioning system is insufficient to slough off all the heat. Her all-glass office is muggy and airless.

She whisks away a Bluetooth earjack as they enter. "Petra."

"Brittany. We have a crisis."

"What other people consider a crisis usually isn't from IT's viewpoint."

Petra says, "We've lost one point three billion dollars over two years to insider theft."

After a beat, Brittany nods. "Okay: crisis."

Petra explains what she's learned from her sleuthing.

Surprisingly, Brittany nods again. "I could've done it. In fact, I'm one of the few who could."

"I know."

She turns to Dez for the first time. "Who's this?"

"Dez. Wotcher."

She nods, an absolute minimum of cordiality. "You should get Frye back from wherever he is. He's probably blowing some diplomat somewhere, but he should get back here. He could've done it, too."

Petra says, "I know. He is."

Dez says, "Blowing some diplomat or coming back here?"

Petra lets free a flash-grin. "The latter. That I know of."

Brittany notices the quick grin, notices Petra drop her shields around Dez, and she stiffens a little. Dez thinks, *Ah*. He couldn't tell if the tech expert had been on high alert because another alpha female had invaded her turf, or if she was sexually attracted to Petra and trying to hide it. It's the latter. Good bit of information to have, Dez thinks.

"You told your dad yet?"

"I have."

"Other than the four of us . . ." Brittany shrugs.

"My father wants to meet with us as soon as Colin is wheels down. He's coming from New York. It'll take a while, even with the corporate jet. Can you stay on campus until then?"

Brittany says, "Is there an FBI agent outside the tech building waiting to read me my rights?"

"No."

"Then I'll come and go as I please until Constantine calls for me. Anything else?"

"Just that we've alerted the Pentagon. This investigation is out of my hands now."

Brittany nods.

Petra nods.

Dez grins. "Well, cheers, then. Been a pleasure."

Outside, Petra circles the electric cart and slides her Ray-Bans down out of her hair.

Dez says, "Your lass there never asked why you contacted the Pentagon."

"No," Petra says. "She did not."

"Anyone else we should visit?"

Petra seems flustered. Dez suspects that she doesn't even know why. Brittany Kinney was fairly radiating pheromones in there.

CHAPTER 33

On the ride back to the main building, Petra's phone goes berserk. She's checking it every fifteen seconds.

"Trouble, then?"

She checks another incoming message. "Alerts from the *New York Times*, the *Wall Street Journal*, *LA Times* . . . Everyone's covering this thing by that power plant."

Dez logs on to his own phone and searches for the news.

"Armed standoff in Central California," Petra says. "South of San Francisco. Some survivalist types, I think. Some soldiers may have snuck onto the property and shot the matriarch of the family, and now there are more casualties. It sounds bad."

Dez sways as the cart rounds a corner. "How's something like that happen?"

She shrugs and pulls up next to the main building. "It happens. It happened in Oregon a few years ago. Ruby Ridge in Idaho. Waco, Texas. It happens."

A train of thunderstorms pummels the Midwest, and the Triton chief financial officer's corporate jet is stuck on the far side of the weather. It's nearly nine at night here, so Petra recommends they return to the Malibu Colony Beach house and interrogate Frye in the morning.

Alonzo makes them a dill and Havarti omelet with bread he'd baked that morning. He's got the news on in the kitchen. Dez spots breaking-news banners and sees the looming cooling tower of a nuclear power plant in the background behind a pretty blond reporter.

The food is perfect and aromatic, the eggs fluffy. Alonzo makes coffee and, without being asked, joins them. Petra doesn't seem to notice.

"Are we under surveillance?" Alonzo asks.

"Not any longer. Created a long, random loop of old footage. Doubt they'll spot it for a while."

At Petra's confused look, Dez says, "I already told Alonzo you'd been under surveillance. He suggested we meet at the Getty."

She smiles a little. "You don't trust a decorated Marine major, but Alonzo you trust."

Alonzo snorts. "Yeah, right. The butler did it."

As Petra laughs, her phone lights up, and Dez, who sits shoulder to shoulder with her, sees the words *Reuters* and *Boca Serpiente, California*.

He tenses up. She catches it. "What?"

"Boca Serpiente?"

"Nuclear power plant, up north somewhere. It's that thing with the survivalists."

Dez drags his own phone out. He brings up Google Earth. He zooms into North America, then into the West Coast, California, Central California, and Boca Serpiente County.

He spots the county seat, Sloatville, population two thousand.

There, to the south of the town, is the Boca Serpiente Valley Nuclear Power Station, owned by the U.S. Department of Energy.

He pulls back the satellite imagery, scans north, then east, then south.

Petra is looking over his shoulder, her chin on his shoulder, and Alonzo hides a smile when he spots their closeness.

"What are you looking for?"

"Joint Base McKinzie-Clark. Remember that Navy bloke I chatted up? The one told me about the conspiracy?"

She nods.

"He's stationed there. Him and his mates. Joint Base McKinzie-Clark."

Petra sits back. "Coincidence?" she says, but it's clear from her tone that she's not buying it herself.

Dez dashes to the guest cottage and retrieves his ruggedized tablet computer. Petra heads to her office and returns with a laptop. They set them up, with their phones and Alonzo's portable TV, and begin scanning every news site. Alonzo had been on Univision but switches now between CNN, Fox, MSNBC, and Patriot Media. They all do.

The standoff at the Ryerson Ranch is the only news that the twenty-four-hour channels are covering. The situation is much worse than they'd initially heard.

Multiple sources are now saying that U.S. Army troops snuck onto the property—the Ryerson family's private property—and shot Molly Ryerson, age fifty-five. Shots were fired by a ranch hand, who was wounded in the arm. There's footage of Molly Ryerson's body. It's clear to Dez that she was shot in the back. There's also footage of the two dead U.S. soldiers. Also, a shot-up four-wheel all-terrain vehicle.

Things have escalated from there.

The Boca Serpiente County Sheriff's Office had been the principal agency in the standoff, which revolved around unpaid property taxes and also brush fires set by the rancher to clear fields, fires that had spread onto federally protected land. The Sheriff's Office has been told to stand down and the U.S. Marshals Service is primary now.

The governor threatens to deploy the National Guard.

The Secret Service is involved—that's according to Patriot Media, a far-right-wing site that has stolen a lot of Fox's swagger. Secret Service gets called in because they provide protection for anything that includes the transportation of fissionable material inside the U.S. That includes Department of Energy sites like the land upon which the state built its nuclear power plant.

Alonzo switches his TV from Patriot Media to CNN. Dez says, "Go back."

"Why? Their news is crap. Racist trash."

And it is. But thorough, racist trash. Patriot Media has people on the ground outside the Ryerson Ranch and in the little town of Sloatville, where a lot of the civilians are taking the side of the ranchers. Emotions are high. In the background, behind a news reporter's head, Dez can make out Jeeps and pickups and even Humvees, parked cheek by jowl on the town streets, plus lots of guys in baseball caps and ballistic vests, hauling shotguns and semiautomatic weapons. He spots AR-15s, MAC-10s, TEC-9s, the odd Armsel Striker, an Israeli Galil or two, a Steyr AUG, and even the odd AK-47.

They switch channels and watch a ninety-second clip of a tearful Joe Ryerson talking into a Patriot Media microphone, holding the shoulder of a ten-year-old boy in front of him, telling about the experience of finding his wife's body and the gunshot wound to her back. Standing to Ryerson's right is a tall man in full, bushy beard and a Detroit Red Wings ball cap, with a bloody gauze wrapped around his left forearm.

Every channel is covering this, but Patriot Media has churned up a graphic for it, superimposing a slowly waving American flag and the silhouette of a fortress rampart. The story has its own theme music.

Petra turns from her laptop, which is set to MSNBC. "Networks are saying militia types from all over the country are pouring into the county to help defend the ranchers."

She and the guys exchange glances.

Alonzo is using his smartphone, too. "Instagram and Twitter are saying hundreds of armed guys have shown up in Sloatville. It's like a damn convention. More of them arriving all the time. *Madre de dios*."

Dez whistles, high-low. "This here's your coup."

Petra smiles at him, but her smile withers when it isn't returned.

Alonzo sits bolt upright. "Coup?"

"At ease, *Primo Ballerino*," she chides him gently, and reaches across Dez to punch her staff in the shoulder. "Desmond has a fanciful idea someone's trying to split off from California."

"Really?"

Petra shakes her head. "He's wrong, fortunately. That town is about two thousand people deep. The joint military base? It's a backwater. It's been BRAC'd."

The men look at her.

"Base Realignment and Closure. First round happened around 2015. The second round is next year. Joint Base McKinzie-Clark is on the list for closure; I looked it up. It's too small and too old for the twenty-first century."

"Who'd get assigned to such a base, then?"

"Well, nobody whose military career is on the rise," she says. "That's a certainty."

The news doesn't ease Dez's worries. She can see that.

She touches his thigh. "I know what you're thinking. It can't happen. It really can't."

Alonzo shrugs. "She is smarter than you, tough guy."

"Goes without sayin'. But hear me out. If you could get a miniature coup started in that town, and at that base, could you hold out for a bit against the might of the U.S. Armed Forces?"

"For days at best," Petra says. "Hours, more likely. Dez, it's fanciful. This is the greatest military power the Earth has ever known. You think they couldn't take Mayberry and the world's least important joint military base?"

Dez says, "Mayberry?"

Alonzo pats his shoulder. "God, he's quaint. Can we keep him?"

The TV, laptop, tablet, and smartphones continue to show the craziness going on in Boca Serpiente Valley.

Petra sees the look on Dez's face. "What aren't you saying?"

"Asymmetrical warfare. It's how the mujahideen bolloxed the Russians in Afghanistan. It's how the Taliban and Al Qaeda and Daesh played merry hob with the Americans. All of 'em stood up against powers far greater than their own and made a good show of it."

"Hit-and-run tactics," Petra says.

"Aye. Guerrilla warfare. Hiding amongst civilians. If them militia types declare independence from California and set up in that flea-speck town, Sloatville, as their new capital, d'you think tanks would roll down Interstate 5?"

Now Petra looks like a little less certain of her argument. "Well . . . they'd have to. Right? Eventually. I mean, they wouldn't pounce on the town like it was D-Day, but . . ."

"Yeah?" Dez stabs his tablet with a stubby finger, all but obscuring the jumpy video image of a cooling tower. "And if the nuclear plant was in play?"

Alonzo says, "You mean, like, if they blew it up?"

"Or threatened to. Or melted it down. Aye."

"That . . ." Petra pauses. Then bolts up from the table, jostling coffee cups in her wake. She paces. Barefoot, her long, long legs chewing up the confines of the kitchen. "It would be an environmental disaster. The prevailing winds all along the Pacific Coast are north-south. The fallout could affect everything from Los Angeles to San Francisco. Beyond."

"Need to remind you," Dez says. "Triton Expediters has a big server farm in the town."

She eyes him critically from the far side of the kitchen. "This really has you worried, doesn't it?"

He shrugs. "There's more t'come, love. We're still left of Boom."

Alonzo leans his way. "Left of . . . ?"

"Military sayin'. A big thing, like, y'know, an invasion or a bomb attack, is Boom. Everything that comes before it is left of Boom, and we can only imagine the future from where we sit. Everything after the big event is right of Boom, and now we're all burdened with twenty-twenty hindsight, and wonderin' how we let whatever-it-was happen. And this now?" He gestures toward the TV and computers and phones. "We're left of Boom."

Petra's laptop is tuned to Patriot Media. Again they hear the stirring, martial-themed music and the breaking-news banner with its unfurled flag and rampart silhouette.

On the Spanish-tile tabletop, Petra's phone vibrates with an incoming call. She ignores it. "I still say it's impossible."

"Improbable," Dez counters. "Not impossible. The ranch shooting was the spark. The right-wing militias are there now. The far-right media is making a cause célèbre out of it. If that military base is compromised, and if they have a billion dollars plus of your money, and if the threat to melt down a nuclear reactor turns Central California into a no-fly zone . . ."

Petra's phone keeps vibrating. She crosses the kitchen, whisks it up. "That's a lot of *if*. Hold on." Into the phone, she says, "Hello? Yes, this is she."

She takes a few steps away from the breakfast nook.

Alonzo speaks low and in Spanish. "You really think this is all that?"

Dez shrugs. "Petra's probably right. What we got here is a bunch of sparks but no explosion. Not really. There's still time for this bit to sort itself out."

"Why isn't that comforting me?"

Dez elbows him in the upper arm. "Cheer up. They bring out the guillotine, it'll be for the rich and powerful, yeah? You'n me will be fine."

Alonzo shoulder-bumps him and grins.

Across the kitchen, Petra speaks softly into her phone, her back to them.

The boys watch the news and sip coffee.

Petra disconnects and turns to them. Her face is drained of color.

"Admiral Gerald Lighthouse is dead. It was a hit-and-run in Maryland."

The guys stare at her a moment.

Dez makes the hand gesture of an explosion.

"Boom."

CHAPTER 34

Dez spends the night in Petra's bed. A week earlier, he'd been sleeping on a camp cot in a room behind a Quonset hut garage in Torrance. This is better.

First thing in the morning, he takes the opportunity to call Captain Naomi Cardona of the LAPD.

The captain says, "I hear you ruffled some feathers in the Nazi bar scene in Los Alamitos."

"Me? I never look for trouble. Listen: I've need of a favor."

"Hang on. I'm waiting for the shock to roll over me. Okay, we're good."

"Can't go into details. Y'know this fecking mob scene in Boca Serpiente County?"

Cardona's tone loses any playfulness. "What?"

"My thing is connected to that thing. I'm thinking of heading north, seeing what there is to see. Could use a guide."

"A guide?"

"Someone there already. Someone lying doggo, eyes peeled."

"I only understand about half of what you say. But . . . I'm not for sure or anything, but maybe I know somebody who knows somebody in the general vicinity."

An undercover law enforcement official, then. Keeping track of the militia types pouring into Sloatville and Boca Serpiente County. Dez says, "Someone you trust?"

"With my daughter's life."

"Think you can make introductions?"

He waits through her pause. "That's a definite maybe, chief. I don't have direct comms, if you follow. I'll have to call in a heaping pile of favors just to see if the lines of communications are even possible. I have to know it's worth it."

"Fair play to you. If I'm right, Petra Alexandris was attacked because she was looking into the funding stream behind them fuckwits up there. She's going t'see if she can choke off the funds. I'd like to be on the ground when she does, throw some spanners in the works."

Cardona says, "What's a spanner?"

"D'you care?"

"Not even a little. Let me see what I can do. Chief? I cannot—repeat— Can. Not. Guarantee that I'll get through to the person who's up there. I give it one chance in . . . ten. Maybe. You with me?"

He laughs.

"What's so funny?"

"One in ten?" Dez says. "My ol' crew, them's the best fecking odds we ever got!"

CHAPTER 35

"You're *what*?"

Petra went for a run on the beach even before the sun rose. She's back now in running shorts, jog bra, and sneakers. She wore weighted bracelets, and her nut-brown arms and long legs glisten with sweat, her hair in a high ponytail. She glugs water and glares laser beams at Dez.

"That's not . . . a . . . plan!" Petra growls. "It isn't even the vague outline of a plan! We think there could be an armed insurrection underway up there. And you want to wander in and see what's up?"

Dez looks a little hurt. "Sounded better when I said it."

"That's the stupidest idea since asbestos!"

"Look, love. Y'see this?" Dez flexes his bicep. "I'm a bruiser. You're gathering your da and two executives to talk about international commerce and high crimes an' misdemeanors, yeah? What d'you want me there for? To beat confessions out of 'em?"

Her glower would peel paint. "That would be suboptimal, *chef*."

"Fairly well put, that. Look, I took a course one summer in economics, online, from a plate-glass college in Aberdeen. And I failed *that*! What good am I gonna do when you and your da and the others start hashing this out?"

She starts a response, but she doesn't actually have one. She glugs water instead.

"Right, then. You go throw punches your way. I'll head north, make friends, influence people, be me usual charming self, yeah? You find the funding for this bloody thing and choke it off. I'll see if I can't make a nuisance of meself up there. And Bob's your uncle."

She narrows her eyes. Dez glances at his chest to confirm that she doesn't actually possess Kryptonian heat vision.

"You'll head up there and, quote, make a nuisance of yourself."

"Yeah."

"How?"

He grins. "Dunno. That's the fun bit, innit?"

They argue a bit more after that, even though Petra has long since come to understand that he's going. She wants to prolong the argument because, well, she's a lawyer. It's how they count coup. Dez lets it ride. There's an old sexist bromide about women being beautiful when they're angry. With Greek women, the cliché's actually true. He doesn't enjoy getting yelled at, but the view can't be beat.

Afterward, while she's showering and changing into her power suit, he packs his duffel, leaving behind his guitar, and heads out to the stolen F-250 Super Duty. He's met behind the garage by Alonzo.

Who also has packed a bag.

"Going up there by yourself would be stupid," Alonzo says in Spanish. "Even by your standards."

Dez surprises the young man by throwing a hug around his torso. He steps back and ruffles Alonzo's hair. "Jaysus, and you've got balls. Coulda used a dozen of you in my crew."

Alonzo looks a little shocked by the hug. And the compliment. "Well . . . so, yeah, am I going?"

"You are hell!" Dez throws his duffel in the back of the pickup. "I'm looking to rile up some racist arseholes. You're a gay Latino. I'm not exactly gonna blend in, but you'd be a fecking disaster!"

Alonzo tries not to look relieved.

Dez opens the passenger door of the pickup, then the glove box. He removes a faded red oilcloth, places it in his upturned hand. He returns to Alonzo and unfolds the cloth, peeling it back in layers, revealing a Smith & Wesson .45 ACP he unknowingly stole when he stole the pickup. After Dez realized it was in there, he took it into the bathroom of the guest cottage, broke it down, and cleaned it thoroughly.

"Know how to use this?"

Alonzo says, "I know how to use YouTube, so, in theory . . ."

"That is, as herself would say, suboptimal. But beggars and all." He rewraps the massive hand cannon and sets it in Alonzo's hands.

Alonzo blanches at the weight of it.

"You keep Petra safe, yeah?"

"Been doing that long before you got here."

Dez offers a hand and the shake turns into a chest bump. "That you have, bruv."

Dez climbs into the pickup, throws it in gear, and leaves Malibu Colony Beach behind.

CHAPTER 36

It's an easy enough drive. Dez heads straight north on Interstate 5, through Santa Clarita, through the lush Los Padres National Forest. He cuts over to the 46 at Lost Hills, moving westward now. He passes through Black-wells Corner and Kecks Corner and connects to the 41, which becomes the 46 again for reasons Dez does not understand. Noon on Saturday, and traffic picks up as Dez hits the edge of Boca Serpiente County, one of the flattest and most arid parts in Central California. From time to time, he can spot the Pacific Ocean and, for the last ten minutes, the cooling tower of the Boca Serpiente Valley Nuclear Power Station.

He notices lots of TV microwave trucks heading into the county. Lots of good ol' boys heading in. And lots of families heading out.

He spots a pickup with a Confederate flag on the bumper and a gun rack in the cab. The pickup pulls into a gas station and an adjacent bar, and Dez quickly follows suit.

Three guys get out: one to pump gas and the other two heading over to the bar. Dez parks behind the bar.

He's been living in the States for months now and has mastered an ironclad American accent that can fool anyone. The value of living his adult life around people from every part of the world; it's given him an unerring ear for dialect. The two guys go directly to the bar and order three Coors from a fortysomething blond waitress attempting to rock cowboy boots and booty shorts and a knotted-off shirt. Dez joins the guys and orders a draft beer with his perfect American accent.

The waitress smiles at him. "Cute accent. Where're you from?"

Dez thinks he might have to reevaluate his perfect American accent. "Australia."

Both guys wear ball caps with Confederate flags. Both are open carrying. One of the guys says, "Didn't you people ban all guns?"

"That's New Zealand, them bastards."

The drinks arrive, along with their buddy from the truck, and everyone gets talking about Boca Serpiente.

"The Ryersons are for real, man," one guy says around a wad of chew. "They got it going on! Fucking cannot wait to wade into that shit."

They fist-bump. Dez, too.

"Can't hold out for long, can they?" Dez sips the absolutely horrible beer.

"Lantree says different."

Lantree? Dez nods. "Well, that's that, then. How many you figure coming to help?"

The tallest guy says, "Don't know. Lots. We're joining the fourth. We was in Iraq. We figure we can use what we know in the fourth."

"Soldiers, you?" He signals the waitress. "I'm buying this round. We've got soldiers here!"

The guys get even more talkative after that. Dez nurses his bottle of horse piss. Thirty minutes later, his newfound friends pile in their truck and keep on heading north.

Dez returns to his F-250 and boots up his tablet. He surfs for *Boca Serpiente* and *Lantree*.

Oliver Lantree, founder and CEO of Patriot Media, has made the standoff in Boca Serpiente County the only news story of the month. It's covered twenty-four seven by the media giant's cable franchise, its radio network and its website, its email newsletters, blogs, vlogs, and podcasts.

Lantree is from Virginia. He's fifty, matinee-idol handsome with a deep baritone voice. Dez learns that he's the new face of the radical right, and quickly becoming one of the most influential people in media today.

Also, that he's barking mad. Dez watches ten minutes of Lantree's screeds on YouTube, and realizes the rich bastard is as crazy as a cat sandwich. But he's a hell of an orator.

Dez googles *Boca Serpiente* and *The Fourth*.

Seems as if someone in the town of Sloatville is organizing all of the militia types that are pouring in. They've created five brigades to protect the town, the Ryerson Ranch, the coastline, Highway 1, and the nuclear power plant.

They're guarding the power plant, he learns from Patriot Media, because *everybody knows* the U.S. Army has been hiding a secret military base in there, ready to back up martial law in California when the United Nations, New World Order, and the Jews take over America. *Everybody knows* a lot of horseshit, but this isn't news to Dez. True the world 'round.

Dez had spotted another bar, three miles back, so he revs up the Ford and reverses course. The second joint isn't overly clean but at least it's humid. The waitress in the *Dukes of Hazzard* cosplay kit is nearly identical to the waitress in the bar he just left. He orders another bad beer. Had he known this investigation would involve drinking American beers, he definitely would have let them kidnap Petra.

He starts chatting up four guys who look like Hollywood Central Casting version of badass bikers with his now newly perfected American accent.

The waitress says, "Where you from?"

Damn it. "New Zealand."

A biker in a long, droopy Fu Manchu says, "Didn't you people ban all guns?"

"That's Australia, them bastards."

"You heading in, dude?"

"Course! Thinking of joining the Fourth."

"We're Third Brigade," a flabby man in leathers says.

"So how the hell did they organize brigades so damn fast?" Dez asks.

One of the guys reaches for a bowl of pretzels. "We first heard about it three weeks ago. Was waiting on Jake. He was doing four at Victorville."

Dez knows that that's a California state prison and he cobbles together the meaning of the rest of the sentence. "Three weeks ago? I just heard about it last week," he says, then hastily adds, "Some fellas and me done a job outside of Oakland. Was laying low. You know."

"Word." The bikers nod knowingly.

They talk and Dez learns from the bikers that this is a wave of West Coast and Southwest white pride types heading in; that a bigger wave is behind them; guys coming from all across the United States, egged on by Oliver Lantree and Patriot Media. They're coming from Appalachia and from Florida and Idaho; from everywhere, really.

Back at his pickup, Dez begins googling again. He learns that Oliver Lantree has relocated his Patriot Media World Headquarters to Sloatville, to be in the midst of this, the Second Great American Revolution.

This whole thing was kicked off by the standoff at the Ryerson Ranch. That was about thirty days ago. Dez learns that the media giant has been in town for about thirty-five days.

He starts reconsidering his notions of cause and effect here.

Someone foresaw this whole clusterfuck before it happened.

Or caused it to happen.

CHAPTER 37

Dez checks his messages, texts, emails, voice mail. Nothing from Captain Cardona or Detective Swanson.

He texts Petra Alexandris: *How going?*

She texts back almost immediately: *Homicide ensues.*

He knows she's been in meetings with her father and the chief financial and technical officers of Triton Expediters. She's about to throttle one or more of them. He grins, thinking about how much he'd give for a tub of popcorn, and to be sitting ringside watching her pistol-whip the lot of them.

Highway 1 runs parallel to the ocean and it cuts between Joint Base McKinzie-Clark to the east, and the Boca Serpiente Valley Nuclear Power Station to the west. The same off-ramp serves both, and the town of Sloatville, a bit to the north.

Outside town, he stops at a convenience store and buys a map published by the Greater Sloatville Chamber of Commerce. It's a single piece of paper, the size of a placemat, and it's a cartoon-drawn map, showing five restaurants, both motels, the historical society, the two-block-long shopping district, the access points to the beach. Dez buys a sandwich and a bottled water and, in the cab of his stolen pickup, compares the chamber's map to the Google Map on his tablet. He finds a ballpoint pen with teeth marks and no cap in the glove box and marks an X on a large, single-story building way to the north, at the very outskirts of Sloatville. It's the size of a warehouse but with little parking.

It's the server farm for Triton Expediters. A massive mess of mainframes with a skeleton crew. A thing like that creates a lot of heat. It uses an excessive amount of electricity and tons of water for cooling. To the west is an ocean, thank you very much.

To the southeast is a nuclear power plant. An aging one, to be sure. Built in the late 1960s and opened in 1971, Dez has learned, and nearing the end of its productive life.

Much like Joint Base McKinzie-Clark, farther to the arid east, although the base dates back to a couple of weeks after the attack on Pearl Harbor.

Another relic of a place, pretty much forgotten by the Pentagon brass. A good place to hide an army in plain sight.

It's about ninety degrees in Boca Serpiente County. If Dez were law enforcement, he'd have blockaded the exit off Highway 1 and kept everyone out of the town of Sloatville. That hasn't happened.

There's an ENTERING SLOATVILLE sign and, right behind it, a gas station/convenience store with Christmas decorations in the window. Christmas was five months ago. The reader board outside reads, GATER'S GAS 'N' GRUB. SEASON GREETINGS: AMMO.

He spots fairgrounds a little outside of the city limits with a sign that reads TIME TO BUCK! BOCA SERPIENTE COUNTY FAIR AND RODEO! But no fair and rodeo this year. The fairgrounds have been turned into a bivouac for arriving men, who have set up a tent camp, or parked RVs, or are sleeping in the beds of their pickups. Dez slows to a crawl and counts scores and scores of vehicles. Well over a hundred.

There's an air of excitement over the tent village. He sees guys laughing and drinking beer and high-fiving. He sees big dogs—shepherds, pit bulls, others—romping about. He sees a lot of family units: moms and little kids but few dads. A long row of porta-potties lines a softball field. *How long would it take for a town of two thousand people to arrange for thirty, forty porta-potties?* he wonders. Then again, they do host a county fair and rodeo. Maybe the town owns them. Or maybe someone was stockpiling materiel prior to the militias' arrival.

He sees TV helicopters circling the city, but he's been seeing those ever since he hit the county border. He sees news crews and microwave transmitter trucks a couple of blocks away. The revolution *will* be televised.

The cooling tower is visible in the distance.

Dez parks amid other pickups in the fairgrounds.

He takes the next ninety minutes to stroll about and engage people in conversation. He doesn't lead with questions. It's a slow way to learn anything, but it also rouses fewer suspicions. He's pretty sure he's honed his American accent to a thing of beauty, but the first two people he chats up ask him where he's from, so he throws out the damn accent entirely.

He finds a keg and a massive pile of red plastic cups, and queues up with a dozen other guys. "Where you from, bro?" says a guy with stringy, shoulder-length hair pulled back into a ponytail. Dez hasn't even opened his mouth yet. What is it with Americans and their radar?

"Tasmania. Is it true Oliver Lantree is broadcasting from here in town?"

The guy uses a rubber hose to pour thin, foamy beer into Dez's cup. "Sure as shit, bro. Patriot Media set up in town. Got reporters, photographers, the whole shebang. See that one?"

The guy points to a specific media helicopter hovering out near the ocean. "That's theirs."

"Well, thank God for them, then."

The guy holds out his own Solo cup and taps it against Dez's. "Last honest voice in the fucking media, bro."

"You know where they're set up? I want to see for meself."

The guy shrugs. "Dunno. In town somewhere. Hey, you just get here?"

Dez nods. He holds the cup to his lips and tries not to swallow the truly craptacular brew.

"You picked a brigade yet?"

"Na. I'll serve where they need me."

"Well . . ." The guy gestures toward Dez's physique. "You got the whole Hulk Smash thing going on. Whatever you pick, bro, they'll take you. Brigade One's gonna protect the town when ZOG shows up."

Dez shakes his head in wonder. "Fecking Zog." He's not certain, but he thinks Zog might've been one of the villains in the Superman comics, though likely that's not who this guy's referring to. "Brigade One for me, then."

"Right on, bro. Fight the good fight."

And Dez realizes that, for them, it is.

The good fight.

Everyone's the hero in their own story.

CHAPTER 38

The people in Sloatville accept Dez's presence, and he quickly figures out why. He's white. He himself never knew if he was of Irish, Scottish, Welsh, or English parentage, but one thing's for certain: He's a fair-skinned guy and he's in a town with absolutely nothing but other white people.

If he started singing in Berber or Arabic, half the heads in this fairgrounds would explode. He's tempted to try.

He checks his phone. No messages.

He leaves the truck where it is and wanders into town. It doesn't take him long to find signs nailed to power poles and fences, welcoming the militia and urging all able-bodied Americans to sign up for a brigade: first for the town; second for the Ryerson Ranch; third to watch the coast; fourth to guard the road leading to the highway; fifth for the power station.

Dez doesn't know, but he suspects the Ryerson Ranch is just the spark to draw people here. It's a diversion. It's not where the real action's going to take place. Too isolated, of too little strategic value.

Guarding the coast? From what, the Spanish Armada?

Same for the road to and from the highway. Dez saw those guys as he drove in and they looked fairly bored.

That leaves the power station and the town.

He knows, for certain, that the nuclear power plant plays a role here, but he thinks it's mostly as a deterrent. The U.S. military won't wade into Boca Serpiente County if they fear the plant has been compromised. But that's right of Boom. Like he told Petra and Alonzo, they're all still left of Boom, the likely assassination of Admiral Lighthouse notwithstanding. That was bad. But it wasn't the big show.

So until Boom, the power plant's just a diversion. Till then, the plant isn't important.

That leaves the town of Sloatville itself.

Well, that and Joint Base McKinzie–Clark, but no militia brigade is assigned to that and Dez hasn't figured out a way to wrangle an invitation there yet. So Sloatville it is.

The town has seen better days, although that might be optimistic. It might never have seen good days at all. Dez suspects the economy here tanked well before the Great Recession and the pandemic, and never truly recovered. It's a town in the center of California with no high tech, no agriculture, no Hollywood, no wine, and no banking. Sloatville is a lactose-intolerant diabetic in the land of milk and honey.

Several hundred white guys open-carrying assault rifles have staged up in this town. Dez spots only a few folks who appear to be residents. Dez brought along his lockbox, with his breaching equipment, his 290-millimeter fixed-blade knife, and the folding Raptor blade clipped to his belt. But he doesn't yet have a gun and he's a little concerned that will look conspicuous.

Towns like this in the Southwestern United States, a largish portion of the population likely would be Hispanic. That may have been true a month or so ago, but if so, they've long since fled or are hiding in their homes.

Dez doesn't spot any actual military types in town, and that's good. He's tangled with a few of them now, and he's not ready to be recognized.

He sees several TV journalists doing what's called stand-ups, holding mics, speaking directly into the cameras perched on the shoulders of cameramen. Other journalists are interviewing people in town. He avoids eye contact with reporters. Then again, who doesn't?

The streets of the urban center of Sloatville—all four of them—are jammed with pickups and Humvees and Jeeps and off-road three-and four-wheel ATVs. People are jovial, grinning, slightly manic. It's all familiar and it takes Dez a moment to realize why: It reminds him of the scene in every American cowboy movie of the Old West town just before the bandits ride in, six-shooters blasting away, bandannas over their mouths, gut-shot stuntmen doubling over and slow-rolling off roofs.

Festive but with a pending air of violence.

Boom is coming.

Dez spots city hall, which includes a municipal building and a police station. A county fire department serves the town, he guesses. The building is one story, bland as oatmeal, and looks like it was built in the 1980s, making it the most modern building he's seen so far by about four decades. It should be closed, this being a weekend. It's not.

Lots of guys coming and going. News crews staging outside. Could be something. Dez rolls that way with his Popeye gait.

The Sloatville City Council is meeting. The city council chamber is a largish meeting room, very plain, that seats about thirty people facing one way, and a raised dais with five chairs and a table facing the other way. This could be an AA room in any church or a Rotary Club meeting space in any office park. There's a round city emblem plaque on the table in front of the centermost chair—the seat of the mayor—but it's plastic and has been mounted slightly crooked. When necessary, he guesses, the plaque gets removed and this becomes the municipal courtroom.

Dez guesses that eighty people are crammed into the hot and airless room.

Up on the dais, the mayor—or the woman holding the gavel at any rate—is maybe in her fifties and Hispanic. She's trying to shout over the roaring crowd. The other people on the dais look pretty shell-shocked. None are leaping to her defense.

The only camera crew inside the council chamber belongs to Patriot Media, according to the logo on the camera and the microphone thrust toward the angry, surging crowd. The camera and the mic are not facing the elected officials, with their shoulders hunched, heads lowered, trying to make as small a target as possible. Patriot Media doesn't much care what they have to say.

The spitting-mad mob, on the other hand? That makes for grand television.

People are standing, the chairs ignored. They shout over one another. Dez, squeezed into the back of the room, hears growls of "go back where you came from" and "real Americans" and "secure our borders." Same old, same old. *It'd be nice,* he muses, *if haters learned a new tune now and then.*

A fortysomething guy leans toward Dez and shouts to be heard. "Showing 'em now!"

The guy's T-shirt shows an American eagle, its talons laden with an AK-47 and a bandoleer of grenades. Dez leans his direction. "What brought this on? What did the city council say to rile everyone up?"

The guy shrugs, then goes back to shouting down the message he (1) is unaware of and (2) vehemently opposes.

Dez can't easily get any closer to the front, nor does he particularly want to. He's got a sense of the dynamics of the room, and that's enough. He edges back out of the chamber.

A quick tour tells him that two-thirds of the building feature the city council chamber and an administrative office that looks big enough for three, maybe four full-time employees. The police station is simply the left-hand third of the building. Dez ambles through a connecting door to see what's what.

The police station is deserted. He spots two desks, a smallish space barred off for a holding cell in one corner, and a small, spare separate office for the chief.

Dez is glad to be out of the roar of the crowd and stands in the quiet for a moment. Someone should be here, even if only a clerk. But nope—not a soul. Maybe the entire force is out trying to maintain calm. Maybe the entire force is in the council chambers yelling along with the others.

The relative silence—he can hear chanting now from the council chamber, "send 'em back, send 'em back"—is a little unnerving. Something's missing.

Dez spots a two-way radio behind a civilian counter. He circles the counter, checks the radio.

It's been unplugged from the wall. Inert.

He doesn't know where the Sloatville City Police are at the moment. But out on patrol isn't the answer.

He rifles through some cabinets. If the station has a weapons locker, he can't find it. He spots a bottle of bourbon and a lot of municipal, county, and state forms that need to be filled out by someone but probably never will now. He sees a pegboard with room for two car keys—stenciled CAR ONE and, weirdly, CAR B. No keys on the hooks over either stencil. He thinks it likely that the same radio that the Sloatville Police would use to communicate internally would be used to communicate with the county sheriff's office and the California Highway Patrol, but maybe not. Either way, there's no second radio to be found.

"You supposed to be in here?"

Dez turns. Two men have entered through the street door. Both wear jeans and boots and untucked shirts, sleeves rolled up. Both look fit and thirtyish. Both wear Glocks on belt holsters at their sides, their shirts rucked up to expose the weaponry.

Dez retrieves the half-full bottle of bourbon from the filing cabinet and smacks it down on the counter between himself and the guys. "Been a long day, now." He beams. "What're ye drinking?"

The two guys are six-two and six-foot. Beyond that, they're pretty interchangeable. Six-Two says, "Asked you a question."

"Are you the chief of police, then? Badges to flash about?" He keeps smiling.

The guys take a step closer. They appear to find Dez not as charming as Dez is quite sure he is.

Six-Two says, "If you don't got business in here, move along."

Dez circles the counter, then hoists himself up onto it, feet dangling. He removes the lid off the bourbon and takes a swig. "Too feckin' crowded in there." He head-jabs toward the sound of chanting. "Can't hear yourself think."

He holds the bottle at arm's length.

Six-Foot steps forward and accepts it. He relaxes a little. "Whole town's getting crowded."

"I want t'see Oliver Lantree," Dez says, letting his legs kick like a little kid on the swings. "That'd be something. Me mum listens to him night and day. She'd love that."

Six-Foot take a swig and gestures with the bottle toward Six-Two.

Who draws his Glock, a quick, professional draw, knees bent, shoulders hunched, body turtled in, left hand supporting his right wrist, finger indexed, and points it at Dez's chest.

"Stand up. Turn around. Hands on the counter. Do it now."

Six-Foot says, "Kyle?" He's frozen, bottle extended, eyebrows raised in surprise.

Six-Two barks, "Do it! Now!"

Dez grins. "Course, mate!" He swings his legs and hops down and, in so doing, brushes the forearm of Six-Foot, nudging his hand and the bottle of bourbon close to Six-Two—Kyle. The bottle jostles Kyle's arm.

Kyle adjusts accordingly, glances reprovingly at his buddy, and Dez uses his left hand to grab Kyle's gun and right hand, both disappearing into Dez's massive mitt. He twists and hears wrist bones break. Kyle's eyes shoot wide.

Dez has very quick hands. His left hand is busy grinding the bones of Kyle's wrist, so he lets pop with his right fist, smacking Six-Foot in the nose, and he still has time to snatch the bourbon bottle out of the air before the man drops it to the floor.

"Waste not, want not."

He releases Kyle's now-useless right hand and punches him in the mouth.

Kyle lands on the floor next to his mate, a wee second after his mate. Both well and truly unconscious.

Dez unclips both guys' holsters, and takes Kyle's Glock off the floor, sets everything on the counter. He takes another hit of the bourbon. He takes the men's mobile phones and hides them in a file drawer.

He grabs Kyle by the shirtfront and deadlifts him up off the floor, dumping him behind the counter. He does the same with his buddy.

He can't kill these two guys—well, *can't* is the wrong word. 'Course, he could kill them. But he won't, and he doesn't want them coming to and telling the world about him. So he clips their holsters onto the back of his belt. Then he circles the counter and squats down. He unbuckles Kyle's belt, unzips his pants, and shoves Six-Foot's hand in the man's pants. He undoes Six-Foot's trousers and shoves Kyle's hand in.

Let 'em wake up and try to explain this, then. Complicates the telling of any tale. Might make one reconsider saying anything at all.

Dez drizzles the bourbon on their shirts to make sure they smell like all have had a good time, then ambles out of the police station.

Town isn't boring. He'll give 'em that.

CHAPTER 39

Time is more of a factor now. Those guys might be too embarrassed by the scenario of rough sex gone wrong, but Dez can't count on that. He needs answers.

He needs the mayor.

The city hall shouting match is breaking up. The woman up on the dais with the gavel—he assumes she's the mayor—looks exhausted. The other two councilors are drifting away, not making eye contact with her. Patriot Media journalists are interviewing the thinning, excited crowd.

Dez waits in the back of the chamber. When the woman packs her tote bag and heads toward an exit near the dais, Dez dashes out and circles the building, to the gravel parking lot shared by the municipal building and a right dodgy bar called Pirate's Booty. Singular possessive. Maybe the proprietor couldn't afford two pirates.

She emerges and vectors toward a twelve-year-old Toyota with a mismatched right front quarter panel. Dez says, "Pardon me," and her shoulders sag.

He knows what this looks like. He's not a resident of the town. He's a white guy, guns strapped on. She says, "Look, whatever you want to add to—"

"There was an attempted kidnapping, Monday last, at the Hotel Tremaine in Los Angeles."

She looks at him for real now, curious. He holds his hands out, palms forward.

"Them bastards in your town attempted to kidnap this woman because she caught onto a scheme to steal . . . well, let's say a lot of money to pay for all this here." He gestures around. "I work with her. She's trying t'stop the flow of money. I'm here to mess with 'em as much as I can."

She studies him. Dez stands there and lets her.

She says, "Are you for real?"

"Aye, ma'am. Between Petra Alexandris—the bird they tried to kidnap—and meself, we've as good a chance as anyone of stopping this lot. But I need to know more."

She nods toward the Toyota. "Come with me."

CHAPTER 40

Her name is Renata Esquivel. When she tells him, Dez says, "Like the bandleader," and she reappraises him. "No relation. But yes."

He finds out she's not the mayor of Sloatville. The mayor split. She's the council president pro tem. Dez doesn't know what that means, but it sounds posh. She could have/should have split, too. But she stayed because this is the town she was born in.

Those chants of *send her back, send her back* must have been painful, given that. He doesn't ask. Seems a stupid question.

Dez likes her immediately.

She's Latina, fifty-five, about five-one, with the hands and wrists and forearms of a baker, which is to say, strong. She invited him to her home, a one-story clapboard affair closer to the ocean. The inside is decorated with tons of images of Jesus and Mary. Dez expected that.

A man sits in an aged, nutmeg-brown recliner and watches *fútbol* on a decent-sized flat-screen TV. He's got a coffee table next to him with an iced tea and a pencil and about a half dozen football publications. Dez can see that the man's been marking them up, making notes with circles and arrows. He has a green-and-yellow afghan over his lap and the recliner is extended, and Dez can see that he has only one leg under the afghan.

Renata chats with him quietly in Spanish for about a minute, and explains Dez's presence. Dez watches the match. It's Liga MX; not Dez's favorite league, although they play damn good football down there. He hears the old man—Dez thinks he's maybe midsixties and as frail as a bird's egg—ask why she would trust another white man with guns. She says she's playing a hunch.

The man looks over her shoulder at Dez with unalloyed suspicion.

Dez juts his chin toward the set.

"Querétaro an' Cruz Azul, yeah?" He speaks Spanish. "Nary a striker for the 'Cement Makers' this year, but their keeper's for real. You see that save against Monarcas last week? Beauty."

The man nods. "You know a little about football?"

"Know enough to put the other side on its hind foot, sir. Looking for the councilor's help on that score."

Renata and the man nod to each other a little. "My name is Hector Esquivel. Welcome to my home."

"Desmond Limerick, sir."

"You are from Spain?"

Dez's accent. "British Isles, sir."

Renata Esquivel says, "Would you like coffee?"

"More'n anything, ma'am."

She leads the way to a very clean and aging kitchen. She gets coffee brewing and gets milk scalded, and presents a plate of concha, a popular pastry from Mexico. They're shaped like a seashell; thus the name. Hers are made with real vanilla and sprinkled with cinnamon, and Dez groans a little when he tastes it.

Renata likes that, he can tell.

She says, "I'm still not sure I should talk to you."

"Smart." He nods, sipping his *café con leche*.

She asks him a lot of good, penetrating questions about himself; about Petra and the attack on the Hotel Tremaine; about the money connection. She's smart. That's in Dez's favor. He could use smart right about now.

The coffee is great.

"How'd all this get started, then?"

She rubs her eyes, fatigued and saddened by what's happened to her town. "That man from the network. He showed up in town last month and started broadcasting. Radio, TV, a blog. He was everywhere."

Dez says, "Oliver Lantree. Patriot Media."

She makes the sign of the cross. "I wish ill on no one, Mr. Limerick. But that man is a cancer."

Somewhere along the line, they'd both slipped into Spanish but Renata only now realizes it. That, more than anything, convinces her to trust Dez.

"Was Patriot Media in town before the standoff started?"

She nods. "A few days before. I thought they were incredibly lucky and Sloatville was incredibly unlucky."

Dez lets that slide for now. "D'you know the family at the ranch?"

"We know . . . we knew Molly. I'd say she was a good mother. She loved her kids. She was a Christian. She was an unrepentant racist but . . . tolerated Hector and me, I think, because I'm strong-willed and speak my mind. And I'm originally from here. She and Joe were survivalists. The ranch is off the power grid; has its own water. Mostly they left everyone alone. Then Joe burned some of his acres to reinvigorate the soil. The burn spread onto federal land. There was a warrant. Shots were fired in the air. A standoff."

"But that happened after Lantree showed up with his media circus?"

She nods, eyes narrowed, following his logic.

"I don't think Lantree was lucky; right place, right time. I think he engineered all this. I think he's got soldiers at that military base out there who're in on it. I think he's looking to create a fifty-first state."

Renata Esquivel says, "Lexington?"

"Aye, that's right. They've the money and the guns and the inciting incident. Maybe they can make it happen."

Renata nods. "There's been lots of talk of that at the town halls." She breaks off a bit of cookie and nibbles it. Dez has gobbled down two-thirds of the plate. "At first, a lot of the residents showed up. Then more of these newcomers. Men with guns. Fewer residents. Today . . . I saw maybe three people I knew. And they wouldn't make eye contact with the spic."

Dez makes a fist and isn't aware of it. He tries to look calm; fails.

She reaches out and cups his fist, or as much of it as she can. "You seem like a nice man, Mr. Limerick."

"Nice won't get me far with this lot, I'm afraid. There's a high like-lihood I'll be meting out violence, ma'am. Sorry, but there it is."

"Violence begets violence," she says. "'Beloved, never avenge your-selves, but leave it to the wrath of God, for it is written, "Vengeance is mine, I will repay, says the Lord."'"

"Paul. Romans." Dez can tell he surprises her. "I'm sorry to tell you this, ma'am, but if you were hoping God sent a pacifist to placate these bastards—sorry—ye'll find he has not. 'Righteous indignation is a mean between envy an' spite. . . .' That's me, then."

She says, "Aristotle."

Dez grins. He's in need of some smart. He came to the right place.

CHAPTER 41

Dez gets to the heart of the matter. "Where do I find this Oliver Lantree and his empire?"

"They've rented space in a server farm, north part of town."

Dez tenses at the term *server farm*.

"Do you know what that is?" Renata asks. "It's just computers. Lots and lots of computers. They suck up ocean water and they run air-conditioning three hundred and sixty-five days a year. They pay well for it all, too. Nearly a tenth of the city's budget comes from their taxes and fees."

"Much staff?" he asks.

"Hardly any. It's all automated. Plenty of room for the news crews to work out of."

"Then that's where I'll start. Thank you, ma'am. I'll do what I can for your town."

She starts taking dishes to the sink, tries not to let Dez spot that she's crying. "Oh, Mr. Limerick. Sloatville's dead. It died when the crazies showed up and the good people fled. Or hid in their houses. It died when the mayor left. When the other members of the city council, and the school board, and the county commission turned their backs and averted their eyes. It doesn't matter now what happens to Patriot Media, or the Ryerson Ranch, or any of these hoodlums. Sloatville is dead."

She's right, of course. Dez saw it at the city council meeting. Anarchy, once in place, is tough to root out. And it kills whatever existed before it. Dez has seen it in the Middle East and in Northern Africa. Fragile things, order and peace.

She looks up at a crucifix on the wall over the kitchen table. "Do you believe in God, Mr. Limerick?"

Dez thinks about it. He could give her a flippant answer, but he won't. He could dodge the question as none of her business, but he shouldn't. "I'm sorry, ma'am. I don't."

"Why not?"

"Because you can put the words *pediatric* and *oncology* in the same sentence. I'm sorry. But if there's a higher being, I fear he's drunk an' mean. And I'd rather imagine no higher being than that one."

Renata Esquivel nods, understanding. She says, "I believe in God. I'll pray for you."

"Thank you, ma'am. I'll take it, and be glad for it."

Dez leaves Renata and Hector Esquivel in their modest clapboard house. He's tempted to tell them to flee but he doesn't.

They won't.

Dez walks back to the fairgrounds and collects his stolen Ford pickup. Then he drives toward the Triton Expediters server farm on the north side of town.

CHAPTER 42

Joint Base McKinzie-Clark

General William Tancredi is in his office, as head of the dilapidated, soon-to-be BRAC'd military base. He's on the phone getting an update from the Pentagon regarding the murder of Navy Secretary Admiral Gerald Lighthouse.

"Lighthouse was asking about your base out there," the caller says.

"How far did his questions get him?"

"Unknown. I've bottled it up, for now. But you need to move quickly. You do not have unlimited time."

"Well, thank you for whatever time you've bought us," Tancredi says. "Things are ready on our end. Our guests are almost here."

They talk a bit more and hang up.

Tancredi is sixty, a short and stocky pit bull of a man, military haircut, and not popular within the Army. Investigations at his last two commands into sexual assault and theft of Army materiel torpedoed his career. Command of a fleabag base, destined to be shut down, is the best he could have hoped for until retirement.

Retirement is Tancredi's plan, as far as the Army knows.

William Tancredi has other options up his sleeve.

He's watched this once-great nation fall apart, under attack from leftists and communists, crime and drugs, an unparalleled invasion by illegals. By abortion and the unchurching of the American populous. By the emasculation of every male role model. Most recently, an African sleeper agent actually made it to the White House. There's almost no America left anymore.

Tancredi wants to do something about all that.

He uses a dedicated website created by one of his coconspirators and initiates a three-way conference call with the two people into whom he's poured a great deal of trust.

Oliver Lantree, one of his coconspirators, is only miles away, on the west side of Highway 1, in the town of Sloatville. He's been doing his job and doing it brilliantly for months now. The powder keg is primed.

His other partner is in an office in Los Angeles. Hawthorne, California, to be exact.

There's a knock at the door and General Tancredi knows who it is before growling, "Come!"

It's Captain Bart Weaver, barely recognizable in his full, bushy beard, civilian clothes, and Red Wings cap. The captain has been deployed to the Ryerson Ranch under the false name of Jones, or Jonesy, for the past month. But his work there is done. His left forearm is wrapped in gauze.

Oliver Lantree takes up half the screen on General Tancredi's computer. Their partner in Hawthorne takes up the other half.

"The Pentagon is sniffing around," Tancredi says. "They know zip. That won't last."

"Things are coming to a head here," Oliver Lantree says. He's barely fifty years old, fit, and recently cultivated a Southern drawl for his ascent to the top of the polls in conservative media circles. He attended Harvard and lived for half his life in New England, but doesn't want people to know that. He's excessively rich, even by American standards, and doesn't want people to know that, either.

"Good Americans are pouring in. Pouring," he drawls. "I admit to bouts of pessimism, friends. Not today. Not today."

"We have some . . . loose ends here," says their coconspirator in Hawthorne. "The faster we move, the better."

General Tancredi glances at Captain Weaver, who nods once.

"We're set at this end. Let's say . . . tomorrow?"

Lantree says, "Indeed. Tomorrow."

The third party on the call says, "Tomorrow," and disconnects.

When she's gone, Oliver Lantree says, "Can we trust her?"

"We won't have to for long," Tancredi says. "Her usefulness is coming to an end."

He disconnects. Then turns to Captain Weaver.

"Trouble?"

"Two guys down," Weaver says, standing at parade rest. "In town. They said they were attacked by a bulky guy with an English accent."

Tancredi rubs his temples, feeling a headache ratchet up. "The same asshole who was at the Tremaine."

"And who attacked our men on the highway, and those guys in Los Alamitos," Weaver says. "For sure."

"Who is he?"

"Don't know yet, sir. He's trained. Special Forces? Someone Admiral Lighthouse sent?"

"Maybe," Tancredi says, pulling on his lower lip. "Find the son of a bitch."

"I've got everyone looking for him, sir."

Tancredi nods and Weaver exits.

He's got some hunting to do.

CHAPTER 43

Petra Alexandris is stalking through the halls of Triton Expediters global headquarters when her phone vibrates. It's Dez.

She slips into an unused conference room. *"Chef?"*

"It's bonkers up here," he says without preamble. "You should see the place. Lunacy."

"It's not noticeably better here. I've been meeting with my father, Colin, and Brittany. Since I don't know who I can trust, we're tracking through all of the evidence of the theft together. I know more than they—presumably. If any one of them tries to hide evidence or obfuscate, I'll know."

He can hear the worry in her voice. He says, "Lovely word, *obfuscate*. From the Latin, meaning *dark*. Jaysus but you're a posh bit."

Despite everything, he makes her smile. "Yes, I am. Are you being careful?"

"No." Why lie? "But I'm making headway."

"Then you're alone. Would you believe, this day of all days, Dmytro Rudko is in Los Angeles? Holy hell."

"An' who's that, then?"

"Russian ambassador to the UN. Triton does a lot of business with Russia. He wants to talk. I can't blow him off."

"Let the record show that it was Ms. Alexandris, and not I, who uttered the words *blow him*. I myself am far too gentlemanly to suggest anything of the sort."

She laughs. "Would that it were so easy. No, I have to go talk business with him. This slows everything down on my end."

"No worries," Dez says. "Plenty to do here. Who knows? Might even get interesting."

CHAPTER 44

Dez needs to meet this Oliver Lantree fella. He's never before met a media star. The guy was here, stirring up trouble before trouble itself arrived. Lantree is one of the people behind this thing. Dez is sure.

He cruises past the Triton Expediters server farm and sees three microwave trucks out front. Two of their long, extendable necks are down, one of them giraffed up, and a pretty blond thing is doing a stand-up with the Patriot Media logo on the side of the van, right behind her very, very feathered hair.

Two other guys are unpacking cases of water and grocery bags from the back of an SUV, carrying them in.

Dez spots soldiers and a government-issued Humvee. He's not ready to meet any real soldiers just yet. So it's time for subterfuge. Dez enjoys himself some subterfuge.

The server farm draws vast quantities of ocean water for coolant, and the town of Sloatville is on a cliff overlooking the Pacific. It's the only beach town he's seen in California without a decent beach. Dez isn't clear why anyone started a town here on this boil on the buttocks of the planet. There had to be some attraction. Dez doesn't see it.

He parks the stolen F-250 near the cliffs and legs his way down to the beach, using waxy weeds as handholds so he doesn't drop ass-over-teakettle to the rocks below. It's slow going.

When he gets to the rocky edge of the Pacific, he walks north until he comes to a gated-off sector and a massive pipe that runs from the ocean, turns ninety degrees, and runs straight up the cliff face, before turning another ninety degrees. A tin sign on the fence says TRITON ENVIRONMENTAL INC.—A WHOLLY OWNED SUBSIDIARY OF TRITON EXPEDITERS.

If you're a gatekeeper, padlocks are like doors. Each represents a challenge, a fun little puzzle. Dez keeps lockpicks in the sheath that holds his folding knife. The padlock on the pipe facility is massive and iron. The size of a lock does not reflect the complexity of the mechanism. He picks it in under five seconds.

Once inside the paddock, he can see that the massive pipe has been secured to the rock face with bolts driven into the cliff. Perfect. They make ideal hand- and footholds.

He looks around to make sure no one's watching. He spots a mega-yacht perched a kilometer off the coast. Too far away to keep an eye on a dull old pipe, that's for sure. The yacht has a tall conning tower and a helipad but no helicopter. Even at this distance, he can spot a bikini and a long cascade of blond hair on the foredeck. The rich never fail to amuse Dez.

Dez adjusts the guns and the knife clipped to his belt, then begins climbing.

It's a fifty-foot climb, using only the hex nuts screwed into the bolts driven into the rock face. He has good boots, Wolverines, which have served him well.

He's caked in sweat and dust by the time he reaches the top.

The water pipe dives into a metal housing, ten meters from the edge of the cliff, and Dez uses that as cover, to rest and get his breath back. He's leaning against it, forearms on his raised knees, feeling his lungs expand and contract. Since meeting Petra Alexandris, Dez has missed a couple of trips to the gym. On the other hand, her calisthenics in bed probably helped increase his lung capacity.

The server farm is an ugly one-story building with no aesthetics to speak of. It was constructed to house a bunch of computers, and the computers sure don't care what the building looked like. Not too many windows; in fact, none back here. The roof is a ragtag jumble of air-conditioning and ventilation mechanics: ripples of heat emanate from them. Also, four huge radar dishes, all facing south.

Dez rises and sprints to the edge of the building, sitting again. He hasn't drawn a weapon. Truth be told, he doesn't much trust the two guns he took off the fellas at the police station, because he hasn't disassembled them and cleaned them. Mostly, they were for show while walking around Sloatville.

There's a maintenance door back here. Dez draws his lockpicks. Beginnings and gates. Transitions and time. Duality and doors. Passages and endings. He glances at the tattoo of Janus and makes easy work of the door.

Inside, he decides to brazen it. He finds a bathroom and gets the dust and sweat off him. Then he stands tall, walks the halls, smiles at whoever he sees. He passes maybe a dozen people. He nods. They nod back. He's a white guy with guns. This is RacismLand. He passes a locked room marked ENVIRONMENTAL SYSTEMS.

The building is hot and humid. All the ocean water and all the HVAC in the world can't stop that. It's about 80 percent computers, full rooms of standing mainframe arrays.

Patriot Media folks have set up shop in the front. They've created a broadcast room out of a reception area, with automatic, robotic cameras, and a big desk with the Patriot logo, and a green screen behind it. Dez peers through a horizontal window in the door and watches two presenters—*anchors,* they'd call them here—talking. Dez wonders what the home audience sees on the green screen. All he sees is, well, green.

"Help you?"

It's a guy with a walrus mustache and a considerable gut. He's mostly bald, with a ring of gray hair that he wears in a ponytail. He's carrying an old-style, long-barreled Smith & Wesson revolver in a lovingly designed holster on his belt, wearing it up front for a cross-body draw.

Dez says, "Model 19 Classic. Very nice."

Walrus Mustache just nods. The mustache itself nods for a half second after his head stops moving.

"Supposed to see Mr. Lantree."

"He's in the office over there." Walrus Mustache gestures to the left. "Where you from?"

"Auckland. Pearl of the Pacific. Me sister was Miss Auckland, two years runnin'."

More guys who look like soldiers in civilian garb arrive. Walrus Mustache says, "Whatever, man," and gestures to his left again before wandering off.

Dez heads the way he was instructed. He sees an office and, outside it, a guy with a full, bushy beard and a Detroit Red Wings hat. The guy says, "Help you?"

"Supposed t'see Mr. Lantree."

"You're not from around here."

"New Caledonia. Pearl of the Pacific."

"He's this way," the guy says. He opens the office door and, as Dez passes through, he presses a Taser against Dez's lower back.

Dez spasms and falls to the floor.

The guy kneels and hits him with the Taser again.

Dez blacks out.

CHAPTER 45

Dez is handcuffed and taken out of the building by several largish guys. He's placed in the back of a truck. He's hit with the Taser a couple more times. It hurts like hell. His phone, the guns he stole, and his folding knife are taken. Though not the olive green, belt-clip knife sheath.

Two guys, including the tall, bearded man in the red ball cap, sit with him the entire trip.

Dez recognizes the truck. Americans call it a Medium Tactical Vehicle Replacement, or MTVR, series. Because Americans are nuts for abbreviations and fancy names. It's an all-purpose-designed truck; simple as that.

He doesn't know where they're going but they leave town pretty soon. He can tell by the sound.

Dez lies doggo. You can learn more that way. Then again, you also can get driven to a shallow grave in the desert that way. Life is not without risks.

The road noises change from urban sounds, to highway sounds, to the sounds of a more isolated road. Dez hears a guard at a gate asking for ID, then the lifting of a guardrail. He's pretty sure they've taken him to Joint Base McKinzie-Clark.

Okay, well, he wanted an invite there anyway.

Dez is hustled out of the military truck and squints at the bright sun. Yes, this is an American military base. It has most definitely seen better days. The place was last remodeled in 1960, he suspects. It's also fairly bustling but the men he sees don't look like regulation soldiers. He thinks a lot of the white pride types have been given billeting here on the base. The fairgrounds he saw earlier might simply be the slop-over for whoever couldn't fit in here. Which means the number of people in the opposition is much higher than he realized.

He spots the driver: the walrus mustache and ponytail he met earlier, who gives him a long look.

He's marched by the two armed guys into a stockade. A third man waits inside, jail door open. Dez is shoved in and the door is locked in his wake. It's a basic cinder-block building, with four sets of cells sectioned off by simple iron bars. Each cell has a cot and a sink and a coverless toilet made of metal. Each cell has a small window, eight feet off the floor and too small for any but the youngest child to crawl through. Each cell has a drain, and the floors slope toward the drains. It's utilitarian as hell. Dez has been in far worse.

"If you think the Sloatville Chamber of Commerce isn't going to get an earful about this . . ."

The men stand guard, do not take any bait from him. They're professionals, these three. Dez stops trying to razz them. The tall fella with the red ball cap speaks to someone on a walkie-talkie. When he does, Dez notices his left forearm wrapped in a stretch bandage. That clicks a memory. He's seen the tall guy before. He just can't remember where. It'll come to him.

A man enters wearing the standard Operational Camouflage Pattern, or OCP, uniform. Anywhere else in the world, and they'd be called fatigues. Americans and their acronyms. U.S. ARMY is stenciled over his left breast, TANCREDI over his right, and he sports a patch with three stars. This is the general in charge of the base, Dez suspects. His uniform is not immaculate: a little rumpled, a little wash-grayed, one collar stay missing.

Dez has rarely been around anyone with the rank of general who didn't present himself or herself in a manner that demands respect. The general in charge of Joint Base McKinzie-Clark—and Dez assumes this is he—is having a bad year.

"This is him, Captain?" The general addresses the tall man with the red cap.

Captain, Dez notes.

"Sir. His name is Limerick."

Now, that is interesting. Dez has a fake California driver's license, given to him by his Ethiopian friend, Ephrem Kebede, when his crew repainted and relicensed the stolen F-250. The license has a fake name. So how is it the captain knows his real name?

Dez remembers reading off his name and basic information to the three men in shackles, in the back of the military prisoner transport vehicle with no tires. It's possible this captain gained access to them. But not likely; after the aborted jailbreak, those guys are being held in maximum security.

Which suggests the captain learned of Dez's background through some other means.

The general studies him. "Who sent you?"

Dez has had no luck razzing the captain and the other soldiers, but the general seems a little tightly wound, a little fractious. So Dez responds, not to the general, but to the captain in the red cap. "Working with the legal counsel of Triton Expediters, Captain. She tasked me with finding out what's going on up here."

His response, the snub of addressing the junior officer, annoys the general. "We know about Petra Alexandris. She's been accounted for."

Dez turns to him and smiles. "By them lads at the Hotel Tremaine?" He winks. "Not likely. That's for feckin' sure."

"They were good Americans," the general snaps.

"They was Muppets. I'd've killed them, but they bored me so bad."

The general bristles. Dez notes that the captain and the other soldiers don't jump to the defense of the guys Dez attacked. He's not sensing much unit cohesion here. Good.

Dez grins at the general. "Fella going by the name of Robert Smith? Kitted up like a lawyer? Him, I killed. I kicked his fat arse off a cliff. Beat up some other of your boys, too. Here and there. Wherever I could find 'em. Didn't work up a sweat. S'no wonder this base is being BRAC'd, Colonel."

That last dig was intentional. "General!"

"If you say so, love."

"You've stumbled into something you couldn't understand. You are less than an inconvenience. Operation Swift Sword has been years in the—"

Dez groans. "You didn't! Tell me you didn't." He lightly bangs his forehead on an iron bar. "You didn't give this pantomime one of your famous Pentagon code names. Did you? They're the laughin' stock of the world, mate! Desert Storm? Enduring Freedom? Just Because?"

Tancredi's face turns red. "That was *Just Cause*."

"Panama?" Dez howls. "It was Just Cocaine! Who're you kidding!"

Tancredi starts to respond, then checks himself. Dez can see the guy's easily tripped. Good to know. The man glances at his watch, turns to the captain. "I need to communicate with our guests. We need to know who this asshole's talked to."

"Creating a fifty-first state?" Dez laughs. "Lexington? That's a daft play, that."

"A fifty-first state?" A muscle in the general's cheek pulses with rage. "You don't know anything, do you? Captain: Use whatever force is necessary. Find out who he's been in contact with."

He starts to leave. Dez says, "General?"

The man turns.

Dez winks. "Give us a kiss, love."

The man damn near shoots him. He is splendidly livid. He steps close to the bars, peers at Dez as if he's an alien species. "I do not understand you. You're a white man. You see where this goddamn world is going."

"Sometimes I do. Sometimes it's murky."

"What we create here will resonate around the world, Limerick.

The world will see us for what we are. Allies will come. Are coming. We are changing the world. It's a shame you couldn't get with the program."

He nods to the captain and leaves.

Dez says, "Changing the world?"

And the captain in the Red Wings hat gives him a slow-burn smile.

Dez is stunned.

"Jaysus," he says. He's rocked back by the realization of what all this—the armed attack on the hotel, the jailbreak, everything—what it's all been about.

And it's not creating a fifty-first state.

Dez says, "You're seceding from the fecking union!"

CHAPTER 46

There's a science, if not an art, to taking a beating. The first secret is: You have to take a lot of them so your body and your mind know what to expect.

Dez has taken lots and lots of hits and he knows exactly what to expect.

Outside of the general, Dez has only seen four people in the stockade: the walrus-mustached driver of the Army truck, who isn't here currently; the tall captain in the Red Wings cap; the guy with the jail keys—and thus, likely, the jailer; and the third guy in the room who Dez decides to think of as The Third Guy In The Room.

They unlock the cell. The jailer and the third guy enter, and both are rolling up their sleeves. Dez has his wrists cuffed behind his back.

They start off with body blows to his torso, his sides. Dez doesn't fight back but rides the blows. They hurt but they do not surprise. Dez is a brawler. This is familiar territory. His brain doesn't panic, he doesn't forget to breathe. He takes a few shots to the head but rides them, staying on his feet. Fall over, and they'll put the boot in. Dez would like to avoid that.

The captain watches from outside the cell, the door open. The other guys lay into Dez pretty well, and two minutes in, Dez can tell that the jailer is out of shape. He's winded. More winded than Dez, in fact. The guy has a lot of muscle but he doesn't know how to use his legs and his hips and his back to really put power into his punches. He winds up, too. Very dramatic, but who does that? It telegraphs your punch.

Dez thinks it's possible the jailer has only ever beaten men wearing handcuffs.

Dez stays on his feet, takes the blows. He's positioned himself with his back to the bars now. He's bleeding from his nose and lower lip. The third guy backs off, takes a breather.

The captain says, "We need to ask you some questions now."

The jailer opts to get one more blow in. He cocks back his fist, aimed for Dez's nose.

Dez dodges at the last split second and the man's knuckles crack into the vertical bars behind Dez's head.

Everyone hears the finger bones break.

As the man freezes in pain, Dez takes a step forward.

He uses his legs, his hips, his back.

He slams his forehead into the jailer's nose.

Bones crunch. Blood arcs everywhere. The man's boots leave the floor and he lands on his back and his shoulders, arms akimbo, the back of his skull bouncing off the cement floor.

The blow might've knocked him out. Might've broken his neck, if the fall itself didn't.

Dez turns to the door and sees the captain slam it shut, take two steps back, draw his Beretta M9, aim it at Dez's center mass. Pro draw. Man knows his weapons.

Dez grins through the haze of blood and bits of cartilage on his face. Easy to grin; most of the gore isn't his. He sees the third man—who's locked in here with him—shudder a little. Dez must look like the devil himself.

The captain bellows orders. "Back up! Against the far wall! Face it! On your knees!"

Dez nods. "Captain." He turns, walks to the far wall, kneels.

He starts humming. Opening licks, Mark Knopfler's guitar intro, "Money for Nothing."

The captain says, "Check him!"

Dez hears rustling. The third man is checking on the health and general well-being of the jailer.

"Jesus! Weaver . . ." The man's voice breaks. "Goddamn it!"

Weaver, Dez notes. *Captain Weaver.*

So the jailer's dead. Shame, that. Fewer men to question.

Dez licks his lips and spits a gob of the other man's blood on the floor. He does it for the macabre effect. "Captain Weaver, sir," he says. "Your general says you've guests coming. What guests might those be?"

"Shut up."

"Not all them poxy little bootlicks spiraling down the drain and gathering on the fairgrounds. They're not guests. They're the civilian shields that'll keep the real army at bay when you make your grand move."

"Shut up."

"Guests, the man said. Plural-like."

Dez hears the Beretta cock.

He has come to believe that Captain Weaver is a good and well-disciplined soldier. It's in his bearing. He was ordered to get answers from Dez. That means he won't shoot Dez until they have those answers. So the cocking of the gun is just noise, is all.

Dez talks to the wall, voice raised. "Now, who'd come to this camel turd of a town who'd be important enough for you to wait on? Not your moneymen. That's Triton. Not your propagandist. That's Lantree and Patriot Media. Not your muscle. That's you an' yours. What'm I missing, Captain Weaver, sir? Who else would you be waiting on?"

Weaver speaks, but it's to the third man. "Get the keys from Davies. Open the door and get out here. Move!"

Dez can't hear the man move. Apparently, he doesn't.

"Goddamn it," Captain Weaver bellows. "Move now!"

Dez hears keys; hears the cell door open and slam shut again.

Dez returns to Mark Knopfler. That wonderful, iconic guitar riff.

The men exit the stockade building.

CHAPTER 47

Dez told the Sloatville city council president pro tem that he doesn't believe in God. But he does believe in the Roman god Janus: beginnings, gates, transitions, time, duality, doors, passages, and endings.

Right after they hit him with the Taser, they took the two guns he'd stolen from the wankers at the police station. They'd taken his folding Raptor blade out of his belt clip.

What they didn't remove was the green canvas sheath for his little knife. That's still on his belt.

Still holds his lockpicks, too.

Getting out of regulation cuffs is child's play with the picks. His hands free, he uses the dead jailer's shirtfront to wipe gore off his face and neck.

That leaves the jail door. And again, these picks will do. Dez gets it unlocked. Which would have been all well and good, but the walrus-mustached driver—the mostly bald guy with the long, stringy ponytail from the Army truck—takes that moment to open the door to the stockade building.

Dez makes a fist the size of a toaster and the guy quick-whispers: "Friend a Naomi! Friend a Naomi!"

Naomi Cardona. Captain Cardona of the LAPD. She'd said there was a slim possibility she could reach an agent on deep-cover assignment up here. Turns out she was good at her word.

Walrus Mustache eyes the cadaver lying on its back. "Is Davies dead? Wait. Never mind. Move it."

And move it, they do.

The guy takes Dez through a rear door, around to a different, smaller, olive-colored truck. This one's more like an ambulance. Dez climbs in the back and notices a messy pile of burlap bags. Walrus Mustache is going to take him out the same way he came in. Dez climbs in, gets settled under the bags.

His ribs are killing him. His lower lip is bleeding. He took a shot directly in his right ear and it's still ringing. But those were just wounds to his body. He kept his brain out of that quaint little back-alley brawl. His body took the hits, but his mind went walkabout; took in the sights. That's the trick.

The diesel truck starts up. Dez hears what he heard before but in reverse: a guard asking for ID, a guard railing being lifted on a squeaky hinge. They are on blacktop, the base two minutes behind them, when Walrus Mustache says, "Got a med kit. Help yourself."

The guy's from the Deep South, Dez thinks. He sits up, cracks open the red first aid box, finds clean cotton and astringent. He starts cleaning blood off his face and neck.

The driver watches him in the rearview. "Most of that ain't yours."

"It is not. It's Dez, by the way. Owe you one."

"You can call me Phil," the guy says, driving with one hand and using the other to stuff chewing tobacco into his cheek. "Ain't my name but you told me yours, so . . ."

"Aye. You a cop?"

"DEA."

Dez isn't sure what that is but lets it slide. "You know the tall fella, bushy beard, red cap?"

"Captain Bart Weaver, Army."

"I just remember where I know him from. Saw him in a news clip with the rancher fella, Ryerson. I think Weaver was undercover at the ranch. Would explain the beard and civvies."

Phil nods. "Makes sense."

"Good soldier, him. Seen his like before. What d'you know of the big plan?"

"I know jack shit. Three months now, them shitsticks been moving regular soldiers out of the base. Been moving in guys who see things their way. Klan guys. White Pride. Proud Boys."

"An' you?"

He grins, showing tobacco-stained teeth. "Lookit me. I'm a fat, white cracker from Mobile, Alabama. I blend, bud."

"Indeed you do, Phil. Hey: *Operation Swift Sword*? Really?"

Phil shakes his head. "Pentagon types do love their freaking code names. Just once, I wanna see them boys invade a pissant country and call it Operation 'Cause We Can, That's Why."

"Be refreshing, that. What's the timeline?"

"Tight," he says. "They got days, not weeks. Shit, man. Maybe hours, not days. Starter gun's gonna go off soon. I can feel it."

Dez feels it, too. He also feels the aches of the fight and dry-swallows three aspirin from the first aid kit. "Step one?"

"I'm low-level around here. I built up some cred, but not enough. My guess: These fuckers'll go full jihadist on us. Hide their troops among the civilians in Sloatville, which'll slow down an armed response. Step two: The military base invades the nuclear plant." He pronounces it as three distinct words: *new cue lar*. "They threaten to melt that bad boy down, the Pentagon's gonna shit their pants. The Army'll start taking orders from the governor of California. That'll really gum up the works."

Dez has figured the exact same game plan, step-for-step.

"They said they've guests coming. Soon. You know who?"

Phil shrugs. "Don't. *Guests* don't sound like the cockroaches they got coming in now. Also don't know what their goal is."

"They're seceding from the feckin' union, man. The general all but said so."

"Well . . . fuck me raw." Phil rolls down his window, spits, and rolls it up again. "General Tancredi?"

"According to his name tag, yeah."

"Jesus H. Christ, bud. Could they do that?"

"Dunno. But if not that, then what? Was working on a theory that they just wanted to create a fifty-first state, but this whole thing's a bit too well funded for that."

"They do got walking-around money," Phil says. "No matter how many cockroaches show up, everyone gets fed, everyone gets a cot, everyone gets ammo. They got money to burn."

They've got something else, Dez thinks to himself. The general said it himself.

They've got guests coming.

CHAPTER 48

The DEA agent not named Phil drives him to his stolen Ford pickup, which is right where he left it, only a couple of blocks from the Triton facility. Only now Dez doesn't have his stolen guns, his folding knife, or, more importantly, his mobile phone. And like most human beings, he never bothered to memorize Petra's number. Why bother? It was right there on his phone. He feels like a proper twit.

"Question for you," he says as Phil parks next to his pickup. "How'd Tancredi and his lot transfer out good soldiers, transfer in racists?"

"The Triton building, where I ran into you? Nothing but a shit-ton of big-ass computers, bud. Somebody hacked the Pentagon from here. Been shifting personnel without nobody knowing."

Well, the hacking certainly points to one Triton suspect in particular.

"Don't have me phone. I got to contact someone in LA."

"You didn't have no phone when they brought you out to the truck," Phil says. "Likely, it's still in the Triton building."

"Then I'll head back there."

"Serious like?"

Dez shrugs. "If they captured you at a building, took you to the lion's den, but you escaped, would you go back to the very first building?"

"'Course not."

"Nobody sane would. They won't look for me there."

Phil weighs that, gives it a what-the-hell shrug.

Dez grins big and climbs out of the rear of the truck. He spots a plaid work shirt back there, and grabs it. "Borrow this?"

"Yours."

There's no way Dez could button it over his fifty-inch chest, but hanging loose, it hides much of the dried blood on his black T-shirt.

He doesn't let Phil see how much his ribs and solar plexus hurt.

Phil stays put, one arm cocked out the downed, driver's-side window. "Look. I ain't no fighter, bud. My thing is, I go undercover. I dig up whatever I can on hate groups. Klan. White Pride, Aryan Brotherhood. These fools here. I write up details reports that the Justice Department uses to put together indictments. Then I get outta Dodge. You get me?"

Dez smiles and offers a hand. Phil rubs his palm on the thigh of his not-too-clean jeans, then shakes. "Ta, Phil. That was gutsy. Captain Cardona picks her friends well."

"She good people," the man says, and spits chew near Dez's boot. "Be seein' you, bud."

Phil drives away.

Dez climbs up into the cab of his F-250. He checks to make sure that his tablet computer and his lockbox are on the floorboard, passenger side. He'd parked behind a cluster of U-Store-It sheds that had gone out of business. He climbs out; climbs up into the bed of the pickup. From up there, he can see over the top of the U-Store-It place; can see the cluster of HVAC and radar dishes on the roof of the Triton Expediters server farm, a half mile away.

Petra says someone used Triton computers to hide the theft of $1.3 billion.

The DEA agent not named Phil said someone used Triton computers to hack into Pentagon deployment systems; to roll good soldiers out of the joint military base and to roll in like-minded racists.

Those computers, honestly, are starting to get on Dez's nerves.

CHAPTER 49

Last time here, Dez used weeds as handholds and climbed down to the rocky beach, then climbed back up using an intake pipe for the server farm's cooling system. But that was before taking a good thumping with his wrists cuffed. His torso already is starting to look like a map of the moon, the bruises spreading like splotchy lunar maria.

There are no soldiers out front this time. And Dez is still a big, strapping white guy in a land full of white pride types. A few people—gun-toting men and well-coifed types from Patriot Media—glance his direction when he walks over from the far side of the U-Store-It and approaches the Triton Expediters facility, whistling a jaunty tune.

He nods and smiles to a couple of people as he strides—bruises be damned—into the building. He spots guys doing maintenance near one of the TV microwave trucks, a small canvas backpack slung over the handles of a handcart. Dez snags the backpack, en passant, and stuffs his tablet computer into it. Now his hands are free.

He spots a red fire extinguisher and, mounted on a wall next to it, behind glass, an ax. That's the second time he's spotted a fire ax since this whole thing began and he could swear he hasn't seen one for years. Funny how patterns emerge when you're looking for them. He takes the extinguisher and uses it to break the glass, then takes out the ax.

This time, alarms go off.

Two armed guys, one with a Confederate flag cap, jog their way down the hall. "What's happening?"

"Fire." Dez points behind them, then swings the red extinguisher in an underhand arc that catches the first guy in the chest and under his chin. He's unconscious before Dez uses the aft end of the ax to, well, poleax the second guy. They slump down together and Dez takes both their guns.

Moving now, he runs into more people. "Fire!" he shouts, racing past them. The ache in his side makes him run like the Creature from the Black Lagoon, which is just embarrassing, but he keeps going.

His first venture here, he'd spotted a locked room marked ENVIRON-MENTAL SYSTEMS. He sets down the ax, lifts the fire extinguisher with both hands, and smashes the doorknob, cracking the doorframe. The door squeaks open a few inches.

A guy rounds the corner from behind him and spots Dez. "What the hell!"

Dez points to the Environmental Systems room. "He's in here!"

The guy draws his Glock, steps forward, past Dez, into the room. "Who is?"

Dez clubs him behind the ear and drags him in. He brings in the extinguisher and ax, too. He uses the guy's unconscious form to jam the ruined door closed. He sets aside the stolen backpack and the tablet computer for now.

It's noisy in here. The whoosh of fans comes from every direction. Dez can see the water intake from the pipe coming from the Pacific. Banks and banks of AC units stand like a stunted forest, and pipes in the ceiling spread every direction, taking cool water and cool air to where it's needed.

Computers get hot.

Coolant keeps them from melting down.

Dez does his sums.

He swings the ax and destroys the closest AC unit to where he stands. Then the next, and the next.

Swinging the ax actually makes the pain in his gut diminish. Calisthenics, this. It's important to stretch after a fight.

He finds some computer controls and empties the fire extinguisher into them. The foam starts to bollox the electronics, and he watches as light after light blinks out. Even if they could repair all the fans he's smashing, without the computers, they'd have no way to control where the cool air flows.

Klaxons begin blaring over the fire alarm. The heat is rising in the mainframe rooms.

Splendid.

The piping system draws tons of seawater up from the ocean and uses it as coolant. *Where is all that water going now?* He studies the controls for the water intake. Then he increases the intake—the pumps down under the ocean, eighty feet out from the rocky shore—to their maximum. He also shuts off the outflow pipes throughout the building.

Basically, he's turned the ocean faucet on full and corked the tube.

The man he coldcocked is rising to his feet, shaking his head. Dez says, "You okay, mate?"

The Klaxons and fire alarms are loud. Steam hisses from ruined air-conditioning controls. The guy says, "Wha . . . happened . . . ?"

"Antediluvian," Dez tells him, and pats him gently on the shoulder. "From the Latin. Means: *before the flood.*"

CHAPTER 50

Los Californio Bar, West Hollywood

Petra Alexandris has taken a meeting, reluctantly, with Dmytro Rudko, Russian ambassador to the United Nations. Now really isn't the time but Ambassador Rudko is someone Triton cannot afford to ignore.

He's ridiculously wealthy, even by oligarchic standards. The Rudko clan was rich at the time of the czars. They hid their money during the time of Lenin and Stalin. They were quietly rich during the Cold War, then got less quiet about it when Russia needed petroleum giants to force a new economy on the vast nation. Russian political systems come and go but the Rudkos and their fortunes have ridden them all out. Whatever comes next for the Russians, Petra thinks, there will be a Rudko somewhere counting gold coins.

This man also is an old friend and a drinking partner of her father. Petra can remember seeing the two of them stumbling-drunk when she'd been a girl.

She orders vodka, as she always does when meeting with Russians. He orders a champagne cocktail. She'd like to not be impressed with his tailor but can't help it. He's thirty years her senior and always hits on her, a not-uncommon occurrence in Petra's world. With men like Dmytro Rudko, her tactic is to flirt back casually, rather than take umbrage, and to never, ever drop her guard.

She dances around his usual come-ons. She smiles and returns serve. She waits until the drinks arrive and he adjusts his onyx cuff links: his tell.

"I want to speak to you about the oil pipeline."

She expects this. Triton Expediters is securing the funding for a pipeline from Volgograd to Odesa, a 12,600-kilometer Russian-Ukrainian endeavor expected to take six years and to cost twenty-three billion in U.S. dollars.

That's why she accepted the meeting. Simple math tells her she has to set aside her missing $1.3 billion to meet Ambassador Rudko.

"We have a . . . minor concern or two about the region outside Khrustalnyi," he says, sipping his drink. "Would you care to eat?"

"I'll nibble on what you're having." Petra smiles. Serene. Show no worry, show no fear.

"Khrustalnyi is a small town in—"

"The Luhansk sector. In the foothills," she says. "The so-called People's Republic."

Dmytro grins. "You just happen to know all that."

"I just happen to know that somebody ordered a seismic survey of those hills. I think I know why."

A waiter swings by and Dmytro orders calamari.

"We might have to consider rerouting the pipeline."

She nods. "If you go to the south, then it's Donetsk instead of Luhansk. It would add . . . four or five billion to the price tag. It would be politically more difficult, what with Moscow's relationship with Donetsk. And it would add close to a year to your timeline. More like a year and a winter."

Dmytro chuckles. "God, you are impressive. Yes. Yes, those are our calculations as well."

"That's a sizable change order," she says.

He nods. "We would not ask for further funds without, ah, how do you say. Sweetening the coffee."

"Pot."

He frowns. "Marijuana?"

"No, it's . . . hardly important. What were you thinking?"

"We were considering asking Triton to back the rerouting. In return for which, Triton would begin to see profits . . . with the first barrel pumped."

First barrel. That's new. That's new and very, very interesting. Under the existing contract, the Russians would be pumping oil for a full year before Triton began to see a return on its investment. This new proposal would mean considerably more money, arriving considerably faster. This is huge. This may be Petra's deal of the year.

She sips her vodka, keeps her poker face. "And it pencils out, to move the—"

Her phone vibrates. She'd laid it to the left of her drink, as she usually does, facedown.

She turns it over. And frowns.

"Trouble?" he asks.

"Alarms have gone off."

"Metaphorical alarms?"

"No, the real kind. At . . . it's a small facility. Central California."

She reaches for her clutch, then her Amex Black Card.

"Surely you're not abandoning me!" Dmytro smiles and finishes his cocktail. "I took my private helicopter to Los Angeles just to see you!"

She touches the back of his hand with the pad of her index finger. "Dmytro, I am sorry. I have to check on this." She catches the waiter's eye.

"This is an important facility?"

"Triton doesn't have unimportant ones."

He nods to her credit card. "This is on me."

"No. But the second, independent seismic analysis of the foothills in Ukraine's Luhansk sector, which I'm about to order, will be on you. I'll get the drinks."

She rises.

"I hope it's nothing too bad," Dmytro says.

"Just . . . alarms."

"What sort of alarms?"

She studies the readout on her phone. "All of them."

CHAPTER 51

All of the alarms go off throughout the Triton facility in Sloatville. Mainframes are shutting down, the heat rising everywhere. Water pipes bursting.

Dez stalks through the tight, low-ceilinged corridors amid the skin-head types dashing around like idiots. He carries the ax and yet another stolen Glock, this one hidden in his stolen backpack. He strides purpose-fully, looking like a man on a mission. Everyone ignores him.

He turns down a maintenance corridor and spots, among other things, a long coil of thick rope, an iron grapnel, and thick leather gloves yellowed by hard work, sun, and grease.

He ignores them and heads up the stairs to the roof. He bounds up them and uses the ax to massacre the lock on the horizontal metal trap door.

Being a gatekeeper isn't always finesse work.

Up on the roof, it's already several degrees cooler than it is inside.

Dez moves to the first massive microwave transceiver dish, winds up, and severs its hydraulics hose with the ax. He grabs the edge of the dish and rotates it about fifteen or twenty degrees, so that it no longer faces a specific communications satellite in fixed-Earth orbit.

Three more dishes. Three more hydraulics.

He can see cables that have stretched to the dishes and now hang off the front of the building like octopi arms. He steps to the edge and looks down.

Patriot Media trucks had been piggybacking onto the building's array of satellite communication dishes. No way their microwave trucks have enough oomph to reach the Patriot Media headquarters on the East Coast.

The official propagandist arm of the newly emerging nation has signed off the air.

He decides he likes this ax, and he doesn't fancy shooting any gun he hasn't maintained, if he can help it, so he takes the ax with him on his journey down the claustrophobic stairs to the ground floor.

The ocean water intake system has begun to collapse. The water at this, the rear end of the building, is already ankle deep.

He sloshes straight toward the administrative wing—calling it a wing is a stretch; it's really just two offices and a private toilet. To get there, he has to pass through the lobby, now turned into a broadcast studio with a Patriot Media anchor desk with the company logo, robotic cameras, and a green screen behind the desk, staffed by a very pretty blond woman and a much prettier blond fella. Both of them are touching their earjacks and yelling angrily as all power in the building dies. Including the Klaxons. The robot cameras slump, unpowered. The building trembles and everyone but Dez thinks, *California equals earthquake*. Dez knows it's just heavy iron water pipes cracking under pressure.

The very pretty boy-anchor jumps up from behind the logoed desk and confronts him. "What the hell's happening?"

He notices the bits of gore and blood on Dez's T-shirt and his neck where he'd missed a couple of gloppy bits. He notices the fire ax.

Dez scratches his head and looks around. "Power out. Floor's shaking. Links to the outside world cut. Flooding." He shrugs. "Dunno mate. Jews?"

The presenter gulps. "Well, I mean, yeah. Of course. But . . ."

" 'Scuse me. Must dash."

He turns to the admin doors and ambles in.

Four people are present. One is fifty and fit, and wears a fine Western suit with a bolo tie and an American flag lapel pin. Dez recognizes him from Google. Oliver Lantree. He holds a cigar that looks like a stick of dynamite. One young woman looks to be his administrative assistant, and she's glaring at her mobile. From her frown, clobbering the satellite dishes on the roof took out their mobiles, too.

The other two men in the room look like skinheads.

Dez reverses the ax in midair with a tennis-racket flip and uses the handle to clock the first fella in the ear. He picks up the second guy by the throat, his boots leaving the floor, spins, and slams the guy, chest first, into a set of metal filing cabinets. The cabinets concave a little; the man's chest more so.

The assistant screams and dances in place.

Oliver Lantree rises and draws a pearl-handled .22 from a belt-clip holster.

Dez, spattered in blood and carrying a fire ax, gives him a slow, simmering grin. "Think that'll do?"

Lantree sets the .22 down on his desk blotter.

"Fair play to ye." He turns to the administrative assistant. "Stop screamin'."

The girl freezes.

Dez circles the desk, sets down the ax, and quickly puts the fifty-year-old man in a chokehold. Oliver Lantree struggles but so does a titmouse when a hawk drops from the sky. "Shh," Dez coos. "Want you to be unconscious for this next bit. Ye've hurt a lot of good people with that voice of yours. Shh."

Lantree lapses into unconsciousness.

The administrative assistant stares with huge blue eyes, tears welling.

When the man's out, Dez remains behind him, one tree-trunk arm around his right shoulder, across his chest, holding his left shoulder. He braces Lantree against his own chest. He lightly grabs the man's jaw with his left mitt and *pop*—dislocates his jaw.

Even unconscious, Lantree twitches.

Dez sets him gently down in his chair. His jaw is off-center two inches to the left.

"Silver-tongued devil. Try using that tongue now."

Dez turns to the administrative assistant. She freezes, a rabbit in headlights. "Sorry 'bout that. Was here earlier. Left me phone and a knife that has sentimental value. The knife. Not the phone."

She blinks at her unconscious boss, then turns to a smaller desk—hers, maybe—and retrieves the Raptor blade. Plus, Dez's phone, which is his link to Petra Alexandris.

Or would be, if he hadn't just knocked out the cell phone reception for this portion of Boca Serpiente County.

Hadn't thought that one through as well as I might've, Dez thinks.

"Ta, love," he says, and nods toward the door. "Off with you, then."

Off she goes.

CHAPTER 52

When Dez searched the facility earlier, among his discoveries had been a long coil of thick rope, an iron grapnel, and thick leather gloves yellowed by hard work, sun, and grease. He'd ignored them at the time, although he had speculated that they'd been a fine way for getting back down the cliff face. Now it dawns on him: That's exactly what they're for. The rope and three-toothed hook are for use by the Triton Environmental Systems maintenance crew, for securing themselves near the cliff-facing pipes when repairing leaks.

The water inside the Triton building is knee-high. He retrieves the items, then exits through the rear door. Outside now, with his finds and his new favorite ax, he notices it's still abandoned back here. And much cooler than the mini-Everglades he'd created inside the building. Thanks to the fences and the cliff, this is a box canyon. Everyone who fled, fled to the front.

Dez finds a metal stanchion standing upright in a circle of cement. He totally missed it earlier that day, but now can see it's designed for the sturdy iron grapnel. He attaches it and kicks the coiled rope over the cliff.

He hears truck tires screeching up to the front of the building, hears soldiers shouting. He tries and fails to slip on one of the leather gloves. They were designed for a guy with normal-sized hands.

He grips the rope and begins the slow, methodical process of lowering himself down the cliff face. Where Dez is from, they called it abseiling, but most everyone else knows it as rappelling. He's done a fair bit of it in his life, and he gets to the rocky, narrow strip of beach in no time. He starts hiking south, in the direction of Sloatville. He needs to get back to his stolen pickup with his kit of door-breaching equipment, which means taking a three-dimensional zigzag tack: south along the coast, then up the cliff and north back to the truck.

The walk along the rocky shore was easygoing; he only had to wade into the ocean, ankle-deep, a couple of times. It takes him fifteen minutes to spot a weathered, wooden staircase heading up the cliffside with a diamond-shaped aluminum sign that says NO ROUGHHOUSING. PROPERTY OF CITY OF SLOATVILLE. He checks his mobile. No service yet. He starts up the stairs, into the weird little town on its deathbed.

CHAPTER 53

Dez keeps to the quieter streets of Sloatville and kneels behind parked cars a time or two, as Jeeps or big trucks rumble past. It takes him ages to reverse course and get back to his truck. It's dusk, so that helps with the skulking. He hadn't killed Oliver Lantree's administrative assistant, nor the fella he clocked in the Environmental Systems room. So there's no question the word has gotten back to Captain Bart Weaver and the soldiers. Most of the loonies in this town are only a threat if they trip and fall, and their ill-maintained guns discharge. Weaver and his lot are soldiers, well and truly. Dez is hoping to avoid Weaver in the short run, and eventually to engage him on his own terms, not Weaver's.

He drives quickly to the home of Renata and Hector Esquivel and knocks on the rear kitchen door. The porch light snaps on. She answers holding a Remington shotgun. Through the pane of glass, Dez shows her his open palms.

She opens the door. She scans his face and neck. "Who did this to you?"

"Looks worse than it is. I've a favor to ask."

She says, "The bathroom is this way. You have blood on you. Shower first. Then ask. I'll get clean towels."

"I'm not sure there's time for—"

City Councilor Renata Esquivel is holding the shotgun like she knows how to use it. "Shower."

"Yes, ma'am."

He retrieves his duffel from the truck. In the bathroom, Dez throws away the gore-specked T-shirt he's wearing. He climbs into the shower.

When he steps out, he finds a faded and threadbare blue towel and a store-bought first aid kit. Also a disposable razor.

He takes care of a couple of deeper cuts and bruises, but they're nothing. He's well pleased to be out of the bits of gore and blood from the jailer. He shaves, careful around his split lower lip. He checks the twin red marks left by Captain Weaver's Taser. The skin around them is puffy and inflamed. He tugs on a clean T-shirt from his duffel, an exact replica of the one he just threw out.

He finds the city councilor and her husband waiting for him in their living room, amid the religious symbolism and the Mexican football magazines. Hector now sits in a wheelchair, but with the same green-and-yellow afghan.

They had dragged in a kitchen chair. It's in front of the deactivated TV. Dez sits there. Renata sits in a second kitchen chair next to her husband. It's not completely dissimilar for elected members of the city council to hear testimony from some flunky sitting at a table opposite the lectern and gavel. This is how the councilor has been gathering information for some years now. It's her method, and that's all right by Dez.

"Thank you for your hospitality."

"English will be fine. What happened?"

"Confronted some of the bastards—sorry—behind this. Learned a bit more about their plan. By the way, is your cell phone service out?"

She nods. "The whole town."

"That's me, then. Apologies. I needed t'get Patriot Media off the airwaves and to shut down the Triton computers. Done that."

She smiles. Hector grins and nods and gives him the thumbs-up. The man doesn't talk much.

"Now I need to get into the Boca Serpiente Valley Power Station."

"Why?"

"I'm removing chess pieces, ma'am. My friend in Los Angeles is doin' the same. She'll be taking care of the money spigot. Patriot Media was another key asset, and it's gone pear-shaped for 'em. The conspirators at the military base are gonna try to take the power station. I need to get there—to get *in* there—first."

"Why?"

He shrugs. "Chess pieces."

"What can you do?"

Hector pats his wife's hand. "He can do plenty. Call Mike."

Renata ponders a bit. Dez gives them the time. *Thus concludes me testimony, Madam President Pro Tem.*

She gets up and leaves the room, likely heading for the bedrooms and, he suspects, a landline in her home office. Hector Esquivel says, "Coffee?"

"A little late for me, sir. Keeps me up."

Hector nods to a stack of football magazines on an end table. "Who's your team?"

"Liverpool."

"May God keep you in his thoughts."

Dez snorts a laugh. "Dunno what's wrong with 'em this season."

Hector Esquivel nods sagely. "Liverpool could not advance down the left side of the pitch if the right side were on fire."

They're still at it when Renata returns with a spiral-bound, faux-leather pad and a pen. "The landlines are fine," she says. "Mike Whitney and I sit on the board of the chamber of commerce. He's in Rotary, too. He hasn't fled, and he hasn't backed down. He's good people."

Dez waits for the relevance.

"He's the executive director of the Boca Serpiente Valley Power Station. He'll be here first thing in the morning."

CHAPTER 54

Dez uses the Esquivels' landline to call Petra but, as he anticipated, it goes straight to voice mail. That's because she doesn't recognize the number. He leaves a message, asking her to call him back.

The city councilor puts out blankets and a pillow on the couch, and they wish Dez a good night. He notices that their bedroom light snaps off the second they close the door. He uses the bathroom again, strips down to just his boxers, climbs onto the couch, and is unconscious inside of five minutes. It's the sun in his eyes, hours later, that rouses him.

Breakfast is a pot of coffee and huevos rancheros and puffy sopaipilla. The Esquivels pray before they eat, and Dez sits politely, but he can't take his eyes off the food. They normally attend morning Mass but, what with a guest hunted by the mob in their house, they've opted for a new plan. He's noticed that Americans hold their forks with the tines curving away from them when they eat, whereas, like many Brits, he holds his fork with the tines curving toward him. He doesn't think it's important but he tends to notice details. He eats like a horse.

The doorbell rings at 8 a.m. sharp. The man at the door, Mike Whitney, looks fit and jovial, with laugh lines and grin-wrinkles around his eyes. He's five-five and, Dez guesses, a scratch golfer and a hell of a doubles tennis player. He's got that overall country-club look to him. He wears khakis and a polo and deck shoes.

Renata Esquivel talks first and Dez is smart enough to keep it shut. Renata and Mike talk for nearly fifteen straight minutes as Hector Esquivel and Dez sit and listen.

Dez keeps thinking back to what General Tancredi had said. About guests coming. What else had he said?

"*. . . Allies will come. Are coming . . .*"

Mike Whitney turns to Dez at one point and says, "Are you insane?"

"As near as the next man, I s'pose. Insane times, these."

"Look: I don't doubt that these kooks are running rampant in our town. They're everywhere. They even have roadblocks, for gosh sakes. But an armed coup? That—"

Renata says, "Roadblocks?"

"On my way here."

"This was Chief Blalock?"

Mike Whitney shakes his head. "I haven't seen the chief in three or four days."

"Neither have I. But there are roadblocks?"

"Two huge pickups, parked in a sort of an arrowhead formation, right at the edge of town on Old Frontage Road. Four men with assault guns. They wanted to check the trunk of my car, for goodness' sake." Mike shakes his head in awe.

They weren't looking for Dez by checking the trunks of inbound vehicles. That wouldn't make sense. They'd assume he's still right here inside Sloatville trying to get out.

More to the point, this is the kind of civil escalation that can't last long, Dez thinks. The county sheriff's deputies, California Highway Patrol, somebody would put a halt to it eventually. Right? So either these White Aryan types are stupid wankers, or they don't want or need to maintain an armed blockade on public roads for long.

Dez believes that only the worst kind of fighter counts on the enemy to be stupid. By far better to assume the enemy is clever.

Another reason to think Boom is closer than he'd hoped.

Mike eyes him. "I'm not yet clear on exactly who you are."

"Workin' with the chief legal counsel of Triton Expediters, sir. Name's Petra Alexandris. Might've heard of her. Armed men tried to kidnap her Monday last at a fancy hotel in Los Angeles."

Mike Whitney squints. "I saw that on TV. That was her?"

"Was. I'm trying to get through to her to tell what I've found, but I can't without cell service, and she doesn't answer calls from an unknown landline."

Mike takes out his flip phone, checks, shakes his head, tucks it back in the pocket of his pleated trousers. "Sorry. Triton owns a server farm—"

"They do, sir, but it's not so much a server farm right now as it is a very hot, very wet slice o' hell. At Petra's request, I smashed the place."

"And now you think these goofballs will attempt a hostile takeover of the power plant."

"Do, sir."

"What do you plan to do about it?"

Dez grins. "Got an idea or two, sir. Forward thinker, me."

CHAPTER 55

Mike Whitney has just about agreed to take Dez to the nuclear power station when they all hear a strange ringing from outside. "What's that?" Dez asks.

Mike dismisses it with a wave. "That's just the sat phone in my car."

Dez blinks at him. "You've a satellite phone in your car?"

"Everyone in top management at the station does. We invested in them six years ago. Got a good price, too. The trick is, if you buy them using a grant from the Department of Energy, you—"

"Mr. Whitney, sir?"

Mike nods.

"Mind if we make a couple of life-altering-event type calls on that device of yours? I can call collect if it helps."

"Oh. Sure."

Mike Whitney leaves to retrieve the phone. Dez rolls his eyes.

Renata says, "He's a good man. He sees the best in everyone. Right now, he's a fish on a planet that has never even heard of water."

Dez nods.

The sat phone has texting capability and Dez quickly texts Petra Alexandris. *dez. got sat phone. u good for call?*

"You type awful fast for a, ah, largish guy," Mike says.

"Guitarist. Piano, too."

"No kidding! I play guitar in our church youth choir. I took it up because it's so darn fun."

"I took it up 'cause a mate of mine said it would improve my dexterity."

"Did it?"

Dez shrugged. "He was teaching me to defuse bombs. I'm still here." Mike gulps.

The sat phone rings. Petra says, "You're still alive."

"'Course."

"What have you learned?"

"The Triton server farm was being used by someone to hack into the Pentagon. Transferrin' out good soldiers from the base, transferrin' in more of them racist bastards."

Petra sighs. "Brittany Kinney?"

"The hacker? My guess, aye."

"Give me the headlines," she says, and she sounds not like his lover, but like a high-powered litigator.

Dez does. He tells her about the real plot: not to create a fifty-first state, but to create an independent nation.

She openly laughs. Until she realizes he's serious.

"Heading to the nuclear power station now," he says. "I need to be there before General Tancredi and his men make their move. And I think that's happening soonish."

Petra says, "Take the city councilor."

"Why?"

"Because the first war you win is the war against the enemy. The second war you win is the spin after the battle. You'll need an elected leader—a woman, a Latina—facing the media if we get out of this."

Dez grins. "You're by far the smartest person I ever met."

"I suspect that's true for most people who meet me." Petra speaks without the slightest bit of irony. "Stay alive."

She rings off.

Dez underhands the sat phone to Mike Whitney. Who drops it.

"Councilor. Would you come with us?"

She says no. Dez explains what Petra said on the phone. Renata Esquivel widens her eyes. "She's smart, that one."

Dez grins. "I know. Dead sexy, innit?"

Hector Esquivel pats his wife's knee. *"Sí."*

CHAPTER 56

Mike Whitney comes across as a little bit of a country-club doofus, but he suggests a way to get Dez and Renata Esquivel past the impromptu neo-Nazi roadblocks outside of Sloatville. He uses his sat phone to whistle up a driver and a van. The van bears the stylized logo of the Boca Serpiente Valley Power Station. And also the stenciled warning HAZARDOUS RADIO-ACTIVE MATERIAL ABOARD.

The van picks up the three of them and they get in the back. It's filled with clean laundry. Mike addresses the driver, who looks to be thirteen, though Dez suspects that's an illusion. "Lonnie, you head through that roadblock. If they ask to see in the back, you tell them you don't have the proper lead-lined apron. You don't want to fry your . . ."

He glances at City Councilor Esquivel, blushes, then leans in and whispers to Lonnie.

"Balls," Renata says.

"That they have." Dez grins at her. "You, too. You don't mind me sayin'."

★ ★ ★

They get through the checkpoint without any trouble. Dez, Renata, and Mike sit in the back on chairs they fashion out of fresh laundry duffels.

"Tell me 'bout this plant, sir."

"Built in 1971," Mike says. Dez can tell he's made this spiel at a hundred Rotary and Lions events. "Generates a little more than three thousand megawatts thermal and about eight hundred and eighty megawatts electrical. The difference is—"

"Know the difference, thank you, sir. Keep going."

"Oh? Well, it's a pressurized water reactor. Uses ordinary water we pump in from the ocean."

"But it still has a cooling tower?"

"Right-o. Unlike facilities like Diablo Canyon. They're close enough, they can draw enough water to use the Pacific as a neutron moderator. The lucky bums!" Mike says. "That means—"

"Know what it means, sir."

Mike winks at him. "You probably think so. A lot of people think they understand this crazy nuclear power stuff." He rotates his fingers near his temple and crosses his eyes when he says *nuclear*. This part of the speech he's given at high school science fairs and career days. "But it's a bit more—"

"You're using the light water as a medium to reduce the speed of the fast neutrons. Changin' 'em into thermal neutrons, yeah? Could use solid graphite, I suppose, or heavy water. Your way's cheaper. Neutron moderation makes better sense in civilian facilities than using neutron absorbers to lower the high reactivity of their initial fresh fuel loads. If you ask me."

Mike and Renata ride their laundry bags and blink at him. Dez doesn't usually show off but time's a factor here. "How big's the facility?"

Mike's a little shaken. "Um, well, we've got a thousand five hundred acres of God's own country. We have a hundred-and-forty-acre pond as a backup emergency water supply. And, as of 2010, we have California's sixth largest array of photovoltaic solar panels! We were fifth, but there's this project . . . doesn't matter. Anyway, at Boca Serpiente Valley, we like to say we're as green as Kermit! The solar panels came from a grant from the State Assembly, but it's really pass-through federal—"

"Sounds a charm. Hell of a plant ye've got." Dez gives him a thumbs-up. "Access points?"

"Well, the land is surrounded by miles and miles and just miles of fence! Very tall. Barbed wire along the top, which is just ugly as sin, but those are federal rules. Only one gate. All access is through there."

My very pale arse it is, Dez thinks.

Now that they're outside of Sloatville, they have cell connectivity and the internet. Dez uses his tablet to bring up satellite image of the facility. He can see the one gate, eight or nine buildings, five roads, the massive cooling tower, the vast stretches of desert broken up only by dark, rectangular fields of solar cells. Power lines lead from the plant northward, southward, and westward. He sees a football pitch worth of transformers. From above, the shadow of the cooling tower makes the whole facility look like a sundial for the chariots of the gods. He sees three parking lots, but only one of them has cars and that one's only half full.

"Staff?"

"We've downsized, with all the modernization and automation and what-have-you. Right now, I'd say we have two hundred, two twenty-five on duty most days."

"How d'you get around to fix everything?"

"We have all-terrain vehicles with sleds for hauling tools."

"You're to be mothballed, then?"

Mike blanches. "We prefer the term—"

"Insensitive of me. Sorry."

"You should see our Visitors Information Center. We have an inter-active video guide that's really something."

The word *visitors* leaves Mike's lips and Dez snaps his fingers. "God, I'm stupid." He draws his mobile and calls Petra again.

The van turns in to the gateway drive of the Boca Serpiente Valley Nuclear Power Station as Petra picks up.

"Hang on," she says after a half ring. He guesses that she has to step out of the room with Constantine Alexandris, Colin Frye, and Brittany Kinney. It's Sunday, which means they've been going at it for more than a day now. She's still trying to winnow out enough evidence to pin the theft on one of them, even though Brittany Kinney has leapfrogged to the top of the suspect list because of her computer skills. "Go ahead."

"Who'd you have drinks with yesterday?"

She says, "It was unrelated to this thing. He's an ambassador. He's having an issue with a Russian–Ukraine pipeline problem."

"Russian, yeah?"

She waits.

"How'd he get to LA?"

"Dez, I have no . . ." Her voice drifts off. "Helicopter. He said he came by private helicopter. Dmytro Rudko is one of the richest men in Moscow."

"An' this helicopter of his could've landed on a kitted-out megayacht, anchored just off the beach from Sloatville?"

Renata and Mike listen, completely lost.

Petra doesn't answer for a while. And when she does, she yells, "Fuck!"

"General in charge of this cluster, he told me they were waiting on guests. Said, an' I quote, 'Allies will come. Are coming.'"

Petra says, "Goddamn it!"

Dez has a night and a day to put it all together. Petra did the same in about three seconds. That, he thinks, is the difference between them, right there.

"Dez, the Russians interfered with American elections in 2016."

"That they did."

"They tried in 2018 and 2020, too. The GRU, Russian military intelligence, has been attempting to undermine U.S. elections for years now."

"An' what would happen if General Numb Nuts and his merry band of racists declared independence from the United States? The two of us, we listed the assets they'd need, remember?"

She does, of course. "A constitution, governance, infrastructure, an economic plan, trade deals, law enforcement, a military, and funds."

"An' allies," Dez says.

"Dmytro Rudko has a megayacht. With a helipad. I've been on it myself."

"Seen it with me own eyes. It's here."

"Dez, if the conspirators declare independence and threaten the meltdown of a nuclear power plant, that would stop the military from a *quick* response. But not from *a* response. But if a foreign power acknowledged them . . . set up a delegation, assigned an ambassador . . ."

"Then Congress would screech to a feckin' halt." Dez covers his mobile with his palm and winces at Renata Esquivel. "Sorry." He returns to the call. "Congress would hesitate. An' my all-time-favorite time-wasting organization, the United Nations, would get involved."

"Being acknowledged by a permanent member of the UN Security Council would be a game changer."

"They wouldn't be a bunch of upstarts waiting to get smacked about the ears," Dez says.

"No," she agrees. "They'd be a nation."

CHAPTER 57

Triton Expediters Headquarters, Hawthorne, California

". . . They'd be a nation. Damn it. Dez, I have to go. We're very, very short on time."

Petra disconnects. She stands in the corridor a moment, forehead against the wall, eyes squeezed shut.

This. Is. Not. Happening.

This whole scheme has been more than two years in the making. And the Main Directorate of the General Staff of the Armed Forces of the Russian Federation, the goddamned GRU, has been secretly backing it. Why not? They successfully jinxed America's 2016 election. They sowed the seeds of doubt about the election processes in 2018 and 2020. Each time, they harnessed right-wing media to make it happen. If Russian intelligence discovered a nascent proposal by white supremacists to split off from the union, of course they'd intercede. Why in the world wouldn't they?

And Petra Alexandris, whose claim to fame is that she plays three-dimensional chess on the international stage, got caught flat-footed.

It's a Sunday morning at the world headquarters of Triton Expediters and she's in her usual weekend power uniform—that's an oxymoron only if you're not in the international finance world—of fitted jeans, boots with blocky heels, and a man's dress shirt.

She returns to Constantine's office, tucking her phone in the back pocket of her jeans.

"Trouble," she says.

All four of them have been poring over the evidence of the $1.3 billion theft for the entire weekend, using the conference table in Constantine's spacious office. They're on day two of it. Petra is taking them step-by-step through the months of research she did into the theft. And as she does, she narrows the cover for the conspirator in their midst.

The one person here who could hack the Pentagon.

The pompous Colin Frye is looking ragged. Colin hasn't done a decent day's work for decades. He's the chief financial officer of the company but it's been clear for years that his staff does all the real work. His job is to go out and glad-hand worldwide clients. He sees and gets seen with sultans and senators, with oligarchs and petrogarchs, with Indian and Chinese billionaires. They are almost a team, Colin Frye and Petra. He sets up the relationships; she's the closer.

Today he looks fatigued, his bottled tan a little jaundiced, his jawline sagging. No one in his department could have been the coconspirator without alerting Colin. But that's not the same as saying he's used to putting in arduous hours anywhere but the golf course.

Sitting opposite him with her usual Vulcan cool is Brittany Kinney, chief technical officer, in a plain white tank, black yoga pants, and black sneakers. The same uniform she's worn every day since taking the job at Triton. Petra herself stole Brittany away from Boeing, who stole her away from NASA. Petra doubts the woman could put together the financing for a Philly cheesesteak and a bag of chips, but she knows how to route money everywhere, at all times, with such a steely web of spaghetti logic that Triton has leapfrogged ahead of the world's competition, year after year. Brittany is the secret sauce. She's the computer who controls all the other computers.

Petra plays a mean hand of poker. But she has never sat across a card table from Brittany Kinney. Now, that would be a challenge, she suspects. And it saddens her to think that the evidence Dez has uncovered points directly to her.

There is no smoking in the Triton Expediters headquarters. There is no smoking in any public building in California. Constantine Alexandris regularly smokes in his office. He pays a fortune to import a bespoke blend of Papastratos Athens Hellas. They are foul and hideous, but Petra has never known a time in her life when her father didn't smoke the Greek cigarettes. He filled his ashtray to brimming on Saturday and it's already halfway there today. He's poured himself an espresso while she was out, and he sips it at the head of the table.

Petra snatches a bottled water, cracks it open, drains nearly a quarter of it, standing. The others watch her.

She works to regain her cool. She does not speak until she has to.

"That was Desmond Limerick. He's calling from a nuclear power station in Central California. He's made some discoveries. He—"

"Petra," her father cuts in. He had been looking tired the past few hours, but now he looks . . . impatient?

"What?"

Colin and Brittany exchange quick glances.

Constantine inhales deeply, snuffs out the cigarette, reaches for the next. "Enough. Dmytro Rudko told us you already have your suspicions about Sloatville. We know that idiot Englishman is up there. Rudko claims I've always underestimated you. I believe he's right. But enough. Enough."

Petra studies the old man as he taps a cigarette against the heel of his hand to tamp down the tobacco. He puts it to his lips, uses the tarnished, hard-knocked, brushed steel lighter he's had since he was twenty, inhales again.

"Father?"

Colin Frye stands and moves to the wet bar. "I for one could use a Bloody Mary."

Brittany Kinney keeps her head down and thumb-scrolls on her phone, as she has all weekend.

Constantine sucks down that cigarette and stubs it out. He stands and moves to the window, to the view of all of Los Angeles and the ocean.

Petra feels gravity shift under her heels.

"Who are the Founding Fathers of America?" Constantine asks. "Washington? Jefferson? Madison? No. The Founding Fathers were Cooke in finance. Crocker in railroads. Carnegie in steel." He ticks them off with his fingers.

"Father. What the hell are—"

"And after them came John D. Rockefeller and Henry Ford and J. P. Morgan and Andrew Mellon and all the others. Those are the Founding Fathers of the real America. Those were the men with the foresight to see an isolated, rudderless new nation, afloat in a world of international giants like England and France and Germany, and to turn it into the dominant power on the planet."

The room seems to shimmer and it takes Petra a moment to realize the illusion is caused by tears welling. "Dad?"

He stares out at his view. He nods to his own reflection.

What was it Dez had said, standing in the exact same spot, about Alexander the Great?

Constantine makes a dismissive gesture around the room. "We've been buying time, Petra. We've been keeping you sidelined because, at long last, you truly were the only one smart enough to wreck everything."

"I'm not sure she hasn't," Brittany Kinney says, eyes locked on her phone, thumbs flashing across the keyboard.

"No," Constantine says. "We're close enough now. Everything's in place."

Brittany says, "If everything was in place, I'd still be connected to the Pentagon. Which I'm not. And to General Tancredi at Joint Base McKinzie-Clark. Which I'm not."

"Why not?" Colin Frye speaks from the wet bar, where he's mixing a drink.

Brittany shrugs.

Constantine says, "Get our connection back. The general makes his move tonight."

He makes eye contact with his daughter. He nods once. Reassuringly.

"This is a good thing, Petra. We stand next to Carnegie and Rockefeller and Morgan. Right now. We have played the role of giants. We are Founding Fathers."

Petra is still holding the water bottle but has forgotten about it. She has towered over her father since the age of fourteen, but there's an optical illusion in the room that he's towering over her now. She hears her own voice crack.

"Daddy?"

CHAPTER 58

Unlike most people, Dez has actually been on the campus of nuclear power plants before. So he can say, for a fact, that the Boca Serpiente Valley Nuclear Power Station is the saddest excuse for one he's ever seen.

The place has reached the end of its useful life span. In fact, a quick internet check confirmed that the Boca Serpiente Valley plant surpassed its useful life span five years previously, but a combination of the U.S. Department of Energy, Pacific Gas and Electric, and the governors of the western states, with their blended power grids, prevailed upon regulators to keep it open an extra decade.

The overriding logic seemed to be: Well, it hasn't melted down yet. Here's hoping.

The place feels as old and tattered as did the soon-to-be-closed joint military base. It's been built for a staff of about two thousand but modern advancements mean a staff of fewer than two hundred and fifty can run the day-to-day operations. The cooling tower has been shedding paint for decades. Tumbleweeds bop about, bumping up against diesel storage tanks and transformers and the odd rusty Quonset hut.

The young driver gets the laundry van into the facility and parks in front of the administrative building, which, helpfully, has a largish sign out front reading ADMINISTRATIVE BUILDING. Dez, Mike Whitney, and Renata Esquivel head into Mike's office, which features faux wood paneling, a mounted bigmouth bass on a cedar plaque, and pictures of Mike shaking hands with two vice presidents and one movie star. In one corner is an American flag on a pole, in a stand, the one Mike likely loads into his personal SUV to haul to weekly Kiwanis or Rotary meetings. He's got a trophy on the cabinet with the inscription WORLD'S GREATEST DAD and a coffee cup that reads HAPPY WIFE, HAPPY LIFE. He's got a photo of a woman his age and five youths, midteens to early twenties, plus nearly a dozen other photos of them individually, many in softball and baseball kit. When Mike sees Dez looking at the photos, he beams.

Mike picks up the receiver on a phone so old it still has five clear cubes at the bottom that turn red when one of the lines is engaged. "I'll get the dayshift foremen here. We have six teams."

Dez interrupts him. "Can they meet us at the master control room? Would love to see that. Plus, could be good information for the councilor an' me to have."

Mike shrugs. He makes the call.

"They're on their way. It's a pretty big facility. It'll take a while for them to get there. C'mon."

They exit the office and the building and head to the largest building on the campus. It's two stories tall and made of cinder block. No real effort was made to make it look like anything other than a barricade between the real world and fissionable material.

The master control room looks a bit like you'd expect. A curved bank of fifteen work stations with built-in computers, circa 2000 maybe, all facing a full wall of flat-screen monitors that gauge every conceivable metric. Nine of the fifteen workstations are in use; people hunched over them, looking bored; looking a bit more attentive since Mike Whitney walked in. Not a necktie to be seen. At some of the workstations, people have clipped-out comics of Homer Simpson fumbling his famous glowing ingot of uranium, or Mr. Burns gloating over a disaster. The classics.

Six people show up; four men, two women. Some wear jeans and polo shirts. Some wear one-piece coveralls that, when Dez was growing up, were called boilersuits. He's not sure what Americans call them.

Mike Whitney has everyone meet in the single saddest conference room Dez has ever been in. He can see from the mismatched, sun-faded floor that the room used to include vending machines for drinks or maybe snacks. Austere times; the machines are long gone. One wall of windows facing the backs of the crew staffing the master control room.

Mike Whitney is about to address the lot but Renata Esquivel says, "Do you mind?"

Mike gestures to give her the floor.

"Thank you. Some of you know me. I'm on the city council in Sloatville. Before we get started, I should tell you that I am of the opinion that the city has been taken over by a criminal, anarchistic gang of white supremacists. If you think I'm wrong, then you won't be receptive to what this man here, Desmond Limerick, has to tell you. It would be good to establish this up front. Who here stands with Patriot Media and the people who've descended on our town?"

The six staff leaders stay very, very quiet. One guy in coveralls raises his hand, as if he's in a high school classroom. "I guess, some of what they say, you have to admit is true. The invasion by illegals. Drugs and crime and everything . . ." He shrugs.

"Some of what they say *is* true," Renata agrees. "America has problems. America has always had problems. By and large, Americans have risen to the task of solving these problems. Not overnight. Not without setbacks. Not without errors. But America is the land of accomplishing great things, and America is the land of immigrants, and those twin truths we hold self-evident."

Not bad, Dez thinks. She rounded that little speech out nicely. Kept it short. Didn't start by arguing the fella down. Mike Whitney looks a little impressed, too.

The coveralls guy is quick to get on the same page with Renata. "Oh, yeah. For sure. I've got, like, German and Polish and Scottish blood in me. Cherokee, too, my mom says."

The woman next to him says, "My grandfather is Japanese. I'm one-quarter Japanese. We're hearing you, Ms. Esquivel. You won't remember, but you came to my high school for career day, like, eight years ago."

Renata smiles. "I don't remember, no. Was I pompous?"

The woman smiles shyly and waggles her hand in midair. She's relieved when Renata laughs a genuine laugh.

A third guy with tortoiseshell glasses frames and a messy blond thatch of hair smiles and gives Renata the thumbs-up.

A fourth guy with a smoker's voice clears his throat. He looks like public speaking is second only to a colonoscopy on his fun list. "I, uh, didn't vote for you, ma'am. Truth is, I don't vote. I've listened to Patriot Media in the car. They're like everyone else; what my old man used to call three-fourths foolish and a quarter flash. Better than listening to easy rock on the commute. We haven't left our jobs or the town, ma'am. We're here for the long haul."

Renata nods. "My father used to say that, too. All right. Thank you. Everyone. Mr. Limerick was sent here to investigate what's going on. He's laid out his case and, to me, it makes a horrible kind of sense. I think we need to listen to him with an open mind. You'll take questions, Mr. Limerick?"

"Course."

"All right," she says. "Just listen. Take it all in. Ask us anything. Mr. Limerick? The floor's yours."

Dez claps his hands together, rubs his palms. "Good. Thank you. Great." He turns to Mike Whitney and the six forepersons. "Folks? Operation Swift Sword is fecked."

Six of the seven blink at him a bit.

The guy in the tortoiseshell frames and curly hair says, "Shit!" and reaches around to draw a .22 from a belt holster.

Dez hits him in the breadbasket and the man folds like paper money.

The guy's lying in the fetal position as Dez claps his palms crosswise, as if smacking off chalk dust. He smiles around.

"Right then. Questions?"

CHAPTER 59

The people in the conference room take a second or two to react. Some step back in fear. One woman kneels next to the guy holding his gut and groaning. The smoker makes a fist, looks at Dez's hands, uncurls his fist.

Dez nods to Renata and Mike. "Ma'am. Mike. Apologies. The bastards behind this have been keen to use inside people. Did it at Triton Expediters. Did it at the joint military base. Stood t'reason they'd do it here. The general in charge of this clusterf—this event told me it had a code name. Operation Swift Sword. Which, say that three times fast, yeah?"

He smiles at them. They don't smile back.

"Point being, the conspiracy had someone on the inside. Had to be. Someone with command authority. Needed sorting out, that." He gestures to the guy still curled like a snail. "Sorted."

The kneeling woman looks up. "Rolly definitely has some way far, right-wing opinions. He used to talk about them all the time."

Renata says, knowingly, "Used to."

The woman stands. Nods. "Yeah. He stopped talking about politics.

I mean, stopped all together. Honest, I was so glad, I didn't think about it twice."

"Again, apologies," Dez addresses the room. "Needed to be done. Joint Base McKinzie-Clark is no longer under the control of the U.S. military. I was there. I've met up with an undercover DEA agent and two Los Angeles Police detectives, and we can prove it."

A lot of that is horseshit. He's met all those people, sure, but they can't prove squat. Also, Dez still doesn't know what DEA stands for but the people around the room seem to.

"Patriot Media is off the air, an' that's my doing. The bastards behind all this have a plan. Take over the town. Take over the military base. Take over this power plant."

The smoker says, "Bullshit."

"I shit you not." He turns to Renata. "Sorry, ma'am." He turns back. "What they got planned requires slowing down the official response from the military and the police. The bastards'll be hiding among civilians in Sloatville. They've got the small-arms supply of the joint military base already. If they can take this power plant, and if they can threaten to melt it down, they'll keep the whole shebang off their asses long enough for the final phase."

"Which is . . . ?" a woman asks.

The guy in the fetal position stays stock-still.

Dez knows that *secede from the union* and *wait for the Russians to help* will sound like a load of crap, so he bypasses the truth. "Dunno for sure. I only know they're coming here. An' soon. An' I need to know how to SCRAM this place."

That sends a bolt of shock around the room. Mike Whitney says, "Whoa whoa whoa whoa whoa there, partner." He makes the T-for-timeout symbol with his hands. "Nobody said anything about a SCRAM. I, um, just thought we were meant to, you know, defend the place."

Someone says, "We are not hitting a kill switch for you or anybody. We don't know you from Adam. You're just some guy comes in here with a wacky story and punched Rolly."

Someone says, "We'd need orders from Sacramento."

Someone says, "We'd need orders from Washington!"

The woman who'd knelt says, "I always wanted to punch Rolly."

Renata Esquivel says, "What's SCRAM?"

Dez makes a throat–cutting gesture with his hand and his own throat. "It's a kill switch, ma'am. Every civilian reactor has a way to take the plant offline in a heartbeat. When the crazies come stormin' the gates, it was me mate Rolly here who was assigned to guard the kill switch; make sure no one else could get to it."

He rolls Rolly over and retrieves the .22 from beneath him. Dez takes the gun, reverses it, hands it to the smoker, who looks more than a little surprised.

Mike says, "Being armed on the premises is against policy!"

"I'd write him up a reprimand, were I you. Look, we got the SCRAM button now. If they come, *when* they come, you'n me can turn this whacking great facility into the world's largest paperweight."

Everyone looks around the room. The smoker looks at the .22 in his hand, then holds it by the barrel and hands it back to Dez. "Hate these things."

But the point—that Dez trusts the guy—has been made. The guy says, "Takes two of us to SCRAM the mains. Two keys, two stations." The smoker turns to Mike Whitney. "I'll take one."

CHAPTER 60

Joint Base McKinzie-Clark

It's well past noon by the time Captain Bart Weaver returns to base and reports directly to General William Tancredi. The general is livid.

Weaver was in charge of interrogating the Englishman. Limerick was handcuffed and under lock and key, but he managed to escape. Weaver immediately began a room-by-room search of the base, eighteen good men assigned to the task, covering every conceivable nook.

They were five-sixths done when word began to drift in from the temporary headquarters of Patriot Media, inside the server farm of Triton Expediters: A considerable amount of shit had hit the fan at considerable velocity.

Weaver had jumped in a Humvee with five of his best men and raced into town.

He'd had a concept in mind of a worst-case scenario.

He hadn't been within a light-year of it.

That was yesterday. The hunt for Limerick is in its second day, and everyone, on the base and in the town, is looking for him.

Bart Weaver heads directly to the general's office. He raps once, awaits the bark, then enters and stands at attention. It feels foolish, doing so in a full, bushy beard and civilian clothes. Weaver had been undercover at the Ryerson Ranch for over a month, and he'd needed to look the part before he got there. He hates the beard and shoulder-length hair. He hates the civvies and he hates the fucking Detroit Red Wings. He'd picked up the cap at random at an airport before his mission. He's been back more than a day but hasn't had the opportunity to get into uniform.

General Tancredi rises from behind his desk. He nods, once.

"The network station is off the air and they're not getting it back any time soon, sir. Also, Oliver Lantree is down."

"Down?"

"His jaw's broken, sir. It has to be wired. He's off the air for weeks, sir."

"Goddamn it!" Tancredi swipes at the papers on his desk, which blizzard away, filtering slowly to the floor. He runs a hand through his flattop cut. "Limerick?"

"Yes, sir. Positive ID. He's destroyed the Triton computers. He's destroyed the uplink dishes. He broke Lantree's jaw, sir. There's . . ."

Tancredi says, "What!"

"There's nothing at the Triton site worth salvaging, sir. Patriot Media can keep broadcasting from Virginia. Given a day, day and a half, and they can get set up in Santa Barbara. That's close enough to get a signal for their trucks here, I'm told. But . . ."

Weaver shrugs.

"But our coverage for Swift Sword is fucked up beyond recognition!" Tancredi pounds his desktop.

Weaver stands at attention. "It might have to be delayed, sir."

They both stand like that for a while. Tancredi works to get his breathing back.

"Where's the asshole?"

"Unknown, sir."

"Search the town!"

"That's underway, sir. We've recruited all of the newcomers. Everyone's looking for him, sir. Everyone."

When Tancredi's breathing has returned to near normal and the color in his face is better, he nods. "Is our man at the power station ready?"

"Yessir."

In fact, Boca Serpiente Valley Power Station is within land owned by the U.S. Department of Energy. Ever since 9/11, such facilities are monitored for nonauthorized radio and telephonic transmissions. Weaver put a damn good man in there, a Navy guy with SEAL experience. But he's not in day-to-day contact with him.

"Secure the power station, Captain. We might have to delay Swift Sword a little. But *only* a little."

"Yessir."

"The situation at Triton Expediters is handled. The civilians pouring into Sloatville are primed. I'll tell Patriot Media, it's tomorrow. They'll do whatever the goddamn hell they need to do to broadcast. And if they don't, heaven help them."

"Sir."

Tancredi studies him. "We go tonight, Captain."

"Yessir."

Weaver swings past the base barbershop and spots an Air Force guy half-way through a haircut. "Up," Weaver says. "Out."

The Air Force guy takes one look at Weaver's face, rises, and leaves the room with half a haircut. Weaver falls into the chair.

"Be quick."

The base barber is. In no time, the beard and the shoulder-length hair are gone. Weaver studies his face in the mirror: half-tanned, half-much paler. Doesn't matter. It'll do.

CHAPTER 61

It's going on 1 a.m. Monday when Weaver and six of his handpicked guys drive carefully through the short viaduct under Highway 1. Joint Base McKinzie-Clark is east of the highway; Sloatville and the Boca Serpiente Valley Nuclear Power Station are to the west. Weaver had been living on the west side of the highway for more than a month, a ranch hand on the Ryerson place, adjacent to the Department of Energy land that surrounds the power plant itself. He's glad to be away from the ranch, although he admired Joe and Molly Ryerson. He admired their concepts of family and loyalty. He admired their razor-keen vision about what's wrong with America, and how to make it better. He felt bad, shooting Molly in the back and killing her. He'd even felt remorse, standing before Patriot Media cameras with Joe and the seven children, Joe openly sobbing at the murder of his wife, the cameras catching the sorrow of those little kids. Remorse was something Captain Weaver thought got burned out of him by the Afghan sun.

Weaver has killed for his country. Many times. He's never happy to do it. Shooting Molly in the back had been . . . distasteful soldiering.

Shooting those two soldiers and leaving their bodies for the TV news helicopters to see had been distasteful, too.

But it got the job done.

Because of Department of Energy communications protocols, Weaver can't call his man working at the power station to let him know they are en route. But he can send a burst transmission, the word *now*. That will be enough to get his inside man moving.

Only a skeleton crew stays on the grounds at night, just to monitor the nuclear power plant and the outgoing energy distribution. Weaver and his guys will take the station before 2 a.m. and will be ready to let the world know that a meltdown is imminent if the weak-assed, bureaucratic, real-echelon bastards of the Pentagon make any move into the valley.

Any move at all.

The Humvee is the only vehicle on the road leading to the power station tonight. Weaver's six-man team is in full battle rattle: Kevlar and pads and gloves and helmets. He's trained these men. He knows their hearts and he knows they've got balls. They'll hold the station, even if a SEAL or Special Forces team is deployed. Weaver had told General Tancredi: *"Trust in God, and trust in my strike team. We will hold the station."*

They can see the first glimmer of the DOE fence now, along with the up-front signage and the main entrance building, a low-slung, 1960s affair, wider at the roofline than at the ground, a five-hundred-square-foot, one-room structure with big, wide windows for a full two-hundred-degree view of incoming vehicles. The rolling gate will be closed at this hour, magnetically locked, electricity running through the gate and the fence, and the station secured. At least, that's the concept.

The world will be a bit surprised to wake up later that Monday and realize otherwise.

They draw closer and Weaver notices the lights are on in the Visitors Information Center, with its lobby and map of the site and visitors sign-in book. The arc lights over the gate—inside and outside the gate—are blazing, too.

They shouldn't be.

They draw closer.

Weaver taps the Humvee driver on the shoulder. "Slower."

He turns to his first sergeant. "This is wrong."

He nods. "Cap." He senses it, too. The top kick is a 75th Ranger. Like Weaver. He knows his shit.

The truck pulls closer to the bright cones of light, lit like a Broadway stage. The Welcome Building has wide, low-slung windows, canted a bit forward at the top to reduce glare. Sometime in the distant past, it looked very futuristic. It's well lit but empty. It reminds Weaver of the Edward Hopper painting. *Nighthawks,* but without the nighthawks.

The top kick says, "Cap?"

He points to the rolling gate. Something's amiss. There should be a triangular metal plate with the logos of Boca Serpiente Valley Nuclear Power Station and the U.S. Department of Energy. Instead, the middle of the gate seems to be . . . a blob.

Something's attached to the gate.

They drive closer. The road curves and so does the horizontal tube of illumination from their headlights.

It's a body.

"Hold."

The Humvee stops, engine purring.

Weaver nods to his first sergeant. "You and me."

The driver and the others stay put.

Weaver and the first sergeant deploy, guns forward, heads on swivels. A human being is chained to the gate. The person is unconscious or dead. Chains crisscross the chest and hold the arms and legs akimbo. The head lolls forward. His shoes dangle a foot off the ground.

This is a trap.

Weaver whispers, "Set 'em up."

The sergeant deploys the men: one guy up top of the Humvee, on his belly, with an M1101 marksman rifle. Two guys circle behind the Visitors Center. The driver checks out the borrow pits to either side of the road.

Weaver alone approaches the body chained to the fence. The man wears civilian clothes. When he's within six feet, Weaver realizes it's his own man. His inside man. The SEAL guy who was supposed to be here to open the gate and usher them in.

Weaver steps closer, his eyes devour every inch of the chained body. The man hangs like an unwanted marionette after a show. Weaver's looking for booby traps.

What he spots is a walkie-talkie, strapped to the man's chest.

He steps closer.

The walkie-talkie squawks and every guy on the strike team tenses. A crackle, then a voice. With a working-class English accent.

"Evening, Captain."

Weaver's knuckles go white. Slowly, he reaches for the walkie-talkie strapped to the chest of the man. The guy's chest moves in and out. He's unconscious, not dead. Weaver toggles the Send button.

"Limerick. Go."

Crackle. "D'you know what a SCRAM is, then? Over."

Weaver stands stock-still and silently curses for close to fifteen seconds.

The news is as bad as bad gets. Limerick has access to the kill switch that could eliminate the threat posed by the nuclear plant.

With his fingerless gloves, he feels for a pulse in the neck of the chained man. It's steady. The guy doesn't move, doesn't moan. Not just unconscious, but probably concussed. Weaver remembers the Englishman using one blow—from his forehead, no less—to kill one of Weaver's guys in the stockade.

He toggles the walkie-talkie. "Speak."

"You an' you alone, Captain. The man-sized gate to your right is unlocked. Humvee stays put. Your lads stay put. You come through, we talk. Over."

Weaver makes eye contact with his top kick. The first sergeant doesn't move, doesn't shake his head or nod or show any emotion. *Your call, sir.*

Weaver lowers his weapon. "You've got the ball, Sergeant."

"Sir."

Weaver toggles the walkie-talkie. "Coming in. Over."

Crackle. "In the admin building. I'll put the kettle on."

CHAPTER 62

Dez watches Captain Bart Weaver make his way cautiously across the empty grounds of the power station, his M4A1 held against his shoulder, eyes everywhere, the carbine tracking with his eyes. He looks a right soldier, Dez thinks. He's not a man to be underestimated.

Dez talked to the others, told them to hide so Weaver would have the campus to himself. Most of the buildings are dark but the administration building is well lit. Dez stands in the doorway until he's sure that Weaver has spotted him. He lifts a coffee cup in Weaver's direction, smiles broadly, then turns languidly and saunters inside.

Come and get me.

The lobby is corporate-bland. It could have been the lobby of an insurance agency or a doctor's office or an architect's firm. It was designed as a welcoming space in a facility at which visitors are not welcome. The overhead fluorescents are achingly bright. Dez has arranged one corridor with eight doors, making sure the final door, the door to the building's break room, is the only one fully open. That room is lit up and the other seven are dark. Dez stands in the break room, holding the .22 he took from Weaver's inside man. He hears Weaver's boots on the yellowed tile. He hears hinges squeak. Weaver is checking out each room he comes to, opening each door, stepping in, flicking on the lights. He's checking his corners. Pro.

The first office is clear. As is the second. As is a storeroom. As are the women's restroom and the men's restroom. Weaver sweeps each one. He checks each stall. He takes nothing for granted. Next to the last darkened room; the door a quarter open. Weaver shoulders it fully open, steps in.

It's a variation on the gag Dez employed a few months ago in Algeria: He perched a small plastic garbage bin atop the door and the doorframe. Push the door open and the bin tips over, dumping its content. Which is gasoline.

Dez hears Weaver gasp and whisper, "Shit!" The soldier backpedals out of the room. Dez moves to the door of the break room, points the .22 at the man.

"Fire your weapon, you become a Roman candle, Captain."

Weaver glares hatred at him and hocks up a gob of gas-tainted spit onto the corridor floor. He slowly unclips the safety harness that connects his M4 to his ballistic vest. No sparks, now. He bends at the knee, gently sets the automatic weapon on the floor. He undoes the Velcro of his gas-soaked vest and slips it off, leaving it on the floor. He uses two fingers to gingerly remove the SIG Sauer auto from his belt holster and sets it down, too.

He rises.

"Well done, squire. Step into my office."

The break room is everything you'd expect: four round tables, un-comfortable plastic chairs, a sink, coffee maker, microwave, and a fridge that evokes memories of bad milk even with the door closed. Mandatory safety posters from the Departments of Energy and Labor decorate the walls. WORKPLACE HARASSMENT IS NOT TOLERATED! Dez stands back by the microwave, lots of distance between them.

"Sorry about the bin-of-petrol thing. Juvenile."

Weaver's face shows zero emotion. "Did you SCRAM the plant?"

"I've a few questions of my own, you don't mind."

The hate is gone from Weaver's eyes now. He's back to being the unemotional professional. "Is the plant still viable? Is the nuclear plant working?"

"Well, I've the gun and you haven't, so maybe we'll stick to my ques—"

Weaver's attack is unbelievably quick. The big man raises his leg and uses the sole of his boot to kick the hell out of the nearest round table; kicks it so hard that it skids back, chairs flying, hits the next table, which also skids back, clipping Dez in the thigh.

It doesn't hurt but as distractions go, it's not half bad. Before Dez can reorient himself, Weaver lifts one of the plastic chairs and hurls it like an ungainly discus, right at Dez.

There's no time to duck. Dez takes the blow, stumbles back into the microwave.

Weaver is on him so damn fast. A roundhouse kick, and the little .22 bounces off a cabinet and skitters away behind a fridge.

Dez squares off.

Weaver kicks him in the gut and, even before his leg comes back down, turns it into a spin kick and catches Dez in the kidney.

The captain dances back out of reach.

The pain in his side is blinding, but Dez ignores it and wades in. He throws a couple of punches, catches Weaver's forearms, which deftly divert the power of both punches. The gasoline makes Weaver's uniform slippery; harder to tag properly.

Weaver makes a sword of the knuckles of his right hand and drives it into Dez's side.

Dez stumbles back, lightning rolling up and down his frame.

"Did you SCRAM the system?" Weaver asks icily. He dances and jukes on the balls of his feet. "Is the power plant operational?"

Dez's voice sounds like that of an old man. He's trying to get his lungs to remember how to inhale. "I scrammed . . . your mother."

He's trying to get Weaver angry again. A calm Weaver is much more dangerous.

"You killed one of my guys yesterday."

"Aye."

"Davies had a wife."

"She coulda done better."

Weaver moves in again.

Dez swings a couple of well-placed kicks. But Weaver is never where he's supposed to be by the time the kick arrives. Dez grazes the man a time or two. That's all. Weaver's not just tall and well built, he's fast as hell. And trained.

An elbow catches Dez in the clavicle and Dez smashes back against a plastic drainer of dishes near the sink. Everything goes flying, glasses shatter. Dez's right arm goes numb.

Weaver dodges another kick and drives his knee into Dez's stomach. When Dez doubles over, Weaver drives his elbow into his back.

Dez hits the floor.

Weaver kicks him in the gut and Dez rides the kick, rolls with it, gives himself some distance.

He's on his feet but wobbly.

Weaver is, simply put, the superior fighter.

"Best . . . ye got?"

Weaver sounds fresh as a prairie breeze. "No."

They plow into each other. Weaver dodges a high kick and a follow-up punch and a follow-up kick and drives his knuckles into Dez's kidney.

Dez bounces off the fridge; knocks it askew.

Weaver moves in, aiming his boot for Dez's knee and, for the first time since the fight began, Dez finally connects. It's a short, swift rabbit punch into Weaver's side.

They separate.

Dez goes to one knee but uses the table to right himself again, gasping, blinking sweat out of his eyes.

So far, he's landed just one blow.

But that one broke two of Weaver's ribs.

The big soldier starts to move in but his entire right side seizes up. He locks up, pain radiating when he attempts to inhale.

Dez gets a second shot in, going for the man's jaw.

Weaver drops like an anchor. He tries to get up and Dez kicks him in the same broken ribs.

The kick is more than Dez's damaged body can handle and he loses his balance, lands on his ass, gasping for breath, right arm numb, his back a growing knot of pain.

He leans back against one of the tables, wiping sweat off his face, breath ragged.

Weaver's out cold.

Renata Esquivel and Mike Whitney find them like that, a minute after the sounds of the fight stop: Dez on his ass, slowly regaining his breath; Weaver unconscious.

Renata and Mike help Dez up. He groans like an old man. "Are you okay?" she asks.

"Not even a little."

Renata finds an unbroken glass and brings him water. Dez says, "Ta," and drains it.

Then he hauls off and kicks Weaver again.

"Hey, hey!" Mike waves him off. "C'mon. He's down."

"Tried kicking him when he was up," he gasps, holding his side. "This way's better."

CHAPTER 63

Dez hurts like hell. And he's tired. He can't believe it's Monday; it was Monday last when a tall, lovely woman stepped onto his elevator at the Hotel Tremaine. The weekend is almost a blur: finding the town, the Triton Expediters server farm, the military base, the Taser and the beating, the return to the server farm, the visit to the power station, the fight with Captain Weaver.

Hell of a week.

His side and his back and his legs ache from the beating he took. Captain Bart Weaver was, simply put, the better man in the ring. Dez barely laid a hand on him.

Good thing he has a hand like a car battery.

He raided the commissary at the nuke plant earlier that morning. They had aspirin and plenty of coffee. Enough to keep him going.

Dez drives an all-terrain three-wheeler with a tool wagon attached. He's got the headlamp on, because the sun isn't up yet and the ground only looks flat from a distance. When you're rolling over it, it's craggy and coarse with great gouges in the earth, waxy weeds as tall as his belt, and bits of debris. He's driving carefully, slowly. Wouldn't do to fall asleep and smash into a cactus.

He's been aiming at lights for the last twenty minutes.

Around 2 a.m., Dez found a tall vertical hole in the Boca Serpiente Valley Nuclear Power Station grounds fence. Likely where the Army had made its incursion last week. He used the tools in the sled to widen the hole and got the ATV through, and has been driving due north ever since. The ocean's on his left but too far away to see. The highway is on his right but too far away to hear. The stars above are bright. The lights ahead belong to a sprawling ranch house and an adjacent red barn and a small silo. Beyond all that is another fence, a civilian fence, wooden and hand-built, and beyond that are police cars and a couple of TV microwave trucks.

The sun will be up soon.

Dez is within forty meters of the house when the front door opens and a big man with an enormous belly steps out with a shotgun. He's followed by five more adults. All of them are armed. Shotguns, rifles, pistols. They'd heard his ATV coming because sound travels forever on this land.

Dez parks directly in front of them. This hasn't been a covert approach; he doesn't want anyone mistaking that.

He shows them his hands.

Under the porch lights, the six people look haggard and angry. Dez recognizes the man who stepped out first. He'd seen him on television, holding the shoulder of a preteen boy while crying into the cameras.

After everyone's had a moment to study Dez's empty hands, he dismounts from the ATV saddle. He's wearing a T-shirt and jeans, so no place to hide a weapon.

"Who're you?" Joe Ryerson's voice sounds like seashells cracking under your boots. The others stand, threatening but quiet.

"Desmond Limerick. You're Joe Ryerson. Read about you."

"What do you want?"

Dez leans his ass back against the ATV in a nonthreatening stance. "Friend of mine found out someone was using money stolen from her company to finance everything that's going on in Sloatville and at the military base. She's pissed off. Wants an end to it. I've been tryin' to help her do that."

"Why are you on my property?"

Dez says, "Tryin' to end this thing. Told you. Think maybe you can help."

The six people on the porch look down at him and wait. Joe Ryerson studies the newcomer, the three-wheeler, the attached sled with its tie-down tarp. "You bring me weapons?"

"I did not."

"You bring us food or supplies?"

"No, sir."

"Then why should I help you? Why should *we* help you?"

"'Cause I think you got played. An' I think it might bring you a measure of closure to know why. An' how. An' by who. Whom. Sorry."

Joe Ryerson watches him without moving. Dez waits.

Ryerson nods.

Dez rises off the machine he's been leaning against. He shows his empty palms again. He moves to the sled and slowly unties the tarp. Slowly. Fatigued and frightened civilians with guns; that's a recipe for accidental violence. Avoiding accidental violence in favor of well-planned violence is one of the things Dez is good at.

He steps back and takes the edges of the tarp and brings them together, the way you fold bedsheets. He does it again, and again, making a tight, neat little packet of blue tarp.

Joe Ryerson steps down off his porch and studies the body lying on the sled. It's a man in Army fatigues. He lies on his back, legs straight, arms folded over his chest like a corpse on display for an open-casket funeral.

He has short hair and he's clean-shaven. Even in the harsh yellow light from the porch, and the light gleaming through the living room windows, Joe can see that the upper half of the man's face is tanned, the lower half pale. The tan line matches the beard line.

Joe notices the bandages on the man's left forearm.

He sees, in his mind's eye, a Detroit Red Wings cap.

He says, "Jonesy."

The others step down now and surround the ATV and the sled. One keeps an eye and a Colt on Dez.

The people murmur.

Joe Ryerson turns to Dez. "Explain."

"Captain Bart Weaver, U.S. Army, 75th Rangers."

"His name is Jones."

"His name is not." Dez shrugs. "He has dog tags."

Someone checks them.

"What happened to him?"

Dez lifts his own shirt and shows Joe the vampire bite marks of Captain Weaver's Taser, plus the bruises from the fight at the power plant. "We tussled."

Someone says, "He's alive."

Dez says, "Needed him alive."

"I . . . Jonesy's a traitor?"

"Captain Weaver's a good soldier. I saw him standin' behind you, on TV, the day your missus passed. My condolences for your loss, Mr. Ryerson."

Joe studies Dez without the slightest hint of emotion. Those reservoirs were used up days before. Joe's been running on muscle memory and slowly diminishing momentum.

"He was assigned t'your ranch by the bastards behind all this. He was the starter pistol."

Someone says, "Starter pistol?"

"Dunno if you're trackin' what's going on out there. Town's filled up with anarchists, white supremacists, neo-Nazi types." A couple of guys grumble but Joe Ryerson just watches Dez. "The death of your wife, shot in the back, was the incitement they needed. Patriot Media kept everything at a boil. The guy in charge of Joint Base McKinzie-Clark's got men loyal to his particular madness, ready to roll. Men like Captain Weaver, here. Jonesy. They tried to take over the nuclear power station tonight, t'use it as a threat."

Joe watches him awhile. Everyone waits for Joe to make the call. Joe says, "Tried?"

Dez shrugs. "Stopped 'em."

"How?"

"Convinced a good man to hit the kill switch and eliminate the threat of the power plant melting down. With that threat gone, the real military can deal with Joint Base McKinzie-Clark and the mad monk who runs the outfit. I took Patriot Media an' its founder off the air. This whole plot's dead in the water, only the folks in town and the soldiers at the base don't know it yet."

He waits.

"Jonesy wouldn't kill my wife."

Dez thinks about it a minute. He'd love more coffee and a couple dozen more aspirins. "Heard the story on TV," he says. "One of the ranch hands, Jonesy, found a dead calf. Your wife went to look. She ran into two soldiers who shot her in the back. Jonesy defended himself, killed the soldiers, told you all about it. Told the media."

Joe Ryerson nods.

"You went out there? Nearer to the power station? Found your wife's body?"

Joe nods.

"You find a dead calf, sir?"

Now the others are murmuring, glancing at one another. To the east, the sky is moving from indigo to navy, and overhead the stars are beginning to fade. Dez is beginning to fade. When this is over, he'll sleep for a week.

Joe Ryerson says, "Jonesy?"

"That was his job, yeah. Light the fuse. Death of an innocent woman, shot in the back. Tell the media. Media tells the world. Hundreds, maybe thousands of people pouring into this county to defend you. Fella name of General Tancredi uses them, uses his loyal soldiers, to take the town, take the base, take the power station as a deterrent. Sets up his own little fiefdom. Hail t'the chief. But it all starts with Captain Bart Weaver shooting Molly Ryerson in the back. For the media."

Nobody moves for a while. Nobody speaks. Dez aches. Captain Bart Weaver groans, his eyelids fluttering. After the fight, Dez had used the walkie-talkie at the main gate to tell the rest of the soldiers from the Humvee that the SCRAM switch—the power station kill switch—had been hit twenty minutes earlier. The station administrator, Mike Whitney, had been on the horn to the U.S. Department of Energy within seconds, using a secure line. Also the governor of California. He'd explained the whole thing to everyone who'd listen.

The other soldiers had no option but to call into Joint Base McKinzie-Clark for new orders.

Meanwhile, Dez sneaked out the back with a trussed-up Captain Weaver and an ATV with a sled.

From the beginning, when he'd asked Mike to bring him to the power station, he'd hoped it would be Weaver who made the approach. What Dez had in mind all along wouldn't have worked without him.

The sky near the horizon takes on a bit of a reddish glow. A bank of low clouds to the east turns salmon and slate. Dez is facing west and Joe is facing east and Dez can see the first hints of sunrise reflected in the bloodshot eyes of the grieving widower with the Benelli 12 gauge.

Joe Ryerson says, "I been burning crops out here for twenty years. Rotating the fields. My burns never crossed into federal land. Never. The whole standoff. The threats. The . . . everything."

"Yes, sir. Inciting incidents. They needed to get the ball rolling. None of this was of your making."

"I never wanted any of this. Molly never wanted any of this. We wanted to be left alone."

Dez juts his chin toward the wooden gate that the man and his wife built by hand decades ago. "Media trucks're here. Fox, CNN, locals. Patriot Media, too, though I can't tell how far they can broadcast." He nods toward the slowly reviving body of Captain Bart Weaver. Now that the sky is lightening, everyone can see that Weaver's wrists are tied together, his ankles tied together.

Joe looks at the shotgun in his hand for a good long while. Dez waits. Joe turns and sets the weapon next to the nearest wheel of the ATV, and swipes his palms against the thighs of his dungarees. Trying to get the gun oil off his hands.

"What do you want?"

"You wanted t'be left alone, sir. Your wife, may she rest in peace, wanted t'be left alone." Dez nods toward the gate. "Tell 'em what happened. A week, maybe two, and everyone drifts away."

Dez steps forward and offers his hand.

After a while, Joe takes it in both of his rough, calloused, farmer hands, closing them around Dez's as if leading him in prayer.

"Tell the truth," Dez says. "It's the one thing them bastards never counted on."

CHAPTER 64

Malibu Colony Beach, California

Monday morning, Petra Alexandris wakes up in her own bed.

She'd slept atop the sheets in her street clothes. *Sleep* being an optimistic way to think about the rough, listless night of blistering anger. She sits up, runs her hands through her straight hair. She reaches out of habit for the tablet computer embedded in her nightstand and presses a fingertip to the screen.

Normally, she would be able to bring up music, open the drapes, start the coffee. Start the hot tub, if she wanted. She'd be able to activate the massive, built-in TV monitor set to capture real-time statistics from the stock and money markets around the world. She'd have been able to make the smart-house dance a jig.

This morning, nothing happens.

Since being escorted to her house under armed guard, upon orders from Vincent Guerrero, late Sunday night, all of Petra's personal household codes had been deactivated. Including the building locks.

Gilded cage.

She changes into togs, does thirty minutes of yoga, hoping it will dispel some of the pent-up anger and frustration. It doesn't, but feels good nonetheless. She showers, making sure to keep her hair dry.

She slips on soft cotton drawstring pants and a tank and pads out to the kitchen.

She spots the roving guards outside the window. The men have been on rotation since she'd been whisked here by her father, Colin Frye, and Brittany Kinney. The coconspirators who had been using Triton Expediters' money and influence to fund an armed coup, the goal of which, she now understands, is to create a small country on the Western coast of North America with unparalleled economic and military might.

She walks into the industrial kitchen expecting to find Alonzo, coffee brewing, chopping onions and jalapeños, wearing skinny jeans and looking fine. But Alonzo has been dismissed. Fired, to be exact. By her father, at the suggestion of Vincent Guerrero. Alonzo's smart-home codes have been deactivated and he's been banned from the grounds. That's what her father told her. She wonders if it's the whole truth.

A young female guard in a black suit speaks into a wrist microphone as Petra enters. "Secondary's up."

Secondary. She figured it out last night, that the guards refer to Constantine as *Primary* and to Petra as *Secondary*. Their jobs are to protect the primary asset. And to make sure the secondary asset does as she's told and makes no trouble.

"Ma'am."

Petra ignores her, gets the coffeepot going. *Thank God you don't need an eight-digit code for that,* she thinks.

The security pad next to the kitchen door, which leads to the garage, blinks red.

The whole house is in lockdown. Petra has had no real understanding of how reliant she's become on the Triton computers that run, well, everything.

Petra pours herself a cup of coffee before the machine is finished and doctors it with half-and-half.

Wordlessly, she pads out of the kitchen and heads to the private office. *Her* private office, or so she's imagined.

Her father stands in the Spartan office, a smart-house tablet computer in hand, stabbing the screen with a nicotine-stained finger. The monitor is recessed into a wall and, when off, almost perfectly resembles the walls around it. Now it's been activated and shows a soccer match. The audio is off. The chyron in the lower-left corner says halftime of a nil-nil tie, Liverpool vs. Havana.

"What the fuck is this," Constantine Alexandris growls. "I can't get this damn screen to change!"

Petra sets her coffee down and reaches out. "May I try?"

He thrusts the tablet computer at her. Petra takes it, turns, raises it over her head, mimics her best tennis overhead smash, and slams it into the corner of a sandstone bookshelf. The tablet screen shatters, glass flying. She turns and hands him the piece of rectangular plastic, now bent like a hockey stick, its screen missing.

She retrieves her coffee, makes eye contact with him, keeps her voice neutral. "Better?"

He takes it. "Petulance ill becomes you. I raised you better."

"Mother raised me. Which is why I have a moral compass."

Constantine moves to the wall-mounted monitor and physically turns off the soccer match by pressing a button. He sighs, as if using such a menial approach is beneath him.

"The others are on their way. We'll explain everything to you. Trust me, Petra, once you see the big picture, you'll understand."

"I understand that greed has driven you insane."

Constantine paces the office, which reflects her tastes, not his. Petra redecorated in her usual way. She has an eye for art and no tolerance for clutter. There are very few actual objects in her office, and nothing that she doesn't need to get her work done. The scattering of glass on the hardwood floor near the stone bookshelf stands out amid the order of her space.

"Dmytro Rudko is waiting offshore," her father says. "When General Tancredi takes the nuclear power plant and decrees an independent nation, the Russians will go ashore and recognize the new country. Sacramento might have been quick to send in the National Guard and stop us. But with the nuclear plant threatened, the response turns from Sacramento to Washington. And they'll pause, analyze the situation, consider their alternatives. Once Rudko recognizes our new country, the United Nations will intervene. That will slow down all responses even further."

He pauses, glares at his daughter, willing her to concede the genius of his plan.

Petra sips her coffee, does not react. Tall, angular, barefoot, serene mask in place. She manages to make sipping coffee look like tai chi. Constantine paces and smokes. His hands gesture as he talks, conjuring images to go with his thoughts. He comes from a long line of Greek laborers and fishermen. He disdains subtlety; mistakes it for weakness.

"Other countries have been lined up to acknowledge our new nation. No, don't ask which ones. It doesn't matter."

She wasn't going to.

"What matters is this: Triton Expediters has been serving as the bank for half of the world's military. We are the ultimate purveyors of war as a commodity. You know that, I know that. The justness of war, the stupidity of it, the idiocy of it, the shortsightedness of it . . . none of that matters to Triton. Who wins? Who loses? Not our concern, so long as we make our profit. We provide the capital for war, but not the reasons for war. Well, no more."

Petra nods. From her face, they might be talking about that year's harvest from one of Constantine's vineyards. "I see."

"Ours will be the new Vatican. A city-state," he says. "A tiny nation on the edge of the Pacific, with billions of dollars already in play throughout first- and third-world countries alike. The finest international infrastructure of computers that call the shots. We get to say who uses our capital to make war, and who doesn't. The Saudi crown prince wants to pulverize some dirt-poor African nation because of this perceived slight or that niggling blasphemy? Well, no more. Thanks to Brittany Kinney, our computers do a lot more than transfer money around the globe. Thanks to the diplomacy of Colin Frye, we have the back-channel communications to parliaments and military leaders across the globe. The Saudis want to act like sandbox bullies? We could turn off all their security mechanisms along the Iranian border."

He reaches for the packet of cigarettes that sits on the desk—on *her* desk—like a cancerous growth.

Petra nods. "That would be handy if Saudi Arabia and Iran shared a border."

"Don't be insolent!" he barks, face flush. "It was just an example! The point is, within weeks, our nation and Triton Expediters will be calling the shots, worldwide. We will be the most powerful city-state since Rome. We will finally wield the kind of power that will truly matter. That's us, Petra. That's me. And when you finally see the full picture, you'll see the genius of it."

"And these racist scum pouring into your spanking new country? These are your honored citizens?"

Constantine grimaces and waves off the thought like it was a mosquito circling his head. "Don't get distracted by that sideshow, Petra. General Tancredi needs them for now. They'll be jettisoned soon enough. They're useful idiots."

Petra gives him a slow-burn smile, eyes boring into him.

"What?" he barks.

"Polezni durak."

"What? Speak English, for God's sake. Or at least Greek!"

She shakes her head slowly.

"Enough with this Cheshire Cat nonsense! Speak your mind!"

But she turns and studies the roiling Pacific Ocean.

One of the guards knocks and steps in.

"Sir? Ms. Kinney is here."

"Show her in."

The guard never makes eye contact with Petra.

The *Secondary* is of no importance to the guardians of the Malibu house.

CHAPTER 65

Malibu Colony Beach, California

Over the next fifteen minutes, Brittany Kinney and Colin Frye arrive at the Malibu estate. Vincent Guerrero lets them in. He has a security team at least eight men deep; that's how many Petra spots, anyway.

Colin, in a summer-weight suit and a silk pocket square, looks nervous. "I just spoke to Dmytro. He's on his way here."

Constantine gives him a glacial stare. "Rudko? Why?"

Why indeed, Petra wonders, but maintains her mannequin face.

"He wouldn't say. He's bringing down the yacht."

Brittany, in her standard black-and-white garb, is scanning her tablet computer. "We're not hearing anything from Boca Serpiente County. Total comms blackout."

"That was the plan." Constantine waves it off. "When General Tancredi makes his move, he wants to be in position before anyone can react."

He glares at his battered old steel watch. Constantine Alexandris could buy the whole Patek Philippe company, lock, stock, and watch springs, but he won't part with that old stem-winder. "It's started. We should be hearing soon."

As the men talk, Brittany puts her computer away and approaches Petra. The tech officer looks flushed. And it's not just because of the conspiracy to commit treason, Petra thinks.

Brittany keeps her voice low. "Are you okay?"

Petra studies her awhile. It's a stupid question, so she doesn't bother answering.

"At some point, you're going to see this is the right thing to do," Brittany says. "We're making the world safer. We'll be the steady hand on the tiller. No more dipshit generals and admirals with their fruit salad medals and spangled epaulets. Constantine is a fucking force of nature. Colin has glad-handed enough political leaders in the right countries to go along with us. You'd be surprised how many of them want their militaries on a leash."

Petra says, "And you?"

Brittany shrugs. "If you used Triton money to upgrade your nation's infrastructure, any time in the last couple of years, then I have a back door into your system. Most of NATO. Japan and Australia. Big chunks of Southeast Asia. People will get in line like this"—she snaps her fingers—"or they'll be using Commodore 64s and issuing their orders on pin-feed paper coming off dot matrix printers. I can turn the clocks back on their technology so bad an OfficeMax in a strip mall will look like NORAD Command."

Petra nods. "That doesn't surprise me. You are that good."

Brittany blushes and uses a finger to brush crimson hair behind her ears.

"It's the fact that you followed my father's idiot scheme that surprises me. I didn't figure you for one of those blind-faith mutts who drink the Kool-Aid."

Brittany looks like she's been slapped. Her cheeks turn pink.

"That's unfair. Petra, we——"

"Orange Department of Correction jumpsuits absolutely will not go with your do. You can use my bathroom if you want to wash the dye out before the CNN perp-walk."

"Shut up." Brittany says it without rancor. She's not angry, she's hurt.

Petra suddenly, in the blink of an eye, figures it out. She's known for a while that her presence makes Brittany Kinney nervous, but she thought it was an alpha-female/turf thing.

It's not. It's unrequited love.

Petra glances at her father and Colin Frye, who are talking business on the far side of the office. She reaches out and touches the back of Brittany's hand with the tips of her fingers.

Brittany pulls her hand back, blushing, eyes on the carpet.

"I'm sorry," Petra says. "I'm lashing out. I'm mad at my father. I apologize."

Brittany looks at the window and the wall and a tall potted bamboo in the corner. "It's not crazy. It's not. I've run the numbers. I've calculated the odds. You know me. I don't do faith. I do facts."

"Just because you can do this, doesn't mean you should. It's—"

Vincent Guerrero raps on the doorframe and steps into the office. He addresses Constantine. "Ambassador Rudko, sir. He's just dropped anchor."

Petra turns from the blushing tech wizard to the big window behind her.

Sure enough, she spots the megayacht, with its three decks, helipad and helicopter, and infinity pool. She has, on occasion, negotiated with Dmytro Rudko aboard the *Os'Minog*. It's a floating corporate headquarters for the Rudko family's petrochemical empire. The ship is parked maybe two miles off the coast, directly opposite the Malibu estate.

Guerrero says, "They're bringing over a launch."

Brittany turns to him. She seems to have regained a little of her usual cool. "Vincent? So who's this Limerick?"

Guerrero eyes her coolly. "Nobody."

"Yeah? Well, *nobody* hacked the shit out of you," she says. "He was in your personal computer. He owned this house. He'd screwed with your surveillance here."

Petra had been counting on all this going unnoticed. She remains stoic.

Guerrero says, "Bullshit."

"I've reset everything. He's locked out. But"—Brittany shrugs—"he made you his bitch, big-time."

Petra enjoys that but doesn't show it. She sees a small motorboat vectoring toward the Malibu Colony dock. She spots at least three people on board.

Guerrero's phone vibrates. He reads the incoming text, turns his eyes to Constantine. "Something on TV we should see. It's about Boca Serpiente Valley."

Colin Frye looks around for the smart-home tablet and doesn't spot it. That's because, after Petra smashed it, her father threw it in the garbage can by the desk.

Constantine stalks out of the office before Brittany Kinney can stop him, his short legs pumping like pistons. After a beat, the others follow.

He reaches the living room and finds another tablet. He activates this room's wall-embedded television. This time he gets nothing but static.

"I tried to tell you," Brittany says. "I had to cut off the cable service. This Limerick guy appears to be a decent hacker. He'd have used that to get in. Here . . ."

She turns on her own phone and uses it as a Wi-Fi hot spot. She brings up MSNBC.

Constantine Alexandris, Colin Frye, and Vincent Guerrero gather in a semicircle around her to watch the tail end of an impromptu, outdoor press conference, shot against the backdrop of a handmade wooden fence and a ranch house beyond. Joe Ryerson, recently widowed patriarch of the Ryerson Ranch, has just exposed one of his followers as an Army mole who shot his wife and two of his own men.

The officer, a tall man with an unevenly tanned face, leans with his chest against a police patrol car, his wrists cuffed behind him. The man looks like he's inhaling with difficulty.

Colin Frye says, "Ah. Well. That doesn't look good."

Constantine snorts. "General Tancredi has to have a contingency plan for this. I'm not worried."

Brittany has moved to the floor-to-ceiling window, looking out at the Pacific. "I wouldn't be so sure of that."

Constantine turns to her. "Why not?"

Brittany points to the motor launch being tied off at the Malibu Colony dock. "Because General Tancredi isn't running things up there. He's here. He came with the Russian."

CHAPTER 66

Shortly after Mike Whitney talked to the U.S. Department of Energy—explaining why he and his senior staff had activated the SCRAM shutoff of the nuclear power station—a bevy of U.S. troops from Point Mugu Naval Air Station, the Marine Corps Logistics Base Barstow, and the Marine Corps Mountain Warfare Training Center rolled down Interstate 5 and the 1, heading for Boca Serpiente County and Joint Military Base McKinzie-Clark.

After the local and federal law enforcement officials on duty at the gate of the Ryerson Ranch took statements from Joe Ryerson and others living in the compound, they booked U.S. Army Captain Bart Weaver into custody on charges of first-degree homicide. At that cue, county, state, and federal law enforcement officials began heading toward the town of Sloatville.

But before all of that occurred, Dez got a ride back into town and was dropped off at his stolen F-250 Super Duty.

He's halfway back to Los Angeles before all of that erupts behind him.

★ ★ ★

The first big problem: Dez can't raise Petra. She answers neither phone calls nor texts. Either she can't or she won't, and Dez is leaning toward *can't*.

When the two of them believed that Triton Expediters' money was funding a bunch of far-right-wing dorks looking to create a fifty-first state, Petra appeared to be in no physical danger. She was confronting her own father, along with her company's tech guru and chief lobbyist. At worst, they'd talk her to death.

Now Dez realizes the stakes are very much higher—life-and-death stakes—played out on a global arena in which real power, and not just money, is on the table. Military types who launched a coup d'etat are involved. Russian military intelligence is involved. Petra's a brilliant legal mind and a dogged investigator but she's up to her eyeballs with a different kind of predator this time.

She's incommunicado, which means she's either being held against her will or she's dead.

Dez compartmentalizes that for now. There's a time for action and a time for mourning.

Dez has tried to raise Alonzo. No luck there. The calls go to a number that has been disconnected.

He stops at a greasy spoon in Lebec. Walking into the diner, every part of his body aches. He orders coffee, two eggs, and bangers. "Sorry, love. Sausages."

There's a sundries dispenser in the men's room and Dez pays for Tylenol. He downs five of them with his coffee.

While he uses the caffeine to fend off fatigue, he pulls out his bespoke, ruggedized tablet computer with the scuffed leather folder and subconsciously kisses the cover before opening it. He tries to access the security system at the Malibu house.

He's been locked out.

He tries to access Vincent Guerrero's computer at the corporate headquarters.

Locked out.

A cursory examination tells him the Triton Security computer protocols have been vastly hardened in the last twenty-four hours. The hacker's tricks of the trade he picked up as a gatekeeper are way too amateurish for the current system.

Someone knows Dez had previously hacked the system. Brittany Kinney, likely.

Dez tucks into the food—it's surprisingly good—and snoops around the security system at Petra's beachfront smart-house. Again, he sees that the security protocols have been improved. With these modern smart-homes, the ways to break in via the so-called *internet of things* has made hacking much easier. Everything from the water heater to the lights to the bloody toaster are on the cloud these days. But Dez hunts around and can't spot any weaknesses in those systems.

Neither Petra's eight-digit security access code nor Guerrero's twelve-digit security access code net him anything but frustration.

Dez does a quick scan of other homes in the Malibu area, looking for someone else piggybacking onto the Alexandrises' internet router. It happens. And lo, he spots an incongruity.

An email is being routed into Petra's home, but not through the home's server. It's as if a secondary server has been installed. And this server is not password-protected.

Dez accesses the server and opens the email to find a looped video, about eight seconds long. It's eight seconds of meaningless football. A bit of play, midfield, nothing of importance happening. Dez recognizes the unis as Club Atlas and someone else—Atlético San Luis?—from the Mexico league.

Words have been photoshopped onto the lower left-hand corner of the image.

Liverpool vs. FC La Habana.

Dez starts to grin.

Liverpool is in the English Premier League. La Habana plays in the Cuban National Football League.

"More coffee, hon?"

"T'go, ta." He digs cash out of his jeans pocket.

Liverpool is Dez's team.

Alonzo is Cuban.

There are only two emails in queue. One has the snippet of a football game. The other has a subject line but no body copy. The subject line is an address in greater Los Angeles.

Dez goes to Google Earth and types in the address. He spots a bird's-eye view of an apartment complex. The image may have been taken last week, last month, or last year. Whenever it was taken, it captured a lavender Mini Cooper with a rainbow flag decal in the window parked in the lot.

CHAPTER 67

Malibu Colony Beach, California

As they wait for Russian Ambassador Dmytro Rudko and General William Tancredi to march up from the pier, Constantine lights up another Greek cigarette. He glances at the inert television monitor embedded in the wall. "If the cable is cut off, why am I getting that damned soccer game in the office?"

Petra maintains her passive face and thinks, *Damn it.*

She'd already figured out Alonzo's chess move.

Brittany Kinney turns to the old man. "No TV signals are coming in. None."

"Tell that to the idiots on my TV."

Brittany heads back toward the office.

She returns in about ninety seconds carrying a cheap plastic router box.

"This was under the desk. We've got a leak. Vincent?"

Guerrero turns to her.

"I'm pretty sure I know who did this. . . ."

CHAPTER 68

Dez hits Los Angeles. He follows the map coordinates to the apartment complex. It's the most generic of structures: five free-standing buildings, each three stories tall, a good twelve to fifteen apartment units in each. Exterior stairs and wraparound, exterior walkways on the second and third floors. Bland as tofu. This could be a subdivision in Boise or Butte or Birmingham.

He spots Alonzo's lavender Mini Cooper, the one he'd borrowed the week prior. It's in a parking space stenciled 535.

Dez finds the apartment building marked NO. 5 and jogs up to the third floor. He finds the door marked 535. He raps twice on the door with a knuckle the size of a bridge rivet.

A curtain twitches.

Dez waits.

The door opens and a stranger stands in the three-inch gap. It's a man, midtwenties, with a mop of curly blond hair and blue eyes.

"I'm Dez."

The man's eyes are red-rimmed and puffy. He's been crying. He pauses, steps back, undoes the chain, and opens the door fully. He wears a hoodie with the Green Lantern symbol and artfully ripped jeans and is barefoot. "He's in there." He head-juts toward a bedroom.

Dez finds Alonzo in bed. He's on his back, his face blotchy and bruised, one eye swollen shut, with an inch-long, vertical split to his upper lip. Far worse, one leg is in a cast. They're using an inverted Postal Service box made of pliant, white corrugated plastic for elevation.

"Jaysus."

Alonzo offers a half smile, trying not to pull on the two stitches in his lip. "It doesn't look worse than it is. It's that bad. Please don't ask about *the other guy.*"

Dez finds a chair at a desk piled with a laptop, reams of papers bundled with brass brads, and used books on screenwriting. He drags the chair over to the bed and sits. The blond man stands in the doorway, hands jammed in his trouser pockets, tears glittering.

"Desmond, Andrew. Andrew, Desmond." Alonzo slurs his words and his one open eye is dilated. He's on serious painkillers.

"Wotcher," Dez whispers over his shoulder.

Andrew says, "Hi."

"It's not my deathbed, bitches. You don't gotta whisper."

Dez nods to the broken leg. "Guerrero's lads?"

Alonzo nods. "I wouldn't leave her there by herself. Petra."

"You planted that looped email before all this, did ye?"

"The . . . oh, that." Alonzo sounds loopy. "*Madre.* I wanted to get her away. I knew they could trace our phones. Wanted to leave you bread crumbs. Holy smokes, that worked?"

Dez rests a hand on his shoulder. "I'm here, aren't I, ye dozy bastard. 'Course it worked."

Andrew inhales sharply. "Such loyalty. For a rich bitch who needs a butler." His voice cracks halfway through.

Alonzo smiles at him. "I should wash your mouth out with a cheap varietal sold in a box, sweetie."

Andrew wipes tears from his cheeks.

Alonzo turns his one good eye to Dez. "They're holding her at the house. I don't have my access card, or my company phone. No way in."

Dez, the gatekeeper, shrugs. "We'll see. Your leg . . . ?"

"Ankle," Andrew interjects bitterly. "After they knocked him down, they stomped on his ankle. They said . . ."

He hiccups, covers his mouth with his palm. Alonzo croons. "Hey. Shhh. S'all right . . ."

"They said, 'Dance this off, faggot.'"

Dez feels a lightness in his chest. A disassociated feeling of serenity. He's felt it before, when facing an enemy it was his job to kill. Experienced killers do it without too much emotion. So, too, do sociopathic killers. Dez is pretty sure he's not a sociopath. But then again, he suspects most sociopaths think that.

A problem for another day.

"Recognized 'em, did you?"

"Guerrero's guys. I've seen them on Con . . . Const . . . the old man's security crew."

Alonzo's open eye is drooping. Andrew walks out and Dez hears the sound of tap water flowing into a glass.

Dez fakes a big grin. "Lucky you. I was looking forward to kicking your arse on the football pitch."

"You . . . and what . . . army . . ." The painkillers do their job. Alonzo drifts to sleep.

Dez feels utterly calm. His breathing is even, his hands steady. He stands and reorients the chair to the desk, as he found it. He steps out of the bedroom, spots the kitchenette.

"You holding up, then?"

Andrew stares out the window over the sink, ignoring him, holding a water glass against his narrow chest. The kitchen is cluttered but clean. A tortoiseshell cat crouches in one corner, eyes on Dez. Dez crouches down and presents two fingers forward. The cat takes a tentative step, sniffs his fingers, settles back down. She allows herself to be scratched between the ears.

"Hey . . ." Andrew says, his eyes on the window, peering down three stories at the complex parking lot.

Dez catches the energy in the man's voice and rises.

"I think those guys are back."

CHAPTER 69

Dez glances out the kitchen window. Three stories below, two black sedans pull into the complex's parking lot. They're well washed and identical. They have tinted windows and stubby antennas on their boots for short-range radio communications. They park at forty-five degrees relative to the pavement stripes, noses canted out for a quick getaway. Pros, them. Dez says, "Andrew, was it?"

The blond kid nods.

"You a dancer, too, then?"

He blinks at Dez. "What?"

"Dancer. D'you dance?"

"Um. No." Andrew watches as four men climb out of the two sedans. "I'm a writer. I *want* to be a writer."

"Good on you. Writing's murder for me. I get the sweats trying."

Andrew is gripping the tumbler so tight his knuckles turn white. He points down to the parking lot. "The guy with the flattop? He's the one who stomped Alonzo."

Dez thinks, *"Dance this off, faggot."* He nods. "Before this weekend, I gave Alonzo something."

Andrew says. "A gun?"

"That's it. Smith & Wesson .45. Yea big. Wrapped in a kerchief. Seen it?"

The four men below consult one another. One of them peers at a smartphone. They are fit, tall, young, dressed well with jackets and shiny shoes and Ray-Bans. The man with the regulation flattop haircut is a bit shorter than the others and looks well put together.

Andrew gulps. "I, um . . . I didn't want it in the apartment. I made him keep it under the seat, in the Mini."

The Mini Cooper. Which is parked two spots over from the sedans.

Dez keeps looking out the window as he nods. "Smart. Nasty things, guns. Wouldn't have 'em in the house, either."

Dez kneels and checks the cupboard under the sink. He moves a lined garbage bin, digs around it and finds a box of small garbage bags, for bathroom-sized bins. He takes one. He spots a bottle of lurid purple dish soap—*For Greasy Messes!*—and takes that, too.

He stands and walks around the partition into the adjoining living room. He pops open his folding knife with the flick of his thumbnail, kneels again, and unplugs a lamp next to the davenport. He slices through the lamp cord near the lamp base.

He stands. "Sorry about that."

He lays the wire on the flecked Formica counter and deftly slices the lower six inches of it, peeling back the insulation, exposing wires. He's done this a thousand times. Did it, recently, at a compound in Algeria, only that time using a car battery. He moves to the front door and ties the exposed wires to the doorknob. The cord dangles to the floor.

"Do us a favor?" he asks casually.

"Um . . . yeah?"

"When I leave—"

Andrew's voice rises an octave. "You're leaving?"

"When I step out, briefly like, plug the cord in, will ye?" Dez pulls out his wallet, digs around, finds a card. "This lady is a police officer, yeah?"

Andrew sneers. "The police can't—"

"She can, and you'd be wise not to speak ill of her in my presence, mate. Beth Swanson. Call her an' tell her what's what. Then call . . . what is it, here? Nine one one?"

Andrew takes the cards. "O . . . Okay . . ."

"Ta. Then go sit with our lad, will ye? Wait for the sirens. There ye go. Cheers."

"What are you going to do?"

Dez slaps him on the shoulder. "Converse."

CHAPTER 70

Vincent Guerrero tasked four good men to track down Petra Alexandris's ex-employee and to ask him the purpose of the hidden router and the eight dull seconds of soccer. These are good men: two ex-Navy, two ex-Army. They've been with Guerrero long enough to be fully trusted. They'll get the job done.

The lead guy, by way of seniority with Triton Security, is Boland. He's Navy. He leads the other three up the exterior stairs of building number 5 to the third floor. Boland is a no-nonsense sort. A lot like Major Guerrero himself. He approaches the door to apartment 535 and draws a thin packet of lockpicks out of his jacket, briefly exposing a Kydex holster and his SIG Sauer P365. He selects two picks. He reaches to jostle the doorknob, to make sure it's really locked first. It happens. You try picking a lock that's already unlocked and you only end up locking it, which is embarrassing and wastes time. Boland grips the knob.

He convulses. It's alternating current, not direct current, so he releases his grip on the knob. His spine arches backward and his muscles shove him away from the door. His butt hits the banister that runs the length of the exterior walkway, around all four sides of the building. His momentum takes him over the edge.

He lands three stories below, his neck cracking like celery.

Alonzo lives in the middle of the north-facing walkway, between apartments 534 and 536. Dez has been hiding around the corner, on the east side with apartments 537 to 539. He hears his electricity trap spring and comes around the corner, arm cocked back.

He's holding a tied-off garbage bag for a bathroom bin. It's sloshing with about two cups of dishwashing liquid.

Two of the three surviving Triton Security guys lean over the railing, as if hoping somehow they could catch the leader, who already lies dead on the sidewalk below. The third guy spots Dez and reaches for his holster.

Dez lets fly with the small, round bag.

Two of the men raise their hands, palms out, the way you do when someone throws anything at you.

The soap bomb explodes, coating the guys and their hands with thick purple liquid.

It's narrow up here. Two men could stand shoulder to shoulder if neither of them moves. The guy nearest Dez is shocked to suddenly find himself coated in lemon-scented liquid. He tries to draw his weapon but only succeeds in elbowing his mate. Dez draws close enough to throw the first punch.

The second guy reacts quicker and actually draws his SIG. But his hands are covered in soap and the gun skitters away, bouncing on Alonzo's Garfield and Odie welcome mat.

Dez hits the nearest of the three in the nose, aiming the kinetic energy of his blow in such a way that this man will ricochet back into his pals, tying everyone up.

They stumble into one another.

Dez drives his fist into the cheek of the fella with the flattop. The one who broke Alonzo's ankle. *"Dance this off, faggot."* The guy bounces into the apartment wall, stunned.

That leaves one, well tangled up in his mates and trying to get soap off his gun hand. Dez hits him in the middle of the chest, a bit lower than heart level. His sternum cracks.

Dez swings his right arm as far to his left as he can, then sweeps his elbow forward, into the ear of the man with the broken nose. The guy's eyes roll up into his skull as his legs give out.

Dez grabs the right shoulder and right wrist of the lad with the cracked sternum. He wonders if the doorknob to Alonzo's flat is still electrified, so he uses the leverage he has on the man's arm to drive the man's cheek and nose into the knob.

Dez lets go before the man makes contact.

The man screams, his long muscles freezing.

Yup. Still electrified.

Dez hears sirens.

The flattop is still on his feet, but stunned. Dez grabs him by the soapy lapels of his jacket and waits until they make eye contact.

"Dance this off, love."

He drives his knee into the man's testicles. So hard, he lifts the man's shiny dress shoes off the third-floor walkway.

He collapses in a pile of lemon-scented, unconscious bodies.

Dez uses the side of his boot to kick all three SIGs into a neat pile atop Alonzo's welcome mat.

Two LAPD cars roll in to the parking lot. Dez leans his forearms on the banister, hands clasped and, more importantly, fully visible to the cops who'll be storming up the stairs any second now.

His hands will be cuffed behind his back soon enough.

Not the first time this week. Not even the third.

CHAPTER 71

Dez doesn't stay handcuffed long. Detective Beth Swanson arrives within ten minutes of the first patrol cars. Captain Naomi Cardona isn't far behind.

Dez warns the first responders about the electrified doorknob. They get dispatch to call Andrew, who disarms the trap and lets everyone in.

The police make themselves at home in the flat. More units arrive to secure the corpse on the ground and the three badly wounded men on the third floor. More units block off the entryway to the parking lot, while others string warning tape up around the whole scene.

Captain Cardona and Detective Swanson ask Andrew to take them in to see Alonzo. The dancer wakes up long enough to slur his part of the story. As he drifts out again, he murmurs, "How come everything smells like lemon?"

When he's out, Naomi Cardona nods toward his ankle. She turns to Andrew. "Mind if I ask you a question?"

"Okay."

"The guy who did this, and who called him *faggot*. Was the guy about five-ten, flattop haircut?"

"That's him."

Cardona had talked to the med techs who'd arrived first. They'd told her about the various injuries. At first, the testicular damage done to flattop had seemed excessive, given what she knows of Dez.

Now it doesn't.

In the living room, Beth Swanson and Naomi Cardona sit with Dez, a little away from the commotion around them.

"All hell has broken loose in Boca Serpiente County," the captain says, hunched in, her voice low. "Military. State and county law enforcement. FBI and DEA. What the hell happened up there?"

Dez lays it out quick-like, with a minimum of unnecessary details. Is there time to explain about the would-be sovereign nation of Lexington? There is not.

"Told you about Petra Alexandris, yeah? She's trying t'stop this thing. Being held against her will at her own house in Malibu. Massive security detail. The house is a fecking fortress. Sorry."

Naomi nods. "I heard from my contact up in Boca Serpiente. He does not impress easily. He says you're for real."

The DEA agent not named Phil. "Says the same of you, guv'nor."

Beth says, "What do you need from us?"

"When Petra was almost kidnapped and them three idiots was arrested, did you authorize the entire LAPD report to be sent to Vincent Guerrero, Triton Security?"

Naomi turned frosty. "No. As in: no goddamn way."

"Yet it was. I hacked my lad Vincent and saw your entire police report. That's how I knew the prisoners were being transferred, so I could warn Beth."

Beth Swanson nods to her boss.

Dez turns serious. "Meaning no disrespect to present company, but Triton Security is inside the LAPD in a big way. If I were to ask for official help, I fear it'd get back to 'em."

Naomi reluctantly nods.

"'Sides, for every military-trained guard at that house, the family can whip up a dozen lawyers. It's Petra's house but the title is in her father's name, she told me. We can't storm the place and we can't lay siege and wait for the lawyers to chew us up."

Naomi nods. "Which leaves . . . ?"

"I have to get them to walk out."

"And how are you going to do that?"

"What I do." Dez smiles. "Open some doors."

CHAPTER 72

Dez takes a cell phone from one of the downed Triton Security guys. He retrieves the hacking/breach equipment lockbox from his truck, pries the back off the phone, and quickly bypasses the phone's lockout.

With the permission of Naomi Cardona, he takes photos of the wounded men being carried onto ambulances. He gets an image of the man whose neck he snapped; in situ, on the pavement, eyes still open, skull no longer spherical, neck broken so badly it's nearly severed.

He texts the photos to Vincent Guerrero.

He and the two cops stand near the two Triton sedans. "Stirring up the hornet's nest?" Captain Cardona says. Skinny as a broom, six-two, she towers over him, peers down at him through her half-glasses.

"Aye, that's right. The lot of them was counting on things going their way in Boca Serpiente County, but that went pear-shaped. Major Guerrero sends his thugs to put the boot into me mate Alonzo. They fail. Again. Get 'em stirred up, they'll have a right bull."

Naomi and Beth Swanson look at each other. Beth shrugs. They look back at Dez.

"Bull," he says. "As in bull and cow."

They blink.

"Cow rhymes with row."

Blink.

"Row means fight."

Beth says, "This is America. Speak English."

The phone in Dez's hand rings. It's Vincent Guerrero.

He ignores it.

The captain says, "You keep pushing them, they're going to get desperate. I don't like desperate people. They do stupid things."

Dez barks a laugh. "This lot led with an armed assault on the Hotel Tremaine and a rolling jailbreak on Highway 1! An' that's when things were going their way! They started at desperate. I want to kick 'em up a notch to berserk."

The phone keeps ringing.

Beth seems unconvinced. "Locked doors work both ways. They can keep us out but it keeps them in, too. We could just go old-school: cordon off the place and drag out the megaphones."

The phone in his hand stops ringing. Dez tucks it away, draws his own phone. "Look at this."

He calls up Twitter. The image on display is a megayacht with three decks, a helipad, and an infinity pool.

"Had an inkling this tug might show up here. It's moored at Malibu, according to Twitter. Belongs to the Russian ambassador to the UN."

Cardona peers at it over the tops of her glasses. "And you know this how?"

"It was moored off the coast of Boca Serpiente County this weekend. Petra told me who owns it. The ambassador is up to his borscht in all this. Means there's a foreign national in the house, an' one with diplomatic immunity, to boot. Means he can come and go on his merry, cordons and megaphones be damned."

The borrowed phone in Dez's pocket vibrates. He pulls it out, checks it.

It's coming from Guerrero.

He ignores it.

Naomi says, "You have a plan?"

"Keep them restricted to the house. Let 'em know they're well and truly fecked . . . sorry. Petra's in there. She's smarter than the three of us combined. If she knows she's got allies, she'll get 'em dancing to her tune."

"What can we do?"

Dez says, "Borrow a boat?"

"A what?"

"Boat. Floaty thing. Prow, aft, starboard . . ."

"I know what a boat is. What do you need a boat for?"

"To sink it."

Naomi opens her mouth. She pauses, then shuts it. There is literally nowhere to go with that. "Can I ask you something? The Russian ambassador to the United Nations is on scene. What aren't you telling us?"

"Some bits," he concedes. "Nothing that would interfere with you and yours, guv'nor. Got my word."

Naomi Cardona studies him, her face as serious as sunstroke. "Are you *sure* you know what you're doing?"

The phone in Dez's hand rings.

He answers it, puts it on speaker mode.

"Who the hell—"

"Hi." Dez goes for totally bland in his voice. "You're reached the office of Desmond Aloysius Limerick. I can't come to the phone right now because I'm in your mother."

He turns and overhands the phone into the wall of the apartment building. Dead center between two arcs of blood from the man who fell. The phone shatters.

Naomi Cardona turns to Beth Swanson.

"Okay, he's sure."

CHAPTER 73

Malibu Colony Beach, California

Vincent Guerrero stares at the disconnected phone in his hand.

He's just been shown a photo of the dead body of one of his most trusted men, his neck broken so badly that a greasy white bit of spine is visible. The left rear quadrant of his skull is staved in.

Guerrero has also seen images of three more of his men, all badly injured.

And he's heard Limerick's voice.

Guerrero's hand shakes. He wishes like hell he hadn't had the phone on speaker mode. He wishes everyone hadn't heard Dez's childish taunt. Standing around him in the living room of the Malibu house are Constantine Alexandris, Colin Frye, Brittany Kinney, General William Tancredi, and Ambassador Dmytro Rudko. They stand, more or less, in a circle around Guerrero. They can see his hand shake in rage. No one speaks for several seconds.

Petra stands barefoot at the far end of the room and chuckles.

"*Goddamn it, Petra!*" Constantine wheels on his daughter. "You laugh? You have no idea the stakes at play here!"

"Do the stakes at play here have anything to do with homicide and conspiracy to commit treason?"

Brittany Kinney freezes up. "Homicide?"

"Two members of my security detail were shot at the Hotel Tremaine. Remember? Military police were shot doing a prisoner transfer on Highway 1. The assassination of Admiral Gerald Lighthouse, secretary of the Navy."

Dmytro Rudko, in an expensive, camel-brown suit and bespoke suede shoes, turns slowly to her and smiles knowingly. Dmytro has always admired Petra's ability to analyze situations and to drill down to the heart of any matter.

Colin Frye, the chief financial officer, blanches. "That . . . none of that had anything to do with . . . you know. All this."

Brittany turns to Constantine. "Does it?"

Constantine ignores them both, approaches Guerrero. "Limerick. You need to send men, now, to—"

"I sent *four* men," Guerrero uncharacteristically cuts him off, then amends, "sir."

"Then send more! Send everyone! That prick is laughing at us!"

Guerrero steels himself. "Sir. Must strongly advise that securing this site is our top priority. The opposition could be here at any minute."

Petra has figured out Dez's game. He wants to turn up the heat? Fine. "And by *opposition,* Vincent means Homeland Security."

Constantine shoots a blizzard-cold glare at his daughter.

Colin Frye looks like his head is about to explode.

Brittany Kinney is recalibrating all these new facts so quickly, the others can damn near hear her brain churning.

Petra says, "I'll be going now, Father. I'm still chief legal counsel of Triton Expediters. With the CEO, CFO, and CTO sharing a cell at Guantánamo Bay, someone needs to salvage as much of the company as possible."

"Actually, no." Dmytro Rudko's voice is melodic and cultured. "You shall not be going now, Petra. My apologies."

He nods to Vincent Guerrero. Guerrero nods to his two security men stationed in the room.

He and the men draw their sidearms.

"Nobody is leaving just yet," Rudko says.

Constantine dismisses this with a wave. "Vincent. Holster your damn weapon. Petra actually has a point about the future of the—"

Vincent Guerrero aims his gun at Constantine's heart. "You heard the man."

Constantine's eyes bulge. "What in God's name do you think . . . ?"

His daughter laughs again and drawls out in Russian, *"Polezni durak."*

Rudko also laughs, shakes his head in appreciation.

Constantine looks staggered.

"You used the term earlier, Father. *Useful idiots.* It's Russian. From Lenin, I think. The concept of the foreign fool who carries water for Russian or Soviet interests, even if it means damaging his own nation."

Rudko nods, smiles.

"I know you and Dmytro meet often, Father. Hours-long dinners with vodka flowing. I know now who first whispered this idea in your ear. Who planted the concept of Lexington. Of a new Vatican. Of a nation-state driving the military and political will of other nations."

Constantine's face turns red. His fists are clenched and pale white. His small body fairly vibrates.

Petra keeps her voice cool. "An Alexandris Center, just like Rocke-feller Center? Only taller? A chain of Alexandris Libraries in every small town, like Carnegie Libraries? That's what he crooned to you, didn't he, Father? A robber baron for the twenty-first century. Statues of you in every town square."

"Shut up," Constantine whispers. "Shut up, Petra. Shut up."

"It wasn't ever the nation-state of *Lexington,* was it, Father? Let me guess. New Constantinople? Or, no, wait! New Alexandria?"

"Shut. Up." Spittle flies from his mouth.

She knows she hit the target with one of those guesses. She can see it in the rage, in the undertone of embarrassment, on her father's face.

"Polezni durak," she says. "Useful idiots."

Dmytro Rudko chuckles. "Petra. My God, you're impressive. Vincent?"

Guerrero nods.

"If she speaks again, shoot her in the stomach, please."

CHAPTER 74

The house in Malibu Colony Beach stands on stilts over the beach, letting the tide sweep in and out beneath the deck and the transparent glass floor of the living room. The walls are alabaster white. The entire west-, north-, and south-facing walls are floor-to-ceiling windows. It's three stories tall, with twin dining rooms, a dozen bedrooms, and an office from which Constantine, once upon a time, and Petra, up until a couple of days ago, could run their entire international empire.

Dez knows there are exterior surveillance cameras; he'd spotted them and mapped them out the morning after his first dust-up at the neo-Nazi bar in Los Alamitos. He also knows they are brand-new. It gives him an idea.

There are several ways to further isolate the coconspirators in the great house, but Dez doesn't know who all is in there. Some of the players seem emotional and squirrelly. For instance, he'd only ever seen Colin Frye, the chief financial officer/lobbyist, via Skype, but the man seemed like a stiff wind would blow him away. Constantine Alexandris is a stick of sweaty dynamite. And Dez has been pushing Vincent Guerrero's buttons pretty hard.

Isolating them will ratchet up their insecurities. But at some point, that puts Petra in jeopardy.

The only way to read the scene, Dez decides, is from inside the house.

Getting in will be the least difficult part of his plan.

Dez taught himself to hack. But he's an amateur. When his skills weren't enough, he learned to reach out to much better hackers across the globe.

Sitting in the cab of his pickup, Dez goes online and connects with an anarchistic hacker collective in Shenzhen, China. They know his alias and he knows theirs, and a certain respect and trust have evolved.

Dez informs the collective that Triton Security, a subsidiary of Triton Expediters, has greatly improved its online protocols in the past seventy-two hours and now claims they are perfectly impervious to any denial-of-service attacks.

Several hackers respond with the equivalent of *oh, is that so . . . ?*

A denial-of-service attack means bombarding a site with so much unwanted traffic that everything online grinds to a halt. The bigger the attack, the slower the internet connection. And Dez has just put a world-wide bull's-eye on Triton Security.

By the time he drives to his next destination, several million attacks have slammed up against Brittany Kinney's cyberbarricades. Kinney is very, very good at what she does. But unless Dez is mistaken, her internet access has just been rolled back to AOL dial-up circa 2002.

Naomi Cardona has seen to Dez's one request. She contacted not her own LAPD, but her counterpart at the Port of Los Angeles Police, the independent law enforcement agency serving the city of Los Angeles and the Los Angeles Harbor Department.

Dez had explained to Cardona—and Cardona to her counterpart—

that he needs to borrow the worst possible, barely floating piece of crap in the agency's stockpile of confiscated boats. Whatever they lend him definitely will be worse for the wear. Dez intends to use this borrowed boat as a blunt object.

CHAPTER 75

Malibu Colony Beach, California

The dynamic inside the estate has changed dramatically.

Dmytro Rudko had been an uninvited guest, an uber-rich petro-chemical industrialist turned diplomat with a long and cordial relationship with the Alexandris family.

Now he's very much in charge.

Vincent Guerrero had been the patriotic, veteran Marine officer and Constantine Alexandris's most loyal watchdog. Discovering that Guerrero and his security personnel are working for Rudko throws a wrench into everyone else's perspective.

Petra has gone very quiet. Partly because Guerrero's man is holding a gun on her. Partly because she's recalibrating all the elements of the quickly evolving situation.

Constantine Alexandris is apoplectic. His daughter now is concerned he'll blow a valve in his heart before she figures a way out of this mess.

Brittany Kinney and Colin Frye are in way, way over their heads. Colin shakes like a pampered Pomeranian. Brittany keeps her eyes on her smartphone and, with every passing minute, her frown grows more perplexed.

General William Tancredi, U.S. Army and, soon, likely to face charges of treason, has folded in on himself. His plan to save America has fallen apart at every single stress point: the murders at the Ryerson Ranch; the propaganda boost by media mogul Oliver Lantree; the taking of the nuclear power plant as leverage; the Russians acknowledging the existence of this new independent nation and establishing diplomatic relations.

All gone to hell.

Every good military commander generates alternative strategies for each engagement. Tancredi had. Every one of his contingencies has evaporated like dew under the gaze of a vengeful god. Now he sits tucked into a corner of the leather couch, feet planted on the clear glass floor of the living room, arms folded petulantly, staring into the middle distance.

Petra stands at the westward-facing windows, watching the ocean and the beach and the private dock. She turns to survey her captors; some of whom, themselves, are now captives.

Brittany's frown almost darkens one corner of the perpetually well-lit room. "Trouble?" Petra asks.

Dmytro Rudko had been on his cell phone, speaking sotto voce and in Russian. He disconnects, glances at Petra and then at Brittany. "Yes," he drawls. "Trouble, Ms. Kinney?"

"We're under attack," she says, eyes on her phone.

Petra says, "I know."

Rudko steps toward Brittany. "How so?"

"Denial-of-service attacks. Not on Triton Expediters. On the Triton Security subdivision. We're being flooded with unique visitors. Tens of thousands per second."

"Surely a woman of your genius has ways to combat such vandalism?" There's no irony in his voice. Rudko sounds kind, almost avuncular.

"Of course we do, but . . ."

"Yes?"

"These are coming out of Asia and Southeast Asia. Now Australia and New Zealand. We're getting . . . thousands of separate attacks. We just became the number-one hacker target on Earth. Our internet access is down to a crawl and dropping fast."

Dmytro Rudko draws his smartphone and attempts to log on to Yandex.ru, one of the top five search engines internationally, headquartered in Russia. The site starts to load and freezes like a Siberian landscape.

Rudko feels his avenues of communication diminishing.

He glances up from his screen to Petra, sun-dappled, backlit by the western windows.

"Petra, darling?"

"Hmm?"

"When Ms. Kinney said we were under attack, you said, 'I know.'"

Petra hears hard-soled shoes pounding their way from another room. "I did."

Rudko waggles his phone in the air. "Did you have something to do with this attack?"

"Hmm? Oh, no. Sorry."

"Then . . . ?"

Two of Guerrero's men burst in and vector toward their boss.

Petra says, "Sorry for the confusion. No, I was just observing that someone rammed into your motor launch and it's sinking."

Rudko and Guerrero rush to the window. Rudko uses his inert phone as a sun shield above his eyes.

They watch as the prow of his motor launch arcs to face the sun, the rear of the boat fully underwater. A greatly rusted, flat-prow scow bobs in the rough waters near it, also taking on water. Rudko can't see his own crew swimming for the dock.

But he does spot Dez, standing on the dock, messenger bag over his shoulder, dusting off his palms and looking pleased with himself.

He begins strolling up the dock and turns toward the Alexandris estate, bowlegged, happy as a clam.

Guerrero draws his phone and toggles it to walkie-talkie mode. "External Westside: Limerick spotted. He's on the dock, heading for the house. Get him."

Petra forces herself not to react. She reaches for her long-empty coffee cup, sets it back down on the fireplace mantle, which puts her within arm's reach of a tall, brass, standing lamp. One swing, and she can hold it around Rudko's neck, press Rudko's body against her own, much-taller body, as a human shield. It might—might—be enough to give Dez time to get away.

Every eye at the window watches as Dez saunters and grins like an idiot. Two Triton Security guys in dark suits, SIGs drawn, sprint up to him.

Dez stops, palms forward. He holds a piece of white paper. Nobody in the house is close enough to see what, if anything, is written on it.

Dez's lips move as he speaks to the guards.

They don't fire. Petra exhales.

After several seconds of dialogue, Dez doffs the shoulder strap of his bag, lets it fall to his feet, and backs up. One of the guards retrieves it and rifles through it.

The other draws his phone.

Guerrero's phone vibrates. He listens for several seconds. "You're shitting me."

Apparently, the guard outside is, in fact, not shitting him.

"All right. But slowly."

The guards pat Dez down, then escort him closer to the great house. They stay well outside his reach, one guard slinging Dez's bag over his own shoulder.

They open the gate to the property and walk closer to the house on stilts.

The three of them mount the stairs up to the deck that dominates the entire western side of the first floor of the house. It's the same deck where Dez and Petra shared drinks.

Now that he's closer, those inside can see he's holding a piece of eleven-by-seventeen standard printer paper. They can see a second piece of paper in his hand, but this one's folded.

Dez speaks to one of the armed guards—those within can hear nothing through the well-soundproofed glass. The guard nods.

Dez winks at Petra, on the far side of the glass.

He takes the piece of paper and, incongruously, licks it.

He turns it around and smacks it up against the great window. His saliva makes it stick.

Written on it in black Sharpie is

MY 1ST BOAT TOOK OUT YOUR LAUNCH.

Dez unfolds the second sheet, licks it, and smacks it up against the glass.

2ND BOAT IS AIMED AT YOUR YACHT.

Dmytro Rudko sighs theatrically. He turns to Guerrero.

"I take it this is your Mr. Limerick?"

Petra answers, "Oh, yes it is."

Rudko sighed again.

"By all means. Please invite Mr. Limerick to join us."

Dez learned early on, during his time as a 'keeper, that there are four primary methods for getting through a door: You can bash your way through, shoot your way through, explode your way through, or burn your way through.

And every now and then, you get invited in.

CHAPTER 76

Interior guards pat Dez down, even though exterior guards already had done so. One of the guards drops Dez's messenger bag upside down on the living room wet bar and two men sort through everything. They find his tablet computer, but not much else.

Dez spots General William Tancredi. He can't believe how bad the man looks. He has, for certain, cracked under the pressure.

Dmytro Rudko and Constantine Alexandris are about to speak when Dez blows past them to Brittany Kinney. Dez's hand is extended and, out of sheer habit, she puts her hand forward, too. He pumps it.

"That was you, yeah? The enhanced online security?"

She nods, uncertain. Two men keep guns turned on Dez and now, by proximity, on Brittany.

"Brilliant. I'm good. No question. But not in your league. You're pro, you."

She's flustered. "I, ah, thank you. The denial-of-service attack?"

Dez rolls his eyes. "Best I could think of. Rubbish, I know. Embarrassing. Show you something?"

He draws his mobile—slowly, making sure the guards are okay with it. He brings up a web page and hands his mobile to Brittany.

Her face morphs from unsure to surprised to pissed off. She uses her thumb to swipe through several images.

"Oh, Vincent." Her voice fairly drips with disdain. "Did you recently add external surveillance to this house?"

Guerrero steps up. "Absolutely. When this whole thing started. Nobody gets near here without my people knowing."

"You didn't tell me."

He stiffens. "I don't need IT's permission to do my job."

"Yeah," Brittany Kinney says, and tosses Dez's phone to him in a high, lazy arc. "You do."

Guerrero catches the phone. He shoots Dez a look, then turns to the screen. The web page cascades from shot to shot to shot, all black-and-white video images, in real time, showing this house.

"I upgraded the house security after Dez hacked you," Brittany snaps. "You didn't tell me you'd added external cameras."

She turns to Constantine and points to the westward-facing window, the one with two sheets of paper still adhered outside, thanks to saliva. "Some of the cameras show windows. Including this one. He's been watching us all day."

Guerrero tries to think of something to say but nothing comes. He's fuming. Dez turns to Brittany, rolls his eyes, jabs a thumb at the major. "Wanker."

"If that word means what I think it does," Brittany deadpans. "Yes."

Dez turns and, in turning, gives Petra the quickest of winks. He's ignored her so far since being escorted in. He wants her to know he's got a plan.

Dez and Brittany almost sound like they're bonding—she even called him *Dez*—and it all adds to Constantine's raging anger. "Why are we even talking to this fool! He is nobody!"

Dmytro laughs. He eyes Dez shrewdly. "I think perhaps that is not true, Constantine."

Dez grins at the perpetually angry tycoon. "Dunno all the players here, but I'm betting you've been thinking of yourself as the boss man. Imagine my surprise, watching the video, seeing our lad Vincent here pull a gun on you. Shocking, that."

Constantine sputters. "Shut the fuck up! What are you? You have no idea . . . !"

Dez waves him off. "Suck me." He turns to the Russian. "Don't know you, sir. You'd be the Russian gent whose boat I sank?"

"I would. Dmytro Rudko. And you're the young man who made such a mess of things up north. I believe you broke Oliver Lantree's jaw, took his radio station off the air, destroyed our uplink to the Pentagon. Yes?"

Dez offers his hand and the Russian shakes.

"You impress me, Mr. Limerick. And the nuclear power plant?"

"Aye, that was me."

"That is . . . not unimpressive," the Russian says, and sounds like he means it.

General William Tancredi rises from the couch, eyes feverish, skin clammy and pale. "You . . ."

Dez thinks the time is right to push the general as far as he can. "Billy! That you? Didn't see ye there. Been a day. Get us a drink, will ye? Beer for me." He turns to Petra. "Whiskey?"

Tancredi rocks back as if facing a headwind.

Petra follows Dez's lead. "A little early, but why not. The Tullamore, not the Jameson, I think. Lots of ice."

Constantine looks like he's within a hair's width of a stroke. "Stop this fucking insanity!"

Dez nods. "Ice in good Irish whiskey? I'm with your da there. Fecking insanity."

Constantine's face is the color of a ripe tomato. He advances on Rudko, fists cocked. "This is my house! I want that bastard dead! Now! This entire thing, this was my plan! And you!" He jabs Rudko in the shoulder with a stubby, yellowed finger. "No mincing little comrade treats me like this! I want you out! Now!"

He spins on Guerrero. "You're fired! Take your men with you. I built my company from nothing! I drove the first truck our company ever owned! I cleaned the toilets in the first office! *I* tell *Russia* what to do and how to act! Not the other way around! Out! Now!"

Colin Frye gulps down a drink nobody saw him pour; his hands are shaking, his eyes red-rimmed.

Dmytro Rudko laughs.

Brittany Kinney runs a hand through her crimson hair, turns to Petra, mouths, *I'm sorry!*

General William Tancredi draws a holstered SIG from one of Guerrero's men, thumbs off the safety, puts the muzzle under his chin, and pulls the trigger.

The explosion is deafening within the living room.

People shriek, people duck. Tancredi falls straight back onto the see-through glass floor, the one that shows the tide when it's in. Part of his skull detaches with the bullet's exit. Blood and brain matter splatter across the furniture, across the floor, across Constantine Alexandris's trousers and shoes.

Brittany falls to her knees and pukes into the terra-cotta bowl of a rubber tree plant.

Colin faints.

Dez turns to Dmytro Rudko and finds the Russian already looking at him. Rudko nods a little.

"Master plan's falling a bit off the rails there, mate."

"It is." Rudko sighs. "A bit."

Petra studies the carnage around her. She turns to Rudko.

"We should talk. In my office," she says. "I have a counterproposal for you."

CHAPTER 77

Petra's comment catches most everyone by surprise. Not Dez.

He's dead brilliant at stuff like getting the door to the Alexandris house open, emotionally separating Brittany Kinney from Guerrero, irritating Constantine, and identifying General Tancredi as the weakest link.

Or like manipulating Brittany into handing Dez's own phone to Guerrero. Yes, he'd brought up the pirated, black-and-white feeds from Guerrero's exterior surveillance cameras, but a subroutine in the phone also has been transmitting audio to LAPD units parked three blocks away, a massive SWAT presence ready to drop like an anvil on Captain Cardona's signal.

But that's all battlefield tactics. Not campaign strategy.

You want to win a brawl, Dez is your man.

You want to defeat an army, he thinks, you call in Petra.

Dmytro Rudko studies the carnage around him: the dead body on the floor, the blood and viscera splattered about. And he says to Petra, "I am open to suggestions."

Barefoot, sans her usual Armani armor, Petra circles the splotches of

Tancredi's blood and pads toward the living room entrance. She walks deliberately, in no hurry. A few of the others start to move as well.

"Desmond." She gestures to the wet bar. "Bring the whiskey. *And* the ice bucket. Elitist."

Dez grins. "Aye, ma'am."

"Father," Petra says en passant. "You're not invited."

He starts to bawl her out.

She gives him a look that brings him up short.

And she sweeps out.

Dmytro murmurs to Vincent Guerrero, then follows her.

Dez grabs the bottle of Tullamore, glasses, and ice on a lacquered tray and follows.

He doesn't ask Guerrero for his phone back. Whatever Petra is planning, this part probably shouldn't be transmitted to the police.

In the office—Petra's office, in case anyone was ever in doubt—she pours whiskey and ice for herself, and straight whiskey for the men. Dez says, "Cheers."

Rudko pulls up a chair near Petra's desk and eases himself into it.

Dez stands off to the side. This isn't his show anymore.

Petra sits atop her desk, spine straight, legs folded into the lotus position. She swirls her drink, admires the viscosity and color, and sips.

Dez suppresses a grin. She's the caterpillar sitting atop its psychedelic mushroom, about to show Alice how shit gets done.

She addresses Dez first. "Are you planning to destroy Dmytro's yacht?"

"No. Bluff, that. Had only the one boat and it was shite. Sorry."

Dmytro removes a handkerchief from a jacket pocket, bunches it, and bends to wipe a spot on his Italian loafer. The spot used to be a bit of General Tancredi's brain. "I am fond of that yacht. Thank you. Ah, the crew of my motor launch?"

Dez shrugs. "Dunno. Drowned, like as not."

Dmytro takes in his lack of caring and nods.

Petra says, "Sun Tzu tells us it's okay to burn your enemy's bridges, but always to leave one bridge intact for the enemy to retreat. Your yacht is that bridge."

"Is that what you imagine I'll do next, Petra? Retreat?"

"Yes."

Dmytro ponders that, fiddling with the onyx cuff of his dress shirt. The way they are sitting—he in a comfortable, low-slung chair, she atop her desk—creates an elevation differentiation for their eyes. It's a subtle power move by Petra. Dmytro has to look up to her. Figuratively and actually.

"We flirt, you and I," Dmytro says, smiling slyly. "I hope it is all right to say that in front of the help."

Meaning Dez. Petra studies her drink.

"I've always wondered what would happen if that intensity of yours—your drive—were matched with my skills, dear Petra. Together, we would be . . . formidable."

"Your interests in me have always been crystal clear, Dmytro. About that retreat . . . ?"

"I'm the one person coming out of all this unscathed, dear. I have diplomatic immunity. Your government won't want me here. My government needs me back because I know so much about this plan. And so many, many other plans. Also, because they've already tried to nationalize my oil company and failed. Triton Expediters is the bank for much of the world's military. My company is the bank for what you would call the KGB."

"FSB. Yes, I know."

He lifts his glass an inch toward her in a salute. "I'll be departing. Not retreating. There's all the difference in the world."

"Let me tell you what you did," she says. She speaks without any hint of anger, or judgment, or malice, or surprise. She's laying out a legal brief. "Russia used the 2016 elections to sow discord in America. You did the same thing in Britain and Germany and elsewhere. You've mastered the art of mining social media to salt your enemy's earth. You've weakened NATO and the European Union, and you've manipulated the destruction of several international trade agreements. But in my father, you found a fulcrum for an even greater political disruption to America. I don't yet know who first mentioned the concept of a New Alexandria; of a financial and technical city-state with Constantine Alexandris on the throne."

Dmytro savors his drink. "Constantine did. Although, to be fair, we were exquisitely drunk at the time."

Petra smiles from her perch. "You weren't so drunk you couldn't see the potential. My father's boundless egotism, Triton's money and influence. You could manipulate him into the kind of minor coup d'etat that would have America reeling."

Dmytro smiles, serene.

"It's unthinkable that anyone in America could split off from the union in the twenty-first century," Petra continues. "But if it happens once, it would happen again. The neo-Nazis and white supremacists, they'd soon realize they'd been manipulated. They'd split off yet again. Other factions would as well. The American military would have to move in to stop it, and those images would run twenty-four seven online and on TV. You'd further erode people's faith in America. It's a great strategy. Honestly. A bold move. As much coup de théâtre as coup de main."

"You are too kind."

"But there is no nation of New Alexandria. There is no coup. Desmond, here, stopped you cold. My father will not be the cyberpope, ruling from on high and granting papal dispensations for those who act contrary to the canon law of the World Bank. It's all . . ."

Petra purses the tips of five fingers together, puts them near her lips, and blows, spreading her fingers apart: a dandelion in the wind.

Dmytro finishes his drink. He makes eye contact with Dez, who says, "Oh! Aye, sure," and splashes more whiskey in his glass. "Cheers."

"Thank you. You'll be surprised to hear this, Mr. Limerick, but I actually heard your band play once. I didn't remember it was you on guitar until a few minutes ago. It was a little club in Hollywood. This was perhaps five weeks ago. A very lovely vocalist with an amazing, deep, and resonant voice. Quite a beauty. My driver gave her my card after the show. I thought, p'raps . . ."

He gives Dez a meaningful, man-to-man look. He's talking about

Raziah Swann, who's all of twenty. Dez manages not to pinch his head off.

"She's exquisite," the oligarch says, his voice sounding the way velvet feels. "You were all quite good."

"Hope you bought the CD and T-shirt. She's half-starved, half the time."

Dmytro chuckles, turns to their host. "Petra. The political disruption is accomplished. Did it go as far as I had hoped? No. But that is fine. There will be other days. I shall be leaving after I finish this drink. I truly—and I mean this—I truly wish you the best of luck. You are a most amazing woman."

Petra smiles from atop her lotus-position perch. She raises her glass. "To endeavors."

Dmytro raises his glass. "Endeavors."

"In September, two years ago," she says, squinting and peering out the window, as if dredging up a fond memory, "you fucked the daughter of the chief of police of the city of Kharkiv, Ukraine."

Dez watches as the older man's hand freezes, his glass a half inch from his lips. Dez has played a lot of poker over the years, and he knows when an ante has been upped.

"Her name was . . . ah . . . I want to say either Anastasia or . . . Oleksandra? I honestly can't remember." Petra laughs. "Funny. I had it a moment ago."

"My dear, I have no—"

"Kharkiv," she overrides the ambassador, speaking to Dez, "is very much a Russian mafia stronghold. The chief of police has been an enforcer there for years. He came out of the very KGB that Dmytro referenced moments ago. Today, he's a mob enforcer. Now, here's the interesting part."

Dmytro makes to stand up. "What do you think—"

On instinct, Dez puts a meaty hand on his shoulder; no real force, just holding him in his chair.

"The interesting part," Petra repeats to Dez. "My old friend here is sixty-three years old. And Anastasia . . ."

"Or Oleksandra?"

"Right, thank you. She was sixteen. She and some girlfriends were in Kiev to catch a hip-hop show. After her rape, she returned home. She told her father what happened. She, I'm told, attempted suicide. The father—the mob enforcer—has spent quite a lot of money in Kiev attempting to find the monster who raped his daughter."

Dmytro is almost vibrating with fear now.

"A porter at the hotel in Kiev was paid handsomely to slip Rohypnol into her drink and provided Dmytro with a room, and he—the porter, I mean—got the transaction taped on his smartphone. He tried to sell it on the black market. He tried to sell it to the girl's father. But guess what."

She turns to Dmytro, keeps smiling, keeps her voice light.

"I bought it. I bought it, and I've kept it, because Dmytro?" Her smile bleeds away. "In all of our multibillion-dollar dealings, with all of your come-ons and affectations, I always kept in mind that you are an untrustworthy, uncultured little Cossack peasant with a two-inch dick and the cunning of a two-dollar whore."

Dez can feel Rudko's shoulder shaking under his palm. He reaches down and takes the glass from the man's unsteady hand.

"The deal," Petra explains, speaking slowly, "is that you leave here, you leave America, and, when asked, you tell the media your yacht just happened to be off the coast of Boca Serpiente County because it was motoring down to meet you here. You were coming to see Triton Expediters, to negotiate a delay in the oil pipeline project outside of Khrustalnyi. You know nothing of the violence in Boca Serpiente County. You never met General Tancredi. You never met what's-his-name from Patriot Media. You have no reason to think that Triton Expediters had anything to do with anything up there. The so-called coup was a blip on the American political scene; you read about it in USA Today, saw something about it on CNN perhaps, but you have no particular opinion about it. As ambassador to the United Nations, you continue to have the utmost confidence in America. You will return home to Moscow. You will begin the new seismic survey of the pipeline. Triton Expediters will make a very public statement, reiterating our faith in your oil company and in you, personally, and that our offer to finance the pipeline remains as firm as ever. In exactly one year—to the day, Dmytro—you will announce that you are satisfied with the seismic studies, the project is back on, and I will personally sign the contract granting you the money that will keep your filthy little family in processed borscht and half-assed, fruit-flavored Finnish vodka for years to come. If any of this is not followed to the letter, then the police chief of Kharkiv will get a cell phone video. And after that, were I you, I'd quit my day job. I'd live permanently on that charming little yacht of yours, at sea, until the day you die. Please, speak up if any of this is in any way unclear."

Dez walks over to a cabinet to set down his and Dmytro's glasses. He does this to hide the fact that he's about to pee his pants, he needs to laugh so hard. In all his years, he can't honestly say he's ever seen a beatdown as thorough as this.

Dmytro Rudko says nothing. He sits in the chair for a minute. Then two. He's looking at the wall, *through* the wall, and doesn't see Petra make eye contact with Dez and shake her head: *Wait for it.* Two minutes become three, become four. The sphinx sits on her desk, back straight, serene.

The old man draws his handkerchief to wipe his brow but remembers it has a smear of General Tancredi on it. He stands, crosses to a wastebasket, and releases the handkerchief.

It flutters away like his schemes.

He adjusts his cuff links, his pocket square, his tie. He's aged twenty years in twenty minutes. He looks like a man who had a stroke, whose face has forgotten the proper muscles necessary for a smile, but is trying all the same.

He offers Dez a hand. "Mr. Limerick."

"Pleasure, mate."

He nods once to Petra but does not make eye contact with her.

He exits.

When he's gone, Petra sets her drink down and bows low, shoulders hunched together, her head at the level of her sternum.

Dez crosses to her, takes her in his arms, cradles her against his chest. She sits cross-legged on her desk, shivering. He doesn't need to ask why.

There's a dead body bleeding out on the glass floor of her living room. The man shot himself in front of her. Likely the first person she's ever seen die. She needed to take Dmytro Rudko off the chessboard, so she tamped all that down, held it rigidly inside, played the ice queen, decapitated the Russian and his threat to further sully the image of her company and her country.

It was masterful. And it took a toll.

Dez is quiet for a time as she cries without sound.

When she stops, he says, "Go get kitted up. I'll move everyone out of the living room. You're near done, you."

She nods, wipes her eyes. She climbs off the desk, limber and lithe. She straightens, towers over him.

"Thank you," she says. "Give me five minutes. I still need to defeat my father and take back Triton."

CHAPTER 78

Dez stands in the foyer and watches Petra pad up the curving stairs to the second floor and her bedroom.

He turns and finds the gaggle of coconspirators near the main redwood double doors, also in the foyer—at least, he thinks this room is called a foyer, but maybe not. Big room, near the front, no real purpose except to hold a whacking great marble-top table and a sculpture of what appears to be grapes. The rich are hilarious.

Vincent Guerrero and two of his guards are in deep conversation with Dmytro Rudko, near the main door of the house. The Russian, it appears, is making his excuses and heading out. Dez rolls up to the group, smiling.

Both guards swivel and draw SIGs on him.

Americans. Always with the guns.

Guerrero says, "Back off, Limerick. Now."

"Give us the phone, will ye?"

"You're not walking out of here alive. You do realize that. Right?"

"Pretty fabulous phone, that. Got all the bells an' whistles. It's transmitting. Right now. Cops, a couple blocks away."

Guerrero doesn't believe him; Guerrero doesn't want to believe him.

Dmytro Rudko—not at all his usual cocksure self—makes no eye contact with anyone. "Of course his phone is broadcasting. Let him have it, Vincent."

He opens the door and steps out into the California sunshine.

Guerrero draws Dez's bulky phone from his suit coat pocket. He studies it, touches the screen to bring up the black-and-white exterior surveillance images.

Dez raises his voice. "Mornin', guv'nor. Civilian, on his way out. East side. Has diplo immunity, this one. Best leave him be."

Guerrero glowers at him. "How stupid—"

The phone chirps. "Ah, roger that, Limerick. You okay in there?"

"Course! Fella who just said, an' I quote, 'You're not walking out of here alive,' end quote, is named Guerrero. Major Vincent. Retired. Lovely guy. Thick mustache. Betrayed his country. Piece of work, him."

The phone chirps. "Vincent, this is Captain Naomi—"

Guerrero drops the phone on the black-and-white parquet floor with the inlaid gold piping. It bounces quite high and settles. He raises one Oxford shoe and stomps on it.

Dez says, "Vincent?"

Guerrero stomps on it again.

The phone chirps. "Limerick? You all right?"

Dez bends at the waist to get closer to the mic. "Just fine, guv. Butterfingers here just figured out my phone's ruggedized for use in combat. Too precious for words, him. You okay holding position for a bit?"

Chirp. "Negative. We're coming in soon. You've got . . . thirty minutes. Whatever you're doing, be done by then. Out."

Dez bends farther, picks up the shoe-sole-scuffed phone, wipes the surface on his jeans. He shakes his head. "Women. It's always something."

He turns and rolls in to the living room. He also deactivates his audio link with the cops.

The pool of blood around the corpse of William Tancredi has grown considerably. The room reeks of gunpowder and cordite and death. The CEO, CFO, and CTO of Triton Expediters, and the man who guards them, have sequestered themselves behind the wet bar, as far from the cadaver as possible. Colin Frye is drinking. Again, or still; Dez has lost track.

"Petra'd like a word with ye. In *her* office." He puts a little extra mustard on the word *her*.

Constantine throws back an ouzo. "How is it Vincent hasn't killed you yet?"

"Funny story, that." Dez cocks his head toward the entryway and ambles back out.

Brittany and Colin glance at each other, then follow.

The last thing Dez hears as he leaves is Constantine Alexandris pouring another ouzo.

CHAPTER 79

For the next meeting, Petra has returned to her usual superhero costume: fitted black jacket and trousers, four-inch heels, crisp white shirt unbuttoned low. Her hair is up in a chignon with two lacquered Chinese hairpins standing at quadrant points. She has diamond studs in her lobes. If she's wearing makeup, Dez can't spot it but then again, he never has with her.

She is as serene as a brook.

Vincent joins the group. "Police are all over the place. They've been, ah, monitoring much of this."

Brittany Kinney looks at Dez, then at the phone in Dez's hand, and says, "Son of a bitch."

"Rudko left," Guerrero says. "He, ah . . . I don't know what the plan is. I don't know . . ."

His voice peters out.

Petra watches everyone but does not speak.

Constantine walks in, the neck of an ouzo bottle throttled in one liver-spotted fist. He strides up to Dez, cocks back his other fist, and throws a haymaker at his jaw.

Dez catches it in his palm.

The *thwack* sound resonates through the room. Constantine's fist looks like a baseball in Dez's catcher's-mitt hand.

"Decent, that. What you want to do is pivot off your other leg. Put your hip into it."

The old man's knuckles ache from the impact. His elbow aches. His shoulder aches. It was like hitting a tree.

He backs off and gulps directly from the bottle. "Fuck you, you grubby little bastard."

Colin Frye, behind him, is as white as an orchid. "What do we do?"

Petra finally speaks up. "We save the company."

Everyone turns to her.

Colin lights up a little, a ray of possible hope suddenly before him. "How?"

Petra says, "I have a plan."

Brittany sounds contrite. "All respect. But a plan? Everything we worked for. Everything. It all fell apart. You have a plan? It better be bullet-proof. And I don't mean that just metaphorically."

"It is," Petra says softly.

Constantine holds his right side gingerly, body still reverberating a little from smacking Dez's palm. "Well?"

Petra turns to a filing cabinet. She takes out a single sheet of paper. A heavy stock, a Smythson Cream Wove. Also a hefty fountain pen that appears to be made of solid steel. Her modernistic, artsy desk has neither paper nor writing implements, and Dez wonders how the hell that even qualifies as a desk. She sets the paper and the pen on the surface, slides them both to the far side, nearer the C-Suite trio. She lines everything up, squared off. The fountain pen remains capped.

She nods to her father. "But first, you resign."

Constantine snorts a laugh. "Never. I created this company. I *am* this company!"

Her voice is soft and modulated. "You're a homicidal lunatic, Father. You resign."

"Don't be melodramatic!" He laughs. He waves the bottle a bit, gives his daughter a rueful shake of the head. "My faults are legion, but—"

Petra circles the desk at lightning speed and looms over her father.

Constantine takes an involuntary step back.

"A dead body lies on my living room floor! The man shot himself because your insane, megalomaniacal plan for world domination was shit! Your entire plan! It. Was. All. Shit! Dez outthought you, outfought you, outfoxed you, and he's a fucking bass player! If it hadn't been Dez, it would have been the U.S. military! Or the state of California! Or the police! Or the FUCKING BOCA SERPI-ENTE COUNTY SHERIFF'S OFFICE!"

Constantine has taken two more steps back, eyes wide, blood draining from his face. The barometric pressure in the room drops a dozen points.

"A man bled out on my floor! If you were a dog, I'd rub your nose in it! This is your fault! Do you understand me, Constantine? Do you?"

He stares up into her eyes. For the first time, Dez spots real fear in the old man. He looks, finally and for the first time, like, well, an old man.

"Petra? I don't . . . please, you have to understand what I . . ."

She turns to her desk. She lifts the pen, unscrews the cap, sets it down again.

She steps away. Doing so, she clears a path between Constantine Alexandris and the blank piece of paper.

Constantine looks to Colin Frye. He looks to Brittany Kinney.

He steps forward and gingerly sets the ouzo bottle on her desk. He studies the creamy blank sheet, the tabula rasa. He picks up the pen, feels the coolness, the smoothness of its steely shape, in both calloused hands.

He bends at the waist and writes.

I resign.

Constantine Alexandris.

Then caps the pen and sets it atop the sheet.

Dez turns to Petra. "I mentioned I play keyboards, too, yeah?"

She raises her hand, articulates her fingers. "What do you call these? The bones in your fingers."

"Phalanges," he says. "Proximal and intermediate."

"Does it hurt when you break them?"

"A bit. Not as much as other bones."

Petra makes a left-hand fist, spins, and punches Vincent Guerrero smack in the nose.

Cartilage cracks and the big man, surprised, stumbles back. His foot slips and he falls on his ass. Blood seeps into his fine, fine mustache.

Petra wags her hand in the air, eyes screwed shut. "Damn it!"

Dez says, "Whiskey?"

She winces. "I wouldn't say no."

CHAPTER 80

Petra talks quietly to her father in the corner. After that, the old man heads out of the office, onto the deck of the great house, with his bottle of ouzo, to watch the surfers and the beachcombers and the kite flyers.

Petra circles behind her desk. "Vincent?"

The ex-major is holding a handkerchief under his nose. He's on his feet but his stance is anything but aggressive.

"You don't work for Dmytro Rudko anymore, and you don't work for my father. Can we agree that, for now, you work for me?"

Guerrero nods.

"Good. Understand, please, that it will be temporary." She changes her tone, takes in everyone in the room. "I have a way to save Triton Expediters. I'll need everyone to do what I say. To the letter. Are we understood?"

Brittany Kinney and Colin Frye nod.

She turns to Dez. "I owe you everything. Literally everything. But right now, I can either act to uphold the law, or I can act to save my company. I cannot do both. And I need everyone in the room to understand that or . . ." She pauses. She's rubbing her sore left knuckles with her right hand. "Or, simply, not to be in this room. This house. You don't work for me. You're not part of this. You can do absolutely anything you want, Dez."

Dez has poured them both a whiskey. Colin is eyeing the bottle like an old friend. Dez hands Petra the glass with ice. "Fair. I don't like what you're saying, I walk."

She accepts the drink with her unstiff right hand, takes a sip. "I can live with that."

They raise their glasses to one another.

Petra squares her shoulders to begin. "Colin. You head to New York. Triton Expediters is buying Gamelan Avionics. This week. We're offering one hundred and fifteen percent of the last asking price. Have the contact signed by Thursday."

The chief financial officer looks like he's had a quick onset of vertigo. "I'm sorry?"

"I accept your apology," she deadpans. "Fly back to New York. Make the deal."

"We, ah, I need to check with the buying company, to make sure—"

Petra says, "There is no other company. We're buying it for us. Triton is going to begin competing in the military–industrial sandbox for a while. We are no longer just a bank."

Colin and Brittany try to take that all in.

"Triton had nothing to do with the purported coup d'etat in Boca Serpiente County. The conspirators had taken over our facility up there, a server farm, but we'd invited the secretary of the Navy, Admiral Lighthouse, here, to my home, to offer our assistance. The conspirators, led by that dead man on my living room floor, found out and attempted to kidnap me to gain leverage over my father. That is exactly how we are connected to the conspiracy. We were trying to stop it. All of us. Am I clear?"

They nod.

"Today's news will be about nothing but the coup. Three days from now, the financial media will be stunned to find out that Triton is expanding its portfolio to include tech companies. It'll be the biggest news of the week for the *Wall Street Journal*. And that will be the new narrative for this company. Brittany? You worked with the Russians and with this Patriot Media group to create an internet narrative around the new nation that was about to be formed."

"I . . . yes. I did. That was . . . yes." She sounds genuinely contrite.

"You're going to take everything you learned from the Russians and the rabid right, and you're going to create a new internet *truth*. Which is this: The great Constantine Alexandris had a cardiac incident when his only daughter was kidnapped. We kept it secret. It's leaking out. His daughter is in charge now, and she's green-lit a foolish plan to purchase Gamelan Avionics, and to vastly overpay for it. The news will drive our stock into the ground. The board of directors will be outraged. They've felt useless for years. They never dared try to wrest control of this company from my father. They will gather their forces and come after me. *That* will be the narrative for the remainder of this year."

Colin says, "Ah. Wait. That . . . Petra, that would be very, very bad for our company. We would look weak."

Brittany nods. "I'm not sure how we benefit from—"

"A little clarity." She cuts them off. "First, the truth is that, for the last month or so, Triton Expediters has been conspiring with madmen to destabilize the world military ecosystem. That man out there"—she gestures with her glass toward the sliding glass door, and the deck, and the chaise longue, and the slumped shoulders and hung head of her father—"came close to pulling it off. That makes Triton one of the predators in this story. With the coup failed, the government will go looking for those predators the way farmers gather with their guns when a wolf comes down from the hills and slaughters a calf. So, news of his heart attack will make us look less predatory. Less threatening to those investigating the coup. His heart attack is my sheep's clothing."

Dez is marveling at this bit of legerdemain.

"My knee-jerk reaction to overpay for the first tech company to stumble past will make me look weak. The feckless idiots of our board of directors will attack me. I shall not counterattack. That will make me look even weaker. The sleight of hand here, the misdirection, is that I am not weak. But I need to look that way until such time as the insurrection is in the history books. Toward that end, I need you to conjure up whatever propaganda you've learned from the Russian GRU, and from the far-right hate media, and make sure *my* narrative is the one that sticks."

Brittany looks like she's tracking the story better now. "I see."

"Second, I would ask you both to stop saying *our company* and *we* in my presence. As of this moment, I am Triton.

"I need you both, today, to help perpetuate a myth. That will succeed or it won't. Either way, you'll both resign at the end of the calendar year. Do as I say, and I won't tell the government about your participation in the coup. Succeed in my every demand, and you'll stay out of prison. Fail me, and I feed you to the Pentagon. Could you let me know if this is understood?"

Brittany Kinney looks close to crying. She can't make eye contact. But she nods.

"You can do it?" Petra asks. "You can weave my version of the truth—that we're a weak company, a threat to no one—and make the online world believe it?"

"Yes."

"Good. Colin, be in the air as soon as the police are done with us. Begin the process of buying Gamelan. Work quickly. Be your usual obnoxious self. Succeed in looking like the drunken dandy that you are. Or I swear to God I will see you live out your life in Leavenworth prison. Deal?"

Colin Frye looks a bit less drunk now. He nods.

"Fine. Vincent?"

The man with the bloody handkerchief under his nose nods.

"Get the police in here. Tell them that man in there . . . ah . . ."

Dez says, "Tancredi."

"Yes. Tell him he's shot himself, after being confronted with his complicity in my kidnapping and the coup."

Guerrero checked to see if his nose had stopped bleeding. "Before we let the Keystone Kops in here, we should—"

"Vincent? Please stop talking. Brittany?"

She looks up, tears glittering.

"After Vincent makes his statement to the police, he and all of his personnel are fired. All of them. Lock them out of the system."

Guerrero takes a step forward. "Goddamn it, Petra. We—"

"You arranged for me to be kidnapped. You had two members of my security detail shot and killed to cover your complacency, and you sold out both my company and our nation to the Russians. You not only are fired, I intend to blackball you from security work within the United States. Any company that hires you will find its ability to borrow greatly restricted. Now, get the cops in here. And get your men out of my home and out of my company's buildings."

Guerrero says, "We still have the only guns in the fucking place, Petra."

Dez, who'd been quiet throughout, throws an elbow into the face of the only security man in the room. Before the man can fall, Dez snags his Glock from his shoulder holster, pops the magazine, checks it, pops it back in place, and racks the slide.

The guard hits the ground, unconscious.

Dez walks to the desk and sets the gun down in front of Petra. Cocked.

Petra had seen it coming. She never takes her eyes off Guerrero throughout the move. She says, "Want to bet?"

Dez rolls to Guerrero and draws his mobile. He reconnects to Captain Cardona. Guerrero looks from Petra's eyes, to the fully loaded Glock in front of her, back into her eyes. He accepts Dez's phone. "LAPD? This, ah, this is Vincent Guerrero. The front door is open and the coast is clear. Requesting your presence in here, now."

He turns and walks out of the office.

Dez makes a show of disconnecting from the police. Petra says, "Finally. Are you okay with all this?"

He shrugs. "These fuckwits should be in prison," he says, gesturing to Brittany and Colin. "Your lad Vincent as well. An' your da. But it's not my company. Not my call. I'm a gatekeeper, me. I don't set policy. I just open doors for them what do."

CHAPTER 81

Captain Naomi Cardona and Detective Beth Swanson let the hotshot SWAT guys storm the Alexandris compound first. All the personnel therein are secured before the captain and her crew come in.

A crime-scene tech crew is called in for the cadaver in the living room.

Detectives begin interrogating everyone.

Petra explains to the captain that her father had suffered a small cardiac incident and is in a weakened condition. Also, the company chief financial officer, Colin Frye, is scheduled to fly to New York that evening.

Dez backs the story. Naomi Cardona agrees to interview Frye first and to clear him for his flight.

Beth Swanson takes Constantine Alexandris herself, pulling a kitchen chair out by his chaise longue and talking softly to him for a little better than an hour.

Petra had told her father the whole new, essential narrative before the police stormed in. Constantine is nearly catatonic from shock and sorrow and drink. But he knows the lines he's to speak.

Guerrero's men are disarmed and interviewed.

Dez is interviewed. Yet again. It's his first time without handcuffs. He decides he prefers this method.

It takes the captain and her crew three hours to clear the house and to declare the investigation ready to move into its next phase. The district attorney will get involved, as will the California attorney general. And the federal Justice Department. Clearing the path toward the impending court cases will take months.

The narrative begins to stick: LAPD learns that Triton Expediters had been working with the late secretary of the Navy, prior to his murder, to stop the coup launched by General William Tancredi, and Oliver Lantree of Patriot Media, to create a tiny nation of neo-Nazi, white supremacist secessionists in Boca Serpiente County. In Maryland, a white supremacist with ties to Tancredi already is in custody for the hit-and-run death of Admiral Lighthouse. A Captain Bart Weaver, U.S. Army, is in custody for the murder of Molly Ryerson on her ranch in Boca Serpiente County.

The attempted kidnapping of Petra Alexandris; the well-documented meeting with Admiral Lighthouse here, in this very compound; the suicide of General William Tancredi, all lend heft to the tale.

Brittany Kinney fiddles with her phone, right under the noses of the police. She might have been playing *Angry Birds*. She isn't. She's beginning to spread the narrative online. She also locks out everyone connected to Triton Security, from Vincent Guerrero on down. By midnight, Guerrero and his men will find out that their phones, their building passes, and even the computer-controlled ignitions of the Triton Security fleet of vehicles are offline.

Colin Frye is driven to the airport and takes the company jet to New York. He will begin the forceful negotiations to buy an overvalued avionics firm. Within a week, this will be perceived as a major misstep for the new, untried CEO of Triton Expediters. Petra Alexandris will take a drubbing in the financial press.

For the time being, Triton will be perceived as prey, not predator.

There will be little pressure by anyone to more fully examine the company's connection to the Boca Serpiente County situation.

A car is called for Constantine Alexandris and drives him back to the company compound. He keeps an apartment there and often lives on campus. Petra intends for him to do so from now on. His apartment offers every comfort, including his beloved ouzo and his hand-packed Greek cigarettes. In the last couple of days, Petra has become knowledgeable regarding gilded cages.

The military has taken full control of Joint Base McKinzie-Clark.

The U.S. Department of Energy and the Secret Service are coordinating the investigation of a hostile military takeover of the Boca Serpiente Valley Nuclear Power Station by personnel from McKinzie-Clark.

California Highway Patrol, the U.S. Marshals Service, the FBI, the Drug Enforcement Administration, and Homeland Security flood the town of Sloatville and begin enforcing preexisting warrants for dozens upon dozens of the white pride types who'd infested the town. The departing throngs of white guys with Confederate hats and gun racks create a prolonged traffic jam that will lock up Central California highways for days.

The FCC yanks the license of Oliver Lantree. The board of directors of Patriot Media votes unanimously to strip him of his CEO position.

Lantree, hospitalized in Sacramento, his jaw wired shut, issues no statement.

Petra makes a call to have Alonzo and his boyfriend moved into one of the guesthouses on the Malibu compound, and to hire a physical therapist to sketch out a recovery plan.

CHAPTER 82

The police have a lot of questions. So does state law enforcement. And the feds. And the military.

Two days' worth of questions.

At midnight that Wednesday—almost a week and two days to the very hour that Dez and Petra first met—the two of them sit on longues on the deck of the great house. The sun has set. Dez has a bottled Guinness by his feet and his cherry red Gibson Ripper across his knee. He plays it acoustically. He's been thumbing through a wide array of tunes for nearly an hour, singing to himself sometimes, enjoying the night.

He senses that Petra needs many things right now, and that long stretches of not talking are high on the list.

Dez spots security, quite a lot of it, and men he hasn't seen before. Not Vincent Guerrero's lot, new players. He doesn't ask about them.

They listen to the susurrus of the ocean. The tide is in and the ocean sloshes against the pilings under their feet. They see a couple of campfires a half mile or more down the beach. They hear faraway laughter, and the pop of little store-bought firecrackers, and rap music from a cheap speaker.

Petra listens to Dez play. A bit of Eric Clapton, segueing to Isaac Albéniz. He thinks he heard her cry a couple of times but she's really just a silhouette in the night; he didn't stop to find out. Dez has often cried after a battle, after losing people. It's a good thing, crying. The person who takes a loss and doesn't cry is the one Dez worries about.

When he stops and reaches for the neck of his beer bottle, Petra breaks her silence. "How are you feeling?"

"Like a very big an' very skilled fella beat the ever-loving crap out of me, thank you very much."

"You won the fight, though. He's probably feeling worse."

Dez turns to her. Black tank and black yoga pants, dark skin and black hair; he sees her but he can't read her features. "No. Winning the fight woulda meant never gettin' into it. Bein' smart enough that he never throws the first punch. That's winning. Fact is, he was better than me. Good fighter. Good trainin', good disciplined mind. I shoulda found a better way than tradin' punches with that mook."

"You don't sound angry at him. I don't think I've heard you sound angry at anyone, really. You don't sound like you hate these people."

"No one's ever paid me to hate an enemy. Just to beat 'em." He sips beer. "The fella who broke Alonzo's ankle, insulted him. Well, that bastard . . ."

He shrugs.

Petra sips Irish whiskey. "But you *have* been paid to beat enemies."

No response, just more Spanish guitar.

"I did my damnedest to find out who you are, you know. Gerald Lighthouse told me to trust you, but I wasn't exactly satisfied. I called in favors all over Europe. I asked people in high places and low. I wanted to know where you learned to fight. Why Gerald called you *chef*. Who the hell you are."

"How'd that go, then?"

She laughed. "You're a ghost. You show up nowhere."

"I've a sad lack of ambition. Plagued me my whole life." He strums some chords.

"He called you *chef*. That's French for *chief*."

"It's shorthand, I suppose."

"For what?"

Dez strums. "*Sous-chef de cuisine*. I've worked in a lot of kitchens, me. Fairly keen with a paring knife."

"All right, all right," she concedes. "Keep your secrets. You've noticed I have new security?"

"I have, aye."

"They're former Navy. Men whom Gerald Lighthouse trusted. I reached out to them this morning and they had five men here before noon."

"Seems smart."

"Heads are rolling. I don't want to be one of them. The Patriot Media mogul? Oliver Lantree? He committed suicide last night. About twenty minutes after the Justice Department subpoenaed his records. I also heard from Moscow. Dmytro Rudko is gravely ill. In the hospital, in a coma."

Dez turns to her in the dark. "Oh ho."

"You know what polonium is?"

"Aye. It's Russian for 'take the garbage out.'"

She nods. "I don't feel the slightest thing about the GRU poisoning Dmytro to shut him up. I really have become the steely-eyed bitch people have made me out to be."

Dez says, "Funny old world, this. Bunch of aging lions roarin' about, chests puffed up. Masters of industry, of media, of the military, of espionage. End of the day, an' it's you wearin' the crown. Fact is, love, they never even saw you comin'."

She sets down her glass and uses both hands to wrap her hair into a quick knot at the back of her head.

"My father is insane. My company was complicit in a criminal conspiracy and, to clear our name, I will have to make us look weak and rudderless."

"For how long?"

She pours more whiskey from the bottle at the foot of her longue. "I don't know. A year? It's a delicate game, looking weaker than you are.

A single misstep, and we'll face a hostile takeover. Or bankruptcy. Plus, a man might play this game—the feint to draw the counterattack. The parry and riposte, the invited weaknesses to lure an opponent in. But women are never allowed to feign weakness. It will be . . . a challenge."

"Are you up to it?"

He can see the gleam of her smile, even in the gloom. "Thank you for asking." She thinks about it for a while. "Yes. Yes, I am. No one alive is better situated to save Triton than I. I'm not sure I can do this. But I'm sure no one would stand a better chance."

He lifts his bottle. "Cheers, then."

"Also . . ." She pauses, thinking about how to proceed. "Dez, I've always been an advocate for serial monogamy. And I've never stayed connected to anyone very long. My affairs tend to run their course with . . . alacrity."

He laughs. He picks up the guitar and plays the oh-so-familiar tune, Lalo Schifrin's opening beats for the theme to *Mission: Impossible*. Petra recognizes it and laughs with relief.

"I've no interest in settlin' down and raising a passel of Limericks, love. But I can't say it hasn't been fun."

"I also keep business and my affairs separate. And I need a new right-hand man at Triton Expediters. I was thinking of you."

Dez barks a laugh. "Can you imagine me wearin' a suit and tryin' to look all professional an' grown up? Me name on a door? I'd look a prat."

"I need someone to keep me out of trouble. And make no mistake: I intend to get into trouble. As much of it as I can, until I can reshape Triton in my image. I will make enemies. I need someone I can trust."

"Trust Alonzo. He's smart. Smarter'n me. He knows you better'n anyone. And with the state your da's in, Alonzo's about the closest thing you have to family."

She's quiet again. He plucks at the strings, tunes the guitar a little, plucks the same strings. Down on the beach, two drunk guys attempt to harmonize the opening lines from "Born in the U.S.A." Girls cackle with laughter. The Pacific shushes them from beneath the boards of the deck.

"So what happens to you next?"

Dez sets the guitar aside to dig his phone out of his hip pocket. He brings up the email function, then sets the thick phone down on the wooden slats of the deck and slides it across to her, like gliding a shuffleboard weight.

It clacks against the foot of her chair. She bends over, retrieves it. She reads.

"Who's Raziah?"

Dez raises his hand, palm down, five feet off the deck. "Yea high. All voice and hair."

"The vocalist. From your band."

"Her band. Yeah."

Petra reads. "Her sister's in trouble?"

Dez sips beer.

Petra smiles. She sets the phone down and shuffleboards it back. It bounces off his boot. "And you're going to go help."

"In the morning," he says. "Aye."

Petra hugs herself and watches the foam of the surf flare into existence and flicker out, over and over again. She says, "That seems a good use of your skill set. I approve."

Dez smiles at her in the dark. "You're reckless. Oh, you're tough as fuck. An' you're smart as hell. But you're reckless. You court chaos. If it comes calling—*when* it comes calling—ye know how to find me."

Petra lifts her glass and leans far in his direction.

Dez lifts his bottle and leans toward her.

The glass clinks.

"I am," she says. "Reckless and tough and smart. And yes, chaos will come for me."

Dez sips. He sets down the bottle, picks up the Gibson Ripper.

"Then so will I."

ACKNOWLEDGMENTS

It can be daunting for an American writing about a guy who grew up in the UK. It helps that I've been glued to the BBC and Sky News for decades. My Canadian mom, Shirley Haynes, still employs an array of Brit-speak, so all of us kids got teased in kindergarten for ending the alphabet with *zed,* and I get razzed for saying *shan't* and *naught.* For this book, I also got dialect help from Catherine Richards and Meg Gardiner. Thanks for helping. Ta, cheers.

Big thanks to the *Portland Tribune* staff, and publisher Mark Garber, for your patience while I "moonlighted" on this novel. When I was twenty, I wanted to be either a novelist or a print journalist; I'm the luckiest guy on Earth. And thank you to everyone who supports and subscribes to local news media, now more than ever.